Black American
(Amreekie Aswad)

In the Desert Kingdom©

an Adventure Story by Sumanth

3rd Revision

Published by
Sisyphean Tasks, LLC
SAN: 858-1134
P.O. Box 7956
Woodbridge, VA 22195

Copyright © 2008 - Registration Number TXu 1-601-637

www.blackamericanindesert.com

ISBN: 978-0-9824185-2-9

Printed in the United States of America

Note from the Author

Black American (Amreekie Aswad) in the Desert Kingdom is a work of fiction inspired by the years I spent in the Kingdom of Saudi Arabia during the decade preceding the Gulf War of 1991. I am not an expert on that desert land, but this is an adventure story solely based on my personal experiences. However, it is not autobiographical in the truest sense of the word. While it contains anecdotal information that I gathered from conversations with various Saudi citizens, all of the characters in this story are fictitious and any resemblance to persons live or dead is purely coincidental. For the most part events portrayed herein follow in chronological order; however, the timeline on the whole is not in historical sequence.

In 1979 when I signed a contract to work in Saudi Arabia, I had no idea what the country or its people were like. Images of Arabia in my head were based on Hollywood films, or documentaries and news reports. Arabia had always been depicted as exotic and populated by noble Bedouin tribes who traveled the desert sands on camels and majestic stallions. Arabia to me was a faraway place full of adventure, which is why I literally jumped at the chance to go to the Middle East when I was invited.

On my very first morning in the capital city of Riyadh, I walked into a restaurant hoping to get breakfast even though the only Arabic I knew at the time was the expression A-salaam-alekum. Eventually I ended up having to pull out my passport to show I was a foreigner. When the waiter saw that I was a Black American, he turned and announced this to everyone in the place. At that point everyone jumped up and started cheering and chanting 'Amreekie Aswad, Amreekie Aswad....' It was the opening day of my tour and the first thing I learned to say in Arabic was Amreekie Aswad, their words for Black American. That incident inspired the title for this story.

The cheering puzzled me though, because shortly before I left the United States it was brought to my attention that Black slavery had ended in the Kingdom only 17 years earlier in 1962. That information frightened me a little bit and I caught my flight to Arabia with no idea what a Black man born free in a democratic land should expect while living in the Saudi

Kingdom. But I was curious to find out how the lives of Black Saudi citizens had changed after 17 years of freedom.

One thing the incident at the restaurant that first day proved to me was that I had a lot to learn. And there would be many more surprises in the years to come.

There is a timeless truth about Arabia that I learned to treasure, the hospitality of the Bedouin people. They lived up to this legend in spades when dealing with me. I was also surprised, pleasantly so, to discover that Black Saudis have a lot in common with Black Americans. They love our culture and have a great deal of admiration for our historical and other accomplishments.

Black American (Amreekie Aswad) in the Desert Kingdom portrays my Arabian experience through the eyes and actions of a group of rather interesting characters. I am sure readers will find them as unforgettable as I found the individuals and groups they represent. This is a story that pays tribute to two great communities – the Bedouins of Arabia and the community of people of African descent that became Saudi citizens in 1962. I have endeavored to portray Saudis (White and Black), their customs and traditions, accurately and in all sincerity. Readers will find on the pages of this story adventure, romance, drama, discovery, enlightenment, triumphs, humor, fun and disappointments.

It is my fondest hope that this novel spurs young people to travel more. A world of untold adventure is out there waiting to be claimed. Travel gave me the chance to meet ordinary people, people who are not read about in the news or seen on CNN. Today the experiences I had with Bedouins and Black Saudis are among my fondest and most treasured memories.

Sumanth

Dedicated to the wonderful people of Riyadh and Jeddah who opened their hearts and homes to me and made my tour an unforgettable experience

and to

*The U.S. Military Basketball Team that competed in
The International Military Basketball Championship Tournament
when it was hosted by Saudi Arabia*

Chapter 1

An adventure of a lifetime is something most people dream about but few actually get to experience. My name is Adam Sneed, Jr. In the spring of 1979 the chance for adventure in the exotic land of Saudi Arabia came my way when I was recruited to work on a project in that desert kingdom. I was 27 years old, eager, full of energy and not at all intimidated by the prospect of traveling to the other side of the world.

Admittedly I knew very little about the Saudis when I was recruited. Like everyone else I was aware they had a lot of oil. I also remembered the oil embargo against the West that was led by Saudi Arabia a few years earlier and had caused a lot of people, my dad included, inconveniences when they tried to buy gasoline. Arabian society though was a real enigma to me. For one thing, my ideas about Arabia had been influenced to a large extent by the images in the film *Lawrence of Arabia*. But I had been hired to work on a project that was part of the most expensive and extensive modernization program the world had ever seen. Saudi Arabia was being brought fully into the 20th century, and from what I was being told the changes were taking place rapidly. So I knew, even before I got to Arabia, that my perceptions of the country and its people were outdated. Yet, I wondered how much Arabia had actually changed. It was a question I looked forward to being able to answer personally because, despite what I was learning, I still had romantic notions about the Arabian Peninsula. Privately I held on to the hope that some of old Arabia still existed. I wanted to get a glimpse of that magnificent world of desert nomads before it faded into history forever.

As excited as I was about going to Arabia, I nearly changed my mind at the last moment. The date set for my flight was November 9 and up to the last week before my departure, everything went according to plan. Those last six days, however, were tough and twice in that period I faced challenges that were completely unexpected and serious enough to make me consider backing out of the deal. In fact on the morning of my flight, when I woke up I was still debating whether I should go to the Middle East or stay in America.

To understand what led me to that moment of indecision, I have to begin this story on the day I first heard about the Saudi project.

L Street Office Building Construction Site Trailer
Early May, 1979
Downtown Washington, D.C.

A new office building had joined the L Street skyline. I was the Construction Office Project Manager in charge of a staff that processed change orders, requests for information, submittals, schedules, payment

1

applications, performed budget analyses, shepherded shop drawings and provided quality control in various areas of the construction site. The team had done a top notch job. Meetings between the contractor, architect and the owners always took place on schedule, and at the end of the project all disputes that had arisen during the course of the work were resolved. To complete a contract of that size with no arbitrations pending was rare. I was proud of my crew.

The last day had come and I was in the process of clearing out of the construction trailer. Mentally, I was focusing on ratcheting up my search to find my next project. A dozen copies of my resume were already in circulation around the capital region. No offers had come as yet, but I was optimistic.

It was nearly noon when I got down to the final task and once I got that done, I would turn over all project keys still in my possession to Jean Roseboro. Jean was the only other person in the trailer that morning. Two boxes sat at the foot of my desk; a small one for items I would be taking with me and the other was quickly filling up with trash. The messiest job I saved for last and that was cleaning out the big middle drawer. That drawer had saved my hide many times when one of the bosses or representatives of the owner stopped by the trailer unannounced. I cannot count the number of times I opened that drawer, and in one quick motion swept everything into it from off the desktop. Toward the end of the project that drawer was so crammed it always took a lot of tugging to get it open. It stuck that morning too when I tried to pull it out, and the best I could manage was to open it half way. So I reached in as far as I could and snatched blindly at whatever I might be able to grab. I had no idea that with that simple act, I had unknowingly triggered a chain of events that was about to change the course of my life.

Once I pulled my arm free, I noticed a business card jutting conspicuously from the mass of debris in my hand. Turning my wrist slightly I read the name and smiled in disbelief. The card belonged to a long time friend and colleague. I had misplaced it more than a year earlier. Right away I dropped everything and dialed his number. While the phone rang, I tried to think of a good apology for not keeping in touch.

"Tamborini Construction, Jim Lincoln speaking. How can I help you?"

"You can start by telling me how you are," I said with a nervous chuckle.

"Am I hallucinating, is this really the elusive Adam Sneed? What happened to you man? I have been trying to reach you for the past two months. How have you been?"

"Fine Jim, I just finished my latest job here on L Street downtown and I am about to start the hunt for my next project. I guess you know by now my number has changed. Forgive me for not keeping in touch. First I misplaced your card and then the directory I had your name in got lost when I moved."

"You moved again?"

"Yes, I got into this crazy situation a while back with a woman I was dating – things did not work out the way she wanted – she refused to walk away – there was a bit of stalking and … I'm sure you get the picture… I ended up having to move and get a new number."

"When are you going to learn Adam?"

"All right, all right, don't give me your famous marriage speech again. I will get to prison soon enough. As I was saying, I lost your number and that is the only reason I have not called to get you my new information. I was cleaning out my desk just now, because this is my last day in the trailer, and a few moments ago I pulled your card out of the back of the top drawer..."

Teasing, Jim reacted, "At least you kept my card in the *top* drawer."

"Hey, as soon as I found it I dropped everything and called."

"I appreciate that. It is good to hear from you my friend and to answer your question, I am doing fine. So is Patty. I will tell her you said hello."

"Thanks. Jim, you said you have been trying to reach me for two months. Was it anything urgent?"

"Are you sitting down Adam?"

"Should I be?"

"You might want to sit down for this. A couple of months back Dave and Lillian Breckinridge invited me and Patty over for dinner. We joined them and another couple they were also entertaining that night. Dave knew them long before you and I went to work for him when we got out of college. The husband is a head hunter. He works for a consulting firm there in D.C. His name is Carl Scott. They specialize in recruiting candidates for federal projects outside the country. Carl told us about some of the projects they are handling around the world and mentioned a position in Saudi Arabia that they have been trying to fill for some time. Adam, the job is tailor made for what we do. When Carl started filling in the details of the project I got very excited. For a minute there I was thinking seriously about applying for it myself. But then he started listing all the things women are not permitted to do over there, and Patty put the kibosh on any hopes I might have had real quick. But then my wife says, 'Jim has a friend, he is single and I think he might be interested. His name is Adam Sneed. Adam and Jim went to school together and worked for Dave's company for awhile after they got out of college.' Now tell me, you have to be impressed with Patty for bringing your name up like that my friend."

"What can I say? I am overwhelmed. But I wonder why a couple of other people did not mention my name?"

"Trust me, Dave and I would have suggested you for the job. Patty just beat us to the punch. But you will be happy to know Dave and I promoted you big time, so much so that when we got finished building you up Carl was begging for your resume. So Dave tells him, 'you might want to wait until you get back to D.C. to contact him directly. Adam lives in your neck of the woods.' Carl was really pleased to hear that. I wrote down your number to give to him but then I grabbed the phone and suggested, 'Carl, why don't I call Adam now to give him a heads up and maybe you can say a few words to him.' Of course, as you should know, all I got was that recording "sorry, the number you have dialed has been disconnected." So Carl left his card and said once we contacted you to have you give him a call. And that, my friend, is why I have been trying to track you down for the past two months. I even telephoned the contractor you were working for a couple of years back the last time we spoke. They had no idea what outfit you had gone with after you left them."

Jim's news was incredible. The instant the name Saudi Arabia fell on my ears I started seeing images of harems, tents and camels in my head. Although I had never thought about working overseas, Arabia sounded exciting. My enthusiasm, of course, was tempered by the fact Jim's tip was two months old. That is a long time for a recruiter to wait for a call from a prospective candidate, especially in the nation's capital. Every instinct in me said the job had already been filled. As quickly as my excitement had flared, it fizzled.

"Thanks for thinking about me Jim. I appreciate the support. Relay my thanks to Patty and Dave as well."

"Given the amount of time that has passed, I would be surprised if the job was still open," Jim said, echoing my thoughts. "By the way, you said you are working on L Street – guess what, Carl's firm is on L Street."

"You have got to be kidding."

"No, my friend, Carl Scott has probably been a hop, skip and jump from you all along."

That last bit of news was depressing. All I could think was that I had lost out on a once in a lifetime opportunity before getting a chance to hear about it. "What a bummer. I am going to be kicking myself the rest of my life for losing this chance."

Saudi Arabia – at least I it was nice to know somebody had thought about sending me there. "Can you imagine me riding a camel," I joked.

One thing about me, I never give up on anything without a fight. So I said "Jim, I am going to call this guy anyway. Even if that job is filled, they might have another position I qualify for. Nothing beats a failure but a try, right?'"

"Now that sounds like the Adam Sneed I know. If I can't go to Saudi Arabia, maybe my friend will get the chance. Hold on, I'll get Carl's card." Seconds later Jim dictated the number over the phone. "Good luck Adam. Keep in touch and let us know how things turn out."

"Sure will, but Jim before you hang up the phone would you like to write down my new phone number?"

Jim laughed and said, "I think that would be a good idea."

Jim and I graduated from the University of Pittsburgh in 1974 and began our careers together at East Coast Contractors. The Company had projects from Maine to Florida and inland as far as Illinois. Dave Breckenridge, foreman of the Pittsburgh office, took me and Jim under his wing and taught us everything we needed to know about construction site project administration. Jim and I learned a lot from Dave and as a bonus the three of us became good friends.

At East Coast there were postings on the bulletin board from time to time of temporary positions, or TDYs, at various Company sites around the country. Toward the end of my second year, a one year TDY at the D.C. field office became available. This interested me, so I applied. A week letter Dave called me into his office and informed me I had been selected.

Family and friends were sad to see me go, but I was thrilled to be getting a chance to work in the nation's capital. Since Elementary School I had dreamed of seeing the capital monuments and government offices in person. As an adult my curiosity about D.C. increased when I found out it was nicknamed Chocolate City because of its large Black American population. After growing up in Pittsburgh, life in a city where Blacks outnumbered every other ethnic group would be quite a change. The thought of living there, even temporarily, was very appealing to me.

I arrived in the capital in 1976 on a Greyhound Bus that rolled into town just about the time Federal workers were coming out of those famous government buildings to go to lunch. Never had I seen so many Black people in the downtown section of a city before. I knew right then I was in for an experience unlike anything I had ever known.

But do not misunderstand my feelings about Pittsburgh. My hometown will always hold a special place in my heart. Plus there were a number of advantages in growing up there. The education offered in the school systems is second to none. Also, being raised in a blue collar town instilled a work ethic in me that has served me well wherever I have traveled. And I cannot overlook the fact that the Steel City forged me into a lifelong Steelers, Penguins and Pirates fan.

The District of Columbia, on the other hand, was tailor made for energetic young Black males like me looking for excitement. Females in the District outnumbered males eight-to-one, so Washington was definitely my kind of town.

For two months I fumbled around trying to get up to speed with a faster pace of life. There were plenty of clubs to go to on weekends, but I had to learn to discriminate between them because some needed to be avoided. A couple of clubs had reputations for being little more than shooting galleries set to music. What I needed was a guide to show me around safely until I got to know the city better. Barry Shipman became that guide. But the way he and I started out, it is a wonder Barry and I ever became friends.

I met Barry at a neighborhood basketball court my first weekend in the District. A number of guys had shown up looking to get into a pick up game. During the selection process, Barry and I ended up on opposing sides. Everyone there, except me, knew Barry was the best athlete on the court. Either my teammates thought it was a big joke or they sincerely wanted to test my skills when they assigned me to defend against Barry. They probably thought I was not much of a player after the opening play because Barry snatched the ball right out of my hands, raced down court and executed a crushing dunk. 'Get your head in the game,' one of my teammates yelled. I figured out pretty quickly what I was up against. Barry was superb. However, I was not the kind of guy that simply conceded someone was better than me. As far as I was concerned, Barry presented a tougher challenge and nothing more. Following that opening dunk, I hunkered down and forced him to earn every basket he made. Hard as I tried though, I could not stop him from scoring. To be honest I admired his game, but his trash talking irritated me to no end. I hate braggarts and the anger that built up in me actually helped me play better that game than I had ever done before. Needless to say, by game's end I had a low opinion of Barry Shipman. I never imagined our competition that day was only the start of a long running rivalry.

One of the reasons I tried to get out and do something physical every weekend was to compensate for working all week in a sedentary occupation. To keep my body active and in shape, I played basketball, tennis and any other sport that interested me and I found time to learn. In Pittsburgh I knew where the best players went to compete, and I could always find out where the most hotly contested basketball games or tennis matches were being played. Transferring to DC meant learning a new city and starting over in figuring out the best spots to play. Searching for a different court each weekend helped, because it fit with my strategy to learn my way around town faster. But for some odd reason, wherever I went Barry was there. It did not matter if I went out to play tennis or basketball, he and I always ran into each other. We competed against each other so often it was just plain eerie. Barry had the edge over me in basketball, but I got back at him on the tennis courts. Our competition was so intense that the loathing I felt for him that first day developed into an intense mutual dislike. Today when I look back on that period, I am convinced the competitiveness that fueled our rivalry also triggered the friendship.

Our rivalry was so bitter that we would walk off the court at the end of a game without saying 'good bye', 'nice game', or even 'I hate you dude.' We just walked away. After a few months the rancor we felt toward each other began to diminish, but not until we walked off the courts. At games' end we began to find ways to be civil to one another. Then one Saturday after another one of our hotly contested battles, Barry came right out of the blue and invited me to go out with him. "Adam a new club is opening down on the waterfront tonight. The owner is a friend of mine. Do you want to hook up and go check it out?"

That night I discovered Barry was quite popular with the ladies, and he played as hard off court as he did on them. The moment we walked in the door of the club, women swarmed him. Better than that, because I was with him they surrounded me too. Here at last was the veteran of D.C. nightlife I needed. With Barry's guidance, my fledgling social life took a giant step forward. That first weekend we went club hopping all over the District and in the nearby Maryland and Virginia suburbs. Barry knew so many beautiful women that I was content just to be in his shadow. From that first night together, hanging out with him became a regular thing.

When I was a teenager I always had girlfriends. Most of them were members of my church, so our activities were closely monitored. I guess what I am trying to say is nobody could accuse me of being a young Casanova, not by any stretch of the imagination. But in D.C. my personality changed completely. Within weeks I transformed from a bookish workaholic into a man that worked all week so I could afford the lavish parties Barry and I went to on weekends. There were a number of popular songs in those days that celebrated the party crowd and Friday nights. Those songs were written for guys like me and Barry.

In the spring of 1977, the head office notified me that the temporary assignment in D.C. was coming to and end and I should prepare to return to my job in Pittsburgh.

After a year in Chocolate City the person I was when I left Pittsburgh was long dead. If I did return to Pittsburgh, my family and friends would hardly recognize me. So I resigned from East Coast Contractors and settled permanently in Chocolate City. There were plenty of construction jobs underway in the capital region, or scheduled to begin in the near future, so I was not worried about keeping employed.

Over the succeeding months my construction career flourished and so did my social life. I grew more confident in approaching women and soon owned several black books all filled to the max with phone numbers. Weekends were never dull for me and I had become the kind of man I had fantasized about when I was growing up.

That was the lifestyle I was living the day I pulled Jim Lincoln's business card out of the top drawer of my desk and made the call that changed the course of my life.

✧✧✧✧✧✧✧✧✧✧✧

No sooner had I hung up with Jim, I dialed Carl Scott's number.

"Yes, I remember your name. Dave Breckinridge had a lot of good things to say about you."

"Dave is a good guy and a friend. I learned a great deal working with him."

"You are right about that, Dave is a good guy. I suppose you are calling because Dave told you about the job in Saudi Arabia."

"Actually I heard about it from Jim Lincoln."

"Oh yes, I remember Jim. He was at dinner that night too… with his wife… Patty. Yes, that was her name. So tell me, what do you think about the position, now that you have had time to think about it?"

"It sounds like a wonderful opportunity, that is, if the job is still open."

"It is. Are you interested?"

Was I dreaming? After two months, the job was still available. I wanted to shout to high heaven. I collected my thoughts, kept my emotions in check, took a deep breath and said in a calm tone, "Yes, I am interested."

Our conversation lasted ten minutes during which I learned the name of the outfit he worked for was International Projects Consultants, or in D.C. acronym parlance, IPC. Carl was convinced I was a shoe-in for the job and had been eager to hire me from the night of his dinner with Dave. But he cautioned I would still have to go through the process of filling out and submitting an application and being interviewed. Once the application was accepted, IPC would provide me with a laundry list of things I would need to do in preparing to ship abroad. At the very top of that list was getting a security clearance. Because it was a federal job on an overseas project, IPC could not put me under contract until I got clearance. After assuring Carl that I had no criminal record or skeletons in my closet, at least none I was aware of, he told me where to address my resume.

When I hung up the phone, I reared my head back and yelled at the top of my voice. Curious to know what was going on, Jean Roseboro came over and asked "Is everything okay, Adam?"

"Jean, I might not have to apply for unemployment after all."

"You found a job, great. I am so happy for you."

"Technically I have been invited to apply for a job, so I do not have it yet. But my prospects are better than excellent."

"Awesome. What contractor are you going with?"

"It is a little too soon to talk about any details but I can tell you this much, the job is a little farther away from Washington, D.C. than I ever expected to work. I promise, once the ink dries on the contract you will be one of the first people I call."

The task of clearing out the desk got pushed to a back burner as I busied myself tweaking my resume to give it that 'I am willing to travel' spin. Once that was done, I called a courier service. The messenger looked puzzled when he saw the delivery address, but after a wink of my eye and a generous $20 tip he happily trotted off to the building next door to put my resume in Carl Scott's hand that very afternoon.

Two days later, Carl and a second IPC official met with me for the first of the two interviews I would have at the Agency. On that same day I submitted an application to work for IPC and to participate on the Saudi project. A follow up meeting was scheduled for the following day. During the second meeting, IPC tentatively offered me a two year contract on the Saudi project. Finalization of that offer depended on the outcome of the security investigation. Meanwhile, I officially became an employee of IPC and eagerly signed the consent for the FBI to conduct a background check on my life. If I failed to gain clearance, I could continue working for IPC while I searched for a new construction project.

Carl gave me a quick tour of the maze of cubicles, offices and conference rooms at IPC, which he described as 'a magnificent machine that will go into action to get you to post in six months. Believe me we have this process down to a science. So get ready, you are about to ride a whirlwind.'

On my way home that afternoon, I mused over the unpredictability of life. People often say 'you never know what tomorrow will bring.' In my case my life had been completely turned around in the span of four days on the timely happenstance of my finding a lost business card. But it was more than the fortuitous discovery of that card because my initial thought that morning was to dump the contents of that middle drawer in the trash without bothering to sort through them. It's scary to think how close I came to spending the rest of my life oblivious to an incredible opportunity that could have literally slipped through my fingers. Instead, I found myself on the threshold of traveling to a far away place with strange sounding names and an even stranger sounding language.

When Carl said it would take six months to get ready to ship out, that sounded and felt like an eternity. Especially those first two weeks waiting on pins and needles for the FBI to complete its investigation. Government agents spoke with every neighbor I ever had that was still alive and could be found, both in Pittsburgh and in Washington. They interviewed former teachers, professors, employers and scarier yet, a few of the ladies I had dated in the past. How they found out all those things about me, I never knew. Perhaps they found my lost directory. I did find out later that they interviewed my former stalker. A friend that works in the government told me the woman gave me a good character reference. Color me surprised. At any rate, it was a relief when the clearance came through. After that, the ball really started to roll and the reality of what I had gotten myself into began to sink in.

During the early days of preparation, I often had dinner with Carl Scott and his wife at their apartment down near the waterfront in Southwest Washington. Carl shared a lot of good advice, which I appreciated and he never hesitated to get into my personal business when he felt it was necessary. For instance, early in my pre-tour period Carl asked, 'Adam, are you involved in a serious relationship with anyone? The reason I ask is that if you are not planning to get married and you have something casual going on, you might want to start thinking about breaking it off. In fact it would be better for you to end all unnecessary emotional entanglements because they could undermine your commitment to the project.' That was the day I swore off dating and made a vow of celibacy.

Considering my lifestyle over the previous few years, to stop dating cold turkey was not easy. However, I did have a powerful incentive. I was only a few months away from living in a land where strict religious, social and moral standards were rigidly enforced. Sex outside of marriage received the severest punishment possible – death. And it did not matter to the Saudis where you were from. If you lived in the Saudi Kingdom you were required to respect and abide by the local laws. When it came to sexual morality, Islamic law was incorporated right into the law of the land. Yes, I had good reasons to start adjusting my lifestyle and to do so sooner rather than later.

IPC scheduled me for every kind of examination, physical, dental, psychological, medical, and then some. In addition I was inoculated against diseases common in that part of the world, a precaution I would be particularly appreciative of in the not too distant future.

I was one of a number of recruits in Washington that year preparing to ship out to Muslim lands. We attended orientation sessions together at the State Department, taking courses designed to familiarize us with the culture and religious strictures of Islamic societies. They dined us at local restaurants specializing in Arab cuisine and arranged a tour of the big Mosque on Massachusetts Avenue.

Just as Carl had forewarned, the months flew past. Before I knew I was down to the final four weeks until my flight. Conveniently, the lease on my Northwest D.C. apartment ended at the start of that final month. It was perfect timing. The day before I moved out, a team of professionals showed up at the apartment, boxed up whatever household effects I chose to take to Arabia, transported them to Baltimore harbor and loaded them onto a ship that would be sailing to the Middle East. IPC advised me that the shipment would arrive anywhere from two to three months after I reached post. For the remaining days until my flight, I had to live out of three travel bags.

After moving out of my apartment, I stayed with Barry for a week then took two weeks off to visit my folks in Pittsburgh. I gave relatives and friends written instructions on how to contact me overseas. Dave Breckinridge threw a going away party for me at the Hilton Hotel downtown, and I spent the last few hours in the Burgh visiting some of my favorite places in the city. The last stop I made was at the center of the West End Bridge where I stood watching my favorite site in the world – Point State Park at the convergence of the Allegheny, Monongahela and Ohio rivers.

When I got back to D.C., I checked into the hotel where IPC had a room reserved for me to stay that final week before my flight.

After five months, three weeks and a day, the preparation phase for my overseas assignment was to all intents and purposes completed. Six days remained until my flight. It was hard to believe I had finally come to that point. I tipped my hat to IPC because everything had gone smoothly and the Agency had proven to be a magnificent machine just as Carl had boasted. For a fact not a single glitch had occurred in the entire operation.

Physically, I felt great. Emotionally, I could not have been more ready to get underway. In six days I would be leaving the United States to live in a foreign land for the first time in my life. As far as I was concerned the greatest adventure of my life was about to begin. At least that is what I hoped.

On the next Friday of my life, I would be grabbing my travel bags, walking out the front door of the hotel, and whistling for a taxi to take me to Dulles Airport.

જાજાજાજાજાજાજાજાજાજાજાજાજા

Chapter 2

November 3, 1979

D.C. was unseasonably warm the Saturday I got back in town. Temperatures climbed into the low 70s, perfect weather for a basketball game. After checking into the hotel, I took a shower, called Barry and challenged him to a game of one on one. We agreed to meet at Turkey Thicket in northeast DC. It was one of our favorite spots.

After an hour of play, Barry drove me back to the hotel in his convertible Porsche. He loved that car. When he pulled into the driveway, we were both deep in thought. This was the last time we would be seeing each other for the next two years, so when I got out and walked around to the driver's side I was wondering if it would be unmanly to hug my friend goodbye. Since Barry had not gotten out of the car, I figured we would simply shake hands in parting. I extended my hand. Barry did not react. He just sat quietly staring at the dashboard. I figured he too was struggling with the issue of how to say goodbye to a close male friend. Or, maybe he was planning to say something special and needed a moment to get his thoughts together.

Finally, in a casual matter-of-fact manner he remarked, "I met this girl Adam. Her name is Lovelen. We are going roller-skating tonight…"

The glare I gave Barry was so intense he stopped talking in mid-sentence.

Months earlier when I swore off dating, that decision affected our friendship in a big way. Barry and I had been competitors from the day we met, so it came natural to us to try and outdo each another when it came to females. We vied to find the most beautiful women in the city. But there was a catch. The women we dated also had to be smart. A good looking woman without brains did not qualify for our competition. Of course, it was not a matter of simply stating 'my date is smart.' We devised a group of special questions that we were sure could test their intelligence. I am ashamed to admit this now, but I rejected the woman who ended up stalking me because she failed our test.

Barry and I were positive the test was foolproof, until the night both our dates caught on to what we were doing and told us off in the middle of a crowded restaurant. They gave each other high fives and stormed out of the

12

place together. "I guess that proves they were smart after all," Barry joked. "Obviously smarter than us," I conceded.

That is why, when I took the vow of celibacy I had to explain to Barry that our dating competition had come to an end. Barry's reaction surprised me. He was supportive, plus without any prodding he voluntarily stopped sharing the details of his dates whenever we were together. For a guy who loves to gloat this was no minor concession. Yet my friend remained loyal to my situation and we completely stopped talking about women. Understand this was not a formal agreement, just a tacit understanding between us that the topics of women, dating, and anything related thereto were off limits. For nearly the whole period I was preparing to ship abroad, Barry honored our moratorium. Now with less than a week until my departure, he had broken the truce. That is why I glared at him when he mentioned his new girl.

"Hold on Adam. This is not about competition. I am not trying to start that up again. Seriously, Lovelen is truly amazing... beautiful... smart... you will see for yourself when you meet her tonight.... please come skating with us tonight. Please Adam. You just have to meet Lovelen before you leave the country."

"You are wrong about that Barry. I do not have to meet your girl."

"Trust me, you will regret it if you don't. Besides, you actually do have to meet her because I promised I would bring you along tonight. She expects you to show up at the skating rink. If you do not come, I will look like a big liar."

Sarcastically I retorted, "We definitely do not want that to happen, do we. Listen Barry, I am sorry to disappoint you, and your girl, but I am not in the mood to be a third wheel right now, especially since I am about to start two years of enforced celibacy in a land where they flip out if a man even looks at a woman sideways."

"Did I mention Lovelen is a model?"

"Okay Barry, that's enough" I scoffed. There were times when I could just haul off and pop Barry right in the kisser. That was one of those times. Putting up with his arrogance on the court was one thing; this though was more than I should have to deal with. How dare he rub a beautiful model in my face at a time like that? Talk about ruthless. It was not the way a best friend should say goodbye.

"Honestly, I am not pulling your leg man. She models for a living."

"Then why would she be hanging out with ..." I stopped myself. I did not want to ruin our last moments together. The day had been perfect to that point, and good memories were going to be valuable where I was headed.

Barry though had been shrewd in his campaign to get me to go skating. He knew that mentioning Lovelen was a model would pique my curiosity. I stalled a little longer, just for appearances, but in the end agreed to join them.

Had I known the impact Barry's girl was about to have on my life, I might have stuck to my guns and stayed away from the skating rink that night.

We met at a popular rink on the Virginia side of the Potomac in the city of Alexandria. The moment I laid eyes on Lovelen, I knew why Barry was so smitten with the woman. My friend had not come close to describing her beauty. But there was no faulting him for that as the girl was beyond stunning. Even I was at a loss for words. She certainly was nothing like what I had expected. Lovelen was not anorexic by any stretch of the imagination and the young beauty filled out a pair of jeans like the proverbial brick house. Equally alluring to me was her hair. It was styled in matching Afro puffs, which was one of my favorite looks on a sexy Black woman.

"Lovelen Jocelyn Sinclair, this is my best friend Adam Sneed," he introduced with a laugh. Barry was laughing because I was so taken with his girl that I was gawking.

"Hello Adam," she cooed in a voice so sweet it could make angels cry. "I am so happy we finally got the chance to meet. Barry has told me a lot about you."

Okay, saying she cooed might be a bit of an exaggeration but I felt as nervous as a teenager on the first day of school suddenly facing the prettiest girl in class.

"It has been a long time since I went skating. This is really exciting."

Barry and I simultaneously suggested, "Then let's get started!" The two of us speaking at the same time made me feel stupid. Lovelen just giggled and led the way inside.

Being a third wheel had never been so enjoyable. It was a wonderful evening. Triples were called twice and each time, I took the inside - Lovelen anchored the middle - and Barry, the stronger athlete, held down the outside.

Barry said this date was not about competition, but I noticed he kept looking at me the way he always did when he wanted to signal our game was on. With us it was automatic when it came to the women we dated. Now as far as beauty and femininity are concerned, Lovelen passed those marks with flying colors. All that remained was to test her intelligence. A skating rink, however, was not the best venue for giving Lovelen our special test. Unfortunately, Barry and I did not have plans to be together again before my flight.

Being around Lovelen and Barry that night brought back a lot of fond memories and I realized how much I missed dating. I convinced myself that being around my best friend's girl would not weaken my resolve to remain celibate and so as we skated, I started kicking around a few ideas in my head on how I might squeeze them into my hectic schedule over the few days I had left.

By the time Barry dropped me back at the hotel, I had a plan. As we were saying goodnight I suggested, "Why don't you and Lovelen join me for a farewell dinner Wednesday? It will be my treat."

Before Barry could answer, Lovelen quickly agreed "That would be perfect."

"Lovelen and I would be honored to have dinner with you my friend, but you have to let me pay. After all, you are the one going away, so the dinner will be in your honor." As Barry said this he gave me a knowing smile. Oh yes, the game was on and Barry had to know what I was planning. We had gone down this path too many times.

Nevertheless, there was something different about the confidence Barry exhibited in this particular girl. Ordinarily I might have been worried, but on that occasion it did not matter. So long as I got to see Lovelen again, that was all I cared about. A woman with her kind of beauty does not walk into your life every day.

"Fine, you can pay. I will make the arrangements and call you with the details. Good night Lovelen. It was nice meeting you and I look forward to seeing you Wednesday evening."

❧❧❧❧❧❧❧❧❧❧❧❧❧❧❧❧

Chapter 3

November 4, 1979
(Six days before departure)

When I moved to D.C., I broke a long time habit of going to Sunday service every week. I deliberately went to church that final weekend before my flight, because I felt it was an important thing to do since it would be the last time I could do so for the next two years.   Christianity is not practiced openly in Saudi Arabia. It is a Muslim land where all other forms of worship are forbidden. Expatriates were permitted to hold non-Muslim services on private compounds but steeples, organs and mass choirs - none of that existed where I was going. That Sunday I planned to enjoy one final formal worship service before I left the country.

As I sat in the pew, I concentrated on absorbing everything about the church letting all that I saw and felt ooze into my pores. Visually I zeroed in on the minutest details of the sanctuary and the architecture of the building. The sounds and swaying of the choir were extra sweet that Sunday, and I actually stayed awake all the way through the pastor's sermon.

A few hours later when I got back to the hotel, there was a message waiting for me at the front desk. It read, 'Adam – just heard the news – this is bad timing I know, but please do not get discouraged - call me tonight if you feel the need – if not, I will see you in the office first thing tomorrow - Carl.'

Something had happened. Hurrying to my room, I turned on the television. Every station was broadcasting a special report about dissident Iranian students taking over the U.S. Embassy in Tehran and holding our diplomats hostage.

Anger and disgust filled my heart. Not even a year had passed since the last anti-Shah demonstration was held in Washington. There were so many Iranians marching in our streets protesting against their Shah, that traffic often ground to a halt. All of the demonstrators wore hoods to hide their faces because it was rumored that the Shah had sent his secret police to infiltrate the crowds. Protests like that could never have taken place in Tehran, but the Iranians took advantage of our constitutionally protected right in this country to dissent. Even the police were out in force patrolling the crowds to enforce the Iranians right to demonstrate. Unfortunately, for those of us working in the District we faced many inconveniences on account of the protests. Lunch time seemed to be their favorite time to march, and the crowds grew so large that it was impossible for anyone to get anywhere in the afternoons. Once I stepped out of the trailer with the intention of going to lunch, but the sheer volume of the crowd forced me back inside. I missed lunch that day and on many days like it. A friend of mine told me her office finally resorted to having pot luck lunches. Everyone brought a dish from home and they put everything together buffet style in one of the conference rooms. She said the pot luck lunches turned out well, and for a bonus office morale improved because the additional time together helped her workmates to get to know one another better.

As I listened to the television report, my anger increased. What was ticking me off was the audacity of the Iranians to come to America and take advantage of our hospitality and protection, then turn around and disrespect our Embassy and diplomats in their country.

Staring at the TV I grumbled, 'Why did you guys have to start this insanity a week before I am supposed to fly to a country next door to you in the gulf?' Like it or not the Agency, and I, had to factor in the potential impacts of this new crisis on the project in Arabia. If trouble spilled across the gulf into the Saudi Kingdom; that would be a serious escalation and could put me squarely in harms way.

Yes I needed to call Carl. I reached for the phone but when I picked up the receiver Carl was already on the line. We spoke for an hour. At the end of the conversation, I was calmer and Carl felt relieved that the events in Tehran had not rattled me to the point of wanting to drop out of the Saudi Project.

Monday, November 5, 1979

Months earlier a party had been scheduled for that Monday. It was meant to be a celebration for all recruits shipping out that fall. Despite the somber mood prevailing in the capital, as well as at IPC, the party was not postponed. Aside, Carl said to me "Under the circumstances the only thing the nation can do is carry on as usual. As far as the Agency is concerned, canceling the party would be the same as capitulating to the Iranians. I agree, because it would make me feel like our project had been taken hostage not only in Arabia but also right here in Washington. Furthermore, what we do here today serves a useful purpose in that it strengthens the ties between the home office and you recruits shipping out as well as our employees already working in Arabia. This is important because if something does go wrong while you are over there, we do not want any of you to lose confidence in our determination to assist in getting you out safely. Trust me; nobody in this office is going to hang their head in defeat. Everything that can be done to assist you guys, in the event something happens, will be done and life will go on as always. I believe our diplomats in Tehran would be proud of us for sticking to our schedule today and having this party. And I would not worry too much about what is happening with them if I were you Adam. Our country will get through this crisis and all of our people will get out of Iran safely. You can count on that."

Despite valiant efforts to be cheerful, the festivities were lackluster. Then Carl did something absolutely genius, although I doubt he expected things to turn out as well as they did. At some point he got everyone's attention and gave a speech that proved so uplifting it turned the atmosphere of the party around. Carl announced, "Those of you shipping out this month will be happy to know the State Department has not issued any alerts for Saudi Arabia. Americans working there are advised, as always, to keep a low profile. When you new recruits arrive in the Kingdom, make sure you keep in mind what we have been telling you all along - never discuss U.S. policies with Arab coworkers. You can add this Iranian crisis to the list of off limits topics. On a personal note, while there is no credible indications the Iranians will try to cross the Gulf and make trouble with our Saudi allies, I almost wish they would. That scenario would be so much simpler for President Carter, because a crisis involving Saudi Arabia would definitely spark a quick military response by the United States. That is something I am sure most Americans would support."

With that brief statement Carl articulated what most of us were thinking. Our response was automatic – applause, cheers, and whistles. It was the shot in the arm the party needed. Things livened up nicely afterward.

At the hotel that night another message was waiting for me. This one I looked forward to returning. Barry and I confirmed our appointment for Wednesday and I gave him the details of where and the time we would meet.

Barry knew I was super curious about Lovelen. I pressed him for information. "Where is she from? Does she have a sister; or maybe a close friend in the modeling business that might like a new pen pal for the next couple of years? How did you meet Lovelen?" Questions shot out of my mouth in rapid fire fashion.

"Anything personal you want to know about her, you can ask Lovelen directly on Wednesday. But I will tell you how we met." Barry then replayed the events of the previous five weeks of his life. Barry worked for a lobbying group that represented the automobile industry. They had offices near Capital Hill. Lovelen had been hired to work in one of their commercials. "From the moment I saw her I wanted to take her out, but so did a lot of other guys. By the time Jason Whittaker got around to introducing us, I knew I could not waste any time so my first words to her were 'would you like to go out with me?' I know it sounds crazy, but I did not say hello, nice to meet you or anything like that – just 'would you like to go out with me.' Now, if she had turned me down, I am sure Jason would have laughed in my face and I would have died on the spot. But, she said 'sure!' Later she would tell me that she had noticed me too and had hoped I would ask her out."

As I listened to the recap of their first dates together, it was hard to believe he and Lovelen had been out nine times before Barry mentioned her to me. True, if he had told me about her sooner my reaction would not have been any different from the way I responded on Saturday. On the other hand, if he had told me about her sooner I would have had more time to get over my disappointment and that would have given us a few more days to try and get better acquainted. Still I had to respect Barry for sticking to our agreement. It proved he could be loyal when it came to respecting my feelings.

"Adam sometimes I cannot believe my luck," Barry roared in my ear. "I meet a gorgeous model and she actually likes me too. Anyway, it was about our fifth date when I told her about you and that you were going to the Middle East. She asked where. When I said Saudi Arabia, right away she wanted to meet you. Actually she made a big deal about meeting you, and to tell the truth it caught me off guard. I explained to her that you had tabled certain activities because of this assignment and for that reason we had stopped talking about women, romance and dating. She did not understand, but I tried in every way I could to make it clear that if I even mentioned I was dating someone, it might not go over too well with you. She dropped the subject for a few days, but then she brought your name up again. Meeting you seemed urgent. The other day I mentioned that you would be leaving on the ninth and it was like had pushed her panic button or something. I never saw her get so animated. This time she insisted, 'I have got to meet him.' I told her I would try to set something up when you got back from Pittsburgh. When you called Saturday morning I thought, great this is an opportunity to tell you about Lovelen, but all you wanted to talk about was basketball. Before I left to meet you I decided to call Lovelen to let her know you were back in town. I told her we were about to meet to play basketball. That is when she brought up the idea of going skating and suggested I invite you to come along. As I expected, you got upset when I mentioned her. So I cheated a little. I knew how you would react if I said she was a model, and I was right. But your curiosity did get the best of you, just as I thought it would. Even though I had to use my ace in the hole, you saw for yourself I told you the truth."

"You certainly did."

"I bet you are happy now that you gave in and came out with us."

"I gladly own up to that. Lovelen is quite a looker and I am happy for you Barry. You did well."

"Uh-huh," he mumbled suspiciously.

"What? I mean it. I think you found a good one. Who knows, she might be the one."

"That's okay Adam, I know what you are up to but I warn you Lovelen is time enough for you."

"Man I am not even thinking about that stuff."

"Sure, we will see how you play it Wednesday night."

"I am just looking forward to spending an evening with a beautiful woman. I cannot wait to see your girl all dressed up."

"Adam, you have not seen anything until you see Lovelen dressed to the nines. A couple of weeks' back we went to the Kennedy Center to see the Dance Theater of Harlem. My girl was looking spectacular. Every guy in the Center was jealous and women kept cutting their eyes at Lovelen. I strutted around with my chest poked out all evening. But I am not sure she plans to wear anything too formal to dinner Wednesday. If you like, I can discuss it with her between now and then."

"So long as you do it without making it sound like a request, I would appreciate it."

"No problem, I can do that. I tell you what; if she does decide to go all out we are both in for a treat."

"Barry have I told you how glad I am we are friends?"

"Not lately," he laughed.

"Well I am, and I am honored that you introduced me to your lady. I cannot think of a better way to spend my last hours in the country than to be with my best friend and that beautiful lady of yours. Now if I can just figure out a way to find something to wear between now and Wednesday."

"That's right. All your things are on the way to Arabia."

"I think I can work something out. Talk to you later."

Wednesday, November 7, 1979

Lovelen was not my lady, I knew that, but I could not go to dinner with someone as beautiful as she was wearing clothes I pulled out of a duffel bag. This occasion called for something special. Either I had to buy a really nice suit, or find something better. With the help of the hotel concierge, I rented a tuxedo.

Our reservation was in Crystal City, Virginia at an establishment that featured Italian cuisine and had violinists that performed live for the diners. I was first to arrive and felt terribly overdressed as I was escorted to a table. I could feel every eye in the place fix on me with that look of pity guys get when we show up at a restaurant alone in a tux. I am sure they thought I had been stood up.

Moments later Barry showed up at the door. To my relief he was also wearing a tux. Then I saw her. Loud gasps echoed through the restaurant, and me - I literally froze in mid-breath.

The expression 'beautiful to the extreme' was the first thought that came to mind. That is how the Bible describes Abishag, the young maiden brought in to warm King David's bed when he grew old. Lovelen was an Abishag. Her beauty was petrifying. As she walked toward our table my eyes could not decide where to focus because she was delightful from head to foot. Lovelen strode across the room in a full-length red wool outfit that clung to her tight and hung on her right. That night, instead of Afro Puffs her hair hung straight and fell to the small of her back. At her temples the hair was pushed back to showcase red gem stones on her earlobes. Her low-cut décolletage dress highlighted a long slender neck tastefully adorned with a thin chain on which hung a gold ornament with a red stone inset. From head to toe everything was coordinated, the necklace, ear studs, lipstick, dress and heels.

Every eye was riveted as Barry escorted Lovelen to our table. Buoyed that I had made a wise investment in renting a tuxedo, I rose proudly to shake hands with my best friend and welcome the epitome of loveliness at his side. I had barely welcomed them when the restaurant's violinists gravitated to our table and began a performance that was fit for royalty. Barry and I stared in amazement as the regal looking Lovelen listened appreciatively to the music with a smile that seemed to infuse the musicians with a passion beyond anything that restaurant may have ever witnessed. At the end of the concert there was a powerful enchantment emanating from our table and as I looked around it appeared to have affected everyone in the place.

When I was growing up my mother taught me it was ill mannered to stare at people. I set that lesson aside that night. Employing all of my senses, I tried to take in everything about Lovelen I possibly could, from the smell of her perfume and the glow of her flesh in the light of the candle burning on our table to the sweet sound of her voice. Just watching her enjoy the food made my meal taste better and on those few occasions when her hand brushed against mine, its gentle sensual softness sent shivers up my spine. I even liked the way her eyes danced when she spoke. Needless to say, testing her intelligence was the farthest thing from my mind.

Barry knew I was enjoying myself but he also sensed my nostalgia for the heady days of our dating competition when we both had beautiful women at our sides. In an effort to make things a little easier on me, he got me to talk about the Saudi project. This interested Lovelen very much, and with each question from Barry she leaned in close as if to make sure not to miss a single word of what I had to say in response. Desiring to impress her with my eloquence, I waxed extensively about the project. Being long winded has never been a problem for me. But the dinner talk was not going in the direction I preferred. On the inside I kept hoping for an opening to allow me to initiate a more personal exchange.

Dependable Barry, he finally opened a door that took the conversation in a new direction albeit not where I had in mind for it to go. But we would both realize soon enough that it was the precise opening Lovelen had been waiting for. Like fishes into a net, Barry and I swam straight into the trap. In retrospect, what occurred next was the best thing that could have happened to me that week only I would not realize this until several months later.

Barry innocently inquired, "Do you think the hostage situation in Tehran will affect how Saudis treat Americans living in their country?"

Certainly the question was sensible, and appropriate, though I must say I was a little surprised to hear it coming from Barry. Sure we tested our dates, but that was to see if they were intelligent - not because we ourselves were smart. As soon as Barry asked the question, Lovelen pounced. This was the moment she had been waiting for. Barry's beauty had come to dinner with an agenda.

"Excuse me," she interrupted, "I do not think the situation in Tehran is the most important thing Adam should be concerned with right now. Not to burst either of your bubbles, but the two of you seem inordinately excited about Adam going to a country that only recently abolished Black slavery." Turning to me she asked, "Adam, are you sure the Saudis are going to treat you the same way they treat White Americans working in their country?"

Slavery in Saudi Arabia had never been discussed in any of the orientation sessions at the State Department, nor was it mentioned in any of the handouts we were given. That slavery had existed in Arabia, in past centuries, was not news. But I had assumed slavery there had ended long ago. Hearing that the institution persisted into the latter part of the 20th century was upsetting. Without thinking I blurted out, "Recently! What do you mean they recently abolished slavery? I never heard anything about…" I could hear myself ranting even as a voice in the back of my head frantically shouted 'stop talking Adam, you sound stupid … just … shut … up.' So I did.

Barry too was stunned. Neither of us would have dreamed a model could bring a topic that heavy into one of our conversations. At the least I was embarrassed at being so uninformed about a country where I had readily agreed to spend the next two years of my life. Having my ignorance exposed by a beautiful woman only heightened my embarrassment. If turnabout was fair play, Lovelen Sinclair had turned the tables on our intelligence tests. Someone's intelligence was tested that evening but not that of Lovelen Sinclair.

Lovelen, in an effort to assuage my bruised ego consoled "I really hope Saudi Arabia is everything you expect it to be. But Adam, I strongly recommend that you do a little more research before you leave the country."

"I wish I had the time. My flight leaves the day after tomorrow."

"Barry told me," she winced.

Humbly I admitted, "Listen Lovelen, I have been aware for some time that Arabs enslaved Africans but I assumed, with the exception of what is happening in North Africa, that all of that was in the past on the Arabian Peninsula. It is disconcerting to hear the practice continued as long as it did, especially now that I am under contract to work over there."

"You are right about Arabs and slavery in North Africa," Lovelen concurred. "However, most of the nations on the Arabian Peninsula kept slaves until past the mid point of this century. Most of those countries freed their Blacks in the 1960s and the Saudis freed their slaves in 1962. That was just seventeen years ago."

"Seventeen years ago – when you said recently I had the impression you meant in the last couple of years."

"Seventeen years ago is recent. How old are you?"

"Twenty-seven."

"Seventeen years ago you were ten. What do you think your life would be like today if Black slavery lasted until 1962 here in the United States? Do you believe the three of us would have gotten as much schooling as we have? Would you have earned as much money over the past 17 years? How likely is it that any of us would have grown up with both parents and all of our siblings? What kind of houses do you think we would be living in after only 17 years of freedom in this country? If it helps, think back to 1880 seventeen years after Lincoln's Emancipation Proclamation. Our Great Grandparents were alive then. What kind of stories did they pass down through the generations about their lives? Can you honestly believe the three of us would be dining in this restaurant tonight, dressed as we are, if African Americans had just been freed from slavery 17 years ago? How plausible is it that you would have landed a contract to work in Saudi Arabia? Or, what about…

"Okay, stop… please... I get your point. What more can you tell me about Blacks and slavery in Arabia?"

"Beyond the fact Black slavery was ended by Faisal in 1962, absolutely nothing," she admitted

"Then what makes you think this is an issue I should be worried about?"

"Have you ever heard of Black Saudis?"

Quickly I answered, "No."

Lovelen just stared at me and the pause gave her question and my response to it time to really sink in. When I finally made the connection, a low whistle emitted from my lips and I uttered "They are an invisible community."

"Exactly, and nobody has the slightest idea what the quality of their lives is like after 17 years of freedom. Here's another question for you. When the average Saudi sees you on the street, do you think they are going to identify you as American or one of their former slaves?"

There was no need to respond to that question. For the first time since she brought up slavery in Arabia, I began to worry for my safety and status as a free born Black man from the United States.

"It is highly likely that whatever way they deal with Black Saudis and any Africans that may be in the country that is the way you will be treated."

"How large is the Black Saudi community?"

"Those types of statistics, the Saudis do not make public. I do not have a clue about the size of the community."

"The reason I asked that question is because when I was in college, the Arab slave trade was one of my African Studies Professor's pet topics. He said many Black historians believe Arabs began enslaving Africans as much as 700 years in advance of the Europeans. This fact raises a question that had our professor, and many others, baffled. What happened to all those people? You would think that with such a long head start on slavery, there would be at least one or two Black communities in the Middle East the size of the Black American community or even larger."

"Sorry, I have no idea how many Black Saudis there are but it would be interesting to discover they number into the millions like Blacks do here in America."

Lovelen, I am sure, had not intended to darken the mood at our table but nothing can bring an evening out on the town for Black Americans crashing down faster than talk of slavery. In an attempt to lighten things Barry offered, "Come on guys, this is supposed to be a celebration in honor of my best friend. I would like to make a toast." Raising his glass, Barry declared, "To Adam, may you be prosperous in your new adventure."

"And safe," Lovelen attached as the three of us clinked glasses.

"Make sure you return to us in good health," Barry finished.

"Here, here," I echoed nervously.

At the hotel that evening, Barry and I embraced briefly and said our final goodbyes. Lovelen gave me a hug and kissed me softly on the left side of my face. When she pulled away our eyes met and in that brief glance we both knew what I would be doing over the remaining few hours until my flight.

That night before I went to bed, I prayed harder than I had in a long time. Firstly my thoughts were with our diplomats in Iran, only now to depth I had not felt since the beginning of the crisis. I tried to sleep, but I was inundated with imaginings of challenges that I might soon be facing with respect to my status as a free Black man living and working in a land that had until recently kept people that looked like me in bondage.

Not once in the previous six months had I been concerned about the tour or what might be awaiting me in the Middle East. My only impression had been that I was on the threshold of a great adventure. Now, a trip that had begun with so much promise had in the span of four days become fraught with potential perils from outside and from within the desert kingdom.

᪥᪥᪥᪥᪥᪥᪥᪥᪥᪥᪥᪥᪥᪥᪥᪥

Chapter 4

Thursday, November 8, 1979
(Less than 24 hours until departure)

Early the next morning I went for a jog. However, instead of taking my usual route along the tidal basin and across the river and back, I ran the National Mall toward the Capital. At the first pay phone I saw, I stopped and called Carl to tell him about the previous evening and ask if the Agency had any information on Black slavery in Saudi Arabia.

"I am not sure this issue is as big a deal as the young lady thinks. But I admit I had no idea slavery lasted that long in Saudi Arabia or was only recently abolished. You might want to keep in mind though that we have sent half a dozen African Americans over there already and none, as far as I know, have ever complained about the way they are being treated by the Saudis. I do not know to what extent they interact with Saudis outside their places of work, but I think they would have said something to me by now if they were having problems. At the same time, I hear what you are saying and I am in no way insensitive to your concerns. Perhaps this is something we should add to our orientation package to mention specifically to African American recruits… whoa, now that I have said that out loud I am not so sure I like the idea. Mentioning Black slavery overseas to African American recruits might be counterproductive to what I am trying to accomplish. I certainly do not want to say or do anything to scare our people off from working abroad. Besides, you cannot rule out just yet the possibility that this slavery matter could be a false alarm. Frankly Adam, I think you might be worried for no reason. Saudi Arabia is too busy trying to catch up to the 20th century before some enemy nation invades and takes over its oil fields. I am sure they are not wasting time obsessing over past policies and ways of life. No, I think slavery is ancient history to them, even if we are only talking 17 years. Now before you conclude that I am equivocating, let me say that my main concern is for you and whether you are having second thoughts about going through with your contract."

25

"In a word – yes - in fact when I got up this morning I could think of more reasons not to go over there than I could to fulfill the commitment. First there is this thing next door in Iran and now, recent slavery in the Kingdom. Carl, I can remember vividly how shocked and disappointed I was when I first learned the truth about the history of our people in this country. I was in elementary school at the time, but I started having nightmares about slavery, plantations and racial hatred. Those kinds of dreams plagued me for years. What I am trying to tell you Carl is that I already know I cannot survive in a land where the shadows of slavery are shorter than they are in this country. Carl our people have fought too hard for the measure of freedom we enjoy today. I will not surrender the gains we have made or compromise my personal integrity just to earn a bigger paycheck in another part of the world. I have to be honest with you Carl. This morning, I almost made my first act a call to you to say I quit. As soon as you picked up the phone I was going to say 'I quit'. Not hello, just 'I quit.'"

"I think I can understand how you feel."

"Maybe you can, but you are not the one that is supposed to get on a plane tomorrow and fly into only God's knows what kind of situation over there. Now Carl, I do not want you to think I have lost all of my enthusiasm for the job. Deep inside I still want to go. Plus I have this sinking feeling that if I cancel the contract I will find out later Saudi Arabia is not a bad place for Blacks after all. If that happened I would miss out on an opportunity of a lifetime, and we both know I will never get a chance like this again. At the same time it would be foolhardy to gamble with my life and my future. Carl, are you listening to me man? I've got six months of preparation under my belt, today is the day before my flight, yet here I am waffling over whether I should go or stay. This is absolutely nuts. Help me! No, strike that. This is a decision I have to make on my own. I am sorry to lay all this on you at the last minute Carl, but I thought you should know what I am dealing with right now in case I back out of this thing. Carl, my friend, I have to get going. I am on my way to the Library of Congress to see what I can dig up on the Black Saudi community. If their situation appears benign, I will be on that plane tomorrow. But tell me Carl, what do you think? Could Black Saudis be anything like us?"

"Honestly I thought all Arabs were Black. This White Saudi-Black Saudi distinction is going to take some getting used to. You know what Whites call Arabs don't you?"

"Yes I have heard all the epithets, but after last night I am not so sure any of those expressions have anything to do with ethnicity or skin color. I called my sister when I got back to the hotel. She owns one of those Encyclopedia Britannica sets. I asked her to look up Arabs and guess what; ethnically they are classified as Caucasians. But what really worries me is the fact that I have never heard of a Black Saudi community, neither have you or anyone else we know. There have been no news reports about them and I have not read anything about them in any literature. I have seen plenty of documentaries on Arabia but not once did a Black man in Arab clothing walk in front of a camera. In a way it is like they are invisible to the world. Maybe I should wait until Ralph Ellison takes a trip to Saudi Arabia, what do you think about that?"

"That is pretty funny. But you are right, it does sound like they are invisible to the world. Adam, I want you to be careful not to accidentally open a Pandora's Box with this issue - okay. Whatever you find at the Library, before you make any decisions, please give me a call so we can talk. I hate to admit this young man, but you have made me nervous too. At the same time you have aroused my curiosity about Black Saudis. I definitely want to learn more about them."

"Fair enough, I will let you know what I find out."

"Remember, do not let anything you discover at the Library dissuade you about the project, at least not before we have a chance to talk. I am pretty sure it is safe enough over there. I have all the confidence in the world that your tour will be wonderful. Of all the people we have sent over so far, and I am only talking about African Americans, you are by far the best candidate I ever recruited. The others we sent have made out fine and I know you will too. But if you do decide to cancel your contract; I am not going to lie to you, it would be a big disappointment to me personally. But, I will understand. Keep in mind what I said though. None of the African Americans we have sent so far have complained about the way Saudis treat them. In fact, from reports coming back, it looks like the Saudis get along better with Black Americans than they do with White workers."

"That is an interesting observation. It could help. Carl, time is running out. I have to get going."

"Wait! Adam, before you hang up - Malcolm X went to Saudi Arabia a few years back remember?"

"That's right he made a pilgrimage to Mecca in 1964, two years after slavery ended over there. I read his autobiography when I was in college. He was interviewed when he came back but I cannot recall off the top of my head what he said to the reporters. I will look up his trip too this morning. Maybe Malcolm said or saw something that can help me make some sense out of all this. Carl the clock is ticking - I really need to get going."

"Good luck and call me later."

Bounding up the stairs of the Library of Congress, I nearly tripped when I came face to face with Lovelen and Barry. They were grinning as if they had known all along I would show there that morning. Like me, they were dressed for jogging and Lovelen looked fantastic in the yellow outfit she was wearing.

"You know Adam; I would have been very disappointed if you did not show up here this morning. Plus, you would have cost me $20." As she said this, Lovelen held out her palm and Barry neatly laid down a Jackson.

"You two bet I would come here today?"

"Sure did."

"Okay I admit what you said last night shook me up. But there are plenty of other libraries in this town you know. I could just as easily have gone to Martin Luther King or somewhere else."

"But - you didn't," Lovelen gloated waving the bill in my face. "Adam, I have been listening to your best friend talk about you for several weeks now, and I have made a few observations of my own based on our two evenings together. I think I have a pretty good idea what type of person you are. You would never go elsewhere if the Library of Congress was available. Obviously I am right because... here... you... are," she bragged, again flaunting the $20.

"Okay, so you guessed right about the library. But there is no way you could have known what time I would get here. You guys might have been waiting out here a long time."

Turning to Barry, Lovelen chided, "Is it just me or do you not hear that loud sound? You know the sound of that big clock ticking down the seconds until Adam's flight?" Facing me she continued, "Adam you have a plane to catch. You need every minute you can spare to do this research. But do not worry. Barry and I are here to help."

She was right, I had a lot of work ahead and no clue how much research and time it was going to take to find what I was looking for. I did know one thing, unless I found something that screamed loud and clear 'Adam, keep your butt at home' I would be on a 747 in less than 24 hours. The sand in the top of the hourglass was running out fast. Without wasting another second I turned and quick-stepped into the building. Lovelen followed, but first snapped her finger to get Barry's attention because he had gotten distracted by something across the street at the Capital.

Behind me I heard Barry groan, "Are we going to have to do a lot of reading?"

"Buck up," Lovelen barked, "you are not in high school any more."

For the balance of the morning we pored over countless volumes. There was plenty of information about the ongoing enslavement of Blacks by Arabs in North Africa. Even more material was devoted to the history of the Arab slave trade. But after spending the entire morning searching, we came up empty on Black slavery inside Arabia itself with the exception of a few items that were only related peripherally. We confirmed the edict issued in 1962 by Crown Prince Faisal, shortly before he became King that abolished Black slavery in Saudi Arabia. One report we uncovered actually raised additional questions in our minds. It was submitted by a westerner living in the Kingdom who asserted that *de facto* slavery persisted in the country despite Faisal's edict.

Though none of this data specifically mentioned a Black Saudi Community, it was obvious Faisal could not have abolished Black slavery in his country unless Blacks lived there and had actually been enslaved. Our challenge was to find out what became of the Black population in the years following the edict. Clearly there was a story somewhere in all of this. After breaking for a quick lunch we resumed our research.

From the outset, Lovelen led the way in our campaign. In the process she showed remarkable familiarity with the functions and layout of a library. To say the least, Barry and I were impressed. Stereotypes I had harbored for years about models, shattered like glass that day. Unquestionably, there was more to Lovelen Sinclair than physical beauty. After awhile though I began to suspect, regardless of what she had stated at dinner the previous evening that she knew more about Black slavery in Arabia than she was admitting.

Toward mid-afternoon an interesting thought crossed my mind. I suggested "we might be approaching this all wrong. What I mean is this, we have assumed that the Black experience in Saudi Arabia mirrors ours here in the United States. What if we are wrong? That could be the reason we cannot find the information we are searching for, because we could be looking for data that has never existed. For instance some of the starting points in a study of post-slavery society in America might include, those phony 19th century promises of 40 acres and a mule, 20th century policies like welfare and affirmative action, or debates over reparations; you know, the sort of things one would expect to find in a democratic society trying to reverse the impact of slavery on its past, present and future. Saudi Arabia though, is not a democracy. Its citizens, White, Black, or otherwise, are subjects of a monarchy. Guys, we may be comparing apples to oranges here because it took a war to end slavery in America and that is a far cry from ending slavery by royal decree."

"Which is precisely why you should be worried Adam Sneed," Lovelen lamented. "That is the very point I was trying to get through to you last night. Slavery ended there on the whim of an unchallengeable monarch.

The citizens of the country had no say in the decision. Do you realize what that means? It means, one day out of the blue they were commanded 'let your Black slaves go free'. Remember from history the reaction in the southern states when Abraham Lincoln issued the Emancipation Proclamation? They were infuriated, and the Civil War dragged on several more years afterward. Does it not make sense that some Saudis may have been angry over being commanded to release their slaves? Think about it, the enforcement of a royal edict in Arabia could explain why we found that report about *de facto* slavery persisting in the country. That observation might reflect a degree of resistance to Faisal's decision, at least on the individual level. I think we should consider the possibility that the freedom Blacks enjoy there is only on paper, and God knows Black Americans know what that is like. Could that not also be a contributing factor to why the rest of the world does not know about the Black Saudi Community and has never heard their voices? What if only a privileged few Blacks enjoy freedom while the majority remains in bondage? Or maybe there are former slaveholders in Arabia who on the surface appear to honor the edict, but privately continue to treat Blacks like slaves. What if some former slave owners got together and formed a group like the Ku Klux Klan, to keep Blacks 'in their place'? Or maybe they have systems over there similar to sharecropping to keep Blacks in perpetual debt, the way our ancestors suffered after the Civil War. For all we know, Black Saudis might have no choice but to remain economically chained to their former owners. No Adam, I do not think it is a mistake to compare our people's experiences here in America with Black slavery anywhere on the planet. Everything Blacks anywhere go through, or have gone through, is relevant to all of our communities. I also think we should at least presume that the racial climate in Saudi Arabia, following the issuance of Faisal's edict, may have been similar, if not identical to the way things were in the southern states after Lincoln's Emancipation Proclamation."

Logically, Lovelen's argument made sense but unless we found mention of the Black Saudi Community somewhere all the speculation in the world would do nothing to provide accurate answers to our questions. "Maybe you are right Lovelen. But that begs the question what kind of situation am I about to walk into over there? The last thing I want is to pass through some kind of cultural time warp and emerge into a society no farther advanced racially than the one my great grandfather lived through in his time."

Looking me straight in my eyes Lovelen made the sobering comment, "The fact that nobody knows about these people should give you a pretty good idea what kind of place Saudi Arabia is for the Blacks living there. Remember what you said last night about them being an invisible community? Of all people, we do not have to be told what happens when a community is invisible to the rest of the world."

"They are susceptible to just about anything and everything," Barry added. "The most horrible things could befall them and the rest of the world would never know."

Nothing that I had heard to that point had done anything to reinforce my now flagging commitment to the project. I moaned, "Saudi Arabia sounds more dangerous every time you two open your mouths."

Lovelen then asked a question that hit close to a sentiment that had been brewing in my head since she sprung her bombshell the night before. "Are you sure you still want to go?"

Rolling my eyes playfully, I warned, "Stop reading my mind woman."

"Sorry about that, but I do wish you would think about something that has me worried. Faisal was killed after he freed the slaves, maybe not for that reason, but he is dead now. Does anybody know how the current ruler, what is his name… King Khalid, does anyone know how he feels about Blacks? There is no vote. It is not rule by the people or for the people, but rule by a monarch whose word is law. What could Black Saudis do if all of a sudden King Khalid decided to reinstitute slavery? You and I both know that short of rebellion they could do little. More importantly my friend, what would you do if you got out of bed one morning and heard a royal decree proclaiming Black slavery is legal again?"

I could feel the hair on the back of my neck rising. Lovelen had been correct the previous evening when she inferred I should have done my homework before signing the contract. But was it too late to back out? Carl Scott said he would understand if I changed my mind, but what would a last minute pullout from a federal contract do to my career?

Lovelen had played Devil's advocate, played it well, and I was paying the price with a migraine. Still I could not help but admire her passion and perceptiveness. Driving her argument home, she hit me with what would be the golden spike of the afternoon, "Like it or not Adam, the possibility of Black slavery being reinstituted over there is as real as the throne of Saudi Arabia itself. Probably it will not happen but who could stop it if the current, or a future King, decided to put Blacks in bondage again?"

I knew Lovelen meant well, but slavery, past or future was too big of an issue to be dumped into my lap at the eleventh hour. Saudi Arabia was beginning to sound more like the kind of country any sane free Black person would avoid.

Deep inside I was beginning to resent Lovelen for spoiling my naiveté and telling me about Black slavery in Arabia. If I could have turned back the clock and retracted my invitation to a farewell dinner, I might have been tempted to do so. That way I would have left for my assignment blissfully ignorant of Black slavery in Arabia. But it was too late for wishful thinking. In my heart I was beginning to lean heavily toward the thought I had when I got out of bed that morning – call Carl Scott and tell him 'I quit'.

Across the table a wicked leer came on Barry's face. I knew what that meant. Barry was getting ready to say something stupid. When he started snickering, I braced myself. "Just think, if you are forced to become a runaway, you could become the Kunta Kinte of this century. They will recapture you and a guy named Mohamed will cut off your foot and say," then with a mock Middle Eastern accent he continued, "You are going to learn to say your name Ab-doo." The three of us laughed over Barry's gibe, but we were a little too loud for the confines of the Library of Congress. Heads turned and disapproving glares were cast in our direction.

Only a close friend could get away with that kind of taunt without causing offense and as always I got right into the spirit of Barry's jesting and retorted, "I hate Tubob Mohamed." Just then I remembered something from my conversation with Carl Scott that morning and snapped my fingers; also inappropriate in the library. More heads turned. Leaning toward my friends I whispered, "Malcolm X went to Mecca back in the 60s – 1964 to be exact – that was only two years after Faisal issued his edict. What are the chances, do you think, that Malcolm saw evidence of Black slavery while he was in Mecca? I recall he gave several interviews when he got back to the States, but I do not remember what he said. Lovelen, have you ever come across any statements by Malcolm on slavery in Arabia?"

"No, but I know exactly where to find information on his trip. See you guys in a few minutes," she advised and dashed away.

Following a hunch of my own, I took off in the opposite direction. That left Barry sitting alone and looking perplexed. After scratching his head he got up, strolled over to the central desk and asked for assistance in finding information on the pilgrimage of Malcolm X to Mecca. Minutes later when we caucused, all three of us contributed material on Malcolm's trip. It took twenty minutes, but we whittled the stack down to a couple of relevant quotes. None made any specific reference to slavery; however, there was one comment that particularly stood out. In a post-Hajj interview Malcolm stated:

> 'America needs to understand Islam, because this is the one
> religion that erases from its society the race problem.
> Throughout my travels in the Muslim world, I have met,
> talked to, and even eaten with people who in America would
> have [been] considered "white" -- but the "white" attitude
> was removed from their minds by the religion of Islam. I
> have never before seen sincere and true brotherhood practiced
> by all colors together, irrespective of their color.'

"How could he say something like that when Black slavery was only abolished in Saudi Arabia two years before he got there," Lovelen questioned with irritation.

"Perhaps he, like me, was unaware it existed," I suggested. "You have to remember Malcolm was a student of history. I am sure if he knew about slavery in Arabia he would have been on the lookout to spot oppression. And I think we all know how Malcolm would have reacted if he had observed Blacks being abused in any way."

"What if things had settled down by then and were not as bad for Blacks when he got there," Barry asked?

"Two years after God knows how many centuries of slavery," Lovelen trumpeted incredulously, "what planet are you from?"

"What if the things Malcolm said are true? Their religion does prohibit one Muslim from being harsh to a fellow believer, right? The Blacks we are talking about in Arabia, they are Muslim. So Malcolm's statement seems to make room for that possibility. Then again, who really knows what slavery was like for Blacks in Arabia? Maybe the Saudis never committed the kind of atrocities on their slaves that our people suffered here and Blacks suffered in other countries," I hinted.

"Tell that to Black families in North Africa," Lovelen snapped.

"Listen Lovelen, everyone realizes what is happening in North Africa is bad but North Africa is not Arabia. We really do not know what life is like for Blacks in Saudi Arabia, not now or what it was like for them before Faisal issued his edict. Maybe Malcolm did not observe anything out of the way with respect to Blacks there because there was nothing out of the way to be seen. If that is the case, I can live with that. I mean we know Saudi Arabia does not have a free press or anything like that, but the western press covered Brother Malcolm's trip to Mecca. Had any issues come up that embarrassed or upset Malcolm while he was over there, you know the media would have jumped right on them and they would have become public. Besides, look at us. We have searched practically a whole day in one of the most prestigious libraries on the planet and found absolutely nothing about slavery in Saudi Arabia. In fact we know almost as much about it now as we knew when we got here this morning. Maybe it is simply presumptuous to assume the Saudis mistreated their Blacks."

I was trying to be diplomatic, but Lovelen remained resolute in her feelings and said: "Maybe I am being super sensitive about this, but the facts are that the Saudis ended slavery and nothing has been heard from or about Black Saudis since. This indicates to me there is reason enough to be concerned about them. Listen guys, the very word slavery in and of itself has been offensive from the moment it was first spoken. I do not know who that first slave owner was, but you can bet he had no intention of ever trading places with the people he enslaved. Throughout history everyone forced into slavery immediately transferred all of their energies and ingenuity into trying to figure out a way to regain their freedom. This reaction was automatic and you and I would do the same if we were suddenly put in chains. Even if we had been born in bondage, our dreams would be all about gaining our freedom. Whether people call what they do to other humans, slavery, kidnapping, or something else, there is nothing natural about subjecting a fellow human to the kinds of physical, mental, social or psychological restraints that we ourselves would resist. Every human ever born, knows slavery is wrong. Even those who grew up and became slave owners. I can make that statement without fear of contradiction because every slave holding society in history has a record of having fought to keep itself free and independent. The truth is people do not accept slavery as a natural state, especially people misfortunate enough to have been enslaved."

"We agree with you honey, but I still wonder if Malcolm ever saw or met a Black Saudi," Barry pondered aloud. "We all know Malcolm was not the kind of brother who would stand by and watch a Black person being abused and say nothing. Malcolm could not have kept quiet about something like that."

"You may be on to something there Barry," I reacted. "Malcolm saw Blacks in Mecca, there is no doubt about that, the question is were they Black Saudis or, like him, Black Muslims from other parts of the world? According to Malcolm, race did not matter among the people he saw at Mecca, and I think it is statistically safe to presume at least some of the Blacks he saw had to be from Saudi Arabia. That is why it makes sense to me that if race relations were so peaceful two years after Black slavery was abolished in the country, to the extent that Malcolm saw nothing out of the way between the races, then the institution of slavery, as it was practiced in Arabia, must not have been anything like it was here and in other societies."

"I would just love to agree with you both," Lovelen cautioned, "but I think we should also consider the possibility Malcolm might have been blinded by his faith, maybe just a little, at least to the point he could have ignored or saw through horrors that were taking place right in front of his eyes. What? Don't look at me like that Adam. People get swayed by their faith all the time, in all religions."

"Not the Malcolm Little I read about," I objected.

"Okay then, what if the Saudis deliberately kept Brother Malcolm away from areas where their former slaves lived? What if those former slaves lived in ghettos under squalid conditions? Did we not read that the government sponsored his tours and assigned him an official escort? Don't you think it is possible they went out of their way to shield Malcolm, a man they placed on the status of guest of state mind you, from seeing things that he might personally have found objectionable? Barry, how are foreign dignitaries treated when they come to D.C.?"

"A number of factors are involved. It depends on who they are; their rank, the purpose of their visit and other things. Some are met on the front steps of the White House, while others are given formal welcome ceremonies complete with canon salutes. One thing I can tell you, the State Department does not send diplomatic motorcades through certain sections of this city."

"My point exactly, so we can all agree the Saudis controlled where they took Malcolm and showed him what they wanted him to see. I think it is safe to conclude Malcolm never got to see the real Saudi Arabia. For the Saudis, Malcolm was a high profile pilgrim, which is why they put him on VIP status. For them Malcolm's pilgrimage to Mecca was more of a public relations event."

"There is another consideration I think we might be overlooking," I stated. "What if the Black Saudi community is still forming and has not yet been fully established? Think about it. No Black American Community existed, *per se*, right after the Civil War. Our people were leaving plantations or wandering around trying to find loved ones they had lost touch with during slavery. It took our community decades to organize, and in certain areas we are still struggling to develop continuity."

Lovelen's next question really made me nervous. "It sounds like you are suggesting that after 17 years they may still be living close to the way they were when slavery first ended. Or, in other words, that nothing has changed for them. Hopefully you are wrong, but what if you are right. Could you escape from Saudi Arabia if you had to?"

"I am sure the Mission has evacuation plans, but I assume you mean if I had to escape on my own. In that event I have no idea what I would do. I know very little about the country. Before I was recruited, I had never heard of Riyadh or knew it was the capital of Saudi Arabia. I had to look it up in the Atlas. Given my limited knowledge of the country, I would have to say that as of now getting out of there on my own would be impossible. Gosh! The idea of having to run for my life in the middle of a desert gives me the hives. What was I thinking? I cannot believe I signed up to be over there for two long years."

"Plus you do not speak Arabic," Barry offered, not so helpfully. "That would make your flight even more hazardous if you became a refugee."

"Actually I think not being able to speak the language could work to my advantage because that would let people know I am not a local Black."

Barry countered, "But if they brought slavery back and Blacks revolted, government forces would start rounding up Black people on sight. Nobody would take the time to ask your nationality. And if shooting started, you could forget it. Your skin would make you a target long before you could open your mouth and say 'I am an American' in any language."

"Just how helpful do you plan on being with this Barry? Okay, I get it; and you are right. Those guys could take me deep into the desert, just walk away and that would be the end of me forever. Did you know there is a part of the desert over there they call the Empty Quarter? It is supposed to be one of the most desolate places on the planet. People go in but they do not come out." My mind went into overdrive imagining several disasters at once. Then I had a brain flash. There was a hole in our argument, and it was a big one. "Barry and Lovelen, we read that the Saudis have ruled Arabia since 1932. Black slavery began many centuries before the Saudis came to power. What we are really dealing with is not so much how Saudis treat Blacks, but the way Blacks were treated before the Saudis came to power. Guess what? I do not have to worry about the Saudis because thirty years after the family took over the country, they ended Black slavery in Arabia," I said with flourish and a deep sigh of relief.

With a beaming smile of triumph Barry hopped onto my band wagon, "That settles it in my mind too. By Jove I think you have found the answer to your dilemma. The Saudis are the good guys. They are the Abraham Lincoln's of the desert."

"I would not be so sure of that if I were you two," Lovelen cautioned with a wary furrow of her brow.

"Come on Lovelen admit it, Adam can go to Saudi Arabia and he will be safe. Not only that, he is going to get to see the country in the raw and to an extent Brother Malcolm never got the chance. I cannot think of any reason for Adam to be worried. Two years from now he will come home and tell us wonderful stories and everything we want to know about the Black Saudi community." Despite his upbeat manner, Barry added in a concerned tone, "By the way Adam, while you are over there, make sure you keep me posted on what is happening with you okay. Lovelen and I will keep you in our prayers, won't we baby."

"Absolutely," Lovelen agreed.

Something Lovelen mentioned earlier had lingered in the back of my head and though I was more inclined not to bring it up at that point, it screamed for attention. "Listen Lovelen," I said softly, "you made a comment a little while back that I have not been able to stop thinking about. Do you remember when you said, the possibility of the return of slavery in Saudi Arabia is as real as the throne of Arabia itself? Could not the same be said about America? As long as minorities remain underrepresented in this country, how sure can we be that a political system that seems to prefer charismatic leaders, will never allow someone with a secret fascist agenda to come to power? This has already happened several times in western lands. Or, look at the constitutional amendments that have been enacted over the years, which Blacks depend on for many of our freedoms. How certain can we be, that the Constitution is foolproof from malicious manipulation to our detriment? I mean at one point in history each of us were identified right in the Constitution as only 3/5 of a person."

Lovelen and Barry sat straight up in their chairs but said nothing. On their faces I saw the same consternation that had occupied my inner thoughts from the moment Lovelen made her comment about slavery and the throne of Arabia. All Blacks harbor fears about worse case scenarios in America. This is common among minority communities everywhere. Whites sometime accuse us of being paranoid, but paranoia is part and parcel of being the underclass. On top of that, fuel gets added to our paranoia every time a hate crime comes to national attention. Drastic situations like the one I postulated to Barry and Lovelen are the kinds of things none of us prefer to dwell on, but we would be lying to ourselves and everyone else if we denied that we think about them from time to time.

At that point I decided I had heard enough talk about slavery. The headache I had developed earlier had gotten worse, and I doubted it would be going away any time soon. I was highly agitated over the possibility of traveling to the other side of the planet and being treated no better than a third class foreigner. At the same time I was encouraged by the Saudi family's apparent disenchantment with slavery.

"Maybe the whole thing boils down to the fact there are things about Saudi Arabia that are impossible for outsiders to know," Barry offered.

"In other words, the only way I will find out is to go see for myself," I whispered mournfully. "This is just great. I get to play Magellan and if I fall off the edge of the world I will have the comfort of knowing, in my final moments, that at least everybody else will know the planet actually is flat." Looking at Lovelen I confessed, "I think you are utterly beautiful, but before we met I was the happiest person I knew. I was on the verge of flying out of the country to begin an exciting exotic desert adventure, and then I met you. Lovelen I had absolutely no worries about anything before you walked into my life. Now, thanks to you, the Iranians, and possibly the Saudis themselves, I am no longer sure I want to fulfill this contract." Lovelen opened her mouth to speak but I held up a hand, "Hold on, I have more to say. I need to get a few things off my chest before you say another word. A couple of questions have been on my mind since I got home last night, and I feel I must ask them. Please be honest with me when you answer. How long have you known about slavery in Saudi Arabia, and what was your real motive for wanting to meet me and bring it up at dinner last night?"

Lovelen's chest heaved as she took a deep breath and slowly exhaled. This distracted me temporarily. "I wondered how long it was going to take you to get around to asking that question. When I was in college, I was a member of a team of students assigned to prepare a paper on OPEC. The oil embargo was the big news story at that time. We started by gathering material on each member state. I was assigned to research Saudi Arabia."

"I figured it had to be something like that," I said with a quick glance at Barry.

"The country fascinated me, so much so that after we turned in our paper I continued to study Saudi Arabia just for my own edification. There was so much information on the country that I could not decide where to focus first. I literally went on a reading binge. Saudi Arabia became an obsession. What I read was exciting, positive, and forward-looking. King Faisal… he became my hero. All he wanted to do was bring his country into the 20th century. My appreciation for his courage grew as I learned more about the opposition he faced from his countrymen, even members of his own family. After awhile though, I started to get the feeling something had to be wrong. I mean Saudi Arabia was looking a little too good to be true, and everybody knows there has never been a perfect society - right. Then I came across the report about Faisal abolishing slavery. At first I thought, they must be talking about a different Faisal, someone earlier in the country's history, not the one I have been reading about because that would mean Black freedom is very recent over there. Then I saw the date of the edict … I was floored. It was hard to believe that only a decade earlier people who could very well be distant relatives of mine, had been in chains in that country. Naturally from that point my focus switched to searching for information on slavery in Saudi Arabia and what has happened to the post-slavery Black community."

Barry reacted, "So you have done this research before. That is exactly what Adam and I thought."

"Unfortunately, just like today, I ran into a hundred dead ends. Plenty of information was available on slavery among the Arab states of North Africa, but I found absolutely nothing about Black slavery on the Arabian Peninsula."

"I thought you knew your way around this place a little too well," I told her.

"Actually this is my first time in the Library of Congress, but how I love this place. I wish I could have done my research here when I was in college."

"Then you are not from D.C.," I seeded in hopes of prodding Lovelen to tell more about herself.

"No, but this is the first place I would have come given the opportunity. I am from Georgia originally. I attended Southern University in New Orleans. While I was in college I started modeling part time to help pay for tuition. I did not have a scholarship. The money was very good, so after graduating I switched to modeling full time. I figure I will do this until I lose my appeal. When nobody wants to photograph me anymore, I will have my degree to fall back on and maybe a little bit of fame to boost me into a new career. By the way, this is not my first time in D.C. I have been here on jobs before, but this is the longest I have stayed. Thanks to Barry I have had a wonderful time and Adam, meeting you was an unexpected bonus. I will always treasure our time together."

"Where do you go from here?"

"From here I go to Los Angeles."

"I know Barry is going to miss you. By the way, you have no idea how close I came to turning down Barry's invitation to go skating last Saturday. But I think I can safely say that it was lucky for me that I got to meet you before I left the country. Of course, if I change my mind about going to Arabia it will be your fault, and I won't mind flying out to California to blame you to your face."

Lovelen laughed and admitted, "I have a confession to make. When Barry told me his best friend was going to Saudi Arabia, the first thing I asked about you was if you were Black. When he said yes, I made it my mission to meet you. So if you had turned down our invitation to go skating, I would have thought of some other way to get to meet you. I was even thinking about preparing a lunch and having Barry pin you down for a picnic in the park."

"What if I turned lunch down too," I asked to test her.

Laughing lightly she teased, "I have yet to meet the man who can turn down my goodies."

Barry frowned at her joke, but I enjoyed it a lot.

"Adam, my conscience would not let me ignore the possibility you might not know what you were getting yourself into. I needed to know how much you knew about Saudi Arabia. Listening to the two of you in the restaurant last night scared me a little, but not because you were committed to going. It was just that, you clearly were not fully apprised of the situation over there. I felt if I could enlighten you about Saudi Arabia, even a little, I had to try. There was no point in you going over there and saying the wrong thing to the wrong person at the wrong time."

Barry spoke up, "Listen Adam, if there were serious dangers for Black Americans over there I am sure the government would have alerted every worker being sent over there by now. You told me yourself, you are not the first Black American to be sent to Saudi Arabia."

"Carl Scott pretty much made that same argument this morning. Okay guys I am ready to go home – correction, back to the hotel. Thank you for all of your help and especially your concern for my safety. Lovelen, I know you meant well but I have to tell you, I have got one mother of a headache right now. Anyway, I hope you and Barry enjoy the rest of your time together. I also wish you success in L.A. Barry, if I go through with this contract you and I will be keeping in touch by mail. Now, if you get a call from me tomorrow afternoon asking if I can move in until I find a new apartment, you will know I bugged out. Well… I guess that's it."

Lovelen promised "I will definitely be keeping in touch through Barry and if I find any information that I think might be helpful to you, I will pass it on to him so he can send it to you." She kissed me sweetly on the cheek and said goodbye. Because of my headache and the frustration of the day her kiss lost a bit of its zest. Barry shook my hand. We embraced and said a final farewell. It was sad watching my friends walk away for the last time, but I had an important decision to make and not much time to get it done.

Carl had asked me to call and let him know what I found out about Black Saudis; however, since I had nothing to share I did not feel guilty about my decision not to make that call. Besides, I preferred to make the final choice about my future on my own. Men of Carl's stature did not get where they were without being good at what they do, and one thing they did a little too well was talk people like me into doing things we might not do otherwise. A few words from Carl could have me on the plane without giving slavery another thought. No, it would be better for me to meditate privately and pray. If I chose to remain in America, then so be it.

After dinner, I returned to the hotel, showered, set the radio alarm and got into bed. I hoped a couple of hours of rest would refresh me mentally and leave me clear headed enough to make the right choice about my future. For the most part sleep eluded me that night, as I lay in bed tossing and turning over a decision I had to make by the next morning.

Chapter 5

Friday, November 9

When the radio alarm sounded, the song that was playing made me smile. It was Maria Muldaur's popular tune about a desert oasis. I loved that song. I figured being awakened by that song on that particular morning had to be a good omen, so just like that I stopped worrying about going through with the contract. Dismissing all of my concerns of the past few days, I turned my attention toward the two day layover in Paris that IPC had arranged for me as a last fling before I entered the land of enforced celibacy.

After telephoning my parents, I spoke with Barry briefly then listened to a parting pep talk from Carl Scott. Out in front of the hotel, I caught a taxi to Dulles Airport.

Three hours later I was at cruising altitude high above the North Atlantic.

Parisians lived up to their reputation for being impatient with people that cannot speak their language. French attitudes notwithstanding, I enjoyed my two days in the City of Lights. I walked the Champs Élysées, visited the Arc de Triomphe, Eiffel Tower, Notre Dame and the Louvre.

During one of my walking tours I turned down a certain street and found myself suddenly surrounded by prostitutes. They told me their work was legal in Paris so long as a girl was registered with the police and had a valid license. I had to make my way through a gauntlet of solicitations, but I got past them without breaking my vow.

Early on Sunday, November 11, I resumed my journey to the Middle East. Shortly after takeoff, our flight was cruising above the Alps when a French Air Force jet buzzed the 747. I am sure the pilot of that jet was only having a little fun at the expense of the pilots of the 747, but for me it was a rare chance to experience in real time the difference in speeds between commercial and military aircraft. Also, in an analogous way, the incident reflected what was happening in my life at that very moment. Saudi Blacks with their fledgling 17 years of freedom were like a commercial aircraft crawling along, compared to a speedy military jet that in the analogy represented the century long head start in freedom by Black Americans and our struggle for civil rights. Compared to us, Saudi Blacks were just getting started. I felt like I was making a societal transition comparable to slowing down from jet speed to commercial aircraft pace.

Our flight stopped briefly at Rome to pick up additional passengers and from there we soared across the Mediterranean toward Jeddah, my first stop in the Saudi Kingdom.

Midway across the Mediterranean, the sun began to set. Below us the tranquil green sea turned a deep shade of turquoise and tiny dots of light began to appear on the surface of the water. They were the lights of lanterns hanging over the sides of fishing boats. From our height they looked like tiny stars floating on the sea. As the minutes passed, the sky steadily darkened and a dazzling array of red and orange hues slowly turned into a sliver of deep aqua along the edge of the horizon. Natural beauty surrounded me in the heavens above and on the sea below. Enjoying these images got me to wondering what kind of sights awaited me on the Arabian Peninsula. I was curious about what I might see first. Without consciously thinking about it, I let all my worries about racism and slavery slip to the back of my mind. The trepidation I had felt since Lovelen's news flash at dinner Wednesday, gave way to growing excitement. By the time the pilot announced our descent into Jeddah International, my heart was racing with anticipation.

Peering out of the window into the darkness, I expected at any moment to see dunes, palm trees, tents, camels, Bedouins, bevies of beautiful harem women – all of that imagery – suddenly appear before my eyes. But just as I was poised to enjoy my first glimpses of Arabia, a flurry of activity caught my attention from within the cabin. Turning from the window, I saw women filing down the aisles toward the back of the plane. Others were returning to their seats, and these returnees were covered in a black cloth. Later I would learn the cloth is called the Abbaya and it is worn by Saudi females when they go out in public.

Coming out of Europe, I had never given thought to the possibility some of the passengers on the plane might be Saudis returning to their homeland. No one on the plane had looked Arab to me, though I was no expert on how Saudis or Arabs were supposed to look. Nevertheless, this sudden donning of veils astounded me because these women had blended in so completely with the Western world.

This activity also brought home the fact that I was on the verge of entering one of the last genuinely male dominated societies remaining on the planet. To tell the truth the thought did not feel half bad. I actually found it appealing. 'Living in Arabia just might spoil me,' I mused to myself.

The aircraft decelerated another notch, the nose dipped sharply and the sound of lowering landing gear filled the cabin. Then all of a sudden the plane was caught in a huge swath of bright light coming from somewhere on the ground below. Squinting through the glare, I grew tense as I waited for my eyes to adjust and bring into focus my first sights in Arabia.

Like Pac Man caught by the ghosts, all the excitement and anticipation of the previous six months melted in that first glance. Instead of camels, oases, tents and sand dunes, stretched out below as far as my eyes could see, was the ultra modern port of Jeddah. It was the most mechanized and up-to-date port I had ever seen. Large ocean-going vessels and oil tankers lined the docks along the coast of the Red Sea while hundreds of stevedores operating modern machinery loaded and offloaded goods from around the world. There were automobiles and heavy vehicles moving in and out of the port area on well lit paved roads.

I had known all along Saudi Arabia was modernizing. The contract I had signed was for a job working on a construction project building vocational training centers throughout the Kingdom. Young Saudis would come to these centers to learn how to be auto mechanics, plumbers, electricians, and so forth. Reality set in and I had to admit that for the previous six months I had been in a state of denial. My fondest hope was that some of old Arabia still existed for me to see and enjoy. Now it was clear that ancient Bedouin world was a thing of the past. A way of life I had admired from afar had vanished. Like it or not I had traveled half way around the world to work in a modern country. Off in the distance a vast glow spanned the horizon. Nobody had to tell me where that glow was coming from. It was the night lights of a very cosmopolitan downtown Jeddah, the most modern city in Saudi Arabia. Deflated, I sat back and moped in disappointment over 20th century Saudi Kingdom.

Shortly thereafter the wheels hit the tarmac and the plane taxied to a stop. White buses with green Arabic writing pulled up to transport us to the terminal. It took less than twenty-five seconds to step off the plane and board the bus, but for that brief period I was exposed to thick, heavy, humid air. I knew then that ten minutes in that kind of heat would leave me soaked to the bone with perspiration. Considering the proximity of Jeddah and the nearby desert to the Red Sea, the high humidity made sense. Still I was grateful when I stepped onto the bus to find Saudi Arabia had invested in that most wonderful of modern inventions – air-conditioning. Thoughts of riding a camel no longer appealed to me. Not in that kind of heat.

Green and white, the national colors, dominated the airport and its fleet of Saudia Airlines jets. Atop the control tower, the flag of Saudi Arabia flapped lazily on hot air currents blowing out of the desert from the east.

At the terminal our bus was met by a smartly dressed young Arab wearing dark green slacks with black stripes down the sides and a stiffly starched white shirt that had green epaulets on the shoulders. He led us to a quiet corner inside the terminal. Smiling warmly he welcomed our group, first in Arabic and then in English. His English had a lilt to it and R's rolled off his tongue like a Spaniard. P's sounded more like B's, which, I later learned is because Arabic does not have a letter equivalent to the English P. Phonetically his greeting sounded this way: "Ladies and gentlemen, welcome to the Kingdom of Sow-u-dee Arrrrabia and Jid-dah Interrrrnational Airrrborrrrt. Those of you staying in Jid-dah, blease go to customs herrre on my left. Anyone taking connecting flights to Rrrriyath and otherrr cities in Sow-u-dee Arrrrabia may go to the waiting rrrrom therrre on yourrr left. We hobe you enjoy yourrrr stay in the Kingdom of Sow-u-dee Arrrabia and again welcome.'

Everything about the welcome was friendly, from his manner to the tone of his voice. It was a foretaste of the hospitality in store for me over the coming years. The sting of disappointment when we flew over the port diminished a bit and some of my romantic notions of Arabia began to resurface. What revived them was the thought that modern machinery and technology may not have ruined the legendary warmth and hospitality of the people of the Peninsula, after all.

In Paris I had been a tourist for a few days but now things were different. I would be a foreign resident of the Kingdom for the next two years. The expression 'I am a stranger in a strange land' came to mind as I observed the sights and listened to the clamor of a tongue I could not understand.

Passengers from the United States circled the wagons, so to speak, standing together protectively in a makeshift bond of physical, emotional and psychological unity. Other nationalities were doing the same as arrivals from Europe, Asia and the Pacific clustered in isolated groups. All of us waited like obedient lambs for announcements about our connecting flights. There were no complaints or criticisms or the typical brashness western travelers are noted for, only humble cooperation with airport staff.

Two hours later, the young man that welcomed our flight returned and instructed those of us flying on to Riyadh to load back onto the buses.

As our bus crossed the tarmac we noticed a Saudia Airlines jet standing out in the open far from the gates. There had to be at least a thousand people in several long lines attempting to get on board. A fellow passenger joked "whoever ticketed that flight really screwed up." Laughter filled the bus. It was obvious all of those people would never fit on one plane. A better informed traveler explained, "Those people are Muslim pilgrims who have just made the Hajj to Mecca. That is why they are dressed the way they are. Now they are returning to their homelands."

Rather than drive past this scene, our bus veered and stopped at the base of the loading ramp. Stunned speechless, we watched in disbelief as soldiers armed with automatic rifles instructed the pilgrims to stop boarding and then directed us to get off the bus and climb aboard that same plane.

At the top of the staircase the stench hit my nostrils before I could step into the cabin. Far too many people were crammed into that small space. Western passengers started gagging. Those that had them, placed handkerchiefs over their mouths and noses and the complaining began. "This is insane!" "How many passengers do they think they can put on one plane?" Although I said nothing, I too was worried.

Couples and families would not be able to sit together, that was a given. For each of us to find individual seats was going to be difficult enough. We negotiated aisles swollen with sweaty pilgrims wrapped in the Hajj cloth, some of whom appeared to be carrying all of the worldly possessions they owned. Eventually I found an empty seat but it was in the center of a row sandwiched between two men who smelled like they had not bathed for at least a week.

Somehow every passenger from our bus squeezed onto the plane, and then to our dismay the soldiers ordered the stream of pilgrims at the bottom of the ramp to resume boarding.

For the first time in my life, I gave serious thought to unbuckling my seatbelt and getting off a plane before it took off.

❧❧❧❧❧❧❧❧❧❧❧❧❧❧

Chapter 6

Engines strained and the heavily laden aircraft lumbered down the runway struggling to get airborne. Parts of an aircraft cabin that I had never seen move before, on any flight, shook violently. I bowed my head in prayer as the plane slowly inched off the ground.

Fifteen minutes into the flight, cool air dispelled the acrid odors in the cabin and it got easier to breathe. Travel time to Riyadh was less than three hours so I sat back and tried to relax. Had I been more comfortable I might have taken a nap.

Riyadh airport was nothing like Jeddah International. From the moment we landed things were different. First of all, no buses came to transport us from the plane to the terminal. We were instructed to grab our carry-ons and walk across the tarmac to the main terminal. Outside, the temperature had fallen. However, there was no humidity so the hike was comfortable. Parked near the terminal doors was a row of a dozen or so buses all standing idle and unused. From appearances they had been sitting there a long time. So much sand and dust covered them that I hazarded to guess the engines would need an overhaul before the busses could be put back into service.

When I stepped inside the terminal, I finally saw the kind of scenes I had hoped to see in Arabia. It was very much like what I had read in adventure stories, as a much older Arabia appeared before my eyes. Any modern equipment lying around in the terminal, like the buses outside, appeared to be unused. It occurred to me that modernization at the capital must have lagged behind the rest of the country. There was also the possibility resistance to the changes sweeping across the Peninsula was ongoing at Riyadh. Reports we read at the Library of Congress told of riots being sparked in Riyadh when television was introduced into the Kingdom. That was 13 years earlier in 1966. That night I wondered if, on some levels, defiance to change was still taking place at the capital.

Each step I took seemed to confirm my impression that advancement toward modernization had been slow in the capital city. The return of my romantic expectations of Arabia was speeding up.

Getting through Riyadh Customs, however, would prove to be an experience. All of the inspectors spoke Arabic exclusively and this really slowed the process. Plus they manhandled our belongings. When I stepped forward and handed my passport to a short angry looking inspector, I placed my bags on the table fully expecting them to be treated as shabbily as the bags of the passengers that had preceded me.

The agent returned my passport, seized my bags and began clawing through them as if he had been ordered to sift dung. Then he started shouting. I had no idea what he was saying or what was wrong. If he had pointed to something specific among my possessions I might have had a clue as to what he was raving about. At first I tried to ignore him, but the guy got louder. Getting that much attention at Customs in a foreign land made me nervous, and it was embarrassing. At the same time, I was getting annoyed. Finally out of frustration, I shouted back at the guy but I immediately regretted my reaction. Carefully, I looked around fearing something really bad was about to happen. Nobody seemed to have noticed what was going on between me and the agent, and if they did it was apparent they did not care. The mean inspector continued berating me, and since nobody seemed to mind I felt free to lash out back at him. Our confrontation heated up quickly. He got louder and rougher with my things and in retaliation, I beat him down verbally. Before long I forgot where I was and stopped holding back and ended my ranting against him in a flare saying "you baboon-butt faced idiot, you need to show more respect for my things." The agent never batted an eye or reacted in any way. He just kept up his tirade and continued roughing up my possessions. For all the attention he paid me, I could just as easily have been talking to a deaf mute. But I did not care that he could not understand what I was saying. I was just relieved I could let off some steam.

After all was said and done the agent only confiscated my Bible. I protested a little, but it was just for show. I had another Bible packed in with my household effects coming by sea. If that Bible also failed to survive Customs, I could always have Barry mail me one through the diplomatic pouch, and that service did not fall under Saudi scrutiny.

When the agent completed his task, he grinned wide. I noted he had a gold crown on one of his front molars. Meanwhile, I busied myself stuffing items back into my bags as he turned to the next person in line. Motioning to them he yelled "The next berrrrson in line can step forrrwarrrrd now." As soon as he said this he turned quickly to catch my reaction. Needless to say my jaw had dropped. He winked and whispered, "You baboon-butt faced idiot – that was good. I can't wait to use that one. Now let me see which one of these stubid forrreignerrrrs is next?" With a grim leer he tore into the next passenger's bags. I really felt bad and totally responsible for what was about to happen to some innocent fellow traveler.

My experience at Customs started me to thinking, if getting into the country is this dramatic what could possibly lie ahead? Exactly what kind of place is Saudi Arabia? Then it struck me that if Blacks were being oppressed in the Kingdom then what happened between me and the Customs Agent should have turned out very differently. On the other hand, was it possible I had only gotten away with my theatrics temporarily? After all, was I not coming in the country? If I were leaving the country, I would soon be beyond their reach. But that was not the case. I was just arriving. 'How stupidly I have acted,' I confessed to myself. 'If these guys want to, they can get their hands on me anytime.' Eager to put distance between myself and Customs, I quickly headed toward the exit to meet the person that had been assigned to be my welcome sponsor. It had been arranged for us to meet outside the terminal. I just hoped he was still waiting, because my flight had been delayed.

Along the way I noticed there were many Africans in the crowds. Apparently a large contingent of Blacks from the continent worked in Arabia. Besides their dark skin, some had tribal markings cut into their faces to distinguish themselves from other groups. Arabs were easier to pick out, the Saudis easiest of all in their traditional dress and headgear.

The terminal had the feel of a baseball game during the seventh inning stretch when thousands of males rush to the restrooms at once. There was a lot of pushing and shoving as I made my way through the crowds.

Some people say Saudi males are effeminate because they wear dresses. All I can say to that is those people have probably never been to

Arabia. There was a popular perception in the minds of a number of people that I met in the States, that homosexuality was widespread among the Saudis. I encountered this mindset the day I started at the Agency when Carl Scott took me around to introduce me to the staff. One of the cubicles was occupied by a middle aged man who was hunched over his computer when Carl announced our presence. He pushed his chair back to where we were standing, gave me the once over literally looking me up and down, emitted a loud harrumph, rolled back to his computer and mumbled, 'some Arab must really be lonely in the desert.'

As we walked away Carl explained, 'that guy has been trying to get sent to Saudi Arabia for years. We reject his application every time, but he will not take the hint. The only reason he said those things to you is because he is jealous of our recruits.'

I did not mention it to Carl, but the guy's comment made me wonder about his motives for wanting to go to Saudi Arabia.

There certainly were no gay vibes in the airport terminal at Riyadh that night. Rather, it was like swimming in a sea of testosterone. The main impression the Saudis gave me was that they were not thrilled with foreigners. I was shoved harder and more often than I thought necessary, and received the same kind of stares I used to give foreigners back in America.

I spotted the exit doors and paused before opening them just to reflect a moment and take stock of what I was about to do. Once I walked through those doors a new chapter in my life would begin. I felt like an explorer at the portal of a new world that was unlike anything he has ever seen. It was the moment I had waited for the past six months. Now it was within reach. What would I see first? Whatever that first sight might be, I knew it would stick with me the rest of my life. Taking a deep breath, I opened the doors and walked into the capital city of the Kingdom of Saudi Arabia.

A broad overcrowded plaza fanned out from the terminal building. In the center of the plaza there was a small island with palm trees that was also overrun with people and baggage. I was standing on the walkway that ringed the plaza. The entire area was clogged and busy with activity. Scores of vehicles were picking up arriving passengers or dropping off departing travelers. A cacophony of sounds pounded on my ears, horns honked and the din of unfamiliar tongues rose from the crowds.

There was a parking lot on the opposite side of the plaza and beyond that a wall that separated the airport from a residential section of town. From the looks of things the airport appeared to have been built in the middle of the city. Or it was possible the airport had originally been built on the outskirts of Riyadh but was eventually engulfed by the fast growing city.

Then I saw it, my first since landing on the Arabian Peninsula... a camel. This camel, however, was not following tradition. Rather than entering the airport plaza carrying a sheik on its back, it was resting comfortably in the bed of a pickup truck that was likely being driven by the Arab it once transported. East had truly met west in this instance, and both the camel and the Bedouin were enjoying the best of both worlds.

Since I was trying to see and absorb everything, in my excitement I forgot to keep tabs on where I was stepping. Without realizing it, I reached the curb and the next thing I knew I was falling to the ground. While picking myself up, a frightening sound hit my ears. I looked up and saw an automobile careening toward me at full speed. In that split second I thought I was about to be killed. But the driver slammed on brakes and the car came to a screeching stop mere inches from my head.

With a sigh of relief, I braced myself on the bumper, climbed back to my feet and brushed sand and dust off my clothing. Meanwhile, the driver jumped out of the car and raced toward me. I thought, 'How kind of him to be concerned.' But he brushed right by me calling out 'taxi, taxi, taxi,' and grabbed the bags of a nearby traveler. I growled, "Taxi drivers are the same everywhere I see."

While the hack tended to his passenger, I gathered up my bags and resumed my scan of the area. To my right I could see the entrance to the airport. My sponsor was not supposed to meet me there but I headed in that direction because I was drawn by the sights of the city. There was a broad avenue running through the heart of town that forked on either side of the airport entrance. Hundreds of cars were literally racing along the avenue at speeds I had never seen before in city driving. So many motorists were ignoring stop signs and traffic signals it was a wonder the avenue had not turned into a demolition derby with nonstop collisions. During orientation we were warned that the Saudi's had bad driving habits. Seeing it in person was far worse than I had imagined. In contrast to the frightful traffic, the north and south bound lanes were separated by a beautifully landscaped median with manicured grass, flowers and palm trees. On one side of the avenue there was a bustling business district with a colorful array of bright flashing neon lights. On the other side, the buildings were drab in appearance and I assumed were government offices.

Eventually my gaze down the avenue extended as far as I could see and just above the median and palm trees I saw an incredibly bright crescent moon and star hanging over the city. Equally striking was the backdrop upon which the moon hung. Looking at that sky was like being transported back to a time before light existed. The sky was the purest black I had ever seen and the celestial bodies radiated like it was their very first time appearing in the expanse of heaven. The sight was unforgettable. In my heart a snapshot of that moment was captured forever. I will never forget that first look at the night sky over Riyadh and I understood why the crescent moon is so highly honored in the Arab world. That was the kind of sky a man could fall in love under. I would have been content to stare at it for hours, but my sponsor was expecting me. Reluctantly I turned my head away, but I had the comfort of knowing many moonlit Arabian nights awaited me in the months and years ahead.

Moments later I came upon two obvious Westerners, each holding a sign. One had my name on it. Walking up to them, I extending my hand and announced "I am Adam Sneed, Jr." One of the men took my hand and responded "Hi there, my name is Walter Daniels. You and I will be working together at the same Ministry. For the next few days I am going to be your sponsor. I have the job of helping you to get settled in. This is Herbert Wilson. Herbert works for one of our sister projects. As you can see, Herbert is waiting for a man named Samuel Greene."

"How are you Adam?"

"Fine Herbert, it is nice to meet you."

"So what do you think of Saudi Arabia so far," Walter asked?

"Right now I am just excited to be here but I should be able to give you a more informed answer to that question in a couple of months. We shall see."

"I'm Sam," a burly voice bellowed from behind us. We turned just as a tall wide bodied fellow stepped up. He was wearing a large hat exactly like the ones you hear people describe when they speak of Texans. There is no way I would have missed this guy had he been on the Jeddah flight and frankly speaking, I doubt he could have fit on the plane. It turns out he came into the Kingdom through Dammam on a Pan Am flight. Pan Am was one of the few foreign carriers the Saudis permitted to land in the Kingdom, but they were restricted to landing at Dammam or Jeddah.

Introductions were made all around and Herbert asked, "Sam, did you notice any military activity in the Gulf?"

"No I did not, but I don't mind telling you I was quite nervous that we might be within range of Iran's anti-aircraft missiles."

Herbert invited Sam "come with me. My wife and I are going to be your hosts for tonight. In the morning I will take you to Headquarters and they will assign you to a villa. Adam, I am sure we will be seeing each other around Headquarters. It was nice meeting you. Good night."

At the parking lot, Herbert and Sam went one direction, Walter and I the other. On the way to the car Walter informed me "a new compound is under construction to house bachelors. It should be ready any day now. In the interim you will be staying at the Transient Apartments a few blocks down Airport Road there. It will only take us a few minutes to get there from here."

Walter helped me toss my bags onto the back seat and we were on our way. After driving through the gate at the airport entrance, Walter coolly navigated his car into the stream of traffic and quickly matched the speed of other vehicles. We headed south on Airport Road. Sensing my nervousness he remarked, "Traffic is as bad as it looks, but you get used to it. You have to, there is no other choice."

Describing some of the sights along the way, Walter explained "Airport Road is the main street in Riyadh. Everybody gets their bearings off this road. When someone asks for directions we orient them to where they want to go based on the proximity of that destination to Airport Road. The buildings to the right are Saudi Ministries. That one," he said pointing a finger "is the Ministry that sponsors our project. Tomorrow when you are officially processed in, you will be assigned a car and at that point you will be able to get around town on your own. It will probably take a day or two for you to learn your way around to the places in the city you will need to go, but if you ever get lost or need directions my phone number is highlighted in the directory in your welcome kit. The kit is on the back seat. I will hand it to you when we get to the Transient Apartments. Adam, make a mental note of this corner" he advised as he slowed down and pulled over to the curb. "Headquarters is about four blocks in that direction on the right side of the road. The Transient Apartments where you will be staying temporarily are just on the other side of the Avenue from here so you will be within walking distance of Headquarters until you move to the bachelor compound."

Knowing I had somewhere close by to run to if anything drastic happened that night was comforting. I studied nearby landmarks carefully to make sure I could find that corner again in the event of an emergency. Half a block later Walter made a U-turn around a median and pulled up to the front of a building that looked like it might have started out as a decent looking hotel 20 or 30 years earlier.

"Here we are. Tomorrow I will pick you up around 8:30 to take you to Headquarters. We will get breakfast at the Snack Bar and then I will turn you over to Madeline to get your paperwork started. That should keep you busy for a couple of hours. While you are doing that, I will be over at the new office. That reminds me, the department we work for at the Ministry is moving to a new building. I will be at the new site tomorrow, but I am not sure for how long. If for some reason you do not get your car tomorrow and I am not back when you are finished with your paperwork, you can either walk back to the apartment or get a ride from the Motor Pool. Madeline will show you how to fill out a request for a car. After that you can expect me back here to pick you up around 5:00 tomorrow afternoon."

"What is happening tomorrow at 5:00?"

"Albert Dennison, our Director, is hosting a welcome dinner for you, to introduce you to the staff. The whole Engineering Department will be there, our families too. You will get to meet everybody."

"That sounds nice."

Along with my bags, Walter retrieved a valise off the back seat and handed it to me. "This is your welcome kit. Inside you will find a map marked to show how to get to Headquarters from here. It also notes the locations of every Western facility in the area. The key to the apartment is in there as well. I think they put you in Number 2. You will notice there are two names highlighted in the phone directory. One is mine and the other Albert Dennison's. Those are the most important names you will need to remember for now."

One by one I pulled items out of the packet as Walter described what they were and their importance to me over the next few weeks. When I grabbed a fistful of local currency he informed me "that is a complimentary one hundred riyals to hold you until your first paycheck. It is only worth about thirty of our dollars but you will not need much money over the next week or so. The cost of living here is very low. Gasoline is only 25¢ a gallon, so it is not expensive to drive. Surviving the traffic is the only problem with driving. Any maintenance required on your automobile will be taken care of at Headquarters. When it is your turn to take your car in, your name will be listed on a schedule published in the *Weekly Newsletter*. We get the *Newsletter* in our mailboxes every Saturday. You will be assigned a mailbox tomorrow and more than likely your first *Newsletter* will be in it. They will also set up an account for you at Headquarters so you can cash checks, and there will be other stuff but I am going to stop now. There is no point in overwhelming you with a lot of details tonight. Okay, that is all I have to say for now. Did I mention you will be in Apartment 2? I did? Good, then do you have any questions for me?"

"I cannot think of any right now, but I am sure a few will come to mind as soon as you drive away."

"Good, I will see you tomorrow morning at 8:30. By the way, have you reset your watch to local time?"

"Thanks for reminding me. What time do you have?"

"Its 2:00 a.m. Geez, it is Monday already. I knew your flight was delayed coming from Jeddah, but I had no idea it was this late. Oh yeah, you should be aware that today is the third day of the workweek. Saturdays are the same as Mondays in the States; Sundays are Tuesdays and today, Monday, is their Wednesday.”

“They explained all of that to us in orientation, but it does feel a little weird now that I am here.”

“Tomorrow morning is going to be pretty hectic so try to get some rest, especially your writing hand because you will be filling out a ton of forms and signing a lot of papers.”

“I figured as much. Thanks for all of your help Walter, I appreciate it. I guess I will be seeing you in a couple of hours. Good night.”

Spartan was the word that came to mind when I laid eyes on the apartment. I could have searched the seven seas and been hard pressed to find blander furniture. The walls were bare. There were no mirrors or pictures, and of course no greenery to liven up the place. Out of curiosity I went into the kitchen and opened the refrigerator and all the cabinet doors. Every cupboard was empty and the shelves were covered with dust. When I opened the last cupboard, I came eye to eye with the largest cockroach I had ever seen. I never knew they could grow to that size. This behemoth of an insect did not react like its smaller cousins in the States. The sudden intrusion of light into its dark world did not send it scurrying for cover. Instead it flared its antenna at me as if it was trying to figure out what kind of hideous creature I was. I had no pressing need to contest ownership of the shelf, or the roaches’ willingness to defend it so I slowly closed the door and whispered ‘please excuse me Mr. Cockroach for disturbing your evening.’

It had gotten very cold, much cooler than when I landed. There was a blanket covering the twin sized bed but it was thin to the touch. I would definitely have to sleep in my clothes to keep warm that night.

About that time, hunger pangs hit and I got the most powerful urge to eat something. I regretted that I had not taken advantage of the chance when I had it, to grab a snack at the airport in Rome. But then I remembered what happened at Riyadh Customs. That mean agent might have confiscated any food he found in my bags just for spite.

I was so hungry that for a brief moment I considered going out to find a late night place to buy a snack. The thought of our diplomats in Tehran squashed that idea. I shuddered to think what might happen to me on my first night in Saudi Arabia if I were kidnapped. Even if I survived such an ordeal, I would never be able to live it down. They would be talking about me at Headquarters, State Department, the Agency and everywhere in between for years to come. God knows I did not want to be the center of another international incident. At any rate, debating whether to go out or not was a waste of time because we had been warned not to eat the local food or drink the water. I only had one option and that was to stick it out until morning and have breakfast with Walter at Headquarters.

Chapter 7

Monday, November 12

For the second time in a week, I lay restless in bed. This time I was much too excited to sleep. At sunrise I would get to see Riyadh in full daylight. It was awesome knowing I was in the capital of the nation that brought the industrial world to a standstill with an oil embargo merely six years earlier. I recalled the lines at gas stations and how dad always crossed his fingers hoping there would be enough fuel left when it was our turn at the tank.

Though I did not speak Arabic, I was looking forward to learning my way around town and I had a lot of questions. What were the Saudis like? How different were they from Americans, beyond the way they dressed and their religious practices? What was a typical day in the life of a Saudi man my age? Now that I was living in Arabia, what sort of things could I do in my spare time? What hobbies did people enjoy in the desert? Arabs liked soccer; that much I knew, but were they interested in any other sports? What kind of jokes did they tell? Were city-dwelling Saudis anything like the famous Bedouin nomads of the desert? Were there any nomads left, still dwelling in tents and practicing the ancient traditions of their forefathers? A million questions swam in my head and I never fell asleep.

A couple of hours later I decided to stop wasting my time and got out of bed. For a few minutes all I did was pace around the desolate apartment. Then I checked my watch and realized it was close to daybreak so I figured I might as well take a shower. Twenty minutes later I stepped out of the shower and as I reached for a towel an ear splitting scream rocketed through the apartment. It was so loud and shrill that I dropped to one knee and clasped my hands over my ears. Either some nut had escaped the lunatic asylum and gotten hold of a megaphone or something worse was happening. Odd fears ran through my head. Had the crazy Iranians completely lost their minds and attacked Saudi Arabia? Swiftly I went over in my head the way to Headquarters. I was also thinking, if something tragic was happening so soon after getting to post then I was going to be terribly disappointed. Once I pinpointed the direction the sound was coming from, I crawled toward it and ended up at the back of the apartment. At a rear window I looked outside and immediately solved the mystery of the loud alarm. The back of the apartments were adjacent to the rear of a Mosque on the next street. I was hearing was my first prayer call in Saudi Arabia.

Shaking my head, I told myself 'this is going to take some getting used to and just think four more of those are coming today.' Counting in my head, I calculated, based on five calls a day that I had 3,649 prayer calls to go until the end of my contract. Never having lived near a Mosque, I had not been aware the calls started that early in the morning or that electronic amplification was used when summoning the faithful to pray.

Still it amazed me that such large numbers of men were out at that early hour obediently entering the Mosque. How many men in the West, I wondered, would willingly sacrifice the best sleeping hours of the morning to perform a religious ritual and do it every day of their lives?

When my ears adjusted to the call, I was able to distinguish similar echoes from other Mosques across the city. Once I got used to the sound, the calls were not all that bad on the ear. There was a symmetry to them that was peaceful and melodic. At least the Saudis do not need alarm clocks, I reasoned, not with Allah waking them up like that every morning.

I got dressed and rechecked the time. An angry reaction came out of my stomach indicating that at 6:30 a.m. it was not willing to wait another two hours until Walter came before we got something to eat.

During the drive down Airport Road the previous evening, I had noticed a neon sign on a building that looked like it could have been advertising a restaurant. If I was correct, it was not too far from the apartment. The only question was whether it was open that early in the morning. With so many men on the streets going to pray, I figured chances were good that it was.

Grabbing my welcome kit, I stepped out to the front of the building. Instantly my nose picked up the wonderful aroma of bread baking in an oven. My mouth watered and a roar of approval welled up from the pit of my stomach. Warnings against eating the local food came back to mind – but only briefly. I had noticed the location of a medical facility for U.S. personnel on the map in my welcome kit. So if anything I ingested made me sick, I had somewhere to go. I was crazy hungry and at that moment the most important task at hand was to get some food in my belly.

Without the neon lights, Airport Road did not look as flashy in the daylight. Dust was everywhere, but this was to be expected. Riyadh is a desert town.

I followed my nose straight to the restaurant five doors up the street from the Transient Apartments. The establishment was clean on the inside and had a decor that reminded me of saloons from old western films. Only a handful of patrons were in the restaurant but they seemed to be enjoying their meals and that was good enough for me.

I looked around for a place to sit where I would feel comfortable, meaning somewhere obscure so as not to bring any attention to myself or the fact I was a foreigner. A helpless feeling came over me as I listened to surrounding conversations. Nobody in the restaurant was speaking English and I could not make heads or tails of the noises coming out of their mouths. I needed to figure out a way to let someone know I wanted to buy a meal. There were fewer people on one side of the room. That is where I chose to sit. Now all I needed was a cooperative waiter.

No sooner had I sat down, a waiter came over and began jabbering away in Arabic. I had anticipated this. Motioning with my finger I signaled him to lean in close and whispered, "I am sorry sir, I do not speak Arabic. I speak English."

He was gracious enough to speak softly when he responded. "La Saudi… Inta Inglizi… na'am?"

Inglizi sounded like the appropriate word, so assuming its meaning I said "Yes, Inglizi, I speak Inglizi."

More gibberish followed, none of which sounding even remotely familiar. I was ready to give up at that point but the waiter, after a momentary pause, started making movements with his hands. He seemed to be indicating he wanted me to give him something. Nonplussed, I stared blankly and shrugged my shoulders. Slowly he started repeating "bitaka, bitaka, hut al bitaka." Again I shook my head. Folding his arms, the waiter bowed his head thinking contemplatively while tapping on his chin. Then his face brightened. Leaning toward me he enunciated very slowly "bass aborrrt, hut al bass aborrrrt."

Ah, I got it. He wanted to see my passport. But wait a minute; this was not a good thing. I could not simply hand my passport over to someone in a foreign country, and a waiter at that. James Bond would laugh his socks off.

The thought of losing my passport that first day in the Kingdom was totally unacceptable. It seems I had gotten myself into a bit of a pickle. So how could I get out of it? Walk out of the restaurant! That is what I would do. Surely the waiter could not be offended. He already knew I did not understand his language. But the guy kept smiling and repeating his request, only now he was alternating between the words "bass abort" and "bitaka." I figured bitaka was their word for passport. Because he was so polite, I became convinced he was harmless. Even so, when I reached for my passport I did so cautiously and remained on the alert in case I had to snatch it back and run out of the place.

The waiter fanned through my passport and when he reached a certain page he stopped and smiled. Like the Customs Agent, he had a gold crown on one of his front molars. Turning to other patrons in the restaurant he shouted, "hatha Amrrreekie Aswad, Amrrrreekie Aswad hunak!" Everyone in the place rushed over and grabbed at my passport. It was as if each person wanted to see for himself if what the waiter had said was true. Baffled, yet intrigued by this turn of events, I stood up to get a better view so I could keep my eyes on my passport. I followed it as it floated from one hand to the next.

Once everyone had seen or touched the passport, the waiter, to my relief, politely returned it to me. Then something astonishing happened. All of the patrons in the restaurant began applauding and chanting - 'Amrrrreekie Aswad', 'Amrrrreekie Aswad...'

Clearly, Amreekie was their word for American and it was a reasonable conclusion to assume Aswad meant Black. What threw me for a loop was that they were applauding a Black American. What did it mean? Did every Black American that came to Arabia get this kind of welcome? I could not wait to meet other Black Americans to compare notes. But there was something even more interesting about this reception. Could this prove once and for all that Blacks had never been treated harshly in Arabia? Barry did say, 'Maybe the whole thing boils down to the fact there are things about Saudi Arabia that are impossible for outsiders to know.' Why though would citizens of a land that had only recently abolished Black slavery, so readily fête a Black American? Or was their reaction based on the fact I was American, as opposed to a Black man from Africa, Arabia or some other land? Or maybe it was time I accepted Malcolm X's attestation that the so-called 'white' attitude had been removed from the minds of Muslim people.

That incident on my first morning in Riyadh, led me make the decision to give the Saudis the benefit of the doubt. Until I saw evidence to the contrary, I would accept Barry's proposition that the Saudi Arabian brand of slavery had not been harsh and oppressive. Yes, it was optimistic to think that way after only my first encounter with the locals. But I was not about to forget it was day one of a two year stretch. I knew I still had a lot to learn. Many questions needed to be asked, both to former slaves and former slave owners. Another thing that incident made me realize, was that I needed to learn the local language. Because I did not know Arabic, I could not question the people in the restaurant about their reaction to me. For the kind of research I had in mind, learning the native tongue was a top priority.

The waiter motioned for me to have a seat. I wondered what was going to happen next. As I waited, I began formulating in my head the opening lines of my first letter to Barry. I could not wait to share my experiences thus far, and tell him and Lovelen how I had been received by the locals that first morning.

It would have been a waste of both our time had the waiter handed me a menu. Instead he went to the kitchen and brought out a steaming hot plate of food. Although everything looked appetizing, I did not recognize any of the items on the plate except the olives. But the odor was inviting, and once I began I did not stop eating until everything was cleared off the plate. Not once did the possibility of getting sick cross my mind. The food was tasty and delicious and I was satisfied and full. When I sat back and grinned, the waiter smiled too pleased that I had enjoyed the food.

How much I owed for the meal was my next question. I pulled one of the Ten Riyal Notes from my welcome kit and handed it to the waiter, at least that is what I attempted to do. Vigorously he waved the money off, refusing to accept payment. One of the other patrons walked over, took the money out of my hand and stuffed it back into my kit. Through hand motions and a few English expressions that they knew, they made it clear that I had been their guest and was welcome to return at any time.

Getting out of the restaurant was no less eventful. People shook my hand or patted me on the back. I got the feeling they needed to touch me just to make sure what had taken place in the restaurant was real. No doubt they would be telling families and friends they had actually laid their hands on a Black American, or as they were again chanting, 'Amrrrreekie Aswad.' I felt like a celebrity trying to squeeze past walls of fans.

As I left the restaurant, Carl Scott's words came to mind, 'From what we are hearing the Saudis get along better with Black Americans than they do with our White workers.' Perhaps that explained the treatment I had received in the restaurant.

Instead of waiting for Walter inside the apartment, I sat on the front stoop to enjoy my first Middle Eastern morning. Aromas wafting on the breeze from the restaurant added to the pleasantness of my wait. The sun was higher in the sky now and daylight gave me a clearer view of sights along the avenue. Traffic volume had picked up and I could see the Saudis were driving as fast in daylight as I had observed them doing the previous night. As I took in the sights, I thought about the fear I had felt a week earlier just before my flight, and how close I had come to backing out of the contract. Considering what had happened in the first few hours of my arrival, there was no telling how much more I would have missed had I turned down the chance to spend two years in Arabia. I shook my head and laughed about all the energy I wasted worrying about what might happen to me in the Middle East. Because if these early moments in the country were any indication of how life was going to be over the next two years, a great adventure was definitely about to unfold.

The drive to Mission Headquarters took less than a minute. As Walter directed me to the Snack Bar, I kept thinking 'there is no way I can eat a second breakfast'. Fortunately, Walter did not order much. Following his lead I limited myself to a boiled egg, a slice of toast and a carton of orange juice. Even with that little, it was tough faking my way through the meal. Walter hardly ate more than a few bites. He appeared to be distracted by the talk in the Snack Bar about the crisis in Tehran. Nothing new was being said, but plenty of suggestions were being bandied about on what President Carter could or should do to resolve the problem. As with conversations of that nature, there was that one expert who dominated the debate. This guy professed to know better than anyone, including the President, how to settle matters with the Iranians once and for all. "If the Iranians had our military might, I know what they would do to us if the situation was reversed and we had grabbed their diplomats," he proclaimed. As I said, Walter seemed to be engrossed in the discussion. But within a few minutes of our sitting down he rose abruptly and said, "We have to get moving".

From the Snack Bar, Walter took me to the main offices. At a central desk an American woman was answering phones and typing at a workstation. In time I would learn that American women could work in Arabia as long as they were employed at a U.S. facility. Doors to several offices lined the wall behind her. Each door had a smoked window pane stenciled with the name and title of a Mission officer.

"Madeleine, this is Adam Sneed. I picked him up at the airport last night and put him in the Transient Apartments. Adam is the newest employee on our project. You are all hers now Adam. When you finish here, Madeleine will show you how to fill out a request for a car to take you back to the apartments. Remember, I will be picking you up at five."

"Right, see you later and thanks again for breakfast."

Walter grabbed my arm, gently steered me aside and whispered, "I usually do not eat here. Most days my wife and I have breakfast at home and occasionally we go to The Empty Quarter Inn. I was hoping to enjoy breakfast with you this morning, but all that talk in the Snack Bar made me lose my appetite. That guy talking the loudest, his name is Erick Elam. You'll hear about him, a lot. As you saw, he can be a real blowhard. It is just like him to think he can do a better job than the President. That man's voice really irritates me. I noticed you lost your appetite too. Maybe things will be quieter the next time and we can have a pleasant meal. Or if you prefer, you could join Vannah and me for breakfast at The Empty Quarter Inn sometime."

"The Empty Quarter Inn sounds perfect. In fact, I promise I will be taking you up on that invitation."

Madeline handed me a list of the officers I was scheduled to meet with that morning. Directly behind her desk was a door labeled, 'Todd Dearbourne, Mission Head.' Todd's name was first on my list.

When Madeline ushered me into his office, there was another man already sitting in one of the chairs in front of Todd's desk. I assumed he was also a new arrival and Todd was either going to speak to us jointly or their meeting was wrapping up.

"Adam, this is Darrell Jenkins. Darrell and I are old friends. We have known each other for many years, long before either of us came to Saudi Arabia. Darrell works at our Embassy in Jeddah. He is in town visiting the Liaison Office. In case you are not aware of it, there are no foreign embassies here in Riyadh. All embassies are located in Jeddah. That is going to change in the future, but for now embassy officials split time between liaison offices here in the capital and their main offices on the west coast. Actually, Darrell will be flying back to Jeddah later this afternoon."

Darrell stood, offered his hand and said "It is nice meeting you Adam."

After Darrell and I shook hands, we sat down and Todd began his speech for new arrivals.

"Although we are guests in the Kingdom of Saudi Arabia, we are first and foremost citizens of the United States. Everything we say and do here, whether it is minor or significant, reflects on our country. None of us are kept under direct surveillance; nevertheless, all members of the project are expected to be circumspect in their conduct and beyond reproach while in the Kingdom. Unfortunately, from time to time a member of the project has had to be sent home because they lost sight of the privilege extended to us by the U.S. and Saudi governments to work in this country. I am confident you will not give us any cause for concern, but it is important that you understand we take the behavior of U.S. citizens, both public and private, very seriously.

"Other than going to work, at whatever Ministry you are assigned, your free time will belong to you. In effect you will have virtually unfettered access to go just about anywhere in the country that you please. You can mingle with the Saudis and other nationals living and working here, if that is what you choose, or, you can follow our recommendation and keep close to the U.S. community. There are Federal workers and independent contractors here from all across America. We have a remarkable pool of talented individuals here and I am sure you will develop friendships among them that will likely last the rest of your life.

"Now, in case no one has mentioned this to you, we are building a new compound for bachelors. It should be ready for occupancy…" after a quick peek at the calendar on his desk, he resumed "probably by this weekend, just a day or two from now. Weekends fall on Thursdays and Fridays here... I guess they told you those kinds of things during orientation back in the States. We learned the hard way that mixing single people with families in the same compound, is not a good idea. So until the new bachelor compound is ready, you will remain in the Transient Apartments on Airport Road.

"Adam, for the most part life in the Kingdom is going to be very different from what you are accustomed to. But since you will be spending most of your time within the U.S. community, culture shock should be minimal. Of course when you go to work, you will have no choice but to interact with the locals. Beyond work though, again, we recommend you limit contact with the indigenous population.

"Some complain that our lives are too cloistered here, but given the propensity for sudden outbreaks of violence in this region of the world, keeping a low profile is the most prudent way to go about our business. Take for instance this crisis in Tehran - that is a prime example of how vulnerable we are. To be brutally honest we are exposed to just about anything every day we are here, which is why the State Department is so keen for Americans to stay close to U.S. facilities. Look at it this way, in the event of an evacuation order it will be easier to get everyone out safely if we are where we should be rather than scattered all over the desert.

"I am sure they told you this in Washington as well, but as a reminder, there are a number of topics we have to be sensitive to here and none more so than the Palestinian issue - specifically our country's policies toward the nation of Israel. I am sure that you, like the rest of us, have personal views on the matter, but as long as you are in the Kingdom it would be best not to express opinions or comments on that topic. I am going to repeat myself on this because it is vitally important that you understand how serious it can be. There are tens of thousands of Palestinians living and working in Saudi Arabia, and trust me when I say you cannot identify them on sight. In my opinion, it is impossible to distinguish one Arab nationality from another, despite the fact they have different ways of practicing the same religion. There are Arabs here from Lebanon, Syria, Egypt, Palestine, Iraq, Kuwait, Yemen, Jordan, North Africa, as well as places you might not commonly associate with the Islamic faith. Nothing about them makes any one nationality particularly more recognizable than the other, with the exception of the Saudis of course, but that is because they still dress the traditional way. Nevertheless, as diverse as the Islamic and political mix here may be one thing all Arabs share in common is hatred for Israel. I reiterate -

avoid political debates - you never know who might be listening. Some casual remark you happen to make could be overheard by the wrong person, repeated in certain circles and you could wind up becoming a target for just about anything, and likely the worst that you can imagine. Again, prudence is our watchword.

"As far as personal needs, food, commodities and the like... Madeleine will issue you passes this morning so that you will have access to the PX and Commissary. There you will be able to buy practically any product available in America. This means you will not have to shop in the local markets, which could save you a lot of money. They like to haggle over prices here, and despite the strong religious undercurrent in the country the Saudis will bilk a foreigner out of his money just as fast as any of us would, given the opportunity. Of course there is nothing wrong with going to the local suqs if you want to pick up a couple of souvenirs to take back to the States. That would be understandable. Everyone does that. By the way, the word suq (sook) is what they call their markets.

"Now, what I am about to say to you is not meant to intrude on your personal life, or choices, so please do not be offended. There are a lot of single women here - from Europe, the United States, the Philippines and other parts of the world. They are here to work in positions that ordinarily would be filled by local women. But as you probably know by now, Saudi culture does not permit their females to work alongside men. Primarily women from abroad come to the Kingdom to serve as nurses, medical attendants and the like. I am telling you this up front because, contrary to what you may have heard, Americans do go to parties here and go out on dates just like back home. However, out of respect for our Saudi hosts, we do not flaunt our lifestyle openly in public. Therefore, and hear me carefully on this, if you meet a woman and want to spend time with her be sure to confine your rendezvous to within the walls of western facilities. And whatever you do, never engage in public displays of affection with a member of the opposite sex. Saudis do not show affection publicly for their own wives, so that kind of behavior is simply unacceptable. On top of that, it is strictly forbidden. Being American or Christian will not make a difference. If you are not married and caught doing so much as holding hands, and God forbid, kissing in public – the two of you will be in for a boatload of problems especially the female. First of all, the girlfriend would automatically be labeled a harlot and probably beaten on the spot by the religious police – a bunch of fanatical, long bearded old men called Mutawahs. They walk around all day beating people with these bamboo sticks and enforcing Sharia, the religious law. In addition to being beaten, men and women caught being affectionate in public are imprisoned, and prison here, well … let's just say you do not want to go to prison here. Bottom line, keep displays of affection private. If you ever have a problem along these lines, try to get in touch with the Mission as soon as you can. Depending on the severity of the case, there may be little we can do, but at the least we would alert the Embassy Liaison Office. Now, on the other hand, if you want to walk down the street holding hands with another man the Saudis are not going to complain about that. Male on male affection is acceptable here. It is part of the culture. And just so you know, the Mission does not concern itself with things like sexual preference or sexual orientation, but I trust we do not have to worry about anything like that on your part."

"Not at all," I assured him.

"Good. You should have found a map in the welcome kit your sponsor handed you when you arrived. The locations of U.S. and other western companies and installations are marked on it for your convenience. Almost all of these places, with the exception of the medical facility, have recreation centers, tennis courts, movie theaters, swimming pools, snack bars and so forth. Headquarters has a recreation center too, probably the finest facility of its kind in the city. Unfortunately it is located miles outside of town in the middle of a Saudi community. Few Americans bother making that long drive but we are working on some things that might draw more people out to the Center and make it worth their while to make that trip. The only reason we ended up building out in the suburbs is because none of the plots available here in town were large enough for our needs. Once you start getting around town, you will see for yourself that a lot of construction is going on. Practically every vacant lot in the city has been purchased by some entity or Ministry and is either already under development or plans are being made to develop the land at some point down the road. Riyadh is expanding fast. The city is literally bursting at the seams. At any rate, I wanted you to be aware that there are places to go and even take a date if you like, including our Rec Center if you are willing to take that long drive. I guess what I am trying to say is, boredom is not inevitable here.

"Of all the things I tell you today the one that could be the most important, in the long run, has to do with our emergency evacuation procedures. Madeline will assign you a mailbox this morning. A copy of the Emergency Evacuation Manual will be in it. Take the time to read over it carefully. Commit as much of the major instructions to memory as you can, particularly the first and alternate extraction points that have been assigned to you personally. You can bet if there is an emergency, things will be moving too fast for any of us to have time to stop and read the manual."

"Adam, Todd's advice to you on that point is very important," Darrell stated as he stood and fastened his jacket in preparation to depart. "I have a secret to tell you young man. As long as Todd and I have known each other, this is the first time I have heard his welcome speech. I trust you did not mind me sitting in."

"Not at all, besides you and I have something in common now – this is my first time hearing Todd's welcome speech too," I quipped.

Darrell chuckled and handed me his business card. "If you are ever in Jeddah, please stop by the Embassy. My wife and I would love to give you a tour of the city and you could join us for lunch or dinner. There is a lovely restaurant just outside Jeddah, called the Red Sea Inn. All of the expatriates go there and it is a favorite of the Embassy staff. You would love it. Remember Adam if you need assistance of any kind do not hesitate to give me a call."

"Thanks, I appreciate this very much."

Todd excused himself to walk his friend out and I put Darrell's card in my wallet. Considering all the services Headquarters provided, I figured I would have to be in pretty desperate straits to ever need assistance from the Embassy all the way in Jeddah. But since I hoped to visit Jeddah while I was in Arabia, it was not out of the realm of possibility I could benefit from having a contact in that city.

Upon returning, Todd spent a few minutes outlining the functions of the various offices at Headquarters. He also gave me a preview of what to expect when I met with other Mission officials that morning.

In addition to acting as in-Kingdom liaison between expatriates and their states-side agencies and various federal departments, Headquarters managed and maintained housing facilities; coordinated with local utilities companies for services to the compounds; arranged for emergency medical assistance, communications, transportation, and commissary and PX privileges. Headquarters coordinated the arrival or packing of household effects shipments at the beginning and end of tours, respectively. Personal checks could be cashed at Headquarters, regular and bulk mail could be posted, and if you needed to be chauffeured around, Headquarters maintained a motor pool. Other benefits provided by Headquarters included *The Weekly Newsletter*, a Snack Bar and the Recreation Center. Finally, Headquarters was our link to the U.S. Liaison Office in Riyadh and through it our Embassy in Jeddah.

Todd concluded with assurances that the U.S. and Saudi governments had spared no expense to make the stay of American workers in the Kingdom as comfortable as possible.

"Okay, that is all I have to say except that if you ever have any problems or questions, my door is always open. Feel free to stop by anytime. Do you have any questions for me before you go to your next interview?"

"Yes, how many Americans work here?"

"In the city of Riyadh on the whole, I have no idea. There are many government programs in operation here and the number of private sector outfits is anybody's guess, and even then I am only talking within city limits. There are U.S. firms out in the rural districts as well. Cities like Dammam and Jeddah also have large numbers of expatriates. There are even more non-U.S. foreign nationals working in Arabia. In fact, they outnumber us by several million. But with respect to projects under the Mission umbrella there are 23, including the construction project you are with. All total I would estimate we are managing approximately 1,200 U.S. workers. Your project, if I remember the latest statistics has about 65 employees. You make 66. Is there anything else you would like to know?"

"Not that I can think of at the moment. Thanks."

Reaching out his hand, Todd expressed warmly "welcome to Saudi Arabia and I wish you a successful and rewarding tour."

When Madeleine showed me how to fill out forms to ship bulk packages, she mentioned "there is an APO Facility down the street that you can use as an alternative to our mail set up. It would probably be better to mail large packages from there. You probably did not notice it, but you passed the APO on your way here this morning when you came from the Transient Apartments." After that she took my picture for the ID cards and assigned me a mailbox.

In the mailbox I found the Evacuation Manual and my first copy of *The Weekly Newsletter*. While waiting for my next interview, I skimmed through the *Newsletter*. Page 1 had a notice identifying the Duty Officer for the week; a list of the newest arrivals from the previous week; and names of individuals returning to the States, either for vacation or because their tours had ended. Information on the second page was dedicated to expatriate schools with ads soliciting bus drivers and monitors to work for the International Community and French schools. Page 3 listed names and telephone numbers to contact in the event of emergencies, like gas or water leaks at a compound, damages to villas, lizard swap-out (whatever that was), and what to do in the event of an automobile accident. An announcement from the Ministry of Interior addressed to expatriates on page 4, explained proper driving etiquette when camel, sheep or goat herds blocked roads. Page 5 outlined the hours of operation of various Headquarters offices and had a printout of the Snack Bar menu for the week. One interesting item mentioned that tapes of the CBS Evening News for the previous week, arrived in-Kingdom every Wednesday and anyone wishing to view the showing should call ahead to reserve seats. This reminded me I would not be watching network television for a couple of years. Want ads filled the next page. Positions were available at Headquarters, other U.S. companies and facilities and the Embassy Liaison Office. The community bulletin board on page 7 offered vehicles for sale, invitations to join chess clubs, bridge clubs, bowling leagues and a hodgepodge of other activities and hobbies. Page 8 was devoted to the Motor Pool and had a list of names and dates for individuals to bring their cars in for maintenance that week. Recreation Center news filled page 9, including titles of films playing at the theater. A watermark replica of Saudi Arabia's crossed swords and palm tree emblem covered the back page of the *Newsletter.* Superimposed over this was The Empty Quarter Inn menu for the week. That week's fare included prime rib, roast turkey, meatloaf, southern fried chicken, duck, barbeque spareribs, steak, lobster, spaghetti, and veal cutlet.

The Empty Quarter Inn was definitely a place I planned to visit often.

By 11:30 I was finished with all of my interviews. Now that I had in-Kingdom identification I would never have to pull out my passport again. U.S. passports were critically important because they were the most trusted piece of identification in the Kingdom, especially when it came to gaining access to U.S. facilities. ID cards worked too, but there is nothing on earth like an official passport issued by the government of the United States of America.

Conversely, Americans working in the private sector, as well as foreign nationals from other lands, were required to turn their passports over to the sponsor or Ministry that invited them to Saudi Arabia. Their passports would be held until it was time for them to return to their homelands. The arrangement did not sit well with the foreign workforce because the names of departing foreigners were always advertised in the local newspapers. Before they could leave the country, they had to settle any claims made against them. Any Saudi citizen could step forward and file a claim against a departing foreigner. For example, an employee could be accused of owing someone a debt. When that happened, the foreigner could not leave the Kingdom until that debt was paid. Foreign workers often complained that the locals routinely exploited them through this process. But complaining that someone was lying on you would be a waste of time. Non-Muslims were considered infidels and liars, which meant fighting against a debt claim by a member of the faithful was useless. U.S. government workers, on the other hand, were permitted to hold on to their passports. This more or less kept control in the hands of the U.S. government over when its federal workers could leave the country. These were just some of the reasons why holding on to my passport was so important.

After my final interview, I headed to the Motor Pool my last stop of the in-processing regimen. The time had come for me to pick up my assigned automobile and get my baptism into the nightmarish local traffic. Though I was not sure I was ready for it, a car was necessary in order to get around town.

A scruffy looking American named Danny, dressed all in black and trying his best to mimic the voice and swagger of Johnny Cash, was in charge of the Motor Pool. As soon as he opened his mouth, I knew I was never going to like this guy. His voice irritated me pretty much the way Erick Elam's voice had irritated Walter. For the most part I tuned him out as he droned on about the services available at the Motor Pool. But then he got to talking about car accidents and mentioned Sharia law and people avenging loved ones in cases of fatal crashes. My ears perked right up. "It works like this," Danny began to explain, "an aggrieved relative has the right to avenge a loved one killed in an accident and can do so right on the spot." With a slimy grin Danny added, "Most Saudis carry knives, in case you didn't know." Reaching behind his back, he retrieved an elaborate looking case out of which he slid a curved blade with a bejeweled ivory handle. "Don't look so worried," he sneered. "You will probably get a chance to prove you are an American before any cutting begins, although I am not too sure about that since you people blend in so well with the natives."

Danny's statements about Sharia law made me uncomfortable and I purposely ignored his 'you people' reference. Still, the high odds of having an accident in the Kingdom meant I had no choice but to pay attention to what he was saying. During orientation in D.C., whenever the topic of driving in Saudi Arabia came up, nobody ever said '*if* you have an accident.' It was always '*when* you have an accident.' They added, 'if you are the kind of person that gets super nervous in traffic or real upset over fender benders, you should probably reconsider going to Saudi Arabia. Taking pills to settle your nerves after an accident is a waste of time and money. You are going to have accidents; in fact you can count on having several while you are over there. When they happen, don't be shocked. As long as you come out in one piece, get over it and go back to work.'

Danny's speech ratcheted up the danger on the streets an extra notch for me on a personal level. Nobody had to tell me that an aggrieved relative, in a fit of anger and loss would hardly take the time to ask for my identification especially since most Blacks they saw were former slaves or Africans. My experience at the restaurant that morning gave me a pretty good idea how rarely Arabs encountered Black Americans. The fact that I did not dress like a local gave me, at best, a chance of being mistaken for African, and I had no idea what blood avengers did in the case of fatal mishaps involving Africans.

As I stood there eyeing Danny suspiciously, I wondered if it was worth it to risk my life in a land where the chances of my getting involved in a traffic fatality were higher than those of being asked to show my 'bitaka' or passport. Needless to say, Danny's words had me worried.

Earlier Madeline had advised me that the Saudi official in charge of issuing driver's licenses to Americans would be at the Motor Pool. She told me 'all you have to do is show him your States-side license and he will provide you with a local license for operating a motor vehicle in Saudi Arabia.' This official walked up to us while Danny and I were talking. Danny introduced him and I handed him my District of Columbia license. The official took a quick glance, handed it back and announced "This is no good. No bicturrrrre."

Shortly before I left the States, the District of Columbia had published a schedule for motorists to exchange their current licenses which had been issued without pictures, for new ones with photographs. The process started too late for me to get a replacement before I left the country.

"Oh no, you don't have a picture on your license," Danny sneered. "That's too bad. I guess you know what that means. You have to go through the whole process of getting a license just like a regular citizen."

As Danny rubbed my misfortune in, the Saudi official handed me a copy of a manual titled - *English Language Guide to Traffic Regulations - Sanctioned by Royal Decree.* "You should study this verrrry harrrrrd," the official counseled.

Nearby a couple of the Motor Pool drivers, all Africans, groaned audibly and started laughing at me mockingly. A young Saudi, apparently the assistant of the licensing official, was very put out by the way these driver's were reacting. Charging forward, he confronted them with a glaring scowl and they quieted down right away. I appreciated the gesture, but did not understand why the young man cared about the way I was being treated. He also gave me the impression he was not too fond of Danny.

Meantime, Danny kept badgering me and making disingenuous offers to help as I walked away. "Make sure you come back when you are ready to take the test. One of my drivers will be happy to take you to the DMV. The number to the Motor Pool is in the Directory included in your welcome kit. If you need a ride anywhere, give me a call. I can arrange for a driver to come pick you up. They will take you wherever you want to go..."

To be honest I was not all that gung ho to get behind the wheel of a car in Saudi Arabia, but it was disappointing to get so close to getting a vehicle only to fail on a technicality.

Other than needing to come back to take the driving test, all my in-processing was complete. I went to the Snack Bar for lunch. It was crowded and the only people I recognized were Madeline and a couple of the officials I had met with that morning.

While eating I heard the second prayer call of the day. It sounded close by, so I assumed it was coming from the Mosque behind the Transient Apartments. Meanwhile, I tried to think up some ideas on how to keep myself busy between then and 5:00.

After lunch I opted to walk back to the apartment rather than ask for a ride from the Motor Pool. I figured the apartments were only a minute away by car, so walking should not take long. My only worry was that it might be too hot outside.

On my way out the front door the first fellow Black American I had seen since arriving walked into Mission Headquarters. The moment we saw each other broad grins spread on our faces. I was so glad to see him that I held on to our embrace for several seconds before letting him go. We shook hands. He was about an inch taller than me at 6'0" and around fifteen years my senior.

"You must be Adam Sneed," he said. "Perry Ferguson told me you were coming. My name is Larry Corbin."

Although I was not too surprised the guy knew my name, I had no idea who Perry Ferguson was.

"Perry Ferguson? I have never heard of him."

"Perry is one of our coworkers. The three of us work on the same project, but on different sides. Carl Scott recruited all of us. I am in curriculum development. You and Perry are on the construction side. The two of you will be working in the same office. Perry and his wife will be at Al Dennison's dinner party tonight. So where did they put you, the Transient Apartments, right?"

"That is correct."

"They put me in there too when I first got here, so I know how you must be feeling about now. I was never happier to get out of a place in my life than when I left that building. I was in Apartment 2 for about three or four days, and that was three or four days too long."

"What a coincidence, I am in Apartment 2. Was that huge cockroach living in the kitchen cupboard when you were there?"

"Maybe, I never looked in the cupboards. If you saw a cockroach it means its time to change the lizard."

"Please explain what that means."

"Lizards eat cockroaches. When you move into your new place a crew from Headquarters will turn a young lizard loose in your apartment. It will keep down the cockroach population. Only problem is the lizards grow so darn fast they get too big to squeeze into tight spaces. From time to time a crew from Headquarters will come by to catch the big lizard and replace it with a new little one. Usually only bachelors get lizards in their places because wives cannot tolerate having them in the house. There is a lot of neat little stuff like that about this place you will learn. Tell you what; if you get bored… excuse me… that was a stupid thing to say… I meant to say when you get bored, give me a call. You can hang out at my place sometimes, and if you like, I will have my maid prepare a nice meal for you. My wife doesn't cook by the way." With a wink he added, "We have to stick together out here, you know what I am saying?"

"I hear you and you have no idea how glad I am that I ran into you. This is a nice lift after my visit to the Motor Pool."

Larry laughed, "Danny gave you the speech about relatives taking revenge if a local dies in a car accident right? He has you wondering if they will recognize you are an American before they take a stab at you. Don't sweat it. Danny likes to rattle newcomers, especially Blacks. There are only a handful of us here, so he doesn't get to give that version of his speech often. The rules here are not as cut and dry as Danny would have you think. Saudi citizens cannot kill anyone without permission from someone in authority. If you have an accident, you will have plenty of time to make a phone call. People will know you are American before anything worse can happen. Even if one of us does get involved in an accident here and someone is killed, there are arrangements in place between the Saudi and U.S. governments to handle that situation."

"Why didn't Danny tell me that, the scoundrel?"

"He was just having a little fun with you. He knew you would find out the truth soon enough."

"It's a relief to hear this," I admitted. "Thanks for the information. By the way, how many Black Americans are there on our project?"

"You make seven, but five of them will be going back to the States over the next few months. Personally I plan on being here another two years at least. Whoa, what is that in your hand? Is that what I think it is?"

"The *English Language Guide to Traffic Regulations*," I answered.

"Oh no, you didn't get your car. You have to take the driver's test."

"My States-side license was rejected. It doesn't have a picture."

"That's too bad. But you haven't started reading that booklet yet have you?"

"Not really. I skimmed through it a little while I was eating lunch."

"Don't waste your time. I guarantee when you go down to the DMV nobody will ever ask you about anything in that booklet. Trust me, if you drive the way that booklet tells you, you will be dead in a week. Nobody drives the way they are supposed to here any way, but I am sure you have figured that out by now."

"Yes, I kind of figured all rules were off the first time I saw the traffic."

"The only thing you need to do is go down to the DMV and drive the same way you do in America. You will pass the first time. Drivers in this country do not have our kind of discipline."

Obviously Larry had never lived in Washington, D.C. or drove on the Capital Beltway to make a blanket statement about Americans being disciplined drivers.

"Adam I have a lot of things to do, so I have to get going. But good luck on your test. I will be seeing you around."

"It was nice meeting you Larry, but you forgot to give me your number or tell me where you live – in case I get bored – remember?"

"My number is in the directory. Tell you what, until you get your car all you have to do is call the Motor Pool and ask for Abdullah. Tell him you want to go to Larry Corbin's place. All of the drivers at the Motor Pool know me. Believe me you can have a lot of fun here if you meet the right people."

"Meeting you is a good start I think. I promise I will stop by to visit you soon."

"You know what, you are right, you should call before you come. I am out a lot. Make sure I am home first. Just get my number out of the directory."

"Thanks Larry. I will be giving you a call soon."

It was 12:30. The sun was at its zenith - and it was hot. The good news was there was no humidity, like at Jeddah, so it was a dry heat. And the lack of humidity meant there had to be few mosquitoes, if any at all, in the city. As I walked toward Airport Road, I noticed that none of the Saudis I passed were sweating. All of them wore the traditional white dress and headgear and looked cool and comfortable. It made sense because white deflects heat, so a white gown was probably the only practical thing to wear in the desert. Perhaps the national attire was worn for more reasons than tradition after all. I was definitely planning to get one of these outfits to take back to America with me as a souvenir.

The APO Facility that Madeline mentioned was three blocks from Headquarters. Saudi military personnel were manning the gate. One of the guards inspected my new identification card, stared at my face a moment then signaled his partners to let me to pass through.

Just inside the compound on the left was the APO building. Across from that there was a recreation center, movie-theater, and a couple of tennis courts. Beyond the APO building an inner wall with a second gate and guard post secured the residential section of the facility. A couple of high-rise apartment buildings stood within the inner compound.

I went into the APO and gave it a quick look over. It was exactly like a typical small town post office. I left to explore the Rec Center, movie theater and tennis courts. Two films were listed on the marquee, both several years old and I had already seen them.

My next stop was the tennis courts. I was happy the courts were close to the Transient Apartments, but sad that my rackets were packed in with the household effects shipment coming by sea. It would be a month or two before I could get on a court.

Unknown to me, someone had quietly approached from behind. I was caught off guard when he asked "Do you play?"

When I turned, I saw a second Black American face.

"Why do you ask," I responded cautiously because the tone of his question indicated he may have been issuing a challenge.

"Guess I am trying to find out if you are a spectator or a gladiator." A wide toothy grin spread over the guy's face as he extended a hand and made his introduction. "The name is Dempsey Stevens. I am from San Diego. I have never seen you around here before, you new in Riyadh?"

"Adam Sneed, Jr. from D.C. by way of Pittsburgh - arrived last night."

"Welcome to the desert Adam. It is always good to meet a brother from the real world. By the way, I was serious when I asked if you played."

"I am no Arthur Ashe, but I know how to get around on the courts."

We were sizing one another up in typical male fashion. Dempsey ribbed "That is the same kind of vague non-answer I give when I am working a hustle. You cannot fool me Adam Sneed. Tell you what, here is my card. Call me sometime and we will play. Even if you are an amateur, that is okay.

In this desert there is so little to do, I can always use another hitting partner. If it turns out you are just plain terrible, I will be happy to give you lessons."

Dempsey had assumed he was the better player without having seen me play. Was Barry ever that cocky? I did not get offended. After a couple of years of being around Barry, I knew how to handle an ego like Dempsey Stevens. "Sounds like you are bragging Dempsey."

"Not really, but I should warn you I have played in a number of prestigious tournaments."

"Did you win any?"

"Yes… well, almost, I came in second once."

We both laughed. I assured him "even if you are a better player you will not be wasting your time with me. Only thing, I have to wait until my rackets arrive before I can play. They are coming by sea. I expect them to get here in about a month."

"Rackets, man I have plenty of rackets. You can use one of mine until yours get here and if you do not like any of mine, there are rackets on sale at the PX."

"That will work. So Dempsey what do you do here?"

"I work in the post office over there. I was in the back when you came in but you were leaving as I was coming back up front. I went to the door to see what direction you had gone and saw you looking at the tennis courts. The way you were staring, I figured you might know a little something about the game so I came over to find out."

"I guess both of us will find out how we match up soon enough. I am definitely going to be giving you a call. You are right about one thing though, there really does not seem to be a lot to do here. What about round ball, does anybody play hoops?"

"See that high rise with the tan balconies over there. A basketball court is just on the other side. Every Wednesday some of the guys get together. We play after sundown. It's the last day of the workweek and temperatures are cooler in the evening. But if you just want to shoot around, run a game of 21, horse, do a little one on one, the two of us could get together any time."

"Sounds decent, when I get settled and have a phone I will get my number to you. In the meantime, we can schedule some tennis matches."

"Good deal. By the way, there is a party tonight at the Rec Center. Stop by if you like. I hear some of the Swedish nurses will be there."

"Now that is something I never expected to hear in this country. Sounds great and I am definitely interested. Only thing, this is my first day in the Kingdom. It will be a minute before I'm set up. Just this morning I had my first meeting at Headquarters down the street there."

"Oh, you work on one of the federal projects run by the Mission."

"That is correct."

"How long have you been with the government?"

"Technically I am not a federal employee, not exactly. I was recruited by a consulting firm that does hiring for overseas federal projects. My government employee status is temporary, just for the length of this contract."

"Don't worry about missing the party. There are dozens of parties every week. If I do not see you tonight we will catch up later." Dempsey signed off with a nod and a half salute.

❧❧❧❧❧❧❧❧❧❧❧❧❧❧

Chapter 8

Boredom, the kind the Mission Head had in mind, was something I never experienced until I sat in the Transient Apartments that afternoon with nothing to do for four hours. That type of boredom I would never endure.

I started wishing I had gotten a car, because I could have gone out and explored the city. Wheels or no wheels, I could still walk. So long as I stayed in the area near the apartment, I figured Riyadh was safe enough for me to go for a short stroll. After freshening up, I stepped outside, looked up the avenue toward the airport and headed in the opposite direction.

Most Saudis were White, just as the Encyclopedia stated. But I also noticed complexions ranging from pale to dark tan and shades of olive and brown. Some could have passed for Indian, Italian, Greek, Turkish, and even African. It was easy to see what Danny meant when he said 'you people' blend in so easily. All I needed to do was put on one of those Saudi outfits, and as long as nobody said anything to me or expected me to answer in Arabic I could probably walk around and go anywhere I wanted. I knew right then without any doubts, that I actually would get to see the country in the raw just as Barry suggested. As soon as I found a tailor shop, I planned to get fit for a Saudi dress.

Armed uniformed men, carrying what looked like AK 47s, patrolled the streets behind the main thoroughfare. Whether they were military or police, I could not tell. Locals did not seem to notice them at all. Everyone went about their business as if the patrolmen and their weapons were background props. For me it was a sobering reminder that I was living in a land ruled by a monarch whose will was unquestioned, and these armed men would fire their weapons on his command. Clearly Saudi Arabia was not a democracy.

Modernization had not made many inroads into the back streets of the capital. Here I found more of old Arabia, as I had hoped to see from the beginning. Block after block there were fascinating sights of bazaars, street vendors, animal carcasses being carved up right out in the open, and herds of goats, sheep and camels being driven along by young boys. Ancient narrow streets wound through tight corridors that could not have accommodated most motor vehicles and the few cars that I did see were barely squeezing through the passageways.

I noticed one youngster overseeing a group of camels had a deformed limb. A chunk of flesh appeared to be missing from his upper left arm. The limb dangled lifelessly at his side as he drove his animals through the street. In time I found out boys like him had been bitten by camels. Camel jaws move sideways rather than up and down, so when they bite strands of muscle and nerves get ripped out all at once.

Thrilling sights, sounds and smells of an ancient culture drew me deeper into the neighborhood and farther from Airport Road. Before long I was lost in a tangle of lanes and streets. On several occasions the street I was on ended abruptly at a solid wall and I was forced to retrace my steps. Somehow I had gotten totally turned around. Rather than panic, I kept my cool. Another glance at my watch showed I had plenty of time to get back to the apartment. Confident I would eventually come across a familiar site and find my way back to Airport Road, I decided to take the time to check out the inside of one of the bazaars.

Incense filled the air. Every vendor had a cassette player that was pumping out Arab music. A large variety of items were on sale, including products manufactured in the United States. Most of the goods were still wrapped in the packaging they shipped out in from factories. An interesting looking sandwich was being made and sold by food vendors. They cut pieces of meat off a slab that was searing on a rotating spit. Whatever it was, it smelled good. They used a kind of bread that opened like a pocket to stuff in meat, tomatoes, lettuce, olives, cheese and other things.

The odor of cooking meat, incense, and new merchandise combined to produce a signature smell that will forever stand in my memory as unique to a Middle Eastern bazaar. I was especially intrigued by the abundance of jewelry stands. Thousands of pieces of gold were displayed right out in the open and it seemed to me anyone could simply pick up an item and run off with it. Proprietors did not appear to be worried at all that this might happen. Their confidence, I would soon learn, stemmed from the fact that in Saudi Arabia the penalty for theft was to get one's hand cut off. That's a pretty good deterrent considering the fact that if you failed to learn the lesson to be honest, you would lose a lot of capacity to steal or do anything else.

Scores of females were strolling through the bazaar, or suq, as Todd Dearbourne had explained they are called locally. Draped in Abbayas and ankle length black skirts, in an odd sort of way they reminded me of nuns. Younger girls walked with their parents while older young girls canvassed the shops together in groups. Unsurprisingly, young males were standing around trying to catch glimpses of these veiled beauties. Both sexes, it seemed, were trying to draw the attention of the other without doing so overtly. However, as I continued to watch I noticed there was a subtle interplay of some kind taking place between them.

Girls were moving their hands in what seemed strange ways, but it dawned on me the girls' hands were the only parts of their bodies visible to the public – ergo to males. Taking advantage of the opportunity that being in the suq provided, they were showing off their thin, soft delicate fingers and well cared for nails. Males looking on from a distance seemed quite appreciative of their efforts. Of course by western standards this activity would not pass as romantic or even exciting, but it was irrefutable evidence that attraction between the sexes was alive and well in the desert kingdom. Months later I would walk through suqs with Saudi friends and watch how closely they paid attention to the hands of young girls, thus confirming the observations I made that first day in the Kingdom. Once a Saudi friend I was walking with saw a young lady's hand and nearly lost his natural mind. He was nearly in tears as he described how lovely and delicate it was. I advised him to never go to a beach in the West.

After a lifetime of being limited to seeing vague outlines of shapes, catching brief whiffs of fragrances when passing girls in the bazaars and obsessing over delicate hands; I could only imagine how strong the attraction between males and females was in the Kingdom.

I decided to play a game with my senses. After closing my eyes for a minute or two, I opened them and tried to pretend that I had grown up in that society. This time I focused my attention on the hand movements of the girls. It was amazing how much a pair of hands told about a young lady. More than the care she took of her hands, the delicacy of her movements made it easy to imagine those hands praying, caressing a face, preparing a meal or cradling a child.

Once again I thought about how much I would have missed had I backed out of the contract. That first day alone had been worth the trip. I walked out of that suq aware of powers of observation that Westerners do not employ for the most part, powers that Arab males begin to develop a fondness for from an early age. But my little experiment by itself convinced me we could become just as adept with these types of observations if western women resorted to wearing veils. Thinking about it made me wonder what might happen if America declared an Abbaya Day on which all females that so chose wore veils. It could be a lot of fun and we might discover we have been missing out on something quite exciting.

When I came out of the bazaar, I was still lost. Another check of my watch revealed I had spent thirty minutes inside. Two hours remained until I had to be back at the apartment.

Every vacant lot I passed seemed to have been taken over by youngsters playing soccer. One hotly contested match had drawn a large crowd. I stopped and watched for a few minutes. Some of the boys wore European style athletic gear with sweat pants, jerseys and had the latest sportswear on their feet. Others hiked up their dress like garments, tied them in knots at the waist, and played barefoot. These kids were like young boys everywhere, happy and full of energy.

At the next corner down from the lot where the soccer match was being played, I turned onto a street that was very different from any of the places I had seen that afternoon. Rows of identical looking shops lined both sides of the block. Scores of males were hanging around inside and on the front steps of these places. Each shop appeared to cater to a particular ethnic group. There were Egyptians, Saudis, Ethiopians, and other African tribes that I could not identify. The shops reminded me of pool halls back in the States. Every shop had a Black and White television set and all of them were tuned to the same soccer match. The game looked and sounded like a BBC broadcast of a match between European teams. Viewers followed the play-by-play by reading Arabic subtitles at the bottom of the screens.

Quite a few of the men were smoking cigarettes, but small clusters of males were also sitting around puffing on an odd shaped contraption that stood about two and a half to three feet tall. A hose with a plastic mouthpiece was attached to one side of the device. As men took turns blowing on the mouthpiece a bubbling sound was generated inside the contraption. It would be several months before I learned that this multi-chambered device was what westerners call a Hubbly-Bubbly. One chamber is filled with water, another with hot coals, and the topmost hollow is stuffed with herbs or some other concoction. Blowing on the hose sends air through the coals, which heats the water thus producing steam that leaches through the herbs, or the concoction. Resulting vapors may have a mild narcotic effect on users, depending on the strength of the herbal mix or concoction put in the topmost chamber.

While observing these activities, the third prayer call of the day sounded and there was a sudden explosion of activity all around me. Although males began scurrying in every direction, I was able to pinpoint the Mosque where the call originated to make sure I stayed out of the way. Droves of faithful Muslims headed to the Mosque while all along the block there were sounds of shop owners shuttering windows and latching doors. The television broadcast had ended abruptly and now a still shot of the Kabba at Mecca was frozen on every screen. The soccer game at the vacant lot was also put on hold as young boys joined the stream of adults advancing on the Mosque. Public faucets, conveniently located all around the area, were used by the faithful to perform ablutions prior to entering the sacred Mosque.

Of course, as a Christian I would not be going to the Mosque but I was not sure of the proper etiquette I should follow in that situation. However, I start to notice that not everyone was heading toward the Mosque. Some were actually running in the opposite direction. Soon I realized they were racing to get inside the shops before the doors were locked. As I was becoming aware of this turn of events, a tapping sound caught my attention. It was coming from behind me. I turned and saw heading in my direction from the other end of the block, two old men with long beards. Immediately I knew who they were. These were the religious police Todd Dearbourne mentioned that morning – the Mutawahs. The tapping sound was being made by thin bamboo canes that they were striking on the ground or on shop doors as they walked along (westerners call these bamboo canes Mutawah sticks). I could not understand the words the Mutawahs were shouting, but the males that had delayed in answering the summons to prayer seemed to know what their arrival meant. Everyone fled at their approach. Those who did not get out of the way in time paid the price when the old men struck them with their canes. As the old men made their way up the street, everybody cleared out before them. They marched tapping their sticks and chanting a mantra I would be hearing many times in the coming months and years. 'Salah ya walad, sully, sully, sully.' Roughly translated they were saying: 'its prayer time young man, pray, pray, pray.'

Three of the young soccer players that I had been watching earlier tried to run inside one of the shops before its doors closed. They did not make it in time. Dejected they sat on the steps. I got the impression that was where they intended to wait out the prayer period. I was only a few feet away from them. But no sooner had they sat on the stairs, the Mutawahs spotted them and headed straight for the boys. None of the boys seemed intimidated by the old men or inclined to go to the Mosque. I looked in their faces and saw all the defiance and hubris of youth. Likely, they ordinarily would never have resisted prayer call, but the game they were playing that day had gotten pretty intense. They were still emotionally charged. The Mutawahs, however, were not concerned about soccer. They closed in on the three boys and the beatings commenced. Sounds of the boys howling, the Mutawah's screaming, and the prayer call in the background all came together in a weird orchestration. Smarting from the blows, the boys raced to a nearby faucet, washed their heads, hands, and feet and obediently entered the Mosque.

Then something really scary happened. I had gotten so focused on watching the boys that I had taken my eyes off the Mutawahs. This was a mistake. By the time I realized they were zeroing in on me, it was too late to avoid a confrontation. I shouted "I am a Christian!" Had I not panicked I might have remembered to call out 'Amreekie Aswad.' Whether that would have helped or not, I do not know. In any event, either my words failed to register, due to the language barrier, or they chose to ignore them. Those dreaded canes shot into the air and this time my head was the target.

Just before their blows could land, I felt myself suddenly propel forward. As this was happening a rush of hot air burned past my ears. It was the Mutawah sticks. They had barely missed striking me. From out of nowhere two young Black males had come up from behind and grabbed me by the arms. By the time I realized what was happening, the three of us were running at a dead sprint toward the stairs of one of the shops. This added to my confusion because the doors had already been closed. Meantime the two old men broke out after us fully intent on chasing us down. For their ages the Mutawahs moved pretty fast and stayed tight on our tails. Up the stairs we bounded and the doors seemed to open miraculously. I and my two rescuers bolted inside while behind us the doors slammed closed right in the faces of our pursuers. The Mutawas angrily pounded on the doors with their canes, furiously screeching their mantra. After a few minutes they walked away and resumed their patrol.

To the delight of the crowd in the shop, the two young Black males who had seen my predicament and rushed over to snatch me out of harms way, were performing a pantomime of me standing like a tourist while the Mutawah's canes narrowly missed my head. After several encores the cheers and applause subsided. My rescuers joined their friends engaged in activities at some of the tables. Though I was puzzled that these men were inside the shop rather than in the Mosque, I found an empty chair near the door and sat to wait out prayer call.

From what I had seen, it was a fair guess that most of the shops on that street were just as crowded as the one I was in; all filled with men who had not gone to pray. I knew why I had not gone to the Mosque, but I was not sure there were that many non-Muslims in that part of town.

Groups of males were playing cards, watching others play or engaging in conversations. The playing cards were identical to the ones we use in the States but these men were playing with many decks at once. The language being spoken was not Arabic, so I assumed it had to be an African dialect.

I checked the time again. In a little less than an hour I had to be back at the apartment to meet Walter. Time was slipping away rapidly now and I had no idea how long prayer periods lasted.

Occasionally one of the guys in the shop glanced over at me but none of them tried to approach or communicate, which was fine with me. All I wanted to do was get out of there and find my way back to the apartment.

Twenty minutes later the television sprang to life and the soccer broadcast resumed. Prayer call was over. The shop owner unlocked the front door and raised the shutters. A collective groan arose from those who had been viewing the soccer broadcast. At the start of prayer call the game had been scoreless. Now each team had a goal. I knew how they felt. Seeing a score on replay is never the same as witnessing it live. And considering the fact it was a soccer game, both teams scoring in the span of 20 minutes could be the only highlights of the match.

On my way out the door the owner stopped me and asked, in English, "Would you like to come back for a visit?"

"How did you know I spoke English," I asked?

"We knew you were American when we saw the way you reacted to the prayer call. The boys who snatched you away from the Mutawahs are my nephews. They were behind you at the time. We were watching through the shutters so I signaled them to help you. My name is Frazier, we are Kenyans. What is your name sir?"

"Adam Sneed."

"Mr. Adam please come back to see us. You are welcome to come to the tea shop at any time."

"Thank you very much Mr. Frazier. By the way, are you guys Muslims?"

"No, we are Christians."

That explained why these men had not gone to the Mosque. In appreciation I told Mr. Frazier, "From one Christian to another, thank you for your hospitality and please let your nephews know I am grateful to them for rescuing me today. I promise I will be back to visit."

After leaving the tea shop, I retraced my steps as best I could remember and thirty minutes later turned a corner and found myself back on Airport Road. How I got there I did not know, but I was happy and relieved to be within sight of the apartment. I got back with ten minutes to prepare. Quickly I showered and dressed. I was tying my shoe laces when the doorbell rang.

It was time to meet my coworkers.

☙☙☙☙☙☙☙❧❧❧❧❧❧❧

Chapter 9

Monday, November 12, 1979

Albert J. Dennison, Director of the U.S. Engineering staff at the Ministry, lived in a compound set aside for married men who held key positions on the Project. Albert was married to a lovely woman named Marlene. Al was tall and burly, possibly of Nordic ancestry, had a habit of laughing at his own jokes and possessed the kind of voice that commanded your attention. Marlene was the polar opposite, petite, soft spoken, and sweet as pie. Of all the wives on the project, Marlene will always stand out in my memory as one of the nicest. But as a couple, the Dennison's made quite a contrast.

In addition to Al and Walter, my other coworkers included Lee Williams, the youngest of the Engineers – Lee served as Al's Deputy Director; Peter Braverman, third oldest on the staff - Peter was flying solo that evening because his family was on the east coast visiting friends at the Aramco compound in Dhahran; and Perry Ferguson, Larry Corbin's friend, a Contract Writer - his wife's name was Angela. They laughed when I told them Larry Corbin called me by my name before I knew who he was. "There is hardly anyone in Riyadh that Larry does not know," Angela chuckled. Walter's wife Savannah was a true southern belle, stately and as charming as any South Carolinian I ever met. Vannah, as Walter called her, taught English at the International School. Lee Williams was married to a gorgeous brunette named Laura. She would be returning to the States in two days. When she and I had a chance to talk, Laura admitted the only reason she came to the Kingdom was to visit Lee. She said "other than spending time with my husband, I refuse to stay in a country that puts such archaic restrictions on women."

At some point before dinner, Al sat me down and went over the tasks I would be performing at the Ministry. Mostly it was the usual stuff I had been doing my whole career, including the hiring of an administrative team. In this case, eligible candidates would be men from developing countries. Al predicted I would have a tough time bringing the staff up to speed with U.S. practices. Al also mentioned a task I had not been apprised of in Washington. The Ministry wanted me to assist in locating an Arab/English computer network. To do this I would likely have to travel to one or more trade shows outside of Saudi Arabia but somewhere in the Gulf region. Where I would be going and when not only depended on the schedules of the major manufacturers, but likely would also be determined based on the status of the hostage situation in nearby Iran.

"Adam you chose a good time to join our staff," Al noted. "The division of the Ministry we work for is moving to a new building, so in a way we are all getting a fresh start. The new building is scheduled to open officially this coming Saturday." To Lee Williams he joked, "What odds will you give me the Saudis never get all our desks and files into the building without breaking or losing half of them?"

Treating the question as rhetorical, Lee smirked and presented me with an interesting invitation. "Adam you should come out with me and my friends to hunt for desert diamonds. Here, let me show you what I am talking about." Reaching into his shirt pocket, Lee pulled out a few pieces of what resembled thin dull shards of glass. "Trust me these are diamonds. Once they are cleaned and polished they shine like regular diamonds. This handful is not worth much but if you get a couple hundred of these together, man you can make a pretty decent chunk of change. So how about it, would you like to come along? We are going out on Thursday. You know Thursdays are the same as Saturdays here."

"Maybe next time" I dodged, then tongue in cheek added "I don't think it would be wise for me to start venturing out like that until I get settled and know my way around a little better."

"That sounds practical and I can understand how you feel. I will let you know the next time we go out."

"Thanks."

A young African male entered the room with a tray and offered drinks to everyone.

"Does he work with us too," I asked Lee?

"No that is Bandar, Al's houseboy," he answered and quickly explained "all of us have house servants. It is not a racial thing or meant to demean anyone or anything like that. A lot of guys like Bandar, come to Saudi Arabia from Third World Countries in search of work because there are no jobs for them in their homelands. They love working for Americans because we pay way more than the Saudis or any other employers here. It helps to have someone doing the things you or your wife might not have the time to get done. I know you are a bachelor, but you would probably find a house boy to be perfect for keeping your apartment in shape and they really do not cost that much."

Privately I wondered if Lee would have given me that speech if I was not African American. Probably not, but I liked him anyway. He seemed genuine and sensitive enough to be trusted. His open invitation to accompany him to hunt desert diamonds was a kind gesture, and later that evening Lee was thoughtful enough to take the time to draw me a map with directions to the new office.

Marlene Dennison served a wonderful meal. The food was excellent. I enjoyed meeting my coworkers and getting a preview of the personalities I would be working with over the next few years. While the evening was winding down, the fourth prayer call of the day rang out in the distance.

When we left the Dennison's, I asked Walter to drop me off at Headquarters rather than back to the Transient Apartments. From there I walked to the APO facility. I wanted to check on the party to see if it was still going. It was. I could hear the music all the way out at the compound entrance. A few of the Saudi guards were bobbing their heads to the rhythms, but I noticed one of them seemed irritated. For a minute or two I thought about going in but changed my mind. I was feeling a little tired. It had been a busy first day and I was still feeling the effects of my long flight to Arabia. There would be other parties. I headed for the Transient Apartments.

Dusk had fallen. Neon lights were coming back on along Airport Road. Soon it would look the way it had the first time I laid eyes on the avenue. Motorists were not driving any slower, but for some reason the traffic did not bother me as much as it had the first night.

Every pedestrian I passed greeted me with the expression 'Al-salaam a lekum.' Familiar with this exchange, I answered 'wa alekum al-salaam.' I am sure they thought I was a fellow Muslim, and though I was not it was nice to be among people who were commonly cordial to one another and to strangers.

The empty apartment offered no outlet for any kind of activity. There was no television or radio. It was too early for bed, so I spent the balance of that evening writing letters to Barry, my parents, and two of my sisters.

When I got in bed, my head had been on the pillow less than ten minutes when the fifth and final prayer call of the day rang out. My day was ending exactly as it had begun with a loud prayer call ripping through the apartment. Only, this time I was only mildly annoyed. It did not have the same affect on me as that jarring predawn call. I did not know it at the time, but I was already growing inured to the calls. After growling a bit, I rolled over and fell into a deep sleep. From that night until I left Saudi Arabia, the early and late prayer calls never bothered me again or woke me up. I slept through them all.

Chapter 10

Tuesday, November 13

After an early breakfast at Headquarters, I reported to the Motor Pool. Danny assigned an African driver named Khalid to take me to the DMV.

When we got there, Khalid parked and grabbed a folder with my files in it off the back seat. He motioned for me to follow him as he moved quickly toward the building. Khalid seemed to be in such a hurry that I began to suspect the DMV in Riyadh might be like the ones back home. If this was true, we were in for a long morning.

Through the front door we walked into a wide foyer at the center of which stood a table piled high and overflowing with folders identical to the one Khalid was carrying. Coming into the DMV right behind us was a Saudi dressed in an expensive looking silk version of the traditional garment. It was the nicest looking one I had seen thus far. The man reeked of wealth and privilege and carried himself with the air of someone accustomed to being treated with deference. He blew past us like we were nobody's and on into the main office. Khalid and I followed. A dozen ragtag rows of men were somewhat lined up behind a long counter where DMV clerks were processing transactions. Unlike everyone else, the fancily dressed Saudi ignored the lines and boldly strode up to the counter and handed one of the tellers his paperwork. Not a single man in any of the lines complained. The clerk set aside the papers he had been working on and completed the transaction for this important looking Saudi. Khalid whispered "he is a Saudi prince. They never wait in line for anything."

Khalid then left me standing at the back of the line and walked to the counter and handed a clerk my folder. When he returned with my pages all properly stamped, I stared at him puzzled. He explained, "You are American. Occasionally this entitles you to some privileges." Khalid took one of the stamped sheets out of the folder and led me back out to the foyer. Walking up to the table overloaded with folders, he tossed mine on top of the heap. With a sober look on his face, he turned to me and said "If you ever have an accident, you might have to come here and dig your file out of that pile." Assuming he was joking I laughed. But Khalid reaffirmed his warning with a stern stare. (By the time I had my first accident, I knew that Khalid had lied to me about those folders. If any American had an accident and his folder was required by the local police, it would be Khalid or one of the other Motor Pool drivers who would have to go down to the DMV and retrieve it.)

Happily, my status as an American allowed us to skip to the front of the next line too. After getting my picture taken, Khalid led me to the room where blood tests were given. Here the line was longer than all the lines I had seen that morning put together. It coiled around the room like a snake and extended through a doorway on the opposite wall. Running interference, Khalid pushed a path through for us to the other side of the room and out the door to the end of the line.

"Do I have to stand in this line," I asked desperately? Khalid shook his head and clarified, "Occasionally... being American entitles you to some privileges. Not this time. Sorry." After this explanation Khalid left me there and walked away.

The line was incredibly slow. It took an hour just to inch close enough to see the testing station. A professional looking medical technician was in charge. At least he looked the part of a technician in his white smock. Conversely, his assistant, the man pricking fingers to draw blood, was gritty and unkempt, not the kind of person one would expect to find anywhere near blood when it was being drawn. I watched him perform his duties for a few minutes and was shocked to see he was reusing the same pin to prick every man's finger that stepped forward. Horrified, I looked around for Khalid. He was nowhere to be seen. As I continued to move forward, my fear increased. Then a Westerner stepped up to have his test. The assistant immediately tossed the pin he had been using into a nearby trash can. Then he reached into a box on the table next to him and pulled out a packet. It was an individually wrapped sterile stick pin for drawing blood. The box of pins had only recently been open because it was full to the top. After tearing off the wrapping he used the clean sterile pin to prick the Westerner's finger. The next man in line was Arab. When this man moved forward, the assistant pricked him with the same pin he had used on the Westerner. He continued to use that same pin until the next Westerner came forward. As the line moved ahead he repeated this pattern enough times to convince me that new pins were reserved solely for use on Westerners. Though I was stunned that new sterile pins, of which there were plenty, were not being used on each applicant, it was a relief to know we Westerners were being treated differently. But it seemed odd that the medical technician was not bothered by what his assistant was doing. Surely he, if no one else in the room, had to know what the box of individually wrapped stick pins was there for and the role medical personnel are supposed to play in helping to prevent the transmission of disease.

As I drew closer to the testing station I started to suspect that this gritty character might take one look at me and assume I was not from the West. If this turned out to be the case, I certainly did not want him to prick me with a pin that had other people's blood on it. Again I scanned the room in search of Khalid. The line moved steadily forward while I kept one eye on the man with the stickpin and the other on the door, in case Khalid walked into the room.

Eventually I reached the front of the line and was forced to confront this despicable situation without Khalid's assistance. As I feared, the assistant did not reach for a sterile pin when he saw my face. Stepping back I complained loudly, "You have a box filled with sterile wrapped pins sitting right there, why are you reusing the same pin on all these people?" If anyone in the room understood English they said nothing. I was alone in this protest. When I did not extend my hand to be pricked the assistant tried to grab for it but I pulled back and explained, "I am an American, Amreekie Aswad. I insist that you unwrap one of those new pins." But the grungy little man jumped at me and grabbed my hand. When he attempted to poke my finger I jerked it away and protested at the top of my voice. Before I could finish what I was trying to say, two large men came up from behind and held my arms as the assistant stepped forward and swiftly pricked one of my fingers with that soiled pin.

Once the deed was done, the men released their hold on me. I was so angry I could not speak. My lips were trembling but no sounds came out of my mouth. Fuming and feeling horribly violated, I stumbled out of the room in search of Khalid. I could not find him. Ten minutes later Khalid nonchalantly strolled up and when he saw my face asked, "What's wrong?" I described what happened as calmly as I could and afterward he acknowledged, "If they had known you were American they would not have treated you that way."

"Then why did you leave me alone in line like that?" Instead of answering my question he said "wait here" and walked away. I was furious with Khalid.

Minutes later I spotted Khalid coming toward me. He stopped twenty feet away and signaled with his arm for me to follow. Khalid never slowed down enough for me to catch up with him. He was deliberately avoiding me because he knew I was angry. I followed him to a different part of the DMV and down a long hallway where he paused momentarily at one door, pointed inside and shouted "go in there to take the road test."

At least I had a heads up on what to expect with the road test, thanks to Larry Corbin. The Saudi overseeing this test only knew a few words of English. After saying hello he motioned for me to get into the car. More gestures indicated I should start the motor and move to the test track. I followed the prescribed course and after a few minutes he indicated I should park. As Larry had guaranteed, the manual was never mentioned.

Ten minutes later a smug Khalid handed me a new license, complete with a photograph. We did not speak on the way back to Headquarters and for the rest of the time I was on the Mission roster I never said more than two words to Khalid.

Danny assigned me a car, but my hands were shaking so badly I had a hard time turning on the ignition. I was terrified. Once I got the car running I drove to the Transient Apartments, ran in and gathered my Certificates of Inoculation brochure, then followed the map to the Medical Facility. I drove so fast I could have been mistaken for a Saudi motorist.

Even though I had never been in that part of town before, I found the Medical Facility on the first try. The doctor on duty was Egyptian but spoke English. He listened patiently as I explained what happened to me at the DMV. After talking me down from hysteria he offered valium, which I refused for personal reasons. I had taken Valium before and within six months was dependent on the drug. Once I accepted that I was addicted, I stopped taking the pills and made a vow not to take them again. When I explained this to the doctor he gave me something else to steady my nerves. The doctor also enumerated a number of symptoms that I should watch for over the next few weeks, but expressed confidence that "based on your inoculation records, unless any of the symptoms I mentioned occur, you do not have anything to worry about."

I think what upset me the most was that I did not walk out of the DMV the instant I suspected they might not handle me the way they were handling other Westerners. Nothing prevented me from leaving the building and there was no reason I could not have come back for a blood test another day. Todd Dearbourne had clearly offered me the option of coming to him with any problems I might have. I know I could have explained the situation to him and he would have arranged for Khalid to do his job properly, or he would have gotten a different driver to shepherd me safely through the blood testing procedure. Hindsight really is 20/20.

There were several lessons in what happened to me that day, including the fact that being a Black American in Arabia was very different from being an American in Arabia. Good moments and bad ones go with the territory if you are a foreigner and Black in any country. The bad moments apparently could be quite risky in Arabia. But to what extent was I at risk? This was something I needed to evaluate seriously because if the tour was in reality a kind of Russian roulette for me, it might be in my best interests to call it off and return to America. Once again I was wavering over going through with the contract, and this after only two days in the Kingdom.

During dinner at the restaurant in Virginia, Lovelen had asked if I was sure the Saudis were going to treat me the same way they treated White Americans. Now I knew the answer to that question. It was interesting though, that I was not the only Black face in the line for the blood test. There were a number of Africans waiting in the blood test line as well, and as far as I knew some of the Blacks I saw could have been Saudi. All of us were handled the same, like we were locals. This meant that I had not been specifically singled out because of the color of my skin. Rather, in their eyes I was a local - one of their own. So the bigger issue was not the color of my skin, or theirs for that matter, but why did they apply western medical procedures when dealing with obvious westerners while ignoring them when it came to handling their own people. A clearer understanding of the expression 'developing land' was coming into focus.

After the events of that morning I knew I could not sit around the apartment the rest of the day. I would be worried to death about my health and running to the mirror every five minutes to see if my face was breaking out or something worse was happening to my body. Technically it was a workday, so I pulled Lee Williams' map out of my wallet and headed for the site of the new office. I figured I could take a quick look around and get an idea of the kind of place I would be working in for the next 24 months; that is if my health held up.

Along the way I saw the wreckage of a car accident that, by its appearance, happened months earlier. I could not imagine why the wreck had not been removed. Whoever was driving at the time of the accident must have been going at a very high speed because the vehicle crashed head on into a wall and crumpled like an accordion. As fast as the Saudis drove, the scene did not surprise me.

As I guided my car past the wreckage I got a better idea of the force of the impact when I spotted the steering wheel sitting in what remained of the frame of the rear window. I did not believe anyone could have survived that accident.

At the new building I pulled into a parking lot overrun with delivery trucks, automobiles, desks, chairs, file cabinets and furniture. Laborers were hauling items into the Ministry and in the middle of all the chaos there stood Lee Williams shouting directions. After squeezing my car into a parking space I joined him.

"Adam you found your way here. Good to see you. We are trying to keep a close eye on these guys because they keep getting our furniture mixed up with the Saudis'. Would you believe we have been yelling at these guys all morning and they are still getting it wrong? Al is upstairs by the way. Run up to the third floor if you want to take a look at our offices. The Saudis have the rest of the building. Minister Al-Naseem and his staff are on the top floor above us."

"I just wanted to stop by for a few minutes and take a look around. I will try to stay out of the way."

"What have you been doing since I saw you last night?"

"This morning I finished up getting my driver's license and I now I have a car."

"I thought you got all that taken care of yesterday?"

"My States-side license was rejected, so I had to go to the DMV this morning to take the test. I finished up a little while ago."

"You had to take the test at the DMV? That must have been painful. Sorry you had to go through all that Adam."

"Lee, the less I talk about it the better."

"Well you have your car now so all that is behind you."

"Hopefully... I am still nervous about driving in this traffic. Man I saw a wreck on the way over here that looked like a guy must have drove straight into a wall at high speed. The car was crumpled like something you see in a cartoon. I have never seen a wreck like that in real life."

"You will get used to that sort of thing. It happens here all the time. I saw the worst accident ever one morning on my way to work. A Cadillac had run into the broadside of a fuel tanker... sheared the top of the car right off killing the driver, his wife and four daughters - all teenage girls. We found out a few days later the guy had put drapes over the windows to keep men from looking in the car at his wife and daughters. Whatever caused the accident, I think it is safe to say the drapes cut off his view from the side and rear windows."

"That is so sad."

"You are right, but like I said that sort of thing is common in this country."

"The accident I saw this morning looked months old. I was surprised the wreckage is still sitting there?"

"Did you see a red X spray painted on the wreck?"

"Come to think of it I did. I thought it was graffiti."

"No, that is how they mark fatal accidents. Wreckage from fatal accidents stays in place for at least a year."

"Why?"

"That I am not sure of. It might have something to do with the way they investigate accidents or it could be connected in some way to their religion. Anyway, that is the rule here when there is a fatality."

I could not decide which was more dangerous – going through the process of getting a license or actually getting a license then having to get behind the wheel and drive on the streets of Riyadh. It was a toss up. Frankly, it did not seem practical to drive at all and the hazardous duty allowance we received did not, in my opinion, come close to compensating us for the level of risk we faced. Unfortunately there were no alternatives to getting around town. In a fast growing city the size of Riyadh you had to have a car. Of course, there was the option of calling the Motor Pool and having Danny assign a chauffeur to take me where I needed to go. The problem with that was it would place my life in someone else's hands, a guy like Khalid for example. At that point I did not think I would ever trust the motor pool again, under any circumstance. Another drawback in depending on someone else to get me from place to place was that it would handicap my efforts to accomplish the personal goals I had in mind.

While Lee and I were talking, a truck pulled into the lot and backed up to the front of the building right at the spot where we were standing. A dozen or so workers jumped off the back and started unloading kitchen furniture. One of them, a diminutive Yemini, placed a full sized refrigerator on his back and started hauling it up the makeshift ramp of plywood boards that had been laid across the outer steps of the Ministry. Thinking he was being helpful, Lee blocked the man's path and motioned for him to put the refrigerator down. The man complied. Next, Lee brought over a dolly and placed it beside the refrigerator and gestured for the man to put the refrigerator on the dolly and wheel it up the ramp instead. The little guy put the refrigerator on the dolly as instructed, then hoisted the dolly and the refrigerator onto his back and resumed his climb up the ramp. Lee felt bad, because instead of helping he had actually added to the worker's burden. Aside he whispered, "New buildings - old minds, that's what we say about them."

Tugging on my arm Lee offered, "Come inside, I want to introduce you to Howard Seymour. He is the big boss over Al Dennison. Howard is the highest ranking American at the Ministry." I followed Lee up to the third floor and at the landing he stopped and informed me "our offices are at this end to the right. Howard is to the left all the way down at the other end of the hall.

The moment I laid eyes on Howard Seymour, I liked him. Howard was blond haired, blue eyed, powerfully built and handsome. What impressed me was that this White American had come to the Ministry that day dressed like a local. There was no way Howard could blend in with the natives the way I could, so his wearing of the local garment was a nice gesture of respect for their traditions. Howard greeted me with a warm smile and squeezed my hand with a formidable handshake. He saw me admiring his get up and proudly explained its different parts. "This long dress like garment is called the Thobe." The headgear was lying on his desk. He picked the items up one by one and said "first I put on this skullcap. It is called the tawkeeya (tah-key-ya). It is worn to protect this next piece, the cloth that covers the head – they call this the gutra (goo-trrra). The tawkeeya protects the gutra from getting soiled with hair grease and sweat. After putting on the gutra I top the whole thing off with this thick black ropelike ring called the ak-gal (ak-gaul). The ak-gal holds the Gutra in place on your head. Check out my sandals" he beamed and lifted the hem of his Thobe to give me a full view. "I am wearing Saudi from head to foot. You should get yourself fitted for this gear while you are here."

"That is exactly what I plan to do."

"Lee why don't we take Adam upstairs and introduce him to Minister Al-Naseem," Howard suggested?

My mouth went dry. This was not something I ever expected to happen. No training had been given during orientation on what protocols to follow when in the presence of Saudi royalty. All government Ministers were Saudi princes related to and appointed by King Khalid, including Minister Al-Naseem.

Lee declined, "I am going back downstairs. I have already met the Minister."

Howard took the headgear off again and urged excitedly, "Come on Adam." During our conversation on the way up to the fourth floor I learned that Howard also played tennis. We agreed to get together soon for a match.

None of the chaos and disarray in the rest of the Ministry was evident on the top floor. Up there the central hallway divided rows of small offices on the right from the Minister's suite on the left side of the building. His suite covered an entire half of the top floor. When we stepped inside, my eyes were immediately drawn to the windows. They rose from the floor to the ceiling and crested at the top in Middle Eastern style arches. The panes were tinted so the glare of the sun was muted filling the room with soft light that was easy on the eyes.

The Minister's suite was separated into two sections - one designed Arab style and the other Western. In the Western half a massive mahogany desk stood in front of a large gold plated replica of the palm tree and crossed swords emblem of Saudi Arabia. Facing the desk were two Chippendale chairs with a fine Persian rug beneath them. Tapestries embroidered with scenes of various Saudi cities, including the holy sites of Mecca and Medina, hung from the ceiling. Incense was burning somewhere. The scent filled the suite with a pleasant odor. Over in the Arab section, a number of guests were being entertained. They all sat cross-legged on the floor and each man had a lavishly embroidered red box shaped pillow to use as an arm rest. Each of the guests wore a high quality Thobe exactly like the one worn by the prince at the DMV. Additionally, these men had beautiful black capes with gold trimming on the edges draped across their shoulders. I assumed all of them were members of the royal family. The floor covering they sat on was as fine, if not finer, than the Persian rug beneath the Chippendale chairs. A servant was distributing hot tea to the Arab guests.

We left our shoes at the door. A staff member directed us to the Western section of the office and seated us on the Chippendale chairs in front of the Minister's desk.

As we waited, my curiosity grew about what was going on with the Saudis on the other side of the room. I tried to guess which one might be Minister Al-Naseem. One man seemed to be the center of attention but like Howard this man was not wearing the traditional headgear, nor did he have a cloak draped over his shoulders. Howard nudged me, nodded at him and whispered "that is Minister Tarik Al-Naseem."

Howard and I sat respectfully, patiently waiting for the Minister to acknowledge our presence. After five minutes he excused himself from his other guests and came toward us with a bright smile on his face. As he approached, I noticed Minister Al-Naseem's skin was swarthy but not too brown. He was what Hollywood might describe as ruggedly handsome. In my estimation he could pass for Greek or Turkish. His smile reminded me of Clark Gable in his opening scene in the film *Gone with the Wind* when he grinned at Vivien Leigh on the grand staircase of the Twelve Oaks plantation. As the Minister neared his desk I tried to guess his age. He was a little gray at the temples, so I figured he was probably in his early to mid forties.

Minister Al-Naseem's Thobe was also high quality like those of his guests. Easily it was more expensive than the outfit worn by Howard Seymour, yet his first words were to commend Howard on his attire.

The Minister had a deep strong voice and spoke English well, with barely a Middle Eastern accent. The same servant who had served the Arab guests came over and offered tea to me and Howard. We accepted this traditional gesture of desert hospitality.

For a person of my lowly status to meet a royal personage my second day in Saudi Arabia was beyond extraordinary. Naturally I was feeling overwhelmed, and the longer we sat there the more anxious I was to get away. Chills ran through me like Olympic relay teams, and I dreaded the possibility that I might be required to say something to the Minister. I sat there hoping neither the Minister nor Howard asked me anything. Those hopes were soon dashed.

"Minister Al-Naseem, thank you for seeing us. We have a new employee on our staff. I would like to introduce to you Adam Sneed, Jr. He just arrived from Washington, D.C."

"Welcome to Saudi Arabia Mr. Sneed."

Oh God, I have to talk. "Thank you Minister Al-Naseem. I am honored to be here." Never had I been so worried that I might say the wrong thing.

"What do you think about Saudi Arabia, Mr. Sneed?"

Good grief, surely this man can see I am a nervous wreck I thought. My mind raced frantically to come up with an answer to his question that would be politically correct, appropriate, and culturally inoffensive. While Minister Al-Naseem waited for my answer, he maintained a steady gaze and warm smile. This calmed me and I regained my composure. Speaking from the heart I responded, "Being here is one of the most exciting things to ever happen to me. I want to learn as much about your country and Saudi culture as I can."

The Minister's face literally lit up and with a beaming smile he exclaimed, "That is wonderful to hear Mr. Sneed. I am very pleased that you have so much interest in my country. Please, if you ever have questions about Saudi Arabia feel free to come to my office at any time. I will leave instructions for my staff so that if I am not here, someone will be happy to speak with you."

Howard stood. I followed his lead. "Adam and I thank you for your graciousness in sharing a moment of your time."

Minister Al-Naseem smiled, rose and offered his hand to me saying "Remember Mr. Sneed, you are welcome to come to my office at any time. I wish you the best during your stay in Saudi Arabia."

I shook the great man's hand and replied humbly "thank you Minister Al-Naseem."

The Minister walked us to the door and said to Howard, "I will see you at the planning meeting Saturday morning."

Although I would see Minister Al-Naseem many times in the years ahead, our conversation that morning was the longest talk we would have together. But I will never forget those few moments in the rarified air on the top floor of the Ministry.

"Well done Adam. He was impressed with you," Howard Seymour commended with a broad grin.

"I have never been that nervous before. That is one powerful man."

"Yes he is. Plus he is probably the nicest Saudi you will ever meet. Adam, I really enjoyed meeting you, but I better get back to my office before the movers completely wreck the place. I look forward to us working together. Don't forget, we will be getting together soon to play tennis." Howard peeled away on the third floor and I went downstairs to rejoin Lee.

As soon as I caught up with Lee, Albert Dennison walked up from behind and pouting said "Lee stole my chance to introduce you to Howard Seymour and I just found out you have already met Minister Al-Naseem. That only leaves me the chance to introduce you to my Saudi counterpart. Come on let's get up to Al-Basheer's office before somebody steals that chance from me too."

The office of Mr. Abdullah Al-Basheer was located directly across the hall from where Al Dennison's new office was being organized. Abdullah Al-Basheer, the only Saudi assigned to work on the third floor, was, according to Dennison, "a watchdog put nearby to keep an eye on us Americans."

Al-Basheer was younger than all of the American Engineers. He and I were around the same age. Compared to the Minister, Al-Basheer was fair skinned - a 'White Saudi'. Minister Al-Naseem had struck me as ruggedly handsome. Al-Basheer was simply a good looking man brimming with the vigor of youth. His facial features put me in mind of the Egyptian actor Omar Sharif (I innocently mentioned this resemblance some months later only to be told that Omar Sharif was persona non grata in the Arab world because of co-starring in a film next to the Jewish actor Barbra Streisand).

Abdullah Al-Basheer carried himself with dignity and inner calm. He and Minister Al-Naseem had a sereneness about themselves that fit well with the magnitude of the task they shared to help lead their country in its race to catch up to the 20th century world. Al-Basheer, also proficient in English, spoke it with a slightly less pronounced lilt than the young man that welcomed my flight at Jeddah.

Al-Basheer offered to have tea brought in but I declined, explaining tactfully "I just had tea upstairs with the Minister a few moments ago."

Abdullah seemed genuinely happy to meet me and our first conversation reflected a personality I would come to enjoy thoroughly over the coming years. "We don't get many Black Americans here," Abdullah forthrightly observed with a hearty laugh. I chuckled and answered, "I noticed."

Relentless, Abdullah persisted, "It is a nice change from only White Americans; do you not you agree Al Dennison?" It was a bold question to throw at my boss, but to his credit Al laughed along with him. Al also knew something about the Ministry that it would take me a few weeks to discover. There were no Black Saudis in our branch of the Ministry. Rather than throw this fact back at his Saudi counterpart, Al chose to be diplomatic.

"I know you just arrived, but what do you think of my country so far Mr. Adam?"

"Your country is beautiful. I am very happy to be here Mr. Al-Basheer."

"Good. I hope you will always think so highly of Saudi Arabia."

"Actually, I have already had some interesting experiences that I am eager to write home about. And one of my top goals is to learn enough Arabic to be able to hold conversations directly with Saudis."

"That is an excellent goal and I can get you started if you like. Ahlan wa-Sahlan – that means welcome. Ahlan wa-Sahlan Mr. Adam. Ahlan fi al Mamlika al Arabia di Saudia. Welcome to the Kingdom of Saudi Arabia."

Abdullah looked at me as if anticipating a response, so I attempted to repeat the words he had spoken.

"My goodness you sound just like a Saudi. Now I know you will speak our language, very well, and real soon. Okay, if you can remember the words Insha'Allah, that means God willing, you will be able to talk with almost anybody in Saudi Arabia. We say Insha'Allah all the time, about everything."

"He said a mouthful that time Adam," Al interjected with a roaring laugh. "We hear Inshallah all the time, especially when somebody mentions a deadline in the planning meetings."

I had to get used to Al laughing at his own humor.

"Now that we have met formally, you can call me Abdullah and if it is okay with you, I will call you Adam."

"That will be fine Abdullah."

"Anytime you have questions about Riyadh or anything about my country, feel free to come to my office and we will talk. Now I will say goodbye to you in Arabic, Ma-al-salaama. Now you try to say it."

"Ma al-salaama."

"Very good. Fi amanila Adam, that means 'go with God.'"

From Abdullah Al-Basheer's office, Al led me to the far end of the hall directly opposite Howard Seymour's suite at the other end of the building. We entered through double doors into a large spacious room with windows on three sides. All of them were non-tinted and the room was flooded with bright sunlight. Other than daylight, the room was empty. It did have a nice carpet though.

"This is where you will be working. I know it does not look like much right now but by Saturday there will be a desk and chair in here for you. Whoopee, right! Since you will also be in charge of our office operations budget, one of the first things you will need to do is order new file cabinets. Our cabinets have gotten so banged up in this move, they are no longer usable. So until new cabinets are purchased our files will have to be brought in and stacked along the walls around this room. They will still need to be organized in some manner so we can get to them when we need to, but I am going to leave that up to you and your staff once you hire some workers. Do not feel discouraged by the way things look right now, or how this place is probably going to look by this time next week. All great enterprises have small beginnings. You already know that from the many construction projects you have under your belt. I read your resume, so I know what you are capable of doing when it comes to organizing offices. I envision the day when this room will be filled with cabinets, computers, desks and a full support staff - everything all nice and orderly. Until then, you can think of this empty space as a canvass upon which you will paint an Adam Sneed masterpiece."

"The way you are talking it sounds like I should start tomorrow. Wednesday's are workdays right? Should I come in?"

"You do not need to worry about coming in tomorrow. Tomorrow is the last day of the workweek anyway. You might as well wait until Saturday to start. Besides, you will probably need an extra day to get set up in your new place."

"My new place?"

"Yes, I got a notice in my mailbox this morning that the bachelor compound is ready for you to move in. Didn't you get a notice?"

"I forgot to check my box this morning when I stopped by Headquarters. It is going to take a day or two for me to pick up that habit."

"Definitely check your box. I am sure Madeline left a note for you too. Okay, I will see you next week. Things should be in a little better shape around here by then."

A move notice and map to Villa 760-D with a key to Apartment B-2 attached, were in my mailbox. After locking the box, I turned and came face to face with a young Saudi who looked vaguely familiar. After a second or two I remembered where I had seen him before. He was the assistant to the Saudi official at the Motor Pool, the young man who glared at the African drivers when they laughed about my having to take the driving test.

"Hello," he said shyly.

"Hello," I answered.

After a quick smile he walked away. I had no idea what that was about and although I dismissed the incident, I had an inkling our paths would cross again.

From Headquarters I drove to the Transient Apartments where I grabbed my bags and was out of the building in all of fifteen seconds. Following the map north on Airport Road, I reached the fork where the avenue divided to the right onto Khurais Road, which I had taken earlier to go to the medical facility. This time I took the left fork past the airport entrance that Walter and I came out of my first night in Riyadh. A quarter of a mile later I pulled into the driveway of Compound 760-D. My new quarters were directly across from a remote airstrip. Other than that strip the view from the front of the compound was nothing but sand dunes and desert as far as the eye could see.

I had hoped the bachelor quarters would be better than the Transient Apartments and they did not disappoint. The compound itself consisted of four multilevel apartment buildings built around a central courtyard with a swimming pool and a patio for cookouts. When I entered my new apartment I smiled in relief. It was on the second floor of Building B. Not only was the place spacious it was tastefully furnished and even had window treatments. Air-conditioning, wall-to-wall carpeting, a master bedroom, a guest room, 1½ baths, a living room, dining area, and kitchen with state of the art appliances, all gave it that made-in-America look and feel. Courtesy bed coverings and complimentary toiletries were added touches that made the place seem like an apartment waiting for someone like me to come along and make it a residence. Once my household effects shipment arrived, I could add a few items of personal nostalgia and the place would really be my home away from home. Al Dennison and the other married workers may have had more, but I felt no lack.

With the help of the map, I made it to the Commissary and PX, which were a little further out Khurais Road beyond the Medical Facility. My shopping list included groceries, cooking utensils, a vacuum cleaner, and an entertainment center complete with television, Betamax player/recorder and an 8-Track player. The selections of movies and music at the PX were disappointing, but I went ahead and purchased a couple of videotapes and an 8-track tape so that I could test out my new equipment. Equally important, I bought a couple of voltage regulators to protect my U.S. manufactured equipment from the frequent electrical surges we had been forewarned about. Power generated by the Saudi Electric Company was produced on the European standard.

As soon as I got the television hooked up and turned on, it picked up a local broadcast. The audio was clear but in Arabic, so I did not understand what was being said. The reception was mostly snow, so the images were too vague to see what was going on. At Headquarters, Marlene had mentioned I would need an antenna to watch local programming. Since I only planned to watch videotapes, I did not give much thought to that idea. The broadcast had English subtitles that came through much better than the picture and at times both Arabic and English subtitles appeared on screen.

Prayer call sounded interrupting the broadcast, and though I could not see it clearly, I could tell the screen was filled with the now familiar scene of the Kabba at Mecca. I turned off the television, set up the Betamax player/recorder and put on one of the videos I had purchased. While the film played I prepared my first meal in the new apartment. Before I went to bed I started a couple of letters that I did not get to finish that night.

Wednesday morning I fixed breakfast and tried to think up some mischief to get into since I did not have to go to work. There was so much to see and learn. I decided to go for a drive, despite the crazy traffic. Believe it or not, having a car was thrilling because it gave me an unlimited range for exploring.

My first goal was to get better acquainted with my new neighborhood. Since there was nothing north of me except the airport and desert, I scoured areas east, west and south of the compound. The bachelor compound was on the northern border of a combination business/residential district.   As Todd Dearbourne had indicated, there were numerous construction projects underway wherever I turned. Riyadh was a construction worker's dream. I had no doubts that in a couple of years the city would be so changed that Westerners currently in the Kingdom would not remember how the place had looked when we first arrived.

Many restaurants operated in the neighborhood and featured a variety of foods including Lebanese, Chinese, Arab, and Ethiopian cuisines. On every block there seemed to be a television or electronics store of some kind, and there had to be at least twice as many gold shops. About a quarter of a mile south of the compound I found a Western style grocery store that was so large it occupied an entire block. Cottage industries dotted the district as well with appliance, repair, and souvenir shops. When I saw a tailor shop I parked, went in, and despite the difference in language, managed to get myself measured for a Thobe. The tailor, using spotty English and hand signals, assured me it would be ready in two days.

After that I came across a large open air market crowded with tents and vendor stalls. It reminded me of a flea market, only twenty times larger. People seemed to prefer the open air market to the modern stores, as many more were shopping under the tents than in all the other shops in the area combined. Southwest of my new villa I saw an amazing looking palace that sprawled over an area approximately the size of two downtown blocks of New York City. The entry gate was tall and imposing. I tried to imagine bygone times when caravans arrived at that gate with important sheiks on camelback who were welcomed as special guests by the occupants of the palace.

Despite the dangers of the roads, I was growing comfortable with the traffic so much so that I drove to the area where I had gotten lost during my stroll on Monday. This time I found my way around much easier. I parked near the teashop and visited the Kenyans as I had promised. Two men approached as soon as I walked in the door. The taller one introduced himself as Ibrahim (ee-bra-him) and his companion was named Owache (ooo-wah-chey). They remembered me from my first visit and invited me to join them at their table. We shared stories about our experiences in Saudi Arabia and Owache tried to teach me the card game they played using multiple decks of cards. They called it konkan. It was an overgrown version of Tonk and I was a terrible student. But that was probably because I like to count the suits when I play cards. Counting cards in konkan was a waste of time. They played with multiple decks but the cards were randomly thrown together and there was no guarantee a complete full deck of 52 could be produced from out of them all.

From the description of their workers' compound I could tell a vast difference existed between living conditions for Americans and that of other foreign nationals working in the Kingdom.

Later on the three of us went for a walk and my new African friends treated me to my first Schwarma (aka Gyro), the sandwich I had observed vendors making when I visited the suq. When I inquired about the meat, Ibrahim explained it could be camel, goat or lamb. The meat cooked as it rotated on a vertical spit in front of a flame. As the spit turned, the vendor sliced pieces of meat off with a long sharp knife. These pieces fell into a tray that he held with his other hand. The meat was then stuffed into the bread pocket along with lettuce, tomato, onion, olives and other items then doused with a generous amount of olive oil. I did not know what to expect with regard to taste, but when I bit into the sandwich – man, it was some kind of good. That was the first of many Schwarmas I would eat in Saudi Arabia.

Around mid-afternoon, I parted company with Ibrahim and Owache. It was just ahead of prayer call. By the time the call rang out I was safely behind the wheel of my car driving around sightseeing. Thirty-five minutes later I came upon an exceptionally large bazaar that looked ancient, possibly old enough to have been around before the original thirteen colonies became the United States. Places like it were disappearing all across the Peninsula. And at the rate new construction was getting underway in Riyadh old sites like this bazaar would not be around much longer. Eager to take a look inside, I looked for a place to park. After circling the block several times I gave up but took note of distinguishing landmarks nearby so I would remember the area if I ever got back there again.

I drove to the corner and this time I turned right. Two blocks ahead of me I saw another incredible sight. The street ended at a T-intersection across from which was a tall wall with a gate that opened to a large complex. The troop of soldiers guarding the entrance, were different from the guards I saw patrolling on the streets and the ones guarding the APO. They were dressed in the traditional white Thobe, but instead of sandals they wore boots and their gutras were red and white checkered. Pinned on the front of their ak-gals was a tiny golden pin of crossed swords. Bandoliers crisscrossed their breasts as well and they carried automatic weapons. It was a troop of royal guardsmen, the first that I had seen since arriving in the country. Behind the guards, at some distance within the complex, there was a grove of palm trees whose fronds were gently swaying in the wind. From the midst of this grove rose a tall white sandstone palace that stretched skyward. Though not as spectacular as the Taj Mahal, the palace was beautiful and reminded me of the enchanting edifices I had read about in Sheherazade's Tales of 1000 Arabian Nights.

At the intersection, I turned left and as I drove past the entrance spotted westerners inside the enclosure taking pictures. Since the palace was a tourist attraction, I planned to take a trip to the PX and buy a camera to keep in the glove compartment. That way I would have it with me the next time I came to that neighborhood. Now I had two places to visit in that area, an old bazaar and a palace.

That day ended well because I made it home without getting lost.

Thursday - November 15, 1979

My fourth day in the country was the start of my first weekend in Arabia. Treating Thursdays like Saturdays felt strange but I knew I would get used to it. After purchasing a camera at the PX, I retraced my route from the previous day with the intention of visiting the palace and the old bazaar. First I would stop at the palace to make sure it had weekend visiting hours. If it did not, I would explore the old bazaar instead and go back to the palace some other time. Getting back to the bazaar was easy. From there I drove to the corner and turned right as I had done the day before. I was confident the palace would be two blocks ahead of me when I turned the corner and I was right. But I did not have time to think about the palace. A wall of traffic was coming right at me. Overnight, the street had been switched to one-way traffic.

As motorists swerved to avoid hitting me, they shook their fists angrily and shouted curses, some of which I did not need to have translated. My heart was racing as I dodged one head on collision after another. Twice I tried to stop and make a U-turn, but drivers were so aggressive in getting around me that I could not get it done. As wild as it may sound, what started going through my mind at that moment was the way I used to react at home when foreign drivers made similar goofs during rush hour in D.C.

The Saudis were not the only ones calling me names that day. I berated myself with the same names I used to yell at foreign drivers in Washington. The situation was so insane it made me laugh. But some of the drivers that saw me laughing must have thought I had driven the wrong way deliberately as some kind of prank and they got even angrier.

A familiar and welcome sound soon fell on my ears. With lights flashing and siren wailing, a police cruiser swerved in front of me and forced the oncoming traffic to come to a standstill. An officer jumped out, rushed over and started talking to me rapidly in Arabic. Slowly I explained "I am American. I came this way yesterday but the street was not one-way then. I am very sorry about causing this mess but something must have happened overnight for somebody to switch the street to one-way."

"Inglizi" the officer asked?

Good, I thought, he realizes I am not a local. "Yes, I am American."

"Amreekie? Amreekie Aswad inta? You are Black American, yes?"

'How about that,' I thought, 'he speaks English.' I had caught a break. "That is right, I am a Black American."

The wide grin he flashed at me also sported the popular gold crown. Pointing to the corner near the bazaar where I had turned into the traffic, the officer explained "See those two large signs. Those are notices that say traffic has been temporarily diverted due to emergency work on an adjacent road. That is the reason this street is one-way today. Just make a U-turn and go back. I will hold the traffic for you," he offered helpfully. His behavior was professional but I could tell he wanted to laugh. This was a story he would be telling and retelling for years to come. After he walked away I laughed too. One of my favorite things to shout to foreign drivers back home had been, 'If you are going to live in this country, learn the language so you can read the signs.'

One antsy motorist tried to squeeze past the cruiser before I could get my car pointed in the right direction, but the officer yelled so harshly at the guy it even made me cringe. After getting out of that situation I drove back to the bazaar. This time I found a place to park.

Inside the bazaar everything was the same as in the first market I visited, only multiplied many times over. As at the first suq, I saw interactions taking place between young men and women. Two incidents that I noticed particularly caught my attention because they both involved Blacks. First, a Sudanese couple was walking through the bazaar when a Saudi called to the husband. Though I did not know what was being said, I got the impression the Saudi had asked the Sudanese for directions. However, what drew my attention to them was that to get the Sudanese man's attention the Saudi called out to him 'ya Abidan.' Several times over my first few days in Arabia, I had heard Saudis use this word when addressing Blacks. It seemed that in Arabia there was some kind of a connection between the word Abidan and Black people. Furthermore, none of the Blacks I noticed being called Abidan were dressed like Saudis, so I figured they were foreign workers like myself. That meant it was only a matter of time before a Saudi addressed me as Abidan. I needed to know what the word meant so I would know how I was expected to respond to them.

The second incident that caught my attention happened when I came out of the bazaar. Several older Black women wearing colorful bandanas had arrived while I was inside and set up camp along the curb outside the market. They appeared to be selling little trinkets and toys. As shoppers passed by them, they held up the toys and cried "Zekki, Zekki, Zekki." Occasionally a Saudi would hand one of the women a riyal or two and take toys. Whether these women were Saudi or African I did not know.

Interaction with locals to that point, including at the restaurant, the DMV and the Ministry, had convinced me there was no racial divide in Arabia, at least not the kind I was familiar with. Visiting that ancient bazaar had me questioning whether my initial perceptions were accurate. I made a mental note of my observations that day and planned to inquire about them later when the opportunity presented itself.

Back at the apartment I prepared a meal and, as had become my habit over the years, sat in front of the television to eat. I did this even though I knew I would get a snowy screen and be unable to understand anything I heard. This time, to my surprise, the local station was broadcasting an episode of 'Little House on the Prairie' with English audio and Arabic subtitles. Being able to hear the program in my language helped me get into the story, despite the blurred visual. Naturally, as soon as the story started getting good the ubiquitous still shot of the Kabba froze on the screen and echoes from scores of mosques filled the air proclaiming prayer call.

Installation of phone service at my place was still a few days away, so after eating I drove to the APO to see if I could talk Dempsey into getting out on the tennis court. He was not at work. I figured he was probably on a date.

A film was playing at the theater so I went inside. It was a small movie house, but other than its size it was no different from theaters back home. The concession stand in the vestibule radiated with the inviting aroma of freshly popped corn. I purchased a box and went in to enjoy the film. Being in that theater reminded me that Headquarters' had its own Recreation Center out in the suburbs. I decided I would attempt the long drive out to the Recreation Center the next day.

Chapter 11

After the film, I stopped by Headquarters to see if any notices had been left in my mailbox. On my way out I ran into Larry Corbin in the parking lot.

"What's up Adam, have you been keeping yourself busy?"

"Pretty much, in fact right after we met I went for a walk and got lost. Finding my way back to the apartments kept me busy for several hours."

"Be careful, you do not want to wander into the wrong area. You might mess around and end up in Chop-Chop square."

"Chop-Chop square? I don't think I like the sound of that."

"That is where they behead criminals. We call it Chop-Chop square. They take a sword and swish, one stroke and off goes the head right at the neck. Man it is gruesome."

"You have seen a beheading?"

"Shortly after I got here somebody talked me into going down there one Friday – executions are done on Fridays. At first I said no, but then I figured what the heck, I will never see anything like it again so I went. To this day I regret that decision. I will never get that image out of my head. By the way, if by some chance you do find yourself down there, whatever happens, never tell anybody you are American or non-Muslim, because the crowd will push you right up to the front. They say we need to get a good look at the justice of Allah. Adam it is like a carnival when a head falls. I am telling you, you would not believe it. They scream and cheer like it is the greatest thing on earth. Blood is spurting everywhere, and they love it." (A Saudi friend explained to me later that from time to time westerners show up at the square expecting to see heart wrenching scenes of prisoners pleading for their lives, protesting their innocence or claiming that they had been falsely accused. 'Nobody is dragged to their execution kicking and screaming,' he assured me. When I asked why this never happens he said, 'condemned men are drugged before being brought out to the square.' If any appeals are made, they have to get them done before the execution date. The fact is, on the eve of the execution the prisoner is numbed, so from that point he loses the capacity to resist or protest. Essentially what the public sees is a body being manipulated by the executioner and his staff. The prisoner is brought out and forced into a kneeling position in front of the executioner. Thereafter the process is a simple matter of physics and timing. The executioner raises his sword. His assistant jabs the prisoner in the side with a pole. This forces the head to lurch forward as a natural reflex and exposes as much of the neck that the expert swordsman needs to carry out his work. In that same instant the sword falls. It is a quick three step process that to all intent and purposes is painless to the prisoner. Typically a decapitation is completed in a single stroke because these guys are the best at what they do. On rare occasions a thin sliver of flesh might keep the head dangling and barely attached to the carcass so the executioner has to take a second swipe at it to sever it completely.)

"Thanks for the graphic description and warning Larry, and trust me your advice is appreciated more than you know." Silently I thanked God that I ran into Larry that evening. As adventurous as I was, I was just the kind of guy to stumble into a place like Chop-Chop Square. I knew if I ever watched a man get separated from his head, it would probably mess me up in the head the rest of my life.

"I see you have your car now. How did your test go at the DMV? They never mentioned the manual, did they?"

After hearing my description of the events at the DMV, Larry commented "That was tough luck. I am sorry you had to go through all of that. But I am surprised Khalid abandoned you like that. He has always been decent when I have had to deal with him. Frankly it sounds like not much good has happened to you since you got here, but I am sure things will pick up. Like I told you the other day, you can have a lot of fun if you meet the right people."

"Not everything has been bad. I have had a couple of nice experiences too. Plus I am learning a lot." I told Larry about my close call with the Mutawahs and how guys at the teashop treated me to my first Schwarma. When I described the incident at the restaurant my first morning in the Kingdom, I asked about the reception he received when he first came to Arabia.

"Like you I did a lot of exploring when I first got here and the locals welcomed me with open arms as well, but I was never cheered or applauded. Carl Scott was right when he told you they like Black Americans. There aren't that many of us in this country, and they seem to be as curious about us as we are about them. By the way, that is not a Saudi restaurant on Airport Road," he corrected. "Those guys are from Yemen. A word of caution though, never hand your passport over to anyone. Most people would probably not snatch it, but what you did was risky. It might have gotten lost or fallen into the wrong hands and that is something you do not want to happen."

"I have in-Kingdom ID now, so I am set if a situation like that ever comes up again."

"That's good. So where are you headed now?"

"Home, but first thing tomorrow I am going to follow the map out to the Rec Center."

"Not much construction is happening that far out of town, so you should not have any problems getting there since you will not have to deal with a lot of detours. Still it might be wise to keep my number with you in case you get into a jam." Reaching into his pant pocket, he pulled out a handful of coins and said, "Here, hold on to these halalas. You can use them at the payphones if you need to stop along the road and call."

As I examined the Saudi coins Larry explained, "They are worthless just about everywhere. Nobody will take them if you try to spend them in any of the stores. About the only thing they are good for is when you have to use a payphone."

"What did you say they are called?"

"Halalas but we call them ha-ha lalas because they are pretty much a joke."

"Hopefully, I will not have to call anybody but thanks for the ha-ha lalas. I guess I will be seeing you around."

Larry walked away. I was unlocking the car door when he turned and said, "Adam hold up. It is still early. If you are not doing anything special, why not come over and hang out at my place for awhile?"

"I'd like that. Thanks for the invite."

I followed Larry to his compound. He lived ten minutes from me west of the airport. His wife's name was Camille. Fifteen seconds into my conversation with her I knew everything I would ever need to know about Camille. She hated living in Saudi Arabia. Ninety percent of her conversation was about her disdain for the culture. Most Western women I met over there felt the same way about the country. Had my friend Jim Lincoln gotten the job, I am certain Patty would have been miserable.

Larry had the largest video collection I had ever seen. Best of all, most of his movies I had never viewed. He let me borrow a stack of them. But there was one I wanted to see that someone was coming by later to get, so

Larry put it in the machine and said I should finish watching it before they came. I tried my best to watch the whole movie but I was too tired. At some point my body stretched itself out on the floor and fell asleep. The next morning I woke up with a blanket over me and a pillow beneath my head.

Larry's housekeeper was preparing breakfast, which is why I woke up when I did because I smelled bacon frying. After a meal of scrambled eggs with cheese, toast and bacon I hurried home to get ready for my trip to the Rec Center.

It was my first Friday in the Kingdom and thanks to Larry Corbin I knew to drive in the opposite direction from wherever most of the traffic was heading. Locals would be going to chop-chop square. Even if a beheading was not scheduled, Larry assured me something was always going on at the square on Fridays. Prisoners from local jails were brought to the square every week and beaten 40 strokes less one. It was the Saudi's idea of rehabilitation. The punishments were administered in a way that they believed incorporated both the justice and the mercy of Allah. Whipping was performed holding a copy of the Quran under the arm to prevent the one performing the task from taking a full swing at the prisoner - that was the mercy of Allah. Forty strokes less one, was the justice of Allah.

The site Wadi Al-Darriyah was annotated on the map not too far from the Rec Center. This Wadi was at the top of my list of places to visit because it was the ancestral home of the family of Saud. For centuries Wadi Al-Darriyah was at the center of a struggle for control in Eastern Arabia waged between the Saud and Rashid tribes. At times the Rashid's dominated the Nejd and at other times the Saudis maintained control. I figured once I learned the way to the Rec Center, finding Wadi Al-Darriyah should be easy.

Thankfully no detours of significance hindered me on the way out to the Center. I was able to follow the map with relative ease, although a couple of times I made the wrong turn and rode into Mexican standoffs on narrow streets. Each time the Saudis waited until I put my car in reverse and backed up. Navigating out of those situations was tricky, but I managed to get it done without scratching the sides of the car. I thought it would be quite ironic if my driving skills actually improved in Saudi Arabia.

Eventually suburban quaintness gave way to rural desert. Roads became dustier and were often blocked by flocks of goats, camels or other animals. Complying with instructions from the Ministry of Interior that I read in the *Newsletter*, I pulled over and waited for the flocks and shepherds to cross the road. All of the herds were shepherded by prepubescent boys. One time I voluntarily pulled over because I was amazed to see a small boy of 5 or 6 years of age leading a full grown camel down the road. The animal literally towered above the child, yet it responded obediently to the boy's tugs on its reigns.

After driving for about an hour, I came upon a sizeable community that, according to the map, was where the Recreation Center was located. Rather than drive into a maze of narrow unfamiliar streets, I decided to first circle the neighborhood because I figured a structure the size of the Center would be conspicuous enough to easily spot even from the outer streets. This turned out to be the best decision because the Rec Center sat on the outer edge of the community along its southern perimeter.

Headquarters' Rec Center was as fine a facility as Todd Dearbourne had described and significantly larger than the one at the APO Facility. Just inside the entrance I passed two professionally laid out tennis courts to get to the main building.

As soon as I entered the main building, two American women jumped up and greeted me with what felt like an exceedingly warm reception. They were so friendly it made me nervous. Sensing my discomfort they apologized and explained, "We rarely get visitors to the Center so please forgive our enthusiasm. This is only shock and joy."

They were ecstatic when I asked for a tour of the facility. "This is so wonderful, the few people that find their way out here usually stay a few minutes then high tail it back to Riyadh," bemoaned one of the ladies.

The movie theater was twice the size of the one at the APO and in addition to a theater, the Center had a lunchroom and, to my exquisite delight, a video game parlor. Playing video games was one of my favorite pastimes. There was also a large swimming pool in back of the building.

The American women were the managers of the facility and they had a full staff of cooks, waiters, projectionists, and a pool maintenance crew. Other than the Americans, every worker was from a developing country. The lunchroom staff was thrilled to have a customer. I was their first in more than a month. They made a big fuss over me. Though I was not very hungry I ordered a hamburger and fries. One bite into the burger and it was a big let down. It looked and tasted like the person who prepared it might have seen a picture of a hamburger once but never actually cooked one. The fries, on the other hand, were pretty good. After the meal I watched a movie and then spent a couple of hours in the video room playing Pac Man, Galaga, and my favorite game of all Spy Hunter.

I was impressed with the Center and sympathized with the staff for their disappointment over the lack of interest in the facility. When the ladies asked if I would be coming back, I assured them "you have tennis courts, a theater and videogames. You bet I will be coming back."

"If you like tennis Adam," one of the ladies reacted, "you might be interested in joining Headquarters' new team. There is a note about it on the Bulletin Board. Come, let me show you. Western companies in Riyadh are forming a tennis league and the Mission is trying to put a team together so we can compete."

I read the announcement with some interest, but decided to wait until I learned more about the league before considering signing up for the team.

On my way out the door the ladies handed me a form that asked for suggestions on activities to increase interest in the Center.

Attempting to drive back to town by going in the reverse direction of the way I came was a mistake. Barricades around construction work, on the return trip side of the road, forced me into detours that took me miles off course. After three hours not only was I lost, I was unknowingly heading west and into the heart of the Peninsula. Vast stretches of sand surrounded me as night fell, but as things turned out the darkness saved my hide. At a certain point I looked in the rearview mirror and caught sight of the glow of the lights of Riyadh fading in my wake. Not only was I heading away from the city but from what I remembered in the Atlas, I was driving into a part of the Peninsula where I would never want to be. Immediately I turned around and headed back to Riyadh. Had I not stayed to play videogames and left the Rec Center sooner than I did, there is a good chance I would have driven too far from Riyadh to have seen the city lights after the sun set. If that had happened, there is no telling how far I might have driven before running out of gas or until I realized I was going the wrong way and turned back.

Riyadh's lights were not my only guides home. Far to my left I saw aircraft descending into Riyadh International. That helped keep me oriented in the right direction because I knew getting to the airport meant finding my compound. For about an hour I drove on a road I thought I had never been on before until I passed Larry Corbin's compound. When I realized I knew where I was, I screamed for joy and ten minutes later was back at my apartment.

That evening I made myself a snack and sat down to finish the letters I started the previous day. To my mother I described the details of my visit to Paris, a city she had always wanted to see. I wrote Barry about the incident at the DMV and described my meetings with Minister Al-Naseem and the engineer Abdullah Al-Basheer. After sealing the envelopes I laid them on the coffee table. In the morning I would mail them from Headquarters when I stopped to check my mailbox.

After a shower and shave I went to bed. The next morning would be the official start of my two year contract at the Ministry.

Chapter 12

Saturday, November 17

No ill effects from the blood test at the DMV had occurred so far and I was happy to be alive after my first week in Arabia. Despite a few emotional roller coaster moments, the start of the tour had turned out better than I could have hoped. Nothing so far had happened to make me feel in any kind of jeopardy on account of the color of my skin. Even the incident at the DMV, while unsettling, reflected more a lack of confidence on the part of the Saudis in Western medical procedures. Changing needles for Europeans was a concession, not acceptance of Western methods. Clearly they were not ready to follow our procedures when handling their own people and since I was mistaken for a local, I simply fell into the wrong category that day at the DMV.

On my way to work I stopped by Headquarters, dropped off the letters and checked my box. The young Saudi that had greeted me previously approached again, said hello, and as he had done the first time, quickly turned and walked away. After posting my letters, I turned in the key to the Transient Apartments and headed for the Ministry.

Al Dennison had advised me ahead of time that Americans rarely wore suits to work in Riyadh. Casual attire was more practical, so for my first day on the job I dressed in jeans and a sports shirt. Howard Seymour pulled into the parking lot just ahead of me. We waved to one another. I was a little disappointed to see that he was not wearing his Saudi outfit. However, I noticed that in addition to carrying his attaché case he had a roll of toilet paper tucked under his left arm. Opening day at a new office building could be a little disorganized, so it made sense a few things might not be in place. But if there was no toilet paper in any of the restrooms, that could be a major problem.

Albert Dennison reviewed with me the tasks he had mentioned at the welcome dinner plus his instructions during my visit to the Ministry on Tuesday. Afterward he took me around to each of the Engineers' offices. Peter Braverman was in a better mood. His family had gotten back from vacation. Perry Ferguson seemed to be brooding over something. Al and I spoke to him, but got little more than a nod and half smile in return. Lee Williams again invited me on a hunt for desert diamonds. Once again I begged off. Walter Daniels was talking on the phone so we bypassed his office and stopped in to say hello to Abdullah Al-Basheer. Al then escorted me to the large room at the end of the hall.

"As you can see, your desk and chair are here as promised. We also scrounged up a typewriter for you, so the room is not as empty as it was last Tuesday. The Saudis told me they are going to start delivering our files this afternoon. All I have to say to that is Inshallah. Like I mentioned Tuesday, our cabinets got busted up pretty bad during the move. When the files and drawings get here you can stack them on the floor until you buy new cabinets. Just make sure they are organized in a way to be accessible to everyone. That should be enough to get you started. Welcome to your new office. By the way, we will be officially calling this the Admin Room."

After Al left the Admin Room, I remembered a question I had meant to ask Al. I knocked on his door, looked in and said "Al, I saw Howard Seymour carrying a roll of toilet paper when I got here this morning. Is that a personal idiosyncrasy or should I have brought a roll too?"

Al's right arm sprang up like a jack-in-the-box in the direction of a nearby table, on which sat - a roll of toilet paper. I had missed it when I was in his office earlier. "The Saudis do not use toilet paper and some of them resent the fact that we do. They believe their way is more sanitary. You will never find toilet paper in their homes, office buildings, or any of the Ministries. That is why Howard Seymour, and every American, brings toilet paper with them when we come to work. Yes, you should have brought a roll. But I take responsibility for not warning you ahead of time. I completely forgot about it. For today you can share my roll, but you only have permission to use it today. Tomorrow you will be on your own. But let me warn you, bringing toilet paper is only the start of the battle. Like I said earlier, some of the Saudis are offended by our custom of using toilet paper. So once you enter this building, keep in mind you are on the front lines of a clash of cultures. Hear me carefully. It has been our experience that if we leave a roll of toilet paper in the restroom when we go back to get it, it will be floating in the toilet bowl. That is why, whatever you do, if you walk into the bathroom with a roll of TP, make doggone sure you have it with you when you come out. If you forget and leave it in there, it would more than likely be a waste of your time to go back for it. Don't fret about it, just go and get another roll. Toilet bowls in bathrooms is another thing that they do not do. You will find toilet bowls here in the Ministry, but that was a concession they made on our behalf. I guess they figure adding toilet paper is going too far. So we bring our own."

"Okay, I think I can deal with bringing my own toilet paper, but you said the Saudis believe their way is more sanitary. What is their way?"

"Raise your left hand," he barked marine sergeant fashion. I complied hesitantly.

"That, my friend, is what they use to clean themselves after defecating."

My stomach did a flip.

"Another thing you should keep in mind, as I alluded to earlier, toilet bowls are a western concept and they definitely do not have them in their homes. If you are ever in a Saudi home and have to go to the bathroom, try not to expect too much when you go in there. A Saudi toilet is just a hole in the floor that you squat over and take a dump, or whatever else you may need to do. Next to the hole you will see a faucet with a hose attached to it. You grab the hose with your right hand, turn the spigot on with your left, bring the hose around behind you then use your left hand to splash water on your 'stuff' until it is all cleared away and washed down that hole in the floor. They say their way is more sanitary because they get everything. Toilet paper, according to them, leaves 'stuff' behind."

"This place is nothing like I expected," I muttered.

"There is a lot about our technology they like, but they draw lines in the sand where you would least expect. Bet you never thought you would be riding shotgun over a roll of toilet paper when you signed up to come here. So you and I will be TP buddies for the day." Pointing at the table he reemphasized, "Make sure you put it back on that table when you are finished and I don't want to hear 'oh Al, I am sorry, I forgot,'" he bellowed in his now familiar jovial way. "Tomorrow you will be on your own, so do not forget to bring a roll with you. I will bite your hand off if you try to touch my TP tomorrow," he teased threateningly.

"I am curious Al, how did you find out about this particular nuance of Saudi culture. I never heard anyone talk about it before. Did you learn about it here at the Ministry or somewhere else?"

"If I told you the answer to that question, I would have to kill you. Let's just say I have first hand knowledge, no pun intended, of how Arabs clean themselves after taking a dump."

I winced.

"What's the matter Adam, I thought you knew you stepped into deep dodo when you agreed to come to this country."

Thusly began my first day at the Ministry, with another stunning revelation about Saudi culture. Reusing needles for blood tests and cleaning feces away by hand. What made it so scary was the fact I was only starting my second week in the country. How many other quaint customs and habits did these people have?

Not wanting to hear another dung joke, I bowed out of Al's office. As I turned in the direction of the Admin Room I heard footsteps on the stairwell. Since our whole staff was already in the office, I assumed whoever was coming was Saudi and on their way up to the top floor. However, the young man that appeared at the third floor landing was neither Saudi nor American. He had a coffee with extra cream complexion and was carrying a camel hair shoulder bag. After a week in the Kingdom I was getting pretty good at guessing a person's country of origin. My instincts told me this young man was from Ethiopia. He smiled, walked up to me and asked, "Could you show me to the office of Mr. Albert Dennison please?" His English had an accent but it was distinctly different from the Saudis.

"Sure, Al Dennison's office is right here. What is your name?"

"Mohamed Al-Hamidi. Excuse me, are you a Black American?"

I chuckled and answered, "Yes, that is what some people call us these days. My name is Adam. Adam Sneed, Jr. It is nice to meet you Mohamed Al-Hamidi."

"I am the new telephone operator slash translator for the American Engineering office in this Ministry. Do you work here too?"

"Yes, I am on the American Engineering staff as well, but this is my first day on the job. I have only been in the country a week."

Mohamed shook my hand and said, "Then I must tell you welcome to Saudi Arabia. You will be my new friend Mr. Adam, okay?"

"That sounds nice Mohamed." I knocked on Al's door. "Our new translator is here Al."

"Oh that's right. I forgot he was starting today. Come on in." Al rose to greet the new employee.

When I got back to my desk it sunk in that Mohamed had introduced himself as a translator. I wanted to learn Arabic – Mohamed was a translator - there might be an opportunity here. I kept the door to the Admin Room open so I could catch Mohamed when he came out of Al's office.

Al and Mohamed came out together and as Al had done with me earlier, he took the new employee around to the different offices to meet the Engineers. They also stopped in to see Abdullah Al-Basheer. Lastly, Al brought the new translator to the Admin Room. "I assume the two of you have already met, but this is your official introduction. Mohamed, this is Mr. Adam Sneed, Jr. Adam is our Office Administrator. He will be your immediate supervisor. I am going to leave you here with Adam. We look forward to working with you. Adam, Mohamed's desk will be delivered either this afternoon or tomorrow morning or sometime this week, like the Saudis say Inshallah," Al laughed. "We are going to have them set Mohamed up in the corridor near the staircase so he can screen visitors for us as well. Until we get his desk in place, I was thinking he could hang out in here with you. The two of you can talk and you can bring him up to speed on what we do around here.”

“Sure Al, I will tell Mohamed everything I know about the office,” I replied with a cheesy grin.

Al snickered. “What Adam just said is pretty funny Mohamed because this is his first day on the job too. Twenty minutes ago I gave him pretty much the same speech I just gave you. That means Adam has about twenty minutes of seniority over you,” Al trumpeted.

Now I had to figure out where to put Mohamed until his desk was delivered. The Admin Room was large enough to accommodate 20 to 30 cubicles the size of those typically found in offices back home so my desk and chair were dwarfed in the emptiness.

Rising up, I said, “Mohamed, excuse me for a moment I have to go find a chair for you somewhere.”

“No, Mr. Adam, you stay here. I will find a chair.”

Mohamed came back with a chair in less than a minute and placed it next to my desk. I admired his resourcefulness but decided not to ask where or how he managed to find a chair that quickly in all the chaos of opening day. Mohamed sat down and stared at me as if expecting to hear something from his new supervisor. It was embarrassing being stared at that way and I did not know what to say to the young man.

Mohamed, however, was not reticent. Initiating a conversation he said, “I am very excited that we will be working together Mr. Adam. Can I ask you something please?”

“Sure.”

“Can I practice my English with you, and if you like I can teach you Arabic?”

“Mohamed you must be reading my mind,” I smiled. “That is exactly what I was planning to ask you.”

“Good, we will teach each other my friend. Do you have a car? What a stupid question, of course you do, all Americans have cars.”

“Yes I have a car, but I am not too sure how I feel about that yet.”

“You can take me home after work and we will make a schedule for study.”

I honestly did not mind Mohamed imposing on me for a ride home, but he would be my first passenger in Riyadh. Adjusting to the traffic was one thing, being responsible for another person's life under local driving conditions – I was not sure I was ready for that.

"Mr. Adam what does contemplate mean," Mohamed wanted to know? "Albert Dennison said he has been contemplating getting an Office Administrator for a long time."

"Contemplating is another way of saying he was thinking about something. In this case he was thinking about hiring someone like me."

"I see. Good. I will use the word contemplate soon; contemplate… contemplating…"

Something told me right then that Mohamed's translation skills might not be at the level our office required. But there was no need for me to articulate any suspicions about his abilities because deficiencies in that area would show soon enough. "Mohamed, are you aware this is the first day our office has opened for business in this building?"

"Yes, they moved here from the old Ministry. I had my interview two months ago. I was supposed to start last month but they told me to wait until this building opened before I came to work."

"Then you understand everything is still being set up. We have to get a desk and a phone for you. I have to order new cabinets for our files, which at this moment are stuck somewhere between the old office and this place. What I am saying is there is not much for either of us to do right now until they start delivering those files. Once they get here, you can help me put them in order. Therefore, until we get some work to do, if you want to read something while you are in the office, feel free to do so. If you have a book in your bag, you can start now."

Mohamed spent the bulk of the day reading a book that was written in Arabic. I had no idea what its topic or contents were about. Meantime, I took advantage of having a typewriter to begin a journal of my experiences, starting from when my flight left Dulles Airport.

Around noon a melodious voice resonated through the corridors of the Ministry singing the now familiar prayer call. Mohamed excused himself. When he opened the door of the Admin Room I spotted Abdullah Al-Basheer, the only other Muslim on our floor, locking his office door. I also spotted what looked like prayer beads in Abdullah's his right hand. Whether the beads were related to Islamic worship, I did not know. I had never seen Muslims carrying prayer beads before.

When Mohamed returned from prayer he invited me to go with him to a nearby suq where we purchased Shawarmas and coca-colas for lunch.

Later that afternoon Mohamed excused himself to go to the bathroom. "In Arabic it is called the hammam (ha-mom)," he explained. Mohamed did not pull a roll of toilet paper out of his bag so I assumed Ethiopians handled their business the same as Arabs. For a brief moment the thought crossed my mind to ask Mohamed what it was like using his hand to clean him self but I changed my mind. That was not the kind of question I ever wanted to ask another man, or anyone else for that matter.

The afternoon dragged along until the midday prayer call sounded. About an hour after that my first workday in Arabia came to an end.

When I pulled out of the Ministry parking lot into Riyadh traffic, I was transporting my first passenger. "Mr. Adam if you are ready to eat dinner I have been contemplating where we can eat." Mohamed said this then let out a high-pitched squeal of a laugh, delighted that he had found a way to use the new word he learned that day. It was the oddest laugh I ever heard and it set me off laughing too. Mohamed's distinctive laugh became his signature for the duration of our friendship.

Mohamed recommended an Ethiopian restaurant not far from the Ministry. He said he knew the owner and ate there often. I had never eaten Ethiopian food but I was eager to find out how it tasted. It was incredible. I really enjoyed using the spongy injera bread to pick up meat, vegetables, and salad the way Mohamed taught me since Ethiopians, like Arabs, eat with their hands.

After the meal Mohamed guided me to his home. He lived no more than ten minutes from the Ministry. Mohamed had two roommates, both much older than him. Neither roommate spoke English so this gave Mohamed the opportunity to showcase his translating skills for me. One of the roommates was Ethiopian but the other was a tall heavyset Egyptian who proudly shared the experience from his youth of having worked as an extra on the film *Spartacus* with Kirk Douglas. Through Mohamed, both roommates plied me with questions about America and seemed to be as curious about my country as I was about Saudi Arabia. I did not stay as long as they wanted me to, and it was a bit of a struggle getting them to let me go home.

A couple of blocks from Mohamed's house I passed a large building where dozens of women were walking in and out of the main gate. It had massive walls with parapets at the top on which soldiers were pacing like sentries. My initial impression was that it had to be a prison, but the presence of so many veiled women made me reject that idea. Curious to know its purpose, I added this building to the growing list of things I would inquire about later.

It was not until I was back in my apartment before it dawned on me that Mohamed and I had never gotten around to planning our language study schedule.

Sunday, November 18

The next morning Mohamed's desk was in place at the top of the landing, complete with a phone console and lines connected to each of our offices so he could transfer calls. Al was shocked the Saudis had delivered it so soon and that all of the lines were working.

Our Engineers had not wasted any time in getting Mohamed work. Handwritten memos were already stacked on his desk to be translated into Arabic. While it was true that most Saudis spoke at least some English, government policy required Ministry documents and all official business and correspondence to be transacted in Arabic. The plan was to establish a procedure whereby Mohamed would translate the work of our staff and deliver the Arabic versions to Mr. Al-Basheer. Mohamed reported for work about a minute after I got to the office. We went over procedures together, including those he would be using for answering the phone, directing visitors to the appropriate member of our staff, and doing translation.

Contrary to our expectations, the files had not been delivered as promised. With so little to do I spent the day writing in my journal. Periodically Mohamed came into the Admin Room. We would spend a few minutes jawing about random matters or he would ask the meaning of various English words. On one of his visits I asked, "Mohamed where are you from?"

"Egypt," he answered quickly. "Why do you ask, Mr. Adam?"

"Actually I thought you were Ethiopian."

"That is because I took you to an Ethiopian restaurant yesterday and I have an Ethiopian roommate. Everybody thinks I am Ethiopian because I have a lot of Ethiopian friends."

"To be honest I thought you were Ethiopian the first time I saw you, but now that you mention it I can see Egyptian features in your face. Not that I am an expert on facial features, but I have noted distinctive characteristics with different groups here." Despite the words coming out of my mouth, in my mind I was certain Mohamed was Ethiopian. Maybe he had to hide his nationality for some reason. After all it was the Middle East. There were rules for survival in that part of the world that I did not know. I just hoped I would never need to learn them.

Later that day Abdullah Al-Basheer brought his translator around and introduced him to the American staff. His name was Aarif al-Alim. "Just call me Alim," he invited. When Americans spoke his name it came out Aleem but Arabs pronounced it Ah'leem, like saying ah followed by a slight catch in the throat then the word leem. Alim had extraordinary skills. He was multilingual and could type faster than any man or woman I ever saw. What impressed me most was that he was equally fast and accurate typing in either English or his native Arabic. But Alim was Palestinian and for that reason the American staff was always careful about what we said in his presence.

The addition of Alim to Al-Basheer's staff completed our internal communications chain. Of course our translator was the weak link in the chain because Mohamed could not type. This shifted the brunt of the work to Alim. Mohamed would write out his translations by hand, handed the pages over to Alim who typed them in Arabic for distribution to Abdullah Al-Basheer. The Saudi Engineering staff gave their handwritten documents to Alim to translate into English and type up for delivery to Mohamed who in turn would distribute them to our Engineers. Although the system worked, Alim always did the bulk of the translating and often had to correct Mohamed's mistakes.

Later that afternoon, Mohamed overheard Al and me chatting about my household effects shipment. At his next opportunity Mohamed came in and asked for an explanation of the expression household effects. Once he understood, he inquired how long had I been waiting for my shipment.

"I have been in the country a little over a week," I answered. "It takes a month or two for shipments to get here."

"You can get your shipment today, if you like. My friend works in the warehouse at the airport where they keep them."

Excited about the prospect of getting my shipment earlier than scheduled, I went to Al's office and told him what Mohamed had said. Al was flabbergasted. "Are you sure Mohamed can get your shipment today?"

"It makes sense to me. They were shipped out a month before I left the United States, so I don't see why they could not have arrived by now. Mohamed says he can get them."

"Good. Go and get your stuff."

The warehouse where the shipments were stored was as long as a football field. Boxes were stacked to the ceiling in dozens of pyramids. Several customers were ahead of us and barefoot clerks were climbing the pyramids searching for their orders. Mohamed called his friend over and explained why we were there. The guy took off his sandals, hiked up his Thobe, tied it in a knot at the waist then scaled a nearby pyramid. Mohamed slipped out of his sandals, hopped over the counter and followed up the pyramid after his friend.

Whatever way the boxes were marked, the clerks apparently had no problem identifying and connecting them with their rightful owners. Still I was glad Mohamed was there to help in the search. Within a relatively short period of time they located my boxes. However, no sooner had Mohamed brought me the good news the mid-afternoon prayer call sounded. He and the clerk scampered away with other members of the faithful, leaving half a dozen of us Westerners waiting at the counter.

It was a relief to finally lay eyes on my boxes. There were things in those boxes I had not seen and clothes I had not worn in nearly two months. The next trick was to get everything through Customs. Fortunately, this time I did not get an angry inspector. The process took longer though because there was much more to check. When the inspector picked up the Bible packed in with my shipment, he merely laid it back down. On the other hand, he took one look at my Donna Summers album and railed, "Hatha mamnua (this is forbidden)… Hatha mamnua… Donna Summer – she sing about sex." I got a kick out of his reaction and fought off the urge to laugh in his face.

Donna Summers' album was the only casualty of the inspection. As Mohamed and I loaded the shipment into my car, I said, "I think someone in Riyadh will be dancing to that album before the night is over." Mohamed erupted with that crazy laugh of his and said, "I agree."

Mohamed and I spent the rest of the evening unpacking and organizing my things. It was late when we finished so I invited Mohamed to stay overnight in the guestroom. The next morning I loaned him a clean shirt to wear to the office.

Monday, November 19

It was midway through my first workweek. So far I had not suffered any ill effects from the dirty needle used on me at the DMV. If I could stay healthy another week I would be able to stop worrying about that incident and focus on what lay ahead.

As a reward for getting my shipment early and helping me unpack, I invited Mohamed to ride out with me to the Recreation Center after work. The lunchroom staff was elated to have two customers. We both ordered French fries and afterward went in to watch a movie. During the film Mohamed got up and left the theater once and returned after thirty minutes. Later he explained he had gone out for prayer.

It was nearly 11 p.m. when I got Mohamed back to his house. He asked me to wait a moment and ran inside. When he came back he had a bag in his hand. "My roommates are not home. Mr. Adam, is it okay for me to spend the night at your place again?" I felt uneasy about it, but said okay. He threw his bag on the back seat and we headed to my apartment.

As I drove home, I got a feeling in my gut that Mohamed was about to become a regular houseguest.

☙☙☙☙☙☙☙❧❧❧❧❧❧❧

Chapter 14

During all the hubbub of the Mecca crisis, I completely forgot I was supposed to be watching for side effects from the dirty needle at the DMV. The doctor had told me to wait two weeks for side effects to show, but I got so wrapped up in the Mecca crisis that the second week passed without the dirty needle crossing my mind. By the time I thought about it or the DMV again, more than a month had passed and physically I was as healthy as ever.

Something else had happened during those weeks that contributed to me being preoccupied. Whether Mohamed planned it or not, for all intents and purposes he had become a live-in houseboy. Every American I had met to that point employed a housekeeper. This, however, was not something I ever planned or thought about doing. Just knowing Mohamed was getting up in the morning and doing housework made me uncomfortable. It was too much like having a Man-Friday. Playing the role of Robinson Crusoe was not my idea of the Arabian adventure I hoped to have.

I tried to explain how I felt to Mohamed, but it was difficult. In his own way he made it clear that what he did around the apartment was his way of expressing thanks for my kindness. "You drive me home; take me to see movies; and let me sleep at your house. I cannot pay you for these things, so I clean. Really, I do not mind."

Out of frustration I sought help from Dempsey. He suggested I could keep the friendship on equal terms by including Mohamed in some of my other activities. That is when we made the decision to teach Mohamed how to play tennis, an idea that turned into a real comedy. Mohamed was not athletic by any stretch of the imagination. The man did not even play soccer, which surprised us since soccer (or football as they call it) is universally loved by males in Africa and the Middle East. Still I did my level best to teach him the fundamentals of tennis. Usually Dempsey and I, and even Mohamed himself, wound up laughing at his clumsy attempts to play the game and that crazy laugh of his had Dempsey laughing even harder than I did.

In addition to cleaning and cooking, Mohamed also did other nice things for me. For instance, he took me to the palace that I had tried to visit the day I got caught in one-way traffic. This beautiful white sandstone

119

Bedouin palace was now a museum filled with artifacts from the nomadic period including ornate camel saddles. Everything in the museum we were free to photograph with the exception of what I thought was the neatest things about the palace - its beautiful inner courtyard. This hidden enclave could only be seen if you were inside the palace and the former residents had used it as a private garden for their harems. Here females could frolic freely out of sight of voyeuristic males.

Another thing about Mohamed that I came to admire and respect was his loyalty to Islamic devotions. Spending time with this faithful Muslim gave me a fuller picture of the daily prayer rituals. When Mohamed was with me, he always stopped to answer the summons to prayer no matter where we happened to be traveling. Many times he walked out of the theater in the middle of a film at the Rec Center to observe Magrib. How he knew it was time to pray during a film was a mystery to me, because it was impossible to hear the prayer call over the soundtrack of the movie.

Mohamed also taught me the names of all five prayer calls. Fajr (fa-jur) rang at dawn (Fajr was the prayer that shook me up that first morning in Riyadh when I stepped out of the shower in the Transient Apartments); at noon came Dhuhr (doo-ur) (this call drew all the Muslims at the Ministry to a special room on the first floor that was set aside for prayer); mid afternoon brought Asr (ah-sir) (the prayer during which I was nearly beaten by the Mutawahs my first day in the Kingdom); Al-Magrib (ma – grib), the sunset prayer often caught Mohamed in the middle of a film at the Rec Center; and Isha (ee shah) the final prayer of the day sounded when the red rays of the sunset faded and the sky turned dark.

The person proclaiming the call to prayer is called the muezzin. He begins the call (or adhan) with the statement - God is great, the familiar 'Allahu akbar'. After repeating this statement the muezzin next recites the Shahadah, or declaration of faith, namely, "I testify that there is no God but Allah, and I testify that Muhammad is his messenger (Ash hadu anlaa ilaaha illallaahu wa ash hadu anna muhammadar-rasulallah)."

Shahadah is the first of the five pillars of faith in Islam. Prayer (or Salah) is the second. Zakat, the third pillar, is the giving of alms or gifts to the poor (the women at the bazaar calling out Zekki, Zekki, Zekki, to passersby were requesting alms, and from what I came to understand the Saudis were generous when giving alms to the poor). Fasting is the fourth pillar. Typically it refers to the holy month of Ramadan during which Muslims refrain from eating, drinking, smoking or engaging in sex from dawn to dusk. These restrictions stay in place for the entire month. The fifth pillar is the Hajj or pilgrimage to Mecca when the faithful circle the Kabba seven times (this trip, or Hajj, every Muslim endeavors to make at least once in their lives. When a Muslim fulfills this fifth pillar he adds the title Hajji to his name. I would find out later in my tour that pilgrims have to pay a levy called the Hajj Tax when they make the pilgrimage). At my apartment Mohamed had a spot reserved in the guest room where he would lay down his prayer rug and kneel toward Mecca to perform devotions.

One of the details of the prayer rituals that I found fascinating was the greeting at the end of the prayer that every Muslim – no matter where he or she happens to be at any moment, and regardless of whether they pray alone or in a crowd – extends to the fellow believers to the right and left of them. Many times this greeting is extended symbolically because the nearest fellow believer happens to be miles or continents away. The fact that this happens on our planet five times a day, all around the world, attests to the force of Islamic unity.

Of course, I did not memorize all of these facets of the faith in a few days, or weeks. It took months, a lot of patience, and repeated reminders from Mohamed before I was able to retain them.

As far as the plan to teach me Arabic, we both forgot about that idea, but I am sure for different reasons. I can only speculate why Mohamed never brought it up again, but I stopped expecting Mohamed to teach me Arabic for a couple of reasons. For one thing there was his constant coming to me during the day to ask the meaning of English words that Engineers had written in correspondence they placed on his desk for translation. But the final glimmer of hope to learn Arabic from Mohamed faded the day he and I had the strangest disagreement about the meaning of an English word. I was visiting him at his home at the time. It was the start of the rainy season so I was wearing a jacket. Though Riyadh rarely gets precipitation, temperatures often fall into the teens or lower after sundown during rainy season. When Mohamed answered the door, he invited me in and offered "let me hang your jacket in the close it."

"What did you say," I asked?

"I said let me hang your jacket in the close it."

"Oh, you mean you want to hang it in the closet."

"No, I mean close it."

That started a debate that lasted half an hour. Everything I tried to say or do to explain the difference between close it and closet failed to get through to him. At first I thought it was a matter of mispronunciation like when a Japanese person uses the letter r when trying to say an English word that begins with the letter l, or when people from India pronounce jeopardy 'g-o-par-dee'. Mohamed also thought our debate was about pronunciation and said "you pronounce it closet because you are American, but to say close it is also acceptable." The real problem though was not about accents. I tried to demonstrate what I meant by walking over to the closet and closing the door. Then I asked, "what did I just do?" Mohamed said, "You shut the door."

"Yes I did and you watched me close it, right."

"No I watched you shut the door to the close it."

I stepped inside the closet and said, "This place where you hung my jacket is called the closet. When I step out, I want you to watch carefully, I close the door to the closet. Did you see me close it?"

"I saw you get into the close it, step out of the close it and then shut the door to the close it," he responded.

"Mohamed, have you ever used the word close when getting out of a car, as in close the door?"

"No, when I get out of a car I shut the door."

Evidently Mohamed had never learned the English word close. As a translator, particularly for a staff of Engineers, Mohamed would need to know the difference between words like close it and closet when he saw them. Though it was not possible for any American to review Mohamed's work for accuracy, Aleem Al-Arif would assuredly know if it was deficient. I had had doubts about the level of Mohamed's translation skills from his first day on the job, but our dispute that night made me even less certain about the quality of his work at the Ministry. As far as him teaching me Arabic, I lost confidence that it would ever happen.

Having had enough of linguistic debate for one night, I called it quits. Mohamed interpreted this to mean he had triumphed. Even so, I went home that night with no disappointments or expectations that Mohamed would ever get around to teaching me Arabic.

One weekend I gathered all of my new local friends, Mohamed as well as Ibrahim and Owache, the two guys from the Kenyan tea house, and treated them to a meal and movie at the Rec Center. As usual we were the only ones there. However, the very next time Mohamed and I showed up to see a movie, the door to the theater was locked. There was a note tacked on the door that read "The Recreation Center and Theater is restricted to use by American Personnel Only."

A couple of days later Mohamed suggested, "Do you remember when I told you about my brother Andome and that he works for an Italian company outside of Riyadh? They show films there too. We can visit him this weekend if you like."

I took Mohamed up on his offer and that weekend followed his directions to the outskirts of town. As soon as I turned on the highway that Mohamed indicated led to his brother's workplace, I recognized where I was and erupted in uproarious laughter. Mohamed wanted to know what I thought was so funny. So I told him the story of the night I ended up on that road when I was attempting to find my way home from the Rec Center for the first time. When I finished the story he let out that squeal of his and we both had a good laugh. Ironically, the company Andome worked for was no more than twenty minutes farther down the road from the point where I turned back to town that night. It would have been wild had I kept going, stopped at that company to ask for directions and been helped by the brother of a man I would meet and begin supervising the very next day. Mohamed really would have been in for a surprise had he introduced me to his brother and discovered we had already met.

Like Mohamed, Andome spoke several languages, including English. But the moment I saw Andome, I knew beyond all doubt he was Ethiopian. Unless Mohamed had lied to me about his ethnicity, he could only be Egyptian if he and Andome had the same mother but different fathers. That would make them half brothers, but siblings nonetheless. Though I came to this conclusion, I kept the suspicion to myself.

The film was already underway when we reached the compound. A sheet stretched between two poles served as the screen. It was an Italian film very poor in quality and not comparable by a long shot to the movies shown at our Rec Center. English and Arabic subtitles appeared in contrasting colors that overlapped and flashed on the screen too briefly for me to make heads or tails of the plot. In addition, the wrong colors had been chosen for the subtitles so that words often blended right into scenery.

Apparently the men at the compound were no more invested in the film than we were. A few workmen sat on benches while most relaxed on blankets laid out on the sand. Most ignored the movie altogether and engaged in lively conversations or played cards. It was an atmosphere exactly like that in the teashops downtown.

At one point Mohamed went to get refreshments for the three of us, and while he was away I had a revealing conversation with Andome. He confirmed that he and Mohamed were brothers but told me they both had been born and raised in Ethiopia. I never mentioned this conversation to Mohamed. Still, I was not surprised that he never invited me to visit his brother's compound again.

1979 was ending. Almost eight weeks had passed since my farewell dinner with Barry and Lovelen, an evening that was still fresh in my mind and

123

seemed like only yesterday. Now, after two months in Arabia fears about racism in the country and possible threats to my status as a freeborn Black American had proven unwarranted. Though I had yet to meet a Black Saudi, I was confident I did not need to worry about racism in this beautiful land of the Bedouins. Nevertheless, finding the Black Saudi community remained an important goal of mine that I wanted to achieve. It was important to me that I find out how much their lives had changed and what progress they had made during the past seventeen years. And even though I had grown confident with respect to race relations in the Kingdom, the fact that Black Saudis were still invisible to me after two months in Riyadh had me a little concerned.

Other than a few personal disappointments and the tragedy at Mecca, I had enjoyed my first months in the desert kingdom. But what would a full year in Arabia bring? I looked to the future with eager anticipation. Sadly, there was a good chance it would be a future without Mohamed Al-Hamidi. At the Ministry his translation skills were coming under increased criticism. The U.S. staff complained openly and within earshot of Mohamed. I feared his days at the Ministry were numbered.

⊱⊱⊱⊱⊱⊱⊱⊰⊰⊰⊰⊰⊰⊰

Chapter 15

1980 could not have begun better. Larry Corbin invited a few of us over to his place to listen to the Armed Forces Radio broadcast of the Super Bowl. My Steelers were competing for the NFL title against the Rams. I got permission to bring Dempsey along and he and Larry hit it off the moment we walked into the villa. Several African drivers from the Motor Pool were there as well, including Khalid. I said hello to him but nothing more. That was also the night I finally met my first Black Saudi. He was a friend of Larry's by the name of Ahdel.

Within minutes I knew Ahdel was not your average Saudi, Black or White. Ahdel was a professional football player and had fans all over the country, even in remote areas of the desert. The Saudi Arabian football league, their version of the NFL, has teams in cities all across the peninsula. Every year at the end of the regular season, the two teams with the best records compete for the National Cup. Ahdel played for the team from Jeddah called Club (or Naddy—nah-dee) Nasser (noss-sir). Naddy Nasser, one of the better clubs in the league, had a bitter rivalry going with Naddy Hilal (hee-lall) the team from Riyadh.

Now that I had the attention of a Black Saudi, I asked "Ahdel, where are all the Black people in Arabia?"

"Everywhere, why do you ask?"

124

"Ahdel, you are the first Black Saudi I have met and it took two months for me to meet you. So where is everybody?"

"I do not know why you have not met Blacks here in Riyadh but there are many more Blacks in Jeddah and Mecca and other cities in the western part of Arabia. If you come to Jeddah you will see many Black people. Are you Muslim?"

"No."

"Then you cannot go to Mecca. But you can come to Jeddah. That is where I live. You must come to visit me sometime."

"I would like that," I said agreeably.

"Why you have not seen Black people in Riyadh, that I don't know but they are here. I have many Black friends here. Perhaps the next time I come to town I can introduce you to some of them. Nassar will be playing Hilal here in Riyadh next season, so when my club comes to Riyadh I will tell Larry ahead of time so he can bring you to the game and you will see me play. There will be many Blacks in the stadium because we have a lot of supporters here in Riyadh too."

"That would be wonderful. Thanks for the invitation."

I had a good time that evening and it ended perfectly. The Steelers won the championship. Now that they had their fourth Super Bowl ring, the team had gone from being the doormat of the NFL to the team with the most Vince Lombardi trophies.

The following week I got a new neighbor. I ran into him while he was moving into apartment B-1 on the floor below mine. We only spoke for a few minutes but in that short time I knew everything I would ever need to know about Mark Parsons. He was a tennis player.

When I mentioned the courts at the Rec Center, Mark asked if he could follow me out to the Center on the weekend so he could learn how to get there. On Thursday we got on the courts. After a couple of volleys I knew Mark was an outstanding player. He was better than anyone in the Kingdom I had played so far, including Howard Seymour and Dempsey Stevens.

Later when Mark read the flyer on the bulletin board recruiting players for the Headquarters' team, he grabbed an application and badgered me until I filled one out as well. It turned out we were the last two players Headquarters needed to complete a roster to qualify to field a team in the new league.

I was not as excited about competing in the league as was Mark, but he sure brought a lot of energy to team practices. Our schedule of matches appeared in the *Newsletter* a week before the first contest and generated a surge of interest that caught everyone by surprise, especially the managers of the Rec Center. Those two ladies were more astonished then anyone to see all the fans that showed up for our first home match. The lunch room staff truly earned their paychecks that day and the Rec Center got the jump start it needed. From that day onward, the Center served the purpose for which it had been built. Personally, I knew the Center's fortunes had changed when teenagers started spending time there on a regular basis because they took over the videogame room. After that I rarely got the chance to play Spy Hunter again.

With Mark's help my game improved and I became more competitive on the courts. We practiced together regularly, but when Mark was busy I went to the APO and worked out with Dempsey. On days when neither was available I drove out to the Center and practiced against the ball machine. On one occasion when I was using the machine, I mishit a volley and the ball caromed off my racket and sailed over the wall. Outside the Center I looked up and down the street but did not see the ball anywhere. While I was panning the street a car pulled up to the Center. An older American couple got out. At that same moment, I noticed that the gate to a Saudi home on the other side of the street was standing slightly ajar. The opening was just wide enough for something the size of a tennis ball to roll through. As soon as I saw the opened gate, I assumed that was where I would find my ball. I headed for the gate. By the time I got across the street the American couple realized where I was going and behind me I heard a loud gasp. I turned and saw the woman staring in shock. She exclaimed, "Oh, no, I would never enter a Saudi home!"

An unveiled western woman entering a Saudi home would surely cause a stir, so to that extent I understood her reaction. But I was not female, and going onto a property to retrieve a tennis ball was not the same as trespassing.

I looked through the gate and sure enough my tennis ball had rolled into the outer courtyard. It was only about ten feet away. Focusing on the ball, I darted in to grab it without noticing that a young Saudi was standing at the entrance of the house on the other side of the courtyard. I caught sight of him out of the corner of my eye just as I bent down to pick up the ball. Startled, I jumped up and in the process left the ball where it lay. The Saudi smiled warmly then gestured with his head that it was okay for me to collect the ball. I picked it up, waved and said thanks. The Saudi waved back and grinned. I was glad he was friendly and took note he did not have a gold tooth in his mouth. I was about to walk out of the courtyard when he motioned in Saudi fashion for me to wait. Walking up to me, he extended his hand and we shook western style. Then in English he said, "you are welcome my friend." Spontaneously we both laughed then said goodbye.

I wanted to share what had happened in the courtyard with the older couple but by that time they had gone inside the Center. Later when I put the ball machine away, I inquired about them and was told they were in the theater watching the film. Since I had other plans that day I did not wait for them, and I never saw that couple again. Considering the many wonderful experiences I had interacting with the Saudis during my stay in the Kingdom, I hope that couple had a change of heart and got the chance to sit down in the home of a Saudi family before they left the country.

Around this time Headquarters announced it was resuming its program of Arabic classes. Until that announcement, I never knew classes had ever been held at Headquarters. Since my hopes of being trained in Arabic by Mohamed had fizzled, I was happy to hear about these classes. Not only did I sign up for them, I talked Mark Parsons into joining as well. We became two of nine students, though most days' attendance fell far short of one hundred percent.

Attending class was challenging for us because it was scheduled to start thirty minutes after our team tennis practice sessions ended. To get there on time, Mark and I had to drive like crazy from the Rec Center to reach Headquarters. Despite the distance, Mark and I never missed a session. We were very loyal to Arabic class. But our perfect attendance had nothing to do with learning the language. Mark and I never missed that class because of an older couple from Texas.

Arabic has been described as a harsh guttural language. Hearing it butchered by Texans with thick accents was as good as going to a comedy club. People often complained there was nothing to do in the desert, but for as long as that class lasted Mark and I enjoyed some primo entertainment. Most days the class was a laugh fest. The wife, to her credit, valiantly tried to repeat the expressions intoned by the teacher. But her husband, that guy was a riot. When it was his turn to recite, he would rub a hand across his mouth and garble something incomprehensible. It was like being in high school listening to the class dunce trying to slide past a question that everyone, including the teacher, knew he could not answer. Our instructor was from Egypt. Usually he walked out of the room when the Texan started his antics. We knew the instructor was somewhere discretely laughing his head off, but my classmates and I were not at all sensitive to the Texans' feelings. We howled openly, right in front of him and nobody laughed louder and harder than my teammate Mark. That class was a lot of fun, but we learned very little Arabic. I did, however, pick up a little skill at writing in Arabic, counting numbers and also some of the linguistic rules of the language. Take the Arabic word for the number two, which is Ethneen. Any time you refer to two pieces of any item you simply add the suffix een from the word ethneen (two). For example, the Arabic words book, hour, car, and house are kutuub, saat, sayara and beyt. In referring to two of these items you would say kutuubeen, saateen, sayarateen and beyteen. Words are pronounced differently as well depending on whether you are speaking to a male or a female. If you heard someone say kuttubak (your book), you would know they would be talking to a male about his book. Or if the person said kuttubik (your book), it would be a conversation to a female about her book. Sayaratak (your car) would refer to a man's car and beytak (your house) a man's house. When a man is talking about his own book, car or house he says kutuub, sayara and beyt. However, a female would pronounce these words kutuubee, sayaratee and beytee. Perhaps sayara (car) is a bad example since females are not permitted to drive.

After a few months, Headquarters suspended the classes again. This, of course, was another setback to my plans to learn the language; however I was managing to accumulate Arabic words and expressions by other means. For instance, during conversations at the Ministry with Abdullah Al-Basheer he continued to drop new words and phrases on me to memorize. Then there was the young Saudi at Headquarters who was in the habit of greeting me most mornings when I stopped by to check for mail. At the start we exchanged simple greetings in English. Then one morning he began a modest effort to teach me his language. That day, after saying "Good morning" to me in English, he explained "bil Arabi (in Arabic), Sabah al-khair. Now, you say, Sabah al-khair." Already familiar with this expression, I repeated it effortlessly. Satisfied, the young man smiled and walked away.

The very next time I saw him, I spoke first. "Sabah al-khair." "Sabah al-khair," he responded happily, then said "Isme Fahad. My name Fahad. A-eesh Ismak? What you name?"

"My name is Adam."

"Ahlan wa sahlan Sayeed Adam. Ahlan fi al-Arabia-di-Saudia. Welcome to Saudi Arabia."

"Thank you Fahad."

"Shukran, thank you. Offwan, you are welcome."

"Shukran Fahad."

Regular exchanges like that with Fahad, along with expressions I was learning from Abdullah Al-Basheer kept my cache of Arabic words steadily growing. Listening to conversations between Saudis was also a big help. As my comprehension of Arabic improved I reached the point where I could understand far more of the language than I could actually speak or write. I was like a child listening to adults talking, then mimicking what I heard based on the context or situation in which those words were spoken. What I lacked was formal rules of grammar and a broader base of Arabic words and expressions.

Like most people living in a foreign country, some of the earliest words I learned from off the street were Arabic curse words. There is no need to repeat any of them here, but I was also becoming familiar with some rather interesting popular slang and expressions. One of my favorites was 'a-eesh feek' which simply meant 'what's up' an expression used exactly the way we use it in America. 'Esh-loon-ak' literally means 'what color are you' but it is not a question about your skin color or ethnicity. It is an inquiry into your state of mind or mood as in 'are you blue' or 'do you feel sunny and bright today.' 'La-ya-sheikh' (lie-yah-shay-ik) in English translates 'no my sheikh'. For Arabs it is their version of the popular English slang 'no way Jose'.

Occasionally, I figured out the meanings of a word on my own through the power of deductive reasoning. For example, the meaning of the word Abidan became evident long before a Saudi formally confirmed it to me. I did it by combining something I had learned in college with an expression that I picked up elsewhere. In college I learned that the name Sudan was Arabic for 'land of the Blacks'- Sud (soil or land) and dan (Black). The first Arabic name I learned the meaning of in Riyadh was Abdullah, which means slave of God - Ab (slave) du (of) Allah (God). Therefore, Abidan had to mean Ab (slave) dan (Black) or Black Slave. This was confirmed later during an unforgettable conversation I would have with Abdullah Al-Basheer.

My knowledge of the language, though rudimentary, really came in handy one day on my way home from tennis practice when I stopped to get gas. Filling my tank had become one of my favorite things to do in the Kingdom simply because gas prices were ridiculously low. Local tradition required foreigners to pay first and then pump their gas, so that day when I pulled up to the pump I waited for the attendant to come out. When he came over to the car, I told him how much gas I wanted and paid him that amount in riyals. It was at that point that I got out of the car and started pumping fuel into the tank. While filling the tank another customer pulled into the station. An unveiled woman was sitting up front on the passenger side. This told me two things. One, they were married and two, they were not Saudis. From their features I guessed they had to be Lebanese or possibly Egyptian. Unlike me, the husband began filling his tank right away. The rules were different for Arabs. Even in America I have seen instances where foreigners had to pay first before being provided a service, so I was not offended by the local rules.

After filling my tank I got in the car, started the engine and was about to drive off when the attendant rushed over demanding, "hut al faloose (give me the money)."

"I already paid you," I said.

In English he screamed, "No, you lie, you pay me now."

For this man to call me a liar, in English, made his vulgar attempt at extortion extra offensive and insulting. Back and forth we argued for several minutes, yelling at the top of our voices. I knew the guy was only trying to hustle me out of a few extra Riyals that only amounted to pennies in American currency, but my sense of fairness would not allow me to submit to his scheme. Finally the attendant threatened to call the police.

"Go ahead," I goaded him. "Call them. I want you to."

"They no believe you, you infidel," he boasted.

He was right. There was little chance I would be believed over a member of the so-called faithful. Nevertheless, I staunchly refused to let myself be swindled by a hypocrite hiding behind religion.

Meanwhile the other customer had been observing our confrontation. When he finished pumping gas, the man came over and asked what the disagreement was about. The attendant switched from English to Arabic explaining 'Kuwajah tibigah ruuh maa faloose fil benzene (This foreigner wants to go without paying for his gas)."

Because I understood most of what he said, I spoke up to refute his accusation. "I paid for the gas when I first drove in. No gas station in this city allows a Kuwajah to pump gas without paying first? Hatha rijal kathabt, (this man is a liar)" I announced in Arabic, much to the surprise of the attendant. Now it was his turn to be incensed at being called a liar in his own language by a foreigner. The guy literally lunged at the car as if he wanted to pull me through the window. That suited me fine. I said, "Oh, you want to fight. Good." I opened the door to get out but the other customer blocked the door closed with his hip. Motioning for me to wait, he turned to the attendant and asked, "Inta Muslim (are you Muslim)?"

"Aiwa, (yes, I am)."

Turning to me he asked, "Excuse me sir, but are you a Muslim?"

In Arabic I answered, "La, anna Mu-see-he (No, I am Christian)."

Back to the attendant he said, "You see he is not Muslim, so... forgive him." Then he waved me on to leave the station.

I drove away from that station a little wiser and more alert to the reality that hypocrisy crosses all cultural and religious lines. There are plenty of people who profess to be Christian that do not live up to the teachings of Jesus of Nazareth and would just as quickly take advantage of a foreigner in a similar situation. Now I could say I had personally met at least one professed

Muslim that did not respect the teachings of the Prophet Muhammad. Fortunately a decent Muslim came into my life at the same moment, and the better man prevailed. Later I learned the Samaritan Muslim may have derived his counsel to the gas station attendant from Surah 60:7, a verse in the Quran that states: "It may be that Allah will bring about friendship between you and those of them whom you hold as enemies. And Allah is Powerful; and Allah is Forgiving, Merciful."

Two days later the inevitable happened. I had my first car accident. I was driving through town when a big Mercedes Benz truck came out of a side street and right across two lanes of busy downtown traffic. The street he came out of was no wider than an alley so I did not see him until the last moment. One second the road ahead was clear and the next I found myself slamming on brakes. The car skidded and bounced off the large rear wheel but the trucker continued on his way as if he had no idea anything had happened. Damaged hood notwithstanding, I chased the truck down. The driver stopped and got out of the vehicle, but only after I pulled in front of the truck and blocked his path. I tried to explain that he was responsible for the damage to my car, but he either did not speak English or pretended he did not. Unfortunately my Arabic was not adequate to get my point across. He jabbered away angrily and incoherently for five minutes before dismissing me with a wave of his hand. Getting back into the truck, he drove up on the sidewalk to get around my car and went on his way.

At Headquarters when I reported what happened, Danny and everyone at the Motor Pool said little but took it in stride. I filled out an accident report, left my car to be repaired and was assigned a loaner vehicle.

Over the course of the time I spent in Arabia I had several accidents. With each I grew less flustered and more accepting of the fact that accidents went with the territory when working in Arabia.

As rapidly as my first months in Arabia had passed by, the exact opposite was the case following the Super Bowl. Time bogged down and life became a slow steady routine. Not everything, however, was dull. There were some interesting moments. For instance, late in January six of the hostages in Tehran escaped. This news made everyone in the expatriate community happy, but we kept our jubilation in check as a tactful reminder, circulated by the Embassy, urged us to maintain a low profile. The local media barely mentioned the escape.

Early in April, President Carter announced that the United States was severing diplomatic ties with Iran. All of us knew what that meant and everyone was nervous. On the evenings of Thursday and Friday, April 24-25, the United States made its move. The result of these actions was immediately felt by those of us in the Middle East. A weekend was beginning in the West but in the Arab world it was the start of a new workweek. That Saturday morning I had only walked through the front door of the Ministry when a couple of young Saudis that I had seen occasionally in passing in the corridors or the parking lot, rushed up and did a weird snapping and popping motion with their hands and crowed "Khomeini he fuck President Carter." I knew immediately this was more than a general statement of dislike for the United States. Something had happened with the Iranians and whatever it was; it was bad news for America. I raced up the steps.

On my way up I tried to imitate the snapping motion the Saudis had done with their hands. Holding my hand in the air kind of loosely, I gave it a sharp down and upward jerk to force the little finger to hit against the other fingers. When the Saudis did it, a loud popping sound occurred like when we snap our fingers. For me the motion barely produced a sound. Mostly I hurt my hand. I was still working on the technique when I reached the third floor.

At the top of the landing I greeted Mohamed, who in turn gave me a strange look as he motioned with his head toward the end of the hall where the whole staff, once again, had huddled in the Admin Room. My stomach twisted into a knot when I saw the grave look on Al Dennison's face.

"Good, Adam is here. Please close the door Adam. I asked all of you to meet this morning because I have received a communiqué from Headquarters that just came from our Embassy in Jeddah. Before I read it, I want to acknowledge that most of you, like me, have probably heard rumblings from the Saudis when you arrived at the Ministry this morning. So you are already aware that something has happened in Iran. With that being said, I will now read the official word from the Embassy:

'On the night of April 24, 1980, U.S. military forces launched a rescue operation to free American diplomats illegally detained and held hostage nearly six months in Iran. Despite the bravery of the personnel involved in this valiant effort, our mission has failed. Although this mission was not successful, when addressing the nation President Carter assured the country and the world that 'the United States will not give up nor will we rest until every American from our Embassy in Iran has been safely returned to their families.' It has been confirmed that U.S. forces have sustained casualties. Our prayers are with the families of the brave personnel involved in this operation, as well as with our diplomats who continue to endure their illegal detainment in Tehran. Americans living and working in the Kingdom are urged to avoid discussions on this matter with Saudi and other Arab and non-U.S. nationals. As always we strongly advise all Americans to keep a low profile.'"

As the engineers filed out and headed back to their offices, Al Dennison grumbled "it never ceases to amaze me how the Saudis hear about things before we do. Al-Basheer asked me about this first thing this morning, long before the courier from the Mission arrived with the message from the Embassy Liaison Office."

Over the next few weeks morale at the office sank to the lowest I had seen it since coming to Saudi Arabia. Unlike the successful escape of the six embassy personnel in January, this failed rescue attempt received generous coverage in the Arab press. Worse yet, keeping a low profile seemed to embolden those razzing us at the Ministry to do so even more. I just hoped it would not take too long for things to settle down, so that interactions between the Saudi and American staffs could get back to normal. In contrast to the general reaction around the Ministry, Al-Basheer did not gloat over the demise of the U.S. rescue effort. Even when he and I spoke privately in his office, Abdullah never commented on it or said anything disparaging about my country. It was as if he was keeping a low profile around us. Whether this had anything to do with the fact he was the sole Saudi working on the third floor, I could not say. Whatever his reasons, the good impression I had of Mr. Al-Basheer grew stronger. I decided I would not mind getting to know this particular Bedouin better.

Shortly after the Iran rescue fiasco, Mohamed Al-Hamidi was fired from his job as our translator. Nobody at the Ministry was surprised by this and I do not think anyone was happier about it than Alim. For a long time he had been feeling overwhelmed and that he was doing the bulk of the translating for both the Saudi and American Engineering staffs, generally making up for Mohamed's deficiencies. Mohamed was replaced by a translator from Somalia named Khaleel.

Playing in the city tennis league took me into sections of the city I had not seen before. We also competed against Western companies out in the suburbs, including sites that did not appear on any of the maps handed out at Headquarters. One weekend we played a company that operated near Wadi Al Darriyah. This gave me a change to visit the ancestral home of the Saud family. I regretted not having a camera with me that day because I would love to have taken some pictures. League play also spiced up my social calendar. All sorts of invitations to dinners and parties were extended to me by people I met on the tennis circuit.

One unexpected but welcome benefit from my increased exposure to the city was that I began to see Black Saudis. Ahdel was right, they were everywhere. Unfortunately, each time I saw them I was driving or riding with teammates in a traffic situation. We passed by them at gas stations and in suqs when they were out shopping. Once I saw a road rage incident that involved two families, one White and the other Black. Both cars had pulled off to the side of the road. As I was waiting at a red light, I saw the Black Saudi father get out of his car, take off his ak-gal, walk over to the other vehicle and start shouting at the other driver. He must have been very angry because he shook his ak-gal, the thick ring that holds the gutra in place, in such a way that I believe if that other guy had gotten out of his car the Black Saudi would have beaten him right on the spot. Whoever was in the other vehicle, they stayed in their car and made sure all the doors were locked. In fact the Black was actually went all around the vehicle screaming, shaking his ak-gal and testing each door to see if he could get inside the car. I would love to have waited around to see how that incident ended but I had to keep moving with the traffic. So even though I was not meeting Black Saudis face to face, I no longer had doubts that they existed in Riyadh. My hopes of meeting them soared.

Our expatriate community was a fish bowl. Everybody knew everyone else, and they knew if and who you were dating. Since I was not dating, suspicions about me spread like a wildfire. The problem for me in Riyadh was that romantic interests often overlapped. It was common for a female to date several guys at once. Sharing a woman was not my style and at that point in my tour I was not feeling a lot of pressure to date. As long as I was content and could hold out, I would be fine. I have never allowed the opinions of others to dictate what I do with my body. Besides, I had prepared myself physically and mentally for a life of celibacy months before I came to

Arabia. Discovering that single western women were in the Kingdom was a nice surprise, but of the few single women I met thus far none had captured my attention.

People, of course, come in all varieties and there was a wild bunch among us that got into just about anything you can imagine. Though I did not go to parties often, I will never forget the night two women and six males invited me to an after party to participate in a no-holes barred orgy. It was an invitation I turned down quick. Later I overheard the two women talking about me and one of them said, "he's a man, he has to be doing something."

A woman more my speed came to my attention on another occasion that I would remember for a long time. While mingling at a party one night I ran into Larry Corbin. "Adam, man where have you been," he asked? "I haven't seen you in ages."

"Playing in the tennis league pretty much takes up all of my spare time these days," I answered.

"Man, you should have come out a few weeks back. This girl, a nurse, very pretty, was asking about you. When she asked me, I confirmed that I knew you, but, and I am sorry to admit this - I was a little out of it that night - I never got around to getting her number. I can't even remember her name. It was something like Lynn, Carolyn or... something like that. I'm really sorry Adam. But if I run into her again I promise I will get a name and number for you."

"How did you say she looked, again?"

"Nice brown skinned girl, rather attractive, not short, but not too tall either, long hair, brown eyes, incredible shape, skimpy amount of makeup, which she did not need at all" he said with a convincing smile. "No, I did not forget I am married, but I was terribly jealous when she asked about you. Honestly, I was."

Momentary shock wore off once he described the girl because it was only then I knew it could not have been Lovelen. Larry's description was way off and much too explicit to mistake her for any other woman and Barry would have said something about her coming to Riyadh in his letters. I was confident that had Lovelen come to Riyadh, Larry would have been tongue-tied trying to describe her.

"Is that the reason you did not get her number for me Larry?"

"No man, you know I would never do you like that. No way. Like I told you when you first came to Riyadh, we have to look out for each other over here."

"So you say she was attractive?"

"Very. And the sophisticated type - if you know what I mean."

"I think so, but Larry you do know that if I do not get to meet this Lynn woman I am never going to forgive you."

"In that case, I will definitely find out who she is. I cannot have you angry with me my friend."

"How do you plan on tracking her down?"

"She is a nurse, remember? There are only so many places she could be, plus I do have connections."

Larry certainly did have connections, which is why I left that party with a fair amount of confidence I would be meeting this mystery woman soon enough. Even so, I decided to be proactive and increase my chances of running into her. After that I must have attended every party given in the city, and kept at it for a long time. I had high hopes of crossing paths with this lovely stranger who was going around asking about me. But weeks passed, weeks became months and still I could not find her. In a short time the woman became a phantom. Imaginations of her haunted me day and night. My head filled with elaborate fantasies. Eventually, my emotional equilibrium began to waver so for the sake of my sanity I took the Saudi approach and told myself Insha'Allah, God willing, we shall meet. Although I went to fewer parties, it took time to wean myself from thinking about her constantly.

One thing this situation did was make me realize my hiatus from dating could not last much longer. I was lonely.

✧✧✧✧✧✧✧✧✧✧✧

Around the middle of May I got out of bed one morning, ate breakfast, dressed, went downstairs to leave for work and walked into the eeriest scene I had ever seen. The air was full of a yellow flaky substance falling from the sky and it was covering everything. It looked and fell just like snow but was not cold to the touch. Everything, even the air, was the color of lemon. As I drove to work I could tell that the Saudis were dumbfounded about the yellow-fall as well, but they seemed excited to be seeing something other than sand and sun in the air. Whatever it was, drivers had to clean their windshields constantly to keep their view of the road clear. The mixture of window washer fluid and the yellow-fall produced a sickly looking sludge that piled up on cars, tires and in the streets. The scenes reminded me of a Dr. Sues story I had read as a child.

Shortly after I got to work Lee Williams came around to all the offices and informed us that the yellow-fall was ash from the eruption at Mount St. Helens that had occurred a few days earlier. Volcanic ash had traveled on air currents in the upper atmosphere all the way around the world to finally fall on the Arabian Peninsula.

Chapter 17

August 1980

Our project was spread across the Peninsula and would ultimately include construction projects at 35 sites in as many cities. The request-for-proposal period had already been completed by the time I arrived in-Kingdom. Submittals were coming in from around the world and winning companies were being awarded contracts that had to meet strict requirements as outlined by the Saudis. Production schedules were tight and only the highest standards of workmanship and quality materials were acceptable. By the time I got to Riyadh, bids had been granted on 18 of the 35 sites and 13 of those got underway from mid-1979 though the early months of 1980. Groundbreaking for the site in Riyadh was scheduled for September and a huge media event was being arranged to kick off the event.

Abdullah Al-Basheer and Al Dennison, along with selected members of their respective staffs were always on hand at groundbreakings. Afterward they returned periodically to the sites to perform inspections and assess progress. Also, from time to time, contractor reps came to Riyadh to meet directly with Ministry officials, answer questions regarding their sites or personnel matters, and advise the staff of any problems they might be having with contract specifications and timelines. They also reported any difficulties they might be having with permits, easements or similar business with local jurisdictions that would require official intervention at the Ministry level.

Two of our contractors flew into Riyadh from one of our remote sites for a quick meeting that August. They were in and out of the Ministry so fast that Al Dennison barely had time to introduce me to them. We shook hands and said goodbye all at the same time.

The very next morning when I arrived at the Ministry, I sensed something was off kilter on our floor as I walked past Khaleel toward the Admin Room. It took a second but I figured out what was wrong. Every Engineer had his door closed. This had never happened before, so it seemed odd to me. Al Dennison was the only Engineer that kept his door closed at all times. At most maybe one of the other Engineers would have his door closed but typically that was when he was on a particularly sensitive phone call. On the odd chance I had missed a message from Headquarters I knocked at Al's door. No sound came from inside, so I opened it and saw Al at his desk shaking his head back and forth. He was mumbling something that I could not make out. I waited until he looked up and noticed me before I stepped inside and closed the door behind me. His face was as ashen as it had been the day we got the notice about the failed rescue attempt in Iran. Something was definitely wrong. I felt uneasy because I knew that whatever had happened, it was bad enough to have affected the whole staff. You know how you get that feeling when you are about to ask a question that you are not sure you really want to know the answer to? That is how I was feeling as I walked up to the desk and inquired, "What's wrong Al?"

"Did you hear about the tragedy at the airport last night?"

"No, but now that you mention it, I did see something odd this morning out on that remote runway across from my compound. I have never known the Saudis to use that runway for anything, but there was a plane parked out there this morning. It looked like it had been hit by a missile or something. Is that the tragedy you are talking about?"

"Right plane; wrong disaster – what you saw is the charred remains of a commercial jet that took off from the airport last night. Fifteen minutes into the flight the pilot reported a fire in the cabin and turned back to the airport. He managed to land safely but it was too late. The fire raged out of control and it got too hot for firemen and rescuers to get anywhere near the plane. They had to let it burn out. There were no survivors. The two contractors that were here yesterday – they were on that flight. Adam… they are dead."

My body went limp and my knees buckled and I reached for a nearby chair and fell into the seat. Nobody is ever prepared for the sudden loss of life and even though I barely knew those men their deaths jolted me deeply.

Al and I were not great friends, but we liked each other for sure. Outside of work we rarely communicated or crossed paths. Still the man was our quarterback. He led our team. We took our cues from him and seeing him in that much distress made me feel hurt.

Out of sheer grief, Al suddenly pounded the desk with his powerful fists and softly complained, "Every time I turn around something else bad happens." Grabbing his head with both hands he cried out, "God, I need a break!"

Al swung between calm and rage for several minutes before he settled down. In time he reassured me, "I will be okay. You can go to your office now. I will not be slitting my wrists or anything like that, but I do appreciate your staying with me through that tirade. It will take time, but I will get beyond this."

Maybe it was callous of me to think the way I did, but I was relieved that I had not gotten to know the contractors better. That would have made their loss harder for me to handle. As it was, a pall hung over our offices, and the whole city, for several weeks.

That was Saudi Arabia's first air disaster and it was hard on everyone. Putting it out of mind was virtually impossible because it seemed every time we turned around, another horrific detail about the tragedy was made public. First we learned that all of the bodies were found piled in a pyramid at the exit door with the stronger passengers at the top because they had climbed over the weak and dying. But the detail that was hardest to bear for many of us was not reported until several days after the disaster. By then the heat from the fire had diminished enough for recovery work to begin. That was the day the official death toll was announced to have increased by one victim. The corpse of an infant was discovered wedged under a seat. Apparently its mother put it there in a desperate attempt to save the child's life. News of the loss of that fledgling life forced us to relive the anguish and horror of the disaster all over again.

On top of all these things, there was that grim daily reminder outside my front window. The burned out fuselage stared at me from the remote runway every morning when I left the compound to go to work and it was there waiting for me when I got home in the evening. It was like a pain that made a fresh wound in my heart twice a day. I was haunted by horrible imaginations of the final agonizing moments of the doomed contractors and their fellow passengers.

How long were the Saudis going to leave the plane sitting on that runway, was a question I asked every day. If wreckage from fatal traffic accidents was not moved for a year, what was the rule for fatal air disasters? Fortunately, depending on how you looked at it, no precedent had been set in this area. So I assumed the plane would remain where it was until the investigation was completed.

Had I stayed at that compound I might have been around the day they moved the plane away, however, my housing situation changed a couple of weeks after the tragedy. One day I stopped by Headquarters to check my mail and found a map and a set of keys in my mailbox along with a note informing me I had been reassigned to a new villa. After work, I followed the directions out Khurais Road to the outskirts of Riyadh and turned on the side street indicated on the map. Two blocks later I pulled up to the gate of my new residence. There were so many tree branches hanging over the wall of the compound that from the outside it looked as if Headquarters had assigned me to a villa inside a small park.

When I unlocked the gate and walked inside I was completely unprepared for what I saw. Two ranch style homes, with a moderate sized swimming pool nestled between them, sat amidst a verdant setting of trees, shrubs and flowers. It was wonderful. I felt like I had stepped into paradise.

But was this really my new residence? Right away I got nervous thinking somebody might have made a mistake. A flood of doubts came over me but just as I was beginning to grow skeptical about this new assignment, Al-Dhuhr prayer call sounded. By this time in my tour prayer calls barely caught my attention but this one was loud, I mean it was as loud as the call I heard in the Transient Apartments my first morning in the Kingdom. This could only mean one thing. Slowly I retraced my steps out to the street and watched to see in what direction men were walking. Because of the tree overhang along the south wall of the villa, the edifice on the corner was obscured from my view. But it did not matter. I did not need to see it to know what it was. Headquarters had assigned me to a compound next to a Mosque. Quickly ducking back inside, I ran to the front door of the villa on the right, unlocked it, stepped in, closed the door and dove onto a nearby couch where I laughed hysterically until I ached. As I lay on the couch, I tried to envision the previous occupants being jolted from sleep every morning by the predawn Al-Fajr summons and again at the end of the day by the Isha prayer call. But I wondered if Headquarters had any idea they had chosen the perfect project member to put in that compound. Prayer calls, early or late, would never disrupt my sleep. Not even if the muezzin himself came into my bedroom with a megaphone.

Once I stopped laughing, I got nervous again. What if this actually was a mistake and Headquarters had not meant to put me in this beautiful place? I raced to the bachelor compound and began the task of transferring my belongings to the new villa. After several trips I was all moved out and, I hoped, permanently entrenched at the new location. First thing the next morning I turned in the keys to Compound 760-D.

There were a number of conveniences that I immediately benefitted from in my new location. For one thing the PX and Commissary were mere minutes away. Also, so long as the other villa remained vacant I would have the compound all to myself. Being able to swim in privacy to my heart's content brought me no little amount of joy. In fact the first thing I did after settling in was go for a swim. I loved swimming and right away established the habit of swimming a couple of laps every day. The effect on my body was amazing and I began to tone up quite nicely. I did not know it at the time, but others in the expatriate community were taking note of my improving physique. One group in particular had actually begun to hatch a secret scheme that, if they had their way, would make me the central figure in the plot. Several months would pass before they were ready to present the plan to me, so I remained unaware of it for a time.

Meanwhile I kept getting stronger. On the tennis courts I became more agile and a better competitor. These physical improvements proved timely because shortly after moving to the new villa, Headquarters announced its first open invitational tennis tournament. Competition was to begin the third week in January. That gave me a little more than two months to get ready.

❧❧❧❧❧❧❧❧❧❧❧❧❧❧❧

Chapter 18

November 1980

It was my anniversary. Hard as it was to believe a year had passed since I landed at Jeddah airport. Interestingly, of all the people I had met thus far it was Abdullah Al-Basheer who had become my closest confidant. I played tennis with tons of expatriates and spent most of the time at the office with our Engineers, yet it was Abdullah who I could talk with like we were old friends. I could tell him anything and he shared a lot of amazing information about his country. We had actually gotten closer than he was to his American counterpart on the Ministry organization chart, my boss Al Dennison. Not long after starting at the Ministry, visiting with Abdullah became a daily ritual. In addition to teaching me Arabic words and expressions, Abdullah shared insights about Saudi culture. He asked a lot of questions about America as well and confided his personal desire to visit my country one day.

One afternoon toward the end of November we were talking in his office when a subtle change came over the usual expression on Al-Basheer's face. I sensed he was about to mention something that was a little off the beaten path from the topics we usually spoke about. I was right.

"Maybe it is a mistake to tell you this, but here in Riyadh we have a term for Americans. We call them Nass Mukhayyam. It means camp people. It is not a compliment. We call them this because Americans go to work at whatever Ministry they are assigned, return to their compounds, and nobody sees them on the street, in the suqs, or other places. This seems so strange to us, you know. Adam I would like to ask you, are Americans afraid to be around Saudi people?"

My initial thoughts regarding his disclosure was that it was ironic descendants of desert nomads with a four thousand year history of living in tents were now calling citizens of the most industrialized nation in the world 'camp people'. As far as his question whether Americans were afraid to be around Saudis, almost anything I said in response to that could spark political debate. I had been in the country long enough to understand why we were told to avoid such conversations.

141

While I hesitated, Abdullah waited for an answer. I knew I had to tell him something. Compromising a little, I offered in explanation, "Personally I have no problem spending time with Saudis, but it is possible the differences in our cultures are too much for most Americans living here. Trust me I can understand there are things about our society that puzzle your people, but Abdullah some things in your culture are just as puzzling to us."

"Really, like what for example?"

What a question. Abdullah did not realize it, but with that question he had opened the door for me to ask something I had wanted to discuss with a Saudi for a long time. However, I was not sure Abdullah was the Saudi I wanted to question about this matter because it was probably more sensitive a topic than politics. Furthermore, I was concerned about offending him. This was something I sincerely wanted to avoid. We had grown close and I did not want to do or say anything to undermine our friendship. Abdullah though, had given me a way to introduce the subject that might make it easier for us both so I figured I would try it because it just might work. "Abdullah a few moments ago you were not sure you wanted to tell me about the Nass Mukhayyam epithet and I can appreciate why you hesitated. Now, to answer your question on what we find puzzling about your country, I find myself in the same position you were in moments ago."

He laughed, smiled, and then got that mischievous look he sometimes gets on his face.

Still, I hesitated because what I was about to ask was not going to be easy.

"Go ahead Adam you can tell me. Whatever it is, it is okay. If it is in your heart, it will be there whether you tell me or not so do not worry. We are friends. You can tell me anything."

I took a deep breath and said, "All right… here goes. I have been bothered by a word I have been hearing since my first day here. But before I tell you what it is, I want to clarify something. Is it true King Faisal ended Black Slavery here in 1962?"

"Yes, that is correct."

"Okay, then Abdullah why when I am in the suqs or walking around town do I hear White Saudis call out to Blacks 'ya Abidan' whenever they want to get a Black person's attention? Doesn't that expression mean 'hey, my Black Slave?'"

Abdullah froze. I could not tell if he was surprised I had found out about this popular expression and what it meant, or was simply unprepared for the question. We sat quietly for what seemed like an eternity, both of us in deep thought. When Abdullah finally opened his mouth to respond, I could tell from his body language that I was not going to like his answer.

"Personally I never say that word, but we have used it so long in this country that now it only means Black person."

A wave of nausea rose inside me like a volcano on the verge of erupting. When I opened my mouth what I said was more of a tirade than an answer one would give a friend who had tried to avoid saying something offensive, but had failed. To this day I cannot remember what I said to him, that is how angry I was. But I do recall how my tirade ended. I closed with the words, "I did not come to this country to offend anyone but I did not come to Arabia to be insulted either or talked to like I am too stupid to know the difference between slavery and freedom." Almost as soon as those words came out of my mouth, I regretted saying them. Not that what I had said was wrong, it was just that I should not have spoken to a friend in that manner. Abdullah looked hurt, and justifiably so, and he seemed surprised I had reacted as I did. After several moments of silence I calmed enough to give him a better response to his statement.

"Abdullah, you probably have no idea how your words make me feel. I did not mean to hurt your feelings, but it's hard to believe you Arabs actually think that way about that word. 'We have used Abidan so long in this country that now it only means Black person?' You can't be serious. Abdullah, the term Abidan has always meant Black people to Arabs. Who else could the term refer to except to Blacks? You are not saying Red slave or Yellow slave or White slave – but Black slave. Do you know what your answer tells me about Arabs? That you guys think we have the label slave stamped on our skin, our culture, our entire history permanently.

"Another thing Abdullah, none of the Black people I have seen and heard being called Abidan here were Saudi citizens. All of them were Blacks from other countries who happen to live and work in Riyadh. These are people like me, who have never been enslaved at any time in this country or anywhere else. So while I can appreciate the fact you do not use the word Abidan, the reality that your countrymen do use that word tells me that it is just a matter of time before one of your countrymen calls me Abidan. When that happens, how do you think I will react? Can you guess? If I accept your explanation, I should let the word roll off my back, as long as I am in this country because it is a tradition here to call Black people slaves. Abdullah I have been called African American, Black American, Negro, Nigger – even Amreekie Aswad - but nobody has ever called me a slave. And I can tell you here and now, nobody had better ever call me a slave – not to my face.

"Abdullah, have you ever heard the expression rag heads?"

"Yes."

"Do you know what it means?"

"That is what some Westerners like to call Arabs."

"Do you find that expression offensive?"

"Of course we do, and yes I see your point."

"Exactly, just because people use a word so many times that its use becomes common, does not mean it is okay to say that word or that it is not offensive. I mean, can you really look me in the face and say you guys never even suspected Blacks were offended by the word Abidan?

"You may find this hard to believe Abdullah, but I have yet to meet a Black Saudi resident of this city. But I am sure of one thing, if a Black Saudi father is walking down Airport Road with his son and a White Saudi comes along and calls out, 'ya Abidan.' the father is not going to look his son in the face and say, 'don't get upset. The word slave used to mean slave, now it means Black people?

"Abdullah, today you shared a local opinion with me about how your countrymen view Americans here in Riyadh. I would like to reciprocate by sharing with you an opinion about slavery from the Black American Community. Shortly before I came to your country, two of my Black American friends went with me to the Library of Congress to do research on Arabia. That is where we found information on Prince Faisal's edict ending Black slavery here in 1962. At the time, however, we had no idea how Saudis treated Black people. But one of my friends suggested you Saudis were probably kinder to your slaves than the way our ancestors were treated in America before the Civil War. The other friend reacted to that by saying it does not matter how slave holding societies treated those they enslaved. And what she said next gets right to the heart of what you and I are talking about. She said, 'the very word slavery in and of itself has been offensive from the moment it was first spoken. Throughout history every human that has ever been forced into slavery immediately transferred all of his or her energies and dreams into plotting ways to regain their independence. This reaction was automatic for them.' Abdullah, when she said this I thought I understood what she was saying. But the funny thing is, that it was not until just now when you explained how Arabs view the term Abidan that I really got what she meant.

"What if you or I were put in chains after we get off work tonight and are dragged away from our lives, hopes and dreams and taken to some strange land far from our families and friends to be slaves? I am sure we would be more upset than either of us could put into words at this moment. But the first time someone called us slave instead of Abdullah or Adam, how do you think we would feel? How would you feel? Would it feel natural to you to be called slave? Say they kept us there until we married and had families and grew old and died. Let suppose our descendants remained in slavery for hundreds of years and then one day many centuries from now, long after you and I are dead and gone, they free our descendants, make them citizens of that land... but continue to call not only our people slaves but anyone that looks like us slaves as well. Would you want your descendants to overlook it because their former enslavers had grown accustomed to calling them slaves? If I challenged you to walk out of this building and stop the first Black Saudi on the street you meet and ask him what he thinks about the word Abidan – would you do it? Have you guys ever thought to do that; to ask your Black citizens how they feel about that word?

"When my friends and I were researching slavery in Saudi Arabia we found reports that claimed *de facto* slavery still exists here. Now I know that mentally, socially, and psychologically it does. There is mental slavery here because from an Arabs perspective their minds are stuck on our skin color and the illusion that being Black identifies us as slaves. That also means you have to have social slavery because you think the terms slave and Black are interchangeable and slaves are not invited to mix with polite society. This probably explains why I have never seen a Black Saudi walk in front of a camera in a documentary. Psychological slavery may be the worst kind because calling a man a slave affects the way he is viewed first of all by his wife, sons and daughters and then by his neighbors, friends, community, hell in this country, probably his camels too.

"Abdullah, one of the reasons words like Abidan and slave are so offensive is that they single individuals out as different from the rest of society. But I will tell you something Abdullah that even you must know is true. The Holy Bible and the Quran teaches that God made humans in his image. Muslims and Christians claim to believe those writings. If that is the case then my friend is right, the word slavery in and of itself has been offensive since it was first spoken. And the reason this is true, is because the image of humans comes directly from God, Allah, Jehovah, Adonai, Elohim, all of the above and Allah... is... not... a... slave.

"Cultures around the world seem to find ways to link the word Black to anything negative and objectionable - from black sheep, black mark, and black day to black slave. Black Americans have stopped accepting negative definitions from other ethnic groups to identify ourselves. Not any more. We embrace our skin, culture and humanity as gifts from God. And when we say we are Black and proud, we mean that from our hearts."

Poor Abdullah, he looked like a ton of bricks had fallen on his head. Here I was his guest, a Black man from a distant land where Affirmative Action and Reparations were commonly discussed, criticizing him and his nation about their long tradition of dealing with Blacks. He sat quietly for a little while then softly uttered, "Hopefully the day will come when nobody will use that word anymore."

I was sad when I left his office that day because I thought our friendship was over. But I was wrong. We actually grew closer. Subsequent visits to his office helped me to understand a little better some of the nuances of the Arab mindset. I was fascinated at how much respect they showed for people who stood up for their beliefs, especially when a person did so against overwhelming odds. Abdullah explained, "We celebrate courage in this country. You have never seen a parade with armies here and there are several reasons for that, but one is because anybody can join an army and attack other people with guns. What we honor is the individual, the single man who is willing to defy millions even when he knows he does not have a chance to win."

As Abdullah was saying this I recalled the way he had conducted himself after the failed attempt to rescue our hostages in Iran. He was the only Saudi that I dealt with on a regular basis, who did not gloat over the failure of our forces. Now I understood his behavior had nothing to do with him being the only Saudi working on our floor. He was simply being true to his heart.

The more time I spent with Abdullah Al-Basheer the more I liked him. When Mission Head Todd Dearbourne spoke about opportunities I would have to form lasting friendships in the Kingdom, he did not have people from the local population in mind; nevertheless, Al-Basheer was becoming just that - a real friend.

One weekend that winter, I was out exploring the local markets around my new compound when I ran into Abdullah. He was shopping for his family. After an initial exchange of pleasantries we came to realize he and I were neighbors. Abdullah took me to his home and introduced me to his parents and a few days later Abdullah came to my villa. We spoke as easily in my home as we did when we sat together in his office at the Ministry. During his visit we even broached a subject I usually avoided with Muslims - religion. My good impressions of Abdullah grew even stronger that day simply because he did not try to convert me to Islam, which I really appreciated. Best of all, he was as relaxed in my home as when we talked at the Ministry. To live as a foreigner in a distant country and be able to invite a local to your house and neither of you feel awkward in any way, is one of the nicest compliments a citizen can give an outsider.

Late that December Abdullah did something so wonderful that it cemented our friendship in a way that left me convinced we would remain friends long after I left Arabia. A couple of weeks before the tennis tournament, I got to the office one morning and had just sat at my desk when the phone rang. It was Khaleel calling to inform me, "Mr. Al-Basheer would like to see you in his office."

Chapter 19

Late December 1980

"Adam, I am going to Dammam this weekend to visit my brother. He is an Engineering student at the University there. Would you like to come along?

A long distance trip with my boss' Saudi counterpart, this was quite an honor. "Yes, I would love to go Abdullah."

"Good, we will drive up together. This will give me a chance to show you some of my country outside of Riyadh and we will have plenty of time to talk. I will be leaving Wednesday after work. All we need to do now is decide whether we will go in my car or yours. What do you suggest?"

"It takes about five hours to drive to Dammam, right?"

"That is correct, but only if you stick to the speed limit. Some Saudis get to Dammam from Riyadh almost as fast as the plane," he joked. When he saw the look on my face he quickly assured, "You do not have to worry about me Adam. I never drive more than the limit."

"Why don't we go in my car and take turns driving?"

He chuckled and agreed, "Okay. I have reserved two rooms at a nearby hotel. We will stay there overnight, visit Majd Thursday morning and drive back to Riyadh later that afternoon."

"Abdullah this means a lot to me. I really appreciate the invitation."

"No problem, my friend. It will be nice to have your company, and like I said we will have plenty of time to talk on the way there and on the trip back."

Horror stories about accidents on Saudi highways ran rampant in the expatriate community. Considering the way Saudis drove in the city, I had no reason to believe anything I had been told was an exaggeration. Needless to say I was a little nervous when Abdullah and I set out that Wednesday. He volunteered to take the first turn driving.

Twenty miles or so outside of Riyadh the posted speed rose to 120 Kilometers/Hour (approximately 75 mph). True to his word Al-Basheer kept to the limit. But every other car on the highway raced by us so fast that the vehicles sounded like aircraft and the slowest driver had to be traveling at a minimum 90 miles an hour.

I disliked the Dammam Highway right away. It was only a two lane road divided by a thin yellow center line. I could see why there were so many accidents on that road. To pass anyone you had to cross that center line. Motorists passed us as we climbed hills and were blind to traffic coming from over the crest. We were passed on wide bends in the road that curved around high sand dunes. Anything could have been coming at them head on from around those bends. Needless to say, passing someone was business.

Abdullah convinced me early in the trip that he was a cautious driver. When drivers took major risks to get by us, Abdullah always slowed down and kept a safe distance. He did this in the event the car passing us got involved in a head on collision. This tactic reduced the possibility of us getting caught up in the backwash of a crash. But I think having Abdullah as the first Saudi driver I rode with was both a blessing and a curse. Not too long after we left Riyadh, I sat back and relaxed with all the confidence in the world that I was riding with someone I could trust. Time would show, however, that Abdullah's good driving habits made me more comfortable about riding with Saudis than I should have been.

Our trip to Dammam was pleasant. Abdullah and I talked about a hundred different things along the way, including, to my surprise, tennis. Abdullah said it was a game he had always wanted to try. Since I had rackets in the trunk, I offered to show him some of the fundamentals of the game when we reached Dammam if the hotel had tennis courts. He agreed to the idea.

The sun was setting when we arrived, but the courts at the hotel had electronic lighting so we would be able to continue playing after the sun went down. I dressed and came out of my room eager to get on the court. Unfortunately the air in Dammam was as heavy and humid as it was at Jeddah airport (Dammam sits on the east coast of the Arabian Gulf – also known as the Persian Gulf). The trip from my room to the courts was like walking on the bottom of a heated swimming pool. By the time I reached the courts I was drenched from head to foot. Sweat was actually draining into my sneakers. Abdullah came out of his room looking quite spiffy in shorts and tennis shoes. I was surprised to see he had brought that kind of attire along for the trip but I have to say my Saudi friend looked like he was about to step onto the courts at Wimbledon. When he reached the court Abdullah was as soaked as I was, plus he was doing something I had never seen a Saudi do before - wiping his brow. We both laughed. "I do not think it is a good idea to play in this kind of heat," I hinted. Abdullah agreed wholeheartedly and laughed even harder when I said, "Man do I miss the dry heat of Riyadh."

Next morning we arrived at the University and were greeted by the young and very handsome Majd Latif Al-Basheer. The two brothers kissed tenderly and then Abdullah introduced me to Majd. The younger Al-Basheer grasped my right hand, placed his left on my right shoulder, leaned forward and kissed me first on my left cheek then on my right while uttering traditional greetings, blessings and inquiries about my health and that of my family. I had grown accustomed to this common greeting ritual. Abdullah was impressed to see that I knew what to do and the appropriate Arabic responses to give in return. He got a kick out of watching us, and commented, "very nice, you did that well. Not only do you sound Saudi, you even act Saudi. If you stay much longer, we will have to make you a citizen."

Abdullah took Majd by the hand and they walked ahead of me through a colonnaded area along one of the University's courtyards. I stayed far enough behind so as not to listen in on their conversation. Not that I would have understood everything they were saying, but I did not want to be rude. I enjoyed their familial interaction and displays of natural affection. That kind of tenderness between males was new to me. Watching them together made me feel even more privileged to have been invited to come along to share such an intimate part of Abdullah's life.

After a meal in the school cafeteria, Majd announced he had a special treat for us. He wanted to show us his favorite place to hang out, but to get there we had to drive.

Following his directions, we drove to the beautiful coastal highway that runs along the Gulf. Some of the most breathtaking seaside sights I had ever seen kept me wide-eyed and in awe along the way. An hour later Majd instructed me to turn off the highway. I pulled up to a mound of sand near a grove of palm trees. After getting out of the car, Majd led us through the grove. We emerged onto a beach at the center of a wide crescent shaped bay. The moment I laid eyes on the gulf, I understood why Majd loved that spot.

There was an ancient looking fishing village along the shore far to the left of us at that tip of the crescent. Further inland behind it stood a palace with massive walls. Between the village and the palace there was a mosque with a single minaret that dominated the skyline. Out in the bay, Dhows had weighed anchor and men and boys were leaning over the sides fishing the warm waters of the Gulf. Around us Saudi families were having lunch on the beach. Some of them were wading in the waters.

The three of us found a private spot, sat and talked until dusk. Although we had not planned to stay that long in Dammam, we spent the bulk of the day on that beach and stayed long enough to see a panoramic view of an amazing sunset across the bay. Dazzling arrays of light cast colorful hues along the beach and on the structures in the nearby village. The stones changed from sand color to a golden yellow and an orange that deepened as darkness fell. Ever so slowly, yet steadily, the moon ascended on a direct tangent with the minaret and climbed to a spot in the sky just above the village. As darkness fell, sailors hung lanterns from the prows of their boats and the fishermen continued plying their trade. I imagined anyone on a flight overhead could look down and see the same sight I saw on the Mediterranean. By the time Al-Maghrib prayer call rolled across the bay, electric lights were shining from within the houses, and the sky darkened as crystal clear and black as the one I had seen over Riyadh my first night in Arabia. From one end of the bay to the other the view was one of heart wrenching beauty. The handiwork of the Almighty left me speechless.

Abdullah and Majd joined other Muslims laying prayer rugs on the sand and as they knelt toward Mecca, I continued to admire the pristine beauty around me and whispered a prayer in praise to the Maker of such glorious sights.

It was hard to tear away from that beach, but a trip that was meant to last half a day had stretched late into the evening. Abdullah and I needed to start for home. We dropped Majd back at his school, where he kissed us both goodbye, then Abdullah and I began the long drive to Riyadh.

For the trip home I had driving duty. Abdullah leaned back and rested his eyes. By the time I reached the highway he was snoring softly. Twenty minutes later the wind picked up suddenly. Thirty seconds later I was driving in a full blown sandstorm. Waves of sand rolled across the highway completely obscuring the road. The only thing I could see was a row of tail lights up ahead. They were about a quarter of a mile up the road, so I sped up to latch on to the end of what I believed was a mobile caravan.

When I got close enough I realized it was not a group of vehicles after all but one of the big Mercedes Benz trucks that the Saudis use to transport goods between cities (the same kind of truck caused my first accident). Expatriates called them Christmas boxes because the drivers strung lights all around the frames of the trucks. The first time I saw one rolling through downtown Riyadh with all those lights, I laughed too. But after that night I would never laugh at them again. I came to appreciate that those lights served a practical purpose in the desert. Thanks to the lights on that truck, I had a guide through that blinding tempest. I latched onto that trucker so fast that if he had made any mistakes or gotten lost, we would have been lost as well or if he drove off the road, we would have been right behind him. That night I learned just how knowledgeable those desert transporters were because his knowledge of the road was like a map burned onto his brain. He was my guardian Bedouin that night and guide through that storm.

Whoever this trucker was, he never veered off the road or led me onto the sand and incredible as it may seem he never slowed down. To keep up with him I had to drive like a bat out of Hades and I can confidently say to this day that I have never driven a car that fast since.

It is hard to admit this, but in the middle of the storm I did something really boneheaded. First I roused Abdullah so he would know what was happening. After his head cleared and he focused on our situation, his eyes grew as large as saucers. Watching his face transform into abject fear did not instill any confidence in me, which was really bad news for both of us because I was the one behind the wheel. The boneheaded thing I did was to ask, "Do you want to take over the wheel? I mean, this is your country so I am sure you know how to drive through this stuff better than me." If Abdullah had fallen for my idiotic idea, I would have had to pull over so we could switch places. By the time we made the exchange our trucker guide would have been long gone. Neither Abdullah nor I were professional drivers with long experience traveling that road, so my idea would have left us at the mercy of the elements.

Abdullah's voice was trembling when he answered, "No, you are doing very well. Just keep on the tail of that truck." There are moments in life when a man finds himself in a desperate situation and the unenviable position of bearing sole responsibility for his life and the lives of those around him. That was one of those moments. Like it or not, I had no choice but to drive like both our lives depended on my actions. And they did.

After awhile I stopped looking at the speedometer. I honestly did not want to know how fast we were going. The only thing that mattered was that I keep on that truck's bumper. I latched on like a racer drafting on the lead car. When the truck sped up, I stepped on the gas. If he applied his brakes, I decelerated. Around bends, up hills, down hills - we punched through that storm like two escapees from the loony-bin.

The storm lasted twenty harrowing minutes, which I thought we might not live through. Then it ended as abruptly as it began. Abdullah and I laughed about it for months afterward, but I know neither of us will ever forget how frightened we were that night.

After the storm lifted the sky cleared and a soft glow fell over the desert. As we continued down the highway I gradually realized this glow was not a mirage. It was very real. On each side of the highway sand dunes shimmered like vanilla ice cream does when it gets that glaze over it as it starts to soften and melt. I was trying to figure out where this glow was coming from when I noticed light was also shining on the hood of my car. Leaning forward, I looked heavenward and above the desert saw the most incredible number of stars I had ever seen. "Wow!" As I shouted I turned the wheel sharply and pulled off the highway. After the car came to a crunching stop on the sand, I jumped out, fell back on the hood and stared into the sky. It was a clear night without a cloud in sight and I could see as far into the heavens as is humanly possible. Billions upon billions upon billions of stars looked down on us from heaven. There were so many stars that my senses went into overload attempting to take in the whole sight. In the meantime, Abdullah had gotten out of the car and rushed to my side. He asked, "What is it? Are you okay?" I could see in his face that he was genuinely frightened.

Pointing skyward I said, "Look"

"Okay, what? What is it? What do you see?"

"The stars! I never knew it was possible to see so many at one time with the naked eye."

"Is that why you pulled off the road… because of the stars? Man you scared me to death. I thought you were having a heart attack or something."

"Sorry Abdullah. I did not mean to frighten you. You guys get to see this all the time. Never in my life have I seen a sky like this."

Abdullah smiled, folded his arms, looked at me, shook his head and started laughing.

As I peered into that vast array of heavenly bodies, it felt like I was getting a sneak peek through a gateway that someone had left open by mistake. Deep into space as far as I my eyes could see, there were layers upon layers upon layers of stars. Nebula from some of the remote regions of the Universe, were also visible. One of the more amazing aspects of what I saw that night was the sight of our moon standing strikingly clear in all its glory right in the midst of this grand heavenly display. Starlight and moonlight blazed together on the blackest and most pristine canvas that heaven had ever produced in my life, and neither outshone the other. As a matter of fact the close proximity of the moon on that backdrop made it seem easily within reach. It was almost as if I could simply reach up and pluck the moon like a piece of fruit. Or, perhaps I could walk over and stand beside the moon and together we would observe the awesome wonder overhead. The sight was both humbling and mind boggling at the same time.

In college my science professor told us 'the Middle East is the best place on earth to observe the heavens.' Now I knew what she meant.

Telling Barry about this was going to be difficult. How could I ever find the appropriate words to describe what I was seeing? Everything that had come to mind so far seemed inadequate. However, several Biblical passages crossed my mind as I looked through this ancient window into heaven. It was as if I could sense what Abraham must have felt when God told him to look into this very same sky and then said "in blessing I will bless thee, and in multiplying I will multiply thy seed as the stars of the heaven." And how

Isaiah's heart must have been filled with awe when the Grand Creator invited him to "Lift up your eyes on high, and behold who hath created these things, that bringeth out their host by number; he calleth them all by name by the greatness of his might, for that he is strong in power; not one faileth." Now here I was staring at the very sky King David praised in Psalm and sang "When I consider thy heavens, the work of thy fingers, the moon and the stars, which thou has ordained; what is man that thou art mindful of him? And the son of man, that thou visitest him?" Like David, the smallness of mankind against the scale and depth of the vast and greater Universe truly hit home that night as I peered into that incredible sky. That night I humbly acknowledged that we humans are the ants of the Universe. And what made that moment even more intense was that I knew I was only seeing what amounted to the bare fringes of His ways.

A few hours earlier when Majd Al-Basheer took us to his favorite bay on the Gulf, I never expected I would see anything that same evening to eclipse those scenes. That desert sky certainly did.

Like the first time I stared into the night sky over Arabia, I wanted to stand and admire the heavens. Abdullah though was anxious to get home. Unfortunately, when we went to get into the car we discovered the vehicle had sunk in the sand right down to the undercarriage. All the wheels were halfway buried and the bottom of my door scraped along the desert floor when I opened it to get in the car. Abdullah looked at me, shook his head and said 'wow'!

I volunteered to wait on the shoulder of the highway to try and flag someone down to help us out of our predicament. While waiting I continued to enjoy the spectacle overhead. As I did so, I tried to envision ancient caravans traveling through the desert under the glow of this very same army of stars.

Not even five minutes passed before an 18-wheel flat bed truck came along. The driver had already delivered his load so the empty truck was moving at a good clip. Fortunately he saw me in time and pulled over. This driver was from Pakistan and spoke English. As soon as he saw my car, he assured me he had seen this situation many times. Thankfully, he was kind enough not ask how the car got in that position and Abdullah and I did not offer an explanation.

From the back of his truck he pulled out a thick rope about six inches in circumference and quickly tied one end to his bumper and the other to mine. Abdullah and I climbed down into my car. The trucker got behind the wheel of his vehicle, turned on the engine and pulled away. As thick as that rope was, it snapped like a strand of spaghetti and my car never budged. Undaunted the Pakistani next pulled out a heavy duty industrial chain with huge hooks on either end and clamped the ends to the truck and to my bumper. Once again Abdullah and I climbed down into the sunken cabin and the trucker pulled off. The chain stretched taut and reached the point of effect just as I realized the car was still set in park. Quickly I jerked the car into gear and in that same instant the vehicle lurched out of the sand like a jack rabbit and we were freed. Abdullah looked at me like he could not believe what just happened. We both knew that if I had not put the car in gear when I did, the chain would not have snapped as the rope had done, but would have yanked the bumper off my car.

Neither of us had much to say the rest of the way home, but we would joke about that night many times in the days and months ahead. An hour later I pulled into the parking lot of the Ministry where Abdullah had left his car. When he got out I said good night. He shook my hand and said 'wow!'

For me it had been an incredible trip. I will always be grateful to Abdullah for inviting me to go along. Who would have guessed that in the course of a single night I would see three glorious displays of God's power – Majd's favorite bay – a fear inspiring sandstorm – and the greatest array of stars a human can see with the naked eye.

A few weeks after our Dammam trip, the Ministry hired a Deputy Director to assist Abdullah Al-Basheer. His name was Barakah Derar. Barakah was younger than Abdullah, extremely shy, and like many of the Saudis I had met, quite proficient with English. Abdullah told Barakah about me and he and I instantly became friends. Every morning Barakah stopped by the Admin Room to say hello and not long after we met he invited me to his home. Over the first few months of our friendship, I visited his home several times. On each visit, he and I watched football matches on television. One of those matches had me riveted because it was a broadcast from Jeddah. Nasser, the club that Larry Corbin's friend Ahdel played for, was competing. But it was not the action on the field that caught my attention. I was focused on the size and makeup of the crowd in the stands. There had to be at least 50,000 fans in the stadium and at least ninety percent of them were Black Saudis. Seeing that many Black citizens in one place made me wish I was in a different part of Arabia to research its post slavery society.

Chapter 20

January 1981

The Steelers did not reach the Super Bowl that year and I did not listen to the game. I tried to be happy for the new champs, the Oakland Raiders, but they were our hated rivals so it was difficult. John Madden though was a good coach. I liked him.

At the end of the tennis league season, attention shifted to Headquarters' upcoming tournament. All the top seeds were clustered in one half of the draw, which allowed lesser talented players like me, in the other half of the draw, a better chance of reaching the later rounds.

Singles competition got underway on Saturday January 17. I was not scheduled to play until the next day, but I drove out to the Rec Center on Saturday after work to watch Mark Parsons play his first round match. Mark won. The next day I played my opening round match and I too came off a winner. Round two on Monday saw another victory for Mark and on Tuesday I stunned my opponent, and a lot of other people, when I successfully moved into the third round. Mark's third round match was set for Wednesday evening. This time he was pitted against the number one seed, a newcomer named Zachary Pierce.

Zach Pierce arrived in Riyadh three weeks before the tournament. Until he showed up, Mark had been the top seed. The first time Zach practiced at the Rec Center he drew a large crowd of spectators. Everyone was curious because talk had already gotten around that he was very good. Watching Zach that day changed everyone's expectations about the outcome of the upcoming tournament. Even Mark realized Zach was far superior to anyone he had played against in the city. But Zach found a way to put Mark on notice, in a personal way, that there was a new top dog in town. It happened a few days before the opening rounds started.

Mark and I were practicing together when Zach walked onto the court and invited us to play a friendly doubles match against him and his partner. We did not know he did not have a partner at that moment, but after we said yes Zach looked around and casually asked 'is there anyone here who would like to partner with me against Mark and Adam?' Eventually he had to recruit someone. He opted for a woman who was waiting for a court to become available. She turned out to be the worst player there, but I suspect Zach already knew that. At first she did not want to play because, as she explained, "I barely pick up tennis rackets. The only reason I came out today is because I was inspired by the tournament." Zachary assured her she would have fun then turned to us for back up, prodding "Tell her guys, this is going to be a lot of fun." Mark and I grinned and repeated, 'this is going to be a lot of fun.' As we walked to the service line Mark mumbled 'when did massacres become fun?' Zach signaled he was ready to serve and asked 'are you ready Mark?' Mark raised his racked to let Zach know he could begin, but under his breath muttered 'we who are about to die salute you.' Zach served. Mark and I almost saw the ace as it zipped past. "Okay, so what's your point," Mark pouted? Zach laughed and set up to serve to me. Zach's partner walked through most of the game like a tourist and essentially it boiled down to a game of 2 on 1 with Zach proving his superiority over me and Mark combined. Anything else that needs to be said about that match, I have already written. The final score was so embarrassing I have not talked about it since.

Mark and I knew Zach had deliberately goaded us into that game, and I had no doubts that my friend would not win against him in their third round tournament match. Despite the predictable outcome, I promised Mark I would be there to support him.

Wednesday morning I stopped by Headquarters to check my mailbox. When Fahad approached, as usual, I assumed he was about to give me another Arabic lesson. Instead he asked "would you visit to my home Mr. Adam?"

I had accepted invitations from Al-Basheer and Barakah Derar to visit their homes, but I worked with those men and we knew each other pretty well. I had visited Saudis with Mohamed Al-Hamidi too, but this was my first private invitation from a Saudi outside of the Ministry. Sure I saw Fahad briefly almost every morning, but for the most part he was still a stranger.

Fahad, seeing I was hesitant pleaded "My little brother, he want meet you. He never meet American before."

Hearing this made me feel honored that he had chosen me out of the entire staff at Headquarters to introduce to his younger brother. "Sure Fahad, when would you like me to come?"

"Bukra, tomorrow… we meet here… Sa'ah wahid (1:00)."

That time would not work for me because my third round singles match was set for 2:00. Though I had no illusions about advancing any further in singles competition, the match would take at least two sets. Factoring in enough time to play and afterward run home to get cleaned up, I countered, "why don't I met you at Sa'ah komsah (5:00) instead?"

"Sa'ah komsah. Okay. See you tomorrow, Insha'Allah."

"Insha'Allah." What a wonderful expression. I was beginning to like the way it fit any situation and could mean just about anything or absolutely nothing.

That night Mark lost to Zach.

My third round match went as expected. Two quick sets and that was the end of singles for me. I was thoroughly beaten in one of the most lopsided matches of the tournament. So Mark and I both bowed out in the third round. Unlike Mark, however, I was also registered for doubles competition so I set my hopes on having a better outcome with my doubles partner.

Traffic was extra heavy that afternoon due to an accident, so I got to Headquarters twenty minutes late. Fahad was still waiting faithfully when I pulled up to the gate. The route to his house went t past a Riyadh landmark I had always wanted to see - the famous TV Tower on Television Street. At the Library of Congress my friends and I had read about the riots that were sparked in Riyadh when King Faisal introduced television into the Kingdom in the early 60s. Now that I had lived in Riyadh for some time, I could easily see Mutawahs and Imams leading demonstrations and denouncing television as a tool of Satan.

Rioting got so bad that King Faisal had to call in security forces to restore order. Several rioters were killed, including a nephew of the King named Khalid. Khalid had a brother who was attending college in the United States at the time – a sibling who, coincidentally, was also named Faisal. Some say the younger Faisal blamed the death of his brother on their Uncle because King Faisal had given the order for the soldiers to fire on the demonstrators. Years after his brother's death, young Faisal returned to Saudi Arabia. At a Majlis, (a ceremony that permits citizens to approach the King and voice private concerns), the young man joined a line of residents waiting to speak to King Faisal. When the King spotted his nephew, he beckoned for him to come forward. As they enacted the traditional greeting, young Faisal pulled out a pistol and began shooting. He was subdued by the guards but not before he shot the King in the face several times at point blank range. As he was dying, King Faisal pardoned his nephew and asked that the young man be shown mercy. The King's dying request did not save young Faisal. The assassin was beheaded.

Faisal's assassination happened four years before I drove past the TV tower with Fahad. But in the years since the television riots a shift in attitude had taken place in the Kingdom with respect to modern technology, television in particular. Had Faisal lived I think he would have been delighted to see how attached his countrymen had gotten to television. But the King might have been amused at the kinds of programming that was most popular in the Kingdom - football broadcasts and cartoons. The *Tom and Jerry Show* for example, drew, by far, the largest television audience in the city. Even in the tea shops, some of the livelier discussions were about episodes of *Tom and Jerry,* or as the Saudis affectionately called them, 'that cat and that rat.'

As I stared at the television tower I thought about the costs the country had paid, and was continuing to pay, for the most rapid adjustment to modern life the world has ever seen. That enduring tower was a fitting reminder of a remarkable man's vision and determination to spark a renaissance in his country because he knew they could not survive in the modern world if the nation remained entrenched in its ancient ways.

The mere fact that I was driving past the TV tower four years after Faisal's death, and there were thousands of foreign workers from the west working in the Kingdom was proof enough that the King's dream did not die with him.

Fahad's younger brother Bashir was a preteen, probably around eleven or twelve years of age. As soon as I squatted on the floor and was served tea, Fahad and his brother revealed why they had been eager to invite an American to their home. To be more accurate, they wanted a Black American to visit. And the reason for their interest in me did not come as too big of a surprise.

Michael Jackson's album "Off the Wall" had been released the previous summer. Sales were brisk all around the world, including among young Saudis. More to the point, because of videos young Saudis got to see Michael dancing to his music. To quote Bashir, who's English was more advanced than his older brother's, "John Travolta is not the king; Michael Jackson is the king." Until the 'Off the Wall' video was released, the film 'Saturday Night Fever' had ruled in the minds of many in the East as the premier example of Western dance. Michael Jackson's videos changed that view.

Bashir pressed the button to a cassette player, the speakers blared with the voice of Michael Jackson, and turning to me the youngster pleaded, "Please Mr. Adam, dance like Michael Jackson!"

I felt bad about it later, but my immediate reaction to his request was to laugh. And when I say laugh, I mean harder than I had laughed in years. In my mind I was thinking, 'this kid thinks just because I am Black, I automatically know how to dance, and on a par with Michael Jackson no less!' Once I got myself under control, I explained that I wished I had half the talent Michael Jackson possesses and assured Bashir there were plenty of Black Americans who could not stay on the dance floor with John Travolta let alone a dance icon of Michael Jackson's stature, who I agreed was the dance king.

Bashir was downhearted. His face had the look of a child whose hopes had been stomped down and ground into powder. I felt like a louse.

Patting him on the shoulder, I stood, smiled, and said in an upbeat tone, "Tell you what Bashir, start the music again." Bashir's face lit up.

Notwithstanding the risk of sounding like a braggart, I admit to knowing how to dance –a little. Maybe better than the average American, however I make no claims when it comes to Michael Jackson. Thankfully the few moves I showed Bashir were enough to satisfy the lad and I actually had a lot of fun showing off for him. By the way, a few years later when the Motown 25 Year Anniversary Special video reached Riyadh, the Saudis went bananas watching Michael moonwalk to the song *Billie Jean*.

"You dance very nice Mr. Adam," Bashir beamed.

"Yes," Fahad agreed. "But you should meet my friend Jabbar. Jabbar he best dancer in Riyadh. When somebody has wedding, they call Jabbar - he come dance for them. He Black man like you."

What? Black like me! Had I heard him correctly, and was Fahad talking about a Black Saudi or a Black African? "Is Jabbar Saudi," I asked hopefully?

"Yes, he Saudi man, Black Saudi man. I call him. He come meet you next week. Can you please to come to my home next Thursday?"

"Yes I can come next Thursday. The same time we met today if that is okay."

"5:00. Yes, we see you Thursday 5:00."

Needless to say, I was floating on clouds during the drive home. I was so elated I did not care that I got lost twice along the way. That evening I wrote to Barry spelling out the events of the day and explained 'this could be the moment the three of us anticipated when we debated the Black Saudi community at the Library of Congress.' In closing I wrote, 'As always I will keep you posted. Take care, keep in touch and give my regards to your lady. P.S. Tell Lovelen I am glad she came back to D.C. after finishing the job in Los Angeles. It sounds like you two are on the verge of getting into something serious. Could Lovelen be the one? Snag her while you can buddy, because I will be home in less than a year and if she is still available – just kidding.'

Doubles competition proved to be more interesting for me than singles had been. My partner was a guy named Ray Jay. Ray and I were the one team everybody predicted would fall in the first round. I could not blame them for being skeptical. Prior to the tournament, Ray and I had only practiced together once and that was in the week before the first round of singles began. With so little practice time together, nobody expected us to get far in the tournament.

Harry Albert worked on a sister project under the Mission umbrella. Mark Parsons introduced us a few months before the tournament. Because Harry had two first names I had a hard time figuring out what to call him. One time I would call him Harry Albert and the next time Albert Harry came out of my mouth. This went on for several weeks. Mark added to my confusion by calling his friend Al at times and on other occasions Harry. One weekend the three of us were at The Empty Quarter Inn when I did something I had heard Mark do plenty of times. I called Harry, Al. Calmly Harry laid down his fork, and as if he were lecturing a five year old corrected me saying, "Adam, my name is Harry Albert. You can call me Harry, or you can call me Albert, but Al does not work." Mark Parsons lost it, howling for several minutes before he settled down enough to tell us why he had gotten so tickled. He looked at Harry and chanted, 'You can call me Ray, or you can call me Jay…' From that day forward Harry Albert came to be known as Ray Jay. Thereafter when new arrivals came to Riyadh, Harry was introduced to them as Ray Jay. I would not be surprised if there are people in America who worked with us on the project in Riyadh and returned to the States without ever knowing there was a Harry Albert in our group.

Two days after my visit to Fahad's home, Ray Jay and I played our opening round doubles match. We were pitted against the number two seed team. To the surprise of a lot of people, we took them out in three of the most grueling sets I had ever played. That win started us on an unbelievable string of victories and we roared into the finals for a match against the number one seed team. The final was set for Wednesday evening, the day before I was to meet Fahad's Black Saudi friend.

Mark and Howard Seymour were in the stands to cheer us on. I served first to start the match. All the hard work Mark had put in working with me over the months, had strengthened my game. In addition, the increased agility gained from swimming regularly kicked in big time during doubles competition. In the title match, I came right out of the gate hitting first serves and they pounded like monsters. I served more aces that match than I had the entire tournament and always, it seemed, at a critical point in a game. Ray Jay and I won the doubles title.

Mark was so excited over our victory that he dragged me and Ray Jay to the weekly Wednesday night party at the Vinnell compound to celebrate. I had not been to a dance in months and after that two week tournament I was looking forward to the change of pace.

Dempsey Stevens was standing near the front door when we walked in. I was happy to see him, but Dempsey was not alone. He was talking to an exceptionally attractive young Black woman. As I walked by, I said hello. Dempsey acknowledged me with a nod of his head. Mark on the other hand said, "Guess what, Ray Jay and Adam won the doubles title. Isn't that great?" Dempsey smiled quickly then turned his attention back to the young lady. His female companion, however, did a little pirouette and called out, "Excuse me... would you happen to be Adam Sneed?" Surprised that she knew my name, I searched her face for familiarity and was about to say something when I noticed the look on Dempsey's face.

It was hard to find a young single Black American woman in Saudi Arabia. One as attractive as the lady Dempsey was talking with was even rarer. Not wanting to give Dempsey any reason to think I might try to steal the young lady away from him I responded in a business-like manner, "I am sorry, but I do not believe I know you."

"Yes... well, actually you don't, but I know you. Okay, not exactly. My name is Jaylynn Sinclair. Lovelen is my sister."

Talk about surprised. It hit me that I had never gotten around to asking Lovelen if she had a sister. This was an interesting turn of events, and for reasons I was sure Dempsey would never appreciate or understand. Poor guy, he looked deflated. "You are kidding," I exclaimed with a toothy grin as we shook hands.

"Lovelen told me you were in Riyadh and said I should look you up. I have been asking around about you for several months. It is nice to finally meet you. How are you?"

"Fine thank you" I answered with a slightly humbler expression on my face than I had with my previous response, again out of concern for Dempsey. I knew exactly how he was feeling and could not blame him for being upset. If the situation were reversed, I certainly would have been. Leaning on an old cliché, I stated flatly "What a small world."

Despite my efforts to tone down this chance encounter, disappointment screamed from Dempsey's face. I wanted to offer an explanation but before I could say anything Dempsey said, "See you guys later" and walked away. I felt bad for him, but my guilt only lasted as long as it took to take a second look at Jaylynn Sinclair.

"So, what do you do here Ms. Sinclair?"

"I am a nurse at King Abdul Aziz Hospital. Lovelen tells me you are with the government working on an Engineering project of some sort."

"To be more accurate I am an independent contractor working with a group of federal engineers who are consulting with the Saudis on construction projects in three dozen cities in the Kingdom."

"That sounds interesting, how long have you been here?"

"I am in the third month of the last year of a two year contract, but I will probably extend to a third year. Some elements of the contract are running behind schedule and have been moved back to begin just about the time my two years will be up. The Saudis have asked me to consider sticking around an extra year to help move forward with those phases of the project. What about you?"

"I have been in the Kingdom about nine months, but I am in the sixteenth month of a two year contract that was begun by a nurse who got kicked out of the country for fraternizing with a man. She had only been in the Kingdom seven months when they sent her home. The man she was with was not her husband. They were caught kissing in public. There were 17 months left on her contract, so I was brought in to finish it out. I have about eight months to go before I return to the States. A friend of mine, who is already working here, contacted me and asked if I was interested. I said yes. She submitted my name as a replacement for the previous nurse and I was chosen. So, you say you might be extending. Sounds like you really like it here."

"Naturally I would like to finish the work I was hired to do but yes I like Saudi Arabia and I also have personal reasons for wanting to stay a little longer. When I first arrived I set a few private objectives for myself that I have yet to achieve. I hope to get them done before I return to the States."

"How long do you think it will take to finish your work at the Ministry?"

"Come on Ms. Sinclair you have been in the Kingdom long enough to know how things go here."

"You are right. How do they say it Insha'Allah."

"Insha'Allah indeed."

"You said you have private objectives that you would like to get done before going back to the States. What besides work attracts you to this country?"

"First of all being here is a heck of an experience, as I am sure you agree. I am learning a lot of fascinating things about this country, things I never knew before or ever saw in a documentary or heard about in the news.

And yet there is so much more to know. I want to learn as much as I can while I am here."

"My God, you are exactly the way Lovelen described. Do you know my sister thinks you bit off more than you can chew by coming here?"

"She almost convinced me of that before I left the country and I nearly canceled my contract on account of your sister. But I do not have any uncertainties about this country anymore, and I can hardly express how happy I am that I got on the plane and came to Saudi Arabia."

Watching Jaylynn smile and her body movements proved the Sinclair genes were strong. Jaylynn was definitely Lovelen's sibling. Both of them were beautiful. Jaylynn's complexion was slightly darker than her sisters and she was shorter in stature, but they shared that same dazzling smile and I loved the way their faces danced when they talked. As I examined Jaylynn's features, I naturally made comparisons to Lovelen. But it must have appeared to Jaylynn that I was staring because she did not react too well to the way I was looking at her face. The enthusiasm she had shown when we first met cooled a bit and she stopped smiling.

Switching gears I inquired with a serious face, "Tell me Ms. Sinclair, what made you leave America and come to King Abdul-Aziz hospital?"

"That is a long story and will take a better setting than this to tell."

"Time is something I have plenty of around here Ms. Sinclair. I am all ears," I offered eagerly.

Jaylynn teased, "Do not waste your charms on me Mr. Sneed. I knew you were good looking before I met you, and I am not impressed."

One of my secret talents is imitating actors. I do a decent Humphrey Bogart. Usually I keep this ability to myself but on that occasion I chose to mimic the great Bogey and bragged, "Yes you are. You were taken with me the moment I walked into the room, even before my friend said my name and you asked who I was. You just refuse to admit what is so obvious. It is as clear as the nose on your face, so stop stalling and admit it - you are impressed with me."

Jaylynn laughed with delight and said, "Oh aren't you full of yourself. Tell you what Adam Humphrey Bogart Sneed, if you really want to hear my story, come to brunch with me on Friday."

"That sounds great. Should I pick you up or do you want to meet somewhere?"

"Let's meet at the APO facility off Airport Road. I assume you know where that is."

"Yes, that is where Dempsey works… the guy you were talking with when I came in…" There was a tinge of concern in my voice because I was wondering if something might be going on between Jaylynn and Dempsey. Dempsey seemed quite upset when he walked away earlier. Did he have a reason to be? Had he been trying to talk to Jaylynn before I entered the picture? If so, meeting at his compound might not be a good idea. Chances were our rendezvous would be observed by Dempsey and that could cause problems.

Jaylynn sensed I was wondering about her relationship with Dempsey and said "not that it is any of your business Mr. Sneed, but the first time I met Mr. Stevens was seven months ago when I went to the APO to mail a package to Lovelen. Since then he and I have run into each other every now and then. Tonight was one of those times. It was mere coincidence, just like running into you tonight was a coincidence. I will see you Friday morning at 8 sharp. Be on time. I will not wait if you are late. Good night Mr. Sneed."

I did not mind Jaylynn being a little miffed at me when she walked away, especially now that I knew Dempsey had never been in the picture. Even better she did not cancel our date. That had to count for something. Although we had just met, I got an early good feeling about Jaylynn Sinclair.

There was one more thing I needed to settle before going to bed that night. I called Larry Corbin. "Sorry to call so late Larry, but I think I met the nurse you told me about – the one you said was named Lynn or Carolyn. Her name is Jaylynn Sinclair. I met her sister Lovelen a few days before I left to come to Arabia. Lovelen is dating my best friend…" After a few minutes of comparing notes we both became convinced Jaylynn was the same nurse he had met. That mystery was finally solved. Deductive reasoning had argued Jaylynn was the same nurse Larry met, but I wanted to eliminate any doubts. If things worked out between us, I did not want anybody walking up on us the way I had walked up on her and Dempsey.

⌘⌘⌘⌘⌘⌘⌘⌘⌘⌘⌘⌘⌘

Chapter 22

Newly inaugurated President Ronald Regan brought the remaining hostages home from Tehran, which was a great relief to their families and friends, the nation as a whole, and every U.S. expatriate in the Middle East.

When I arrived at Fahad's house on Thursday, Jabbar was sitting on the floor smoking a cigarette and talking with Bashir. Jabbar was definitely Black; there was no question about that. His skin was as dark as coal and he had a smile as white as polished ivory. I know that description sounds like a cliché but it is accurate. I might have been a couple of years older than Jabbar but we were in the same age bracket. Jabbar was the first Saudi I met that wore his ak-gal cocked to the side rather than flush on the crown of his head. It reminded me of the way guys in the States point the bill of their baseball caps off to the side rather than over their foreheads. Fahad formally introduced him as Jabbar Al-Bughawi.

We shook hands and started sizing each other up as Black men typically do. When I looked into his eyes I sensed that Jabbar, like me, had not been fooled by Fahad who thought he was being clever when he rigged this dance contest between us, because that is exactly what was about to get started - a dance contest.

Unlike my previous visit, this time I was eager to dance. I could not wait to see how talented the best dancer in Riyadh was.

Bashir started the music. When I began dancing, the only question in my mind was 'how long will this brother from the East sit and watch before he gets up and tries to outdo me?'

Jabbar did not sit still fifteen seconds. No sooner had I begun, an impish grin spread across his face and he jumped up and joined me on the floor. I had expected to see him perform a dance from his repertoire of wedding performances, but the man could have walked into any club in the West and been right at home.

Fahad and Bashir were delirious, applauding and singing along with the music as Jabbar and I danced like we had been dancing together all our lives. When the next song started, Jabbar switched to Bedouin style dance and invited "Come Mr. Adam let me show you how we do it." This time Fahad and Bashir joined us. It was a fun evening that I will never forget. The three of them probably could have gone on until dawn, but I said goodnight around 11 p.m. because I was not going to allow anything to interfere with my date with Jaylynn Sinclair the next morning.

When I said goodbye to Fahad and Bashir, Jabbar asked me to drive him home. Like most Saudis I had met to that point, Jabbar had some English under his belt. He gave directions to his destination and along the way pummeled me with questions about America. Jabbar turned out to be an even bigger fan of Michael Jackson than young Bashir.

It wasn't until we got to the destination that Jabbar admitted it was not his residence, but rather the home of one of his friends. He got out of the car, walked around to the driver's side and said, "You can find your way to your house from here, isn't it?"

"Yes, I think so."

"Good. Come get me tomorrow and I will show you Riyadh."

"Thank you for the invitation, I would like that very much."

"But do not come here. Can you meet me on Television Street?"

"At the tower, okay, what time?"

"1:00."

Since I was having brunch with Jaylynn I wanted to give myself some wiggle room. I suggested instead, "Why don't we meet at 4:00."

"Ah, you have a date tomorrow. I know you Americans."

"I wish - See you at 4:00."

ﻼﻼﻼﻼﻼﻼﻼﻼﻼﻼﻼﻼﻼﻼﻼ

Chapter 23

Friday morning, I got to the APO facility fifteen minutes early. Jaylynn was already there sitting in the back seat of a car parked near the main gate. As soon as I pulled up she got out and came over to my car. When I saw that she was covered from head to shoulder with the traditional Abbaya, I decided to have a little fun with her.

"Good morning Adam."

"Sabah al Khair, ya Habibiti (good morning, my love)." It was an expression an Arab would only say to a girlfriend.

She gave me a strange look then said, "Look, we can do this one of two ways. Either you can leave your car here and ride with us, or you can be my chauffeur for the morning."

Living as a single male in Riyadh had shielded me from most of the inconveniences western women had to deal with in Saudi Arabia. About the only thing I knew about them was that they could not drive, smoke in public, or walk around with their arms and legs uncovered.

I happily consented to Jaylynn's suggestion. "I would love to be your driver today Ms. Sinclair." Participating in the local custom of being a designated driver for a female was another milestone in my tour. And I could foresee that spending time with Jaylynn was not only going to be fun, it would also give me a closer view of how the other sex lived in the desert kingdom.

"Good, I was hoping you would say that. Let me tell Abud he can go. I will be right back."

Jaylynn dismissed her driver, returned, slid into the back seat and instructed, "Take Dammam road please."

166

I was happy to have Jaylynn's company, but the moment she got in the back seat I decided I did not like the arrangement. Forget the debate over whether women should drive, why did they have to sit in the back seat? I wanted Jaylynn up front next to me.

Jaylynn had criticisms about the system as well. No sooner had I pulled off she started venting. "I really appreciate your doing this Adam. I know you did not have to agree to drive me, but I have to tell you this is a nice break getting to ride with a fellow American. You would not believe how creepy some of these drivers can be, and the way they leer at the nurses through the rearview mirror is scandalous. Some of the things they have the nerve to say to women - they have absolutely no shame. The guy I rode with this morning though is very nice. His name is Abud. I am always relieved when he is assigned to be my driver. But the other guys, the way they act you would think they never saw a woman before. If they are not calling me habibiti and inappropriate expressions like that, they are saying much worse."

"Oh, I am sorry Ms. Sinclair. I did not mean anything by what…"

"Adam - I knew you were joking. I am not upset with you and please… call me Jaylynn."

"Okay Jaylynn. None of those guys have ever tried anything with you or any of the other nurses, have they," I inquired delicately?

"Not directly. But most of the drivers are African and speak a fair amount of English. Usually they are polite, but some let it be known, in not so subtle ways, that they are more than ready to offer their 'services,' if you know what I am saying."

"How disgusting, I had no idea you ladies had to put up with things like that."

"In a way it is nice to hear you say that Adam, but I wonder if your not knowing about our struggles is a good thing or a bad thing."

"What do you mean?"

"Well, the fact that you have no idea what Western females go through here could mean you do not date or sleep around a lot, like so many guys are desperately trying to do in this city, or it could mean you do not deal with females at all. I have heard this place is a magnet for guys that do not deal with women."

Having my sexual orientation sniffed out early in a relationship was something I was used to from having lived in D.C., a city where some guys dated women on one side of town and kept male lovers in other parts of the city. Though Jaylynn and I were not in a relationship, I could not blame her for wanting to know up front which flag I served under. All the same, I did not plan to reveal much about myself until I had some idea what direction our relationship might be headed.

"A guy could have legitimate reasons for not knowing what Western women go through here without being stereotyped. But what you are implying is a big topic for a first date, don't you think?"

"Date - you think this is a date? Whatever gave you that idea?"

Oops, wrong direction. Quickly I adlibbed, "We have a couple of guys in our project that everyone suspects are gay, but I have never met anyone here that is openly so Western or Arab."

As soon as the words came out of my mouth I realized my answer sounded vague, and probably in her mind evasive. Chances were she would misinterpret them, so to be more precise in describing myself I said, "Personally, I have been celibate since six months before coming to Arabia. I do not know how much my friend Barry has told your sister about me, but I swore off females and dating in order to center my energies and attention on this project."

"Yes, I heard something about that. So are you saying you have not engaged in any kind of intimacy since arriving in the Kingdom?"

"Plus the six months right before I got here, that is correct."

"How long have you been here now?"

"Like I told you Wednesday night, I have been here a little over a year," I answered.

"Counting the six months in the States, that makes a year and a half. It must be taxing on you having gone this long without intimacy?"

"Not really. I grew up in a strictly fundamentalist Christian household. Extramarital sex was as big a taboo in our church as it is in this country, only we never beheaded or stoned anyone for committing fornication or adultery. Truth is I was still a virgin when I entered college at 18, and remained that way until I moved out of my parents' house."

"How old were you when you left your parents' home?"

"I was a few weeks shy of my 22nd birthday."

"How old are you now?"

"Twenty-eight and I hope you don't mind me saying this, but I feel like I am being questioned rather thoroughly here, especially given the fact this is not a date. You know more about me now than your sister does, and I have only known you less than two days."

"Sorry, my friends say I tend to be overly inquisitive when it comes to people's private lives. But I appreciate your being straightforward with me and I must say I am impressed that you never hesitated with your answers. I have actually learned a couple of things about you that I like."

"Really, pray tell what might they be?"

"Mainly that you are honest, plus you appear to be someone that can be trusted and that is important to me."

"Are you looking for someone to trust Jaylynn?"

"Are you kidding? I am a single woman living 11,000 miles from home, in the middle of a desert surrounded by millions of horny men who rarely see females for the first 20 or 30 years of their lives – you bet I am looking for people I can trust."

"You can trust me."

"Every man says that Adam. Most women find out too late if a guy is in reality, untrustworthy. But like I said I am beginning to think it might be possible to trust you. I guess I must trust you to some extent because I am riding in your car. On top of that I am taking you to meet the man I trust most in this desert."

I was not happy to hear she planned to introduce me to another man, and the fact that he was the one she trusted most in the Kingdom made me wonder what kind of relationship she had with him. Furthermore, what about brunch? Were we still going? I wanted to come right out and ask who this guy was, but I knew that would not be cool. To fish out whether this man she trusted was a relative of hers I asked, "What do your parents think about you coming to Arabia?"

"Lovelen and I are orphans. Our parents died when we were young. They were killed in a car accident when I was four. Lovelen was seven. She remembers their faces and says she will never forget the sound of their voices. But for me they are a blur in my memory. I would not know their faces at all if it wasn't for a couple of fading photographs we have of them."

"What are their names?"

"Dad's name is Lovell Leonard Sinclair and mom, Jane Lynette Sinclair."

It is funny how much a little information can tell about a person, even after they are dead. The names Lovelen and Jaylynn were concatenations of the first parts of their parent's names. What a nice tribute from these devoted parents to their daughters. Based on how beautiful their daughters were, I figured Lovell and Jane must have been a handsome couple. "Did you bring any of those photographs with you to Arabia," I asked?

"I always keep my favorite one with me," she said as she opened her purse. Jaylynn passed an old worn photograph to me over my right shoulder. The Sinclair's were very attractive. Lovell Leonard was handsome, tall and thin. Jane Lynette was short and as stunning as her oldest daughter. The photograph had been taken at a party while the couple was dancing together.

"Your parents were nice looking people Jaylynn."

"Thanks."

Although I could not see her face, I got the feeling the walk down memory lane had triggered a bit of emotional sadness in Jaylynn. She fell quiet and appeared to withdraw introspectively. Out of respect, I stopped talking.

Twenty minutes outside of Riyadh, the outline of a vast compound appeared ahead in the distance. I had missed this site the day Abdullah and I traveled to Dammam. As we drew closer, the complex seemed to stretch endlessly across the sands. Jaylynn directed me to the main gate where she got out, opened the front passenger door and slid into the seat next to me. While making this transfer she flashed her credentials to one of the guards and the bar rose. As I drove into the compound Jaylynn removed her Abbaya. Now that I could see her face again, I realized she was prettier than I had recalled.

"Turn right at the next corner and follow the road around until you get to Arizona Drive," Jaylynn instructed.

The compound was very much like an American suburb. Every home had a front lawn and garage and there were schools, playgrounds and basketball courts which indicated a sizeable population of children in the complex.

Since it was Friday the compound was relatively quiet. A few adults were out jogging, but for the most part the streets were empty.

From Arizona Drive Jaylynn directed me to Blues Alley Lane. After turning off the Lane onto Beverly Hills Circle, we came upon houses that were twice the size of those at the entrance to the complex. Several dozen automobiles were parked at one of the residences up ahead. When we got near to it Jaylynn announced, "This is where we are going. Park anywhere you can find a spot."

I parked as close to the house as I could and we headed for the front door. "Hurry Adam or everything is going to start without us. I hate being late."

"When you said brunch, I thought we would be going to The Empty Quarter Inn or some place like that, not someone's house for a home cooked meal," I mentioned casually. "It looks like they have quite a guest list. Is this a party of some kind?"

Jaylynn did not respond. She rang the bell and instantly, as if we had been expected, an attractive and well dressed middle aged Black American woman opened the door. After giving me a puzzled glance, she welcomed Jaylynn with a warm embrace.

"First Lady Doreen Strong, this is a friend of Lovelen's. She asked me to look him up when I got to Saudi Arabia. I finally ran into him on… yesterday. His name is Adam Sneed. Adam this is First Lady Doreen Strong."

"Welcome Adam. It is always nice to see a new face at the service. Come and meet my husband."

Jaylynn had tricked me into going to church. I wanted to give her the stare of disapproval, but she walked ahead of me and was careful not to look back. I was sure she could guess what I was thinking.

Christian groups met in private homes, out of respect for the fact we were guests in an Islamic country where the open practice of Christianity is forbidden. I was aware of these groups before arriving in the country, but up to that point in my tour had never tried to find them or attend a service.

Pastor Strong looked like a typical Black southern preacher. He was an inch or two shorter than me and weighed around 250 pounds. From his appearance alone I got the impression he spewed fire and brimstone when he preached. It turned out I was completely mistaken about the man. When he opened his mouth, Pastor Strong sounded as gentle as a lamb. His soft, warm voice oozed with fatherly affection. Frankly, the incongruity between the man's physical appearance and the sound of his voice was a little jarring. Looking me straight in my eyes and clasping my hand between his powerful mitts he addressed me in the most peaceful tone, "Hello young man, I am Pastor Phillip Strong. It is so good to have you with us this morning."

Pastor Strong completely disarmed me. I even forgot I was upset with Jaylynn for pulling the rug from under me with her bogus brunch invitation. A powerful urge came over me to confess my sins to this lovable shepherd.

"We had better get to the sanctuary. It is time for the service to begin," First Lady Doreen recommended.

The sanctuary was a converted dining room jammed with a makeshift pulpit and a few rows of chairs for the choir. More seats were available in adjacent rooms into which the congregation overflowed. Every seat was occupied and enough people were standing to fill several more rooms of equal size. Jaylynn and I joined the standees.

Listening to Pastor Strong speak that morning was an enjoyable experience. Particularly interesting was when he spoke about Christian tolerance toward our Muslim hosts. To quote Pastor Strong, "our Muslim brothers have an incorrect view of our Lord Jesus, but they do believe in the Almighty. As they put it, 'Allahu Akbar, ashadu illahu Allah - God is great and there is no God but God.' Their faith in the Almighty Father makes it possible for us to work beside them as brothers in this country. They may not be our brothers in the faith of the Lord, but they are our brothers when it comes to faith in God."

For some reason Pastor Strong reminded me of the Samaritan who rescued me from the clutches of that would-be defrauder at the gas station. I imagined if he and my Samaritan ever met, they would have one incredible spiritual exchange.

As things turned out, Jaylynn had only misled me slightly about brunch. After service when the majority of the congregation departed, selected guests, including Jaylynn and me, were ushered to a back patio where a feast of down home delights awaited. All of my favorite dishes were laid out in a delectable looking array. Potato salad, barbecued chicken, cornbread, rice, string beans, sweet tea, macaroni and cheese, okra and corn, turkey wings, beef short ribs, salmon cakes, mashed potatoes, garden salad, sweet potato pie, and what came as a surprise in a dinner setting, grits. The food was magnificent. Doreen Strong also did something I had never seen anyone do before. She dropped a half pound of cheese right into the large bowl of hot steaming grits. Pastor Strong grabbed a large ladle and stirred the grits until the cheese melted. I had never eaten grits with dinner before and it was my very first time eating them with cheese. It would not be my last. They were awesome. Everything was tasty and quite satisfying, although Doreen Strong repeatedly apologized about not having fresh greens to serve. She said, "I cannot find them anywhere in this country." Brunch was wonderful and reminded me of Sunday dinner at my parents' home when I was growing up.

Pastor Strong dominated the dinner conversation. His soft speech captured my attention as completely as did Al Dennison's booming voice. The pastor was a man of many experiences. He regaled us with stories of births, deaths, weddings and famine from the time when he was a young aspiring minister and member of his father's church in rural Georgia during the aftermath of the Spanish Influenza and the Great Depression.

When Pastor Strong finished sharing his experiences, First Lady Doreen spoke up. From her first words it was clear she was curious about me, specifically my relationship with 'Sister Sinclair'. I knew in her mind she thought she was being protective, but she made me feel uncomfortable and unwelcome.

"How long do you plan on seeing Sister Sinclair? I mean is this a serious relationship or just a fly by night thing for you?"

Was she kidding, asking me questions like that? How could a wonderful man like Pastor Strong be married to such a tactless woman? After knowing me only a few hours she was treating me like a wolf caught trying to steal one of the precious lambs away from the flock. If Jaylynn and I had been dating, her concerns may have been justified to some extent, but even then not because I was a wolf. For all the First Lady knew, this was our first time together. In fact when Jaylynn introduced me that morning, she plainly stated we had just met. Actually Jaylynn stated that we met 'yesterday,' a little white lie that did not throw me at all for reasons I will explain later. So I could not understand why the First Lady assumed something was going on between us or that I had intentions of any kind toward Jaylynn. Besides, it was much too soon for someone that had just met me to be putting me in the hot seat with respect to any possible intentions toward Jaylynn. Even if I were inclined to pursue Jaylynn romantically, I would never have indicated this to her so soon after we met and particularly not to people in her church.

Getting the third degree from First Lady Doreen brought back painful memories. When I was a child any member of our church that got romantically involved with individuals outside the congregation, always caused a stir. I was beginning to think I might have made a mistake in accepting Jaylynn's brunch invitation. Then Pastor Strong whispered something in his wife's ear and the grilling stopped. But I knew the reprieve was only temporary.

Jaylynn took advantage of the lull in the conversation to speak up. Addressing Pastor Strong she explained, "Adam is a friend of Lovelen. Actually, I really do not know him. We only met last… yesterday. When I told Lovelen about the job at King Abdul Aziz hospital, she asked me to look up a friend of hers when I got to Riyadh. She told me his name was Adam Sneed. I asked every Black American I met if they knew him. Those that said they did promised to tell him I was looking for him. I never heard anything until… yesterday afternoon. I happened to be talking to one of the workers from the APO facility, when a couple of guys walked in. One of them mentioned Adam by name so I introduced myself. Adam was very surprised when I told him who I was. I do not think he knew Lovelen had a sister."

Jaylynn was lying like a professional, but I understood perfectly what was happening. I kept a straight face to be as supportive as I could while she weaved this unfamiliar, yet highly entertaining tale about our first encounter.

"So basically he is a stranger to you and you really do not know anything about this man," Doreen responded, insinuating herself back into the conversation while boring her eyes into mine.

"No I never knew him before … his friend mentioned his name. But I think I know more about him than he realizes."

"Really, what do you think you know about this man?"

"For one thing, he and his best friend Barry Shipman used to compete to find the most beautiful women to date, and they had a special test to see if the women were intelligent or dumb."

I bowed my head and silently cursed Barry. Most of all, I wanted to strangle Jaylynn. Knowing about my past was one thing, but why did she have to tell First Lady Strong those details? And why didn't she let me know up front that she had all that information about me?

"Oh no, no, no this man does not sound like the kind of character that should be hanging around a decent Christian woman."

"I disagree. Adam is exactly the kind of man that should be in this church. Do you think I would choose the company of a man like the one I just described unless I had a good reason? I told you those things about his past because I wanted you to know how much Adam has changed. Now he wants the best life for himself, and frankly I would be flattered if he were ever interested in someone like me. You do not know this about Adam, but he subjected himself to a life of celibacy and has kept at it almost two years now without wavering. Nowadays, that is impressive by anybody's standards. On top of that, when I invited him to church this morning he was eager to come."

At hearing about my vow of celibacy the First Lady brightened. "Now that is wonderful news! So tell me Adam, where did you meet Jaylynn's sister?"

"My best friend Barry introduced me to Lovelen a week before I came to Saudi Arabia."

"And this Barry person, how does he know Lovelen?"

Jaylynn broke in before I could say anything in response. "Lady Doreen, I know you are concerned about our welfare, and my sister and I really appreciate you for that, but believe me everything is fine with us. And I…"

Pastor Strong came to the rescue, "What kind of work do you do here in the Kingdom Adam?"

This was a question I did not mind answering. For the next half hour I gave an abbreviated synopsis of my journey from near unemployment to recruitment and, as a bonus, how I met Lovelen, but only the parts about the business relationship between Lovelen and Barry's employer and the three of us going skating together. I ended with a rundown of some of the events of my first year in Saudi Arabia, and since I had everyone's attention shared my adventure at the gas station. "During your sermon this morning that incident came to mind when you mentioned that it is important for us to get along with our Muslim brothers. I think you and my rescuer have a lot in common. Wouldn't it be great Pastor Strong if the two of you got the chance to meet?"

"Thank you for sharing that Brother Adam, and please come back and tell us more of your experiences. I would love to talk with you again young man."

Pastor Strong was cool. If he managed to keep his wife on ice, I could see myself going to their church on a regular basis.

Jaylynn got into the backseat for our return to Riyadh and instructed, "Take me back to the APO facility. I will call for a car from there."

"I do not mind taking you to your dorm."

"Thank you for offering, but no. If I show up at the gate with a driver who is not from our motor pool it will raise all sorts of questions. Then if you are tailed by Saudi agents and they find out you are American and we have been spending time together, that plus the fact neither of us are married, it could put us both in jeopardy. More than likely they would throw me out of the country, just like the nurse I replaced."

"If they think I am a chauffeur, why would they give me a second thought? And unless we get caught kissing or holding hands, why would they care about us spending time together?"

"Maybe they wouldn't. But you have to consider a few things like; first of all, you really do not look like one of the African drivers. And secondly, all it takes is for someone to make an accusation that we are doing things like kissing or holding hands and we would come under close scrutiny. The nurse I replaced had friends in the dorm, so I do not want to take any chances."

"Do you think we were followed from the APO this morning?"

"That is a remote possibility, but even if they did the hospital knows I come out here every weekend. Still, I doubt we were followed because Abud was assigned to drive me this morning."

"But your driver did not take you to church today. Do you think they said anything to him when he got back to the motor pool early?"

"Like I told you this morning, Abud is a good guy. I also consider him a friend. Believe me, Abud is not stupid. He has been dealing with the Saudis a lot longer than either of us, and this is not the first time I rode to church with someone else. The last time it was with a family I know. Whenever Abud is my driver and he does not take me to church, he hangs out downtown to take care of personal business before going back to the dorm. Abud does not want the Motor Pool knowing where he is all the time either. We always work things out to our mutual benefit. That is why I know he would never jam me up or betray me, no matter what."

"You trust him then."

"Yes I do."

"Jaylynn I have to ask, what on earth possessed you to mention that stuff about me and Barry testing our dates and to Doreen Strong of all people? What were you thinking?"

"Forgive me Adam; I was only trying to put her off your scent. She can be a bloodhound when she gets after someone and you would be surprised how many people she knows in the States. Now that she has your name, she will be getting in touch with her First Ladies network. By this time next week they will have tracked down your whole family. A few days from now she will know almost everything there is to know about you, and your brothers and sisters, that is, if you have any. Basically, I was trying to smooth the way before telling her about your vow of celibacy. She would never have believed me if I came right out and said you were under a vow. Guys have walked into our church in the past and claimed they were saving themselves for the Lord. So I thought, why not tell her the worst thing I know about you then neutralize it with your vow? That way she can't fish out anything worse, no matter whom she talks to back in the States unless there are worse things about you that I do not know."

Jaylynn had paused to give me a chance to come clean if I wanted to confess worse sins, but I literally had nothing to add. In fact, secretly I was e turning cartwheels in my head for having neglected church when I left Pittsburgh. The church people in the nation's capital knew anything about me. Lady Doreen could only work with the things Jaylynn found out about me through Lovelen. I was confident that if Jaylynn knew more than she had already revealed that morning, she now understood how important it would be for her to keep it to herself.

Jaylynn went on to say "I figured if the last thing she heard about you was something positive, it could help diffuse any negative thoughts she may have formed in her head."

Her strategy sounded a little quirky to me, but for both our sakes I hoped it worked. Changing the subject I asked, "Tell me about your job Jaylynn. What do you do at the hospital?"

"The same thing nurses do at hospitals in America. Over here I primarily work with female patients. You would be surprised how difficult it is to get women in this part of the world to accept modern medicine. It is a real struggle with some of them."

"I have no doubts about that whatsoever. In fact I could tell you a horror story about medical procedures at the DMV that would make your skin crawl."

"Medical procedures at the DMV; you must mean blood tests right."

"That's right. But tell me something, do you have any friends at the hospital?"

"One of the doctors I work with is especially friendly with me, and because I know you are going to ask yes he's married. Doctor Sayeed talks about his wife and two year old son constantly. I don't think I have ever met a man so much in love with his family. His wife is the center of his life, and his son – he would give his life for that little boy. I have been invited to dinner at their home at the end of this month. I am looking forward to meeting Mrs. Sayeed. Dr. Sayeed showed me a picture of her. She was not wearing her veil. Mrs. Sayeed is gorgeous. You know a veil does not guarantee the woman underneath is a beauty, but Doctor Sayeed found himself a good one. Doctor Sayeed and a few others like him have always been respectful toward me."

"What about Black Saudi doctors? Have you met any?"

"No."

"Have you met any Black Saudis at all at the hospital?"

"I have had Black Saudi patients."

"All of them women?"

"Yes."

"Okay, let's get back to Frau Doreen. What was that interrogation all about? I felt like I was facing the Gestapo."

"What can I say? Doreen has looked after me and Lovelen since our parents died. She is our guardian angel. Maybe I didn't handle things right this morning, but you have to keep in mind I did not know we were going to meet this week. Inviting you to brunch was a knee jerk reaction when you asked to hear the story about how I came to Saudi Arabia. If it makes you feel any better, I admit you have a valid point. In retrospect I might have been better to tell the Strong's about you first, and wait for them to suggest inviting you to church."

"That's another bone I want to pick with you. You never said anything about going to church this morning. You said we were going to brunch. If I had known you were taking me to church, I would have told you it was not a good idea. I grew up in the church, so I know how people like Doreen Strong think when a stranger walks into the congregation. My mother is like that. Now, thanks to you, I will have to attend services several months before she even considers trusting me."

"So you plan to come to church again."

"Do I have any other choice? I mean if I want to see you again, I have to earn the trust of Frau Doreen and that requires going to church regularly and probably a whole lot more."

"So, you want to see me again?"

From past experience I knew the position I would be putting myself in if I answered that question the way she expected. Jaylynn would have the upper hand, and I would be chasing after her like a lost puppy. Not Mr. Sneed, nope, not me. "Just one minute Ms. Sinclair, you and your first lady friend have asked me enough questions for one day. Let me ask you something. Do you want to see me again? How about you answer me that?"

She paused for a moment. I figured it was for dramatic effect. Finally she admitted, "I wouldn't mind."

"Then that is all that needs to be said."

"Okay, but if you are going to convince First Lady Doreen that you are a nice guy that can be trusted, you will have your work cut out for you and that is all I have to say on that."

"Hey, I can do this. Like I told you, I grew up in the church. I know what to expect. That is why I did not say anything when you kept telling the Strong's we met yesterday instead of Wednesday. See, you thought I wasn't paying attention. We both know that if you had said we met Wednesday night the Strong's would have known automatically we met at a party. Then you would have been the one being raked over the coals by Miss Doreen."

"I can see you were not lying about having experience in the church. You are going to need it."

Despite the Abbaya, I could tell Jaylynn was smiling when I took a quick peek in the rear view. She saw me look and made the sweetest comment, "We are probably going to be good friends after all Adam Sneed."

Encouraged by the pleasant way our conversation was going, I grew bolder. "By the way, thank you for that nice cover up this morning."

"What are you talking about?"

"The way you cleaned up after what you said about Barry and me testing our dates. Remember you said I was the kind of man that wanted the best for himself and how you would feel flattered if I ever became interested in you?"

"Oh that. I was really thinking on the fly when I came up with that, so don't hold me to any of it."

"Trust me; I will definitely be holding you to that part. But do you mind if I be very candid with you for a minute?"

"Go ahead."

"I still do not see why you had to tell Doreen Strong about Barry and me testing our dates, which was a bit of information I was not aware you knew I might add. Jaylynn you have known this lady much longer than me, and I am not convinced your tactic to throw her off with that information is going to work."

"Actually that was partly meant for you. It was my way of putting you on notice that I know your tricks and will not fall for any shenanigans. Telling Doreen was a backup for my protection, in case …"

"No, don't stop. Finish what you were saying. In case what?"

"Nothing…"

"Sounds like you don't trust yourself Ms. Sinclair, and that's okay. Sometimes I feel uncertain about a course of action or whether or not I should deal with a particular person. But for the record, I still think it was a mistake to tell the Gestapo lady those things."

"You are probably right. Can you forgive me?"

I was beginning to like Jaylynn's personality. She was fun to be around. But I was not going to let her off the hook too easily. Playfully, I answered her "I will think about it, but I am very, very, very hurt."

"No, what you are is too much."

"I take it the Strong's have no idea you go out to parties."

"Oh God no, you should hear what Pastor Strong calls the Vinnell compound."

"Let me guess, Babylon?"

"That too, but most days he calls it Sodom and Gomorrah."

"Church people are something else."

I could not think of anything more to say, other than things that might get me in trouble with this faithful member of Pastor Strong's church.

Knowing that Doreen Strong was aware I had objectified women in the past, made me feel a little helpless and under the gun. Getting her to get past those details and see me for the nice guy I was, would be a challenge. But I had to win her trust if I wanted to pursue a relationship with Jaylynn. And a relationship seemed to be a foregone conclusion, now that Jaylynn and I had pretty much admitted mutual interest. As far as Barry was concerned, he was due some kind of punishment for violating the man code by telling Lovelen our dating strategies.

"Seriously Adam, would you like to attend church next week?"

"Now if you had asked if I would like to attend church *with you* next week, I would have had a ready answer. But attend church just for the sake of going to a service; that I have to think about. After all, there are other churches here. It might be more practical to check a few of them out first, before I commit to one in particular."

"You are dead set on turning this into a date."

"Date who said anything about dating, I thought we were talking about church."

"Okay Adam Sneed would you like to attend church *with me* next week?"

"That's Mr. Adam Sneed to you, and yes I would be honored to attend services with you next Friday."

"You are so silly Mr. Adam Sneed. If we are going to be that formal you can address me as Ms. Jaylynn Sinclair."

"Nope, just Jaylynn or maybe Jay, yes, that is what I am going to call you - Jay."

"Then I will call you Ad."

"Ad? Why would you call me that?"

"If you can call me Jay, I can call you Ad. Now if you want me to call you Adam, you will have to call me Jaylynn."

"Ad actually does not sound half bad. A little short though, don't you think? I will think on it and let you know my decision next week."

"You do that."

When we reached the APO, I asked the one question I had delayed bringing up the whole trip. "How about giving me your phone number, you know, so I can call if something comes up and I am unable to make it next Friday?"

"Phone number – hmmm – let me see – a male calling me at the dormitory on a phone shared by twenty other women. Forget it - that idea is out of the question. I will be here at the same time next Friday and will wait fifteen minutes. If you do not show, I will have my driver take me on to church. If we are not here when you arrive, because you were running late or something like that... I think you know the way; you can get to church on your own. Now if we miss each other and you get to church and find out I could not get there, for whatever reason; stay and enjoy the service. A little bit of church will not hurt you."

"I can deal with going to church on my own so long as I get to eat brunch afterward. One thing though, if I do show up at the gate by myself will I have any problems getting into the compound?"

"It is a western facility. I am sure you have identification showing you are American."

"That's true, I do."

Jaylynn went into the APO to call her motor pool. Minutes later she returned and advised "I am going to wait here at the gate. Please do not stick around, in case they send someone other than Abud. I will be alright, the guards are on hand. See you next Friday."

I drove around the block a few times until Jaylynn's car came. On my last circuit I spotted Dempsey watching near the guard post. I felt it was time we had a talk. Dempsey stood where he was until I parked. When I approached the front gate he turned and started walking away. He kept several steps ahead of me. I followed him into the Rec Center. He must have turned aside somewhere because when I got inside I did not see him. I waited for five minutes or so before giving up and heading back to the gate.

I had reached the guard post when I heard his voice. Coming up from behind he said, "Okay dude, you have five minutes. Say what you have to say and then be on your way."

"Dempsey listen, we both know what it is like here with there being so few sisters to talk to. But Jaylynn, I never knew she existed before the other night. The only reason she knew me is because I know her sister Lovelen. Lovelen and I met the week before I came to Saudi Arabia. Lovelen had just started dating my best friend but she never told me she had a sister. I admit, I meant to ask if she had a sister, because Lovelen is really beautiful man... it's... its kind of hard to describe how beautiful she is... but that's a different story. Okay, Lovelen was dating my best friend so I was wondering if she had a sister or a friend in the modeling business, she's a model by the way, and I figured I might luck out just like Barry. Like I said I meant to ask her ... if she had a sister or ... a friend ... anyway the three of us ... Lovelen, Barry and me ... we got caught up in some other stuff, time flew by and before I knew it I was on my way out of the country. So after all was said and done, I never got around to asking Lovelen if she had a sister."

Dempsey was turning away. Even though my five minutes had not run out, I pleaded "Come on man, five minutes is not enough time to explain all of this. Everything I just told you is the truth man. I was completely surprised to meet Jaylynn Wednesday night, and even more surprised when she said she was Lovelen's sister. Honestly Dempsey I had no idea she existed, so I never expected to meet her."

"Let me get this straight. The way you tell it, you met a girl and told her you were going to Saudi Arabia. This girl happens to have a sister working in Saudi Arabia, but she does not mention this sister to you. Months later you happen to run across this sister, mind you just as I am trying to talk to her, and now this morning I see the two of you coming back from a date. Oh yes, that sounds like your everyday boy meets girl story to me. No, strike that, it sounds like a lie."

"Dempsey, I have been condensing things here because you gave me so little time. Man if you are going to react this way, I have no choice but to start from the beginning."

"Start from the beginning? That sounds like risky strategy for a liar, don't you think?"

"Be fair Dempsey."

"Your five minutes are almost up."

"Fine, I am going to start at the beginning but I am telling you it is going to take a while to say all that I need to say."

"Tell you what; I will make you a deal. If I am convinced you are saying anything worth listening to, I might stick around a few extra minutes. Beyond that I am out of here, and so are you."

Twenty minutes later I reached the part of the story when Lovelen and Barry surprised me on the steps of the Library of Congress the morning before I flew out of the country. Dempsey was still upset, but I was encouraged since he had stuck around to hear what I had said thus far. Also his demeanor had softened just a little. Emboldened by this slight change in his attitude, I surged ahead with the story.

After I reviewed the events at church that morning, I apologized to Dempsey once more. "Sorry man, I did not intend to ruin any plans you had with Jaylynn."

Dempsey sighed heavily, walked up to me and offered his hand. As we shook, he said "Sounds like I dodged a bullet with this Strong woman. But the way you described Jaylynn's sister Lovelen... whoooo I wouldn't mind meeting her myself. And dude, I did not know all that stuff about slavery in this country or that it lasted for so long. What the heck, do your thing man. I mean that from my heart. Whatever happens between you and Jaylynn … I wish you both the best.”

“Thanks man. Are we still on for tennis Monday night?”

“Sure, but don’t expect me to be easy on you. I have a lot of pent up frustration to vent on a good friend.”

“That is duly noted. See you Monday my friend.”

“All right Adam.”

For the first time since we bumped heads Wednesday night, Dempsey had smiled. I was relieved. The best thing about our reconciliation was that I did not have to pull out my aces in the hole. For one it was obvious that he knew Jaylynn months before I saw them together Wednesday night. So if he was not able to talk to Jaylynn in all that time, yet she went out with me after our first meeting, then they were not meant to be together. Another thing, I could have mentioned to Dempsey that he was wrong when he said Lovelen had a sister in the Kingdom when I met her because Jaylynn did not come to Arabia until several months after I arrived in the country. I also kept to myself what Jaylynn said to the Strong’s about having asked every Black American she met if they knew me. That meant she had asked Dempsey too. Therefore, since she did not know me before Wednesday, Dempsey had to have lied when she asked him about me. Throwing these facts in his face would have been harsh under the circumstances, and probably would have brought our friendship to an end. We were living in a part of the world where anything could happen at any moment. One of the most valuable assets a man could possess in the Kingdom was a good friend. Since his friendship was important, I could let go of any hard feelings about his lying to Jaylynn about me. Of course the main reason I could afford to be generous with Dempsey was because Jaylynn was with me and not him.

That afternoon I picked Jabbar up at our prearranged spot. The man turned out to be quite a character. We spent the evening going from one house to the next visiting what seemed to be an endless number of his friends. The thought crossed my mind that Jabbar might have been taking advantage of my having a car to catch up with people he had not seen in a long time, but I did not mind. Whatever his motives, Jabbar was my first official guide to Riyadh and a conduit to the Black Saudi community. In effect he was about to become to me what Barry had been when I moved to D.C. At the end of the evening I again dropped Jabbar at the home of one of his friends.

On the way home my thoughts were on Jaylynn Sinclair. Jaylynn came to Arabia five months after I arrived and had been in the Kingdom nine months before we found each other. That was plenty of time for Lovelen to tell Barry about her sister. Barry though never mentioned Jaylynn in any of his letters. There was a chance Lovelen did not tell Barry about Jaylynn, but I wondered if she did tell him and then convinced Barry not to say anything to me about her coming to Arabia. If that was the case, she would need to have a reason for holding back information on her sister. But what could that be?

That night I wrote Barry a long letter describing my interactions with Jabbar and the young Saudis we visited together. In a post script I informed him that I had met Jaylynn. I put a second note in the envelope for him to pass along to Lovelen. In it I thanked her for not telling me about her sister ahead of time, and assured Lovelen that meeting Jaylynn was a very nice surprise that came at a good point in my tour.

A week later I got a letter from Barry that also had a note from Lovelen inside. She wrote, "I was relieved to hear you were not angry with me for holding back information about my sister. As you probably know by now, she got to Riyadh several months after your arrival. It was a surprise opportunity for her and everything happened so fast that I really did not have time to get in touch with you beforehand to tell you about her assignment. But I must tell you, I would never have supported Jaylynn going over there had it not been for your letters. The way you described how the Saudis applauded you in the restaurant your first day in the country, reduced a lot of my fears and suspicions. To be honest that story left me speechless. You might also be surprised to know that what you wrote about your mishap at the DMV convinced me Saudi Arabia was precisely the kind of place for Jaylynn. She has always wanted to go to a developing country to help out. But what I love best about your letters is the way you describe the land and the people. Your descriptions of the fishing village nestled in the corner of that crescent shaped bay on the Gulf left me wanting to know more about the country. I would love to see that bay in person one day. But what you wrote about the desert night sky and all those stars simply blew my mind. I also enjoyed your descriptions of the interplay between young males and females in the bazaars. That was terribly romantic. I was right with you when you shut your eyes and imagined you had grown up in Arabia. Adam, the way you talk about Saudi Arabia it makes me want to find a job over there. Given the type of work I do, that would be highly unlikely. The best I can hope for is to enjoy Arabia through your experiences and those of my sister. So please keep your letters coming. By the way Adam, do not think I am trying to be a matchmaker. I always hate when people try to fix me up with the person they think is perfect for me. That is the real reason I never mentioned Jaylynn. I asked Barry to keep quiet about her too because I wanted to leave it up to fate whether the two of you became friends. Or how do your Muslim friends say it, Insha'Allah - God willing? If you and my sister become friends, good, but even if you do not, it might be nice to see each other from time to time while you are over there. Without getting too sentimental, I confess I have a good feeling about the two of you. By the way, it might interest you to know that Barry and I are living together now, but whatever you do, do not mention this to Pastor Strong and especially not to his wife. Jaylynn told me what she said to Doreen and how you reacted. Adam, I agree with you one hundred percent, Jaylynn should never have told Doreen those things about you. Give Doreen some time, she will get over it. While we are on the subject of my sister's conversation with First Lady Doreen, I hope you are not angry with Barry for telling me about the dating competition the two of you had going on before I met you guys. He is still a good man, so try not to think of your buddy as a traitor to the male club. Barry and I are still wondering though, how did I rate on your scale? Did I pass all of your tests?"

I decided to keep Lovelen and Barry guessing a little longer about my impressions of her as a date, but the news about her and Barry cohabitating made me worry what might happen if First Lady Doreen ever found out. Likely she would jump to the conclusion that Jaylynn could end up in the same situation. That would probably push her to step up her efforts to keep me away from Jaylynn. A more pleasant thought also crossed my mind. If Jaylynn and I got close, Barry and I might end up falling in love with a pair of sisters. Of course it was too soon to start thinking seriously along those lines. Jaylynn was not even my girlfriend – not yet.

ઇઉ ઇઉ ઇઉ ઇઉ ઇઉ ઇઉ ઇઉ ઉઇ ઉઇ ઉઇ ઉઇ ઉઇ

Chapter 24

On Thursdays I played tennis with either Mark Parsons or Dempsey Stevens. On Fridays I attended church with Jaylynn and ate brunch with the Strong's afterward. Friday evenings I traveled around Riyadh with Jabbar visiting his friends. That was my routine.

All of the young men that Jabbar introduced me to appeared to be in their early to late twenties. All of them loved cigarettes. Most were chain smokers. They spoke English to varying degrees (English is a required subject in all levels of education in Saudi Arabia). When Jabbar and I entered a room, the host always deferred to my language as a matter of courtesy toward

185

a guest. Of course when conversations grew spirited or turned into heavy debates, they abandoned English in favor of their native Arabic.

Warm hospitality was extended to us wherever we went, and the kindness they showed made a permanent imprint on my heart. Most evenings I drank so much tea that I would be running to the bathroom for days afterward. In time I learned that if I shook my glass from side to side servers would take that as a signal that I had had enough and would stop automatically refilling my glass. From the start, however, when it came to food I staunchly refused when it was offered. With all the tea I was consuming I was forced to ask to use the bathroom, or hammom, in the homes of our Saudi hosts. Having been forewarned about the way they are structured, I was not shocked at what I found in them, or to be more precise, what I did not find in them. I was determined that my experiences in them would remain liquid rather than solid, if you know what I mean. I was not ready to dive that deep into the local culture.

Only one thing disappointed me about the time I was spending with Jabbar. He had not introduced me to his family and gad yet to take me to see any of his Black Saudi friends.

Late that spring I fell head over heels in love with Jaylynn. I did not share my feelings with her at the time, but I remember vividly the moment it happened. At one of the after service meals, a guest spilled ice tea on the floor. First Lady Doreen had her hands full at the time. Out of all the guests enjoying the offerings of Pastor Strong's table it was Jaylynn who got up, fetched a mop and quietly cleaned the floor. This selfless act and her humility awoke something in me and it had a striking physical effect. A kind of darkness seemed to lift from off my head and the best I can explain it is like the arrival of dawn, I saw Jaylynn as if for the first time. Her physical and inner beauty suddenly blended together in my heart and she became the most wonderful person I had ever known. In that single instant of clarity, Jaylynn Sinclair became more beautiful than any woman I had ever met, including her sister and that is something I thought I would never say about another female. From that moment Jaylynn was the pinnacle of femininity and loveliness in my heart.

One of the more interesting things about the time I was spending with Jabbar is that he never took me to see the same friend or group of friends twice in a row. I was meeting a lot of the locals and the weekly excursions were giving me increased insight into numerous aspects of Saudi society. I was fascinated at the lack of consensus among Arab men when it came to just about any topic. Emphasis was placed on the individual. Each man had strong opinions and was willing to hold onto his beliefs, no matter what. They argued passionately about all sorts of things, sometimes to the point that at times I thought a fight would break out. In contrast to this, they were unified in mutual hatred for people and nations they viewed as enemies of Islam or other Arabs. As one young Saudi explained it to me, "Arabs fight against each other, this is true, but we stand together against a common enemy. We have a saying here – me against my brother, but me and my cousin against you."

Conversations during these visits varied from simple matters about food preferences to complex issues such as the growing resentment in the Kingdom over foreigners taking up all the jobs in the country. For the most part these were young men that had finished college and possessed a variety of skills. Evidently many in their ranks were unemployed and the inability to find work was becoming a problem. On the other side of that argument, the expatriate communities argued that Saudi males refused to do hard labor and only wanted to be directors in fancy offices. A popular saying among expatriates was that the least non-office type job a Saudi would do, was drive a taxi. Even among our staff at the Ministry, it was commonly said that we were building vocational training centers that the Saudis would never attend.

Nobody told me that conversations during these visits were open for anyone to participate in but I figured that out for myself. A man could say whatever he felt. The only rule was that you had better know what you were talking about because you could count on being challenged. Most evenings I sat quietly and listened to the discussions, but occasionally I asked questions. Speaking up helped me learn a few additional things about these amazing Bedouins that I might not have, had I remained a passive listener. Once I asked a friend of Jabbar's, "why do Saudis drive so fast?" He answered "We did not know anything about driving until Americans came to Saudi Arabia. So we watch Americans and do what we see Americans do. When light turns yellow, Americans drive faster so this is what we do." The young man had us dead to rights on that, so I could not say anything in rebuttal. Another Saudi explained that he hated traffic signals and said, "When I get to a corner and see this light, I say 'how can this thing control me? Only I can make my car stop, not this light.'" Some of the logic was scary, but I kept in mind it was a developing land. Giant leaps were being made every day toward catching up to the rest of the world but everyone was not advancing at the same rate. Most Saudis that had traveled or lived abroad were ahead of those who had never been outside the Kingdom.

Once a young man tried to draw me out. I think his intent was to embarrass me with his contempt for the West. He boasted "we Saudis do not need modern technology. We do not need oil. Your country needs oil. Yes we get money from the oil, but we do not need money. We can go back to living in tents in the desert, like our grandfathers."

This statement caught everyone's attention, not only because it put me, an American, front and center but also because the young man had articulated one of the more popular concepts in the Kingdom. If my challenger knew me better, he would have known had a ready response to that contention. To answer him I related an incident that happened the day I had to take my video recorder to a local repair shop.

"There had been a power surge in the compound and despite being hooked up to a voltage regulator, some of my equipment was damaged. To find out if the video recorder could be repaired or should be tossed out, I took it to one of the local shops in my neighborhood. There was a long line of customers ahead of me, so I stepped to the back of the line to wait my turn. Less than twenty seconds later a Saudi came into the shop. He had a servant in tow carrying a large television set. This man strode past the line of customers right up to the counter and demanded service as his servant placed the TV set on the counter. The desk clerk left the customer he was waiting on and went over to hear the Saudi explain the problem he was having with his TV. They only spoke briefly but it was clear the clerk was not responding the way the man wanted. The clerk returned to his previous customer after calling to the back of the shop and asking for the manager. The manager came out and listened to the Saudi as he related his urgent need to have his TV set fixed. Once the manager understood the nature of the problem, he assured the Saudi it could be repaired. That much was fine with this Saudi, but what he really wanted to know was when he could get his television set back. The manager said 'it will be ready in two days.' When he said this, the Saudi hit the roof. This man began screaming at the top of his voice and he insisted that he had to have his television back that very afternoon. The problem – a football game was being broadcast and the Saudi did not want to miss it. Twenty minutes later when I left the shop, that man was still fussing about getting his set back that afternoon."

After I finished the story and it was translated for those in the room who did not have enough English to follow along, I concluded with the observation, "Say what you will, but you Saudis are not going back to living in tents like nomads." Lo and behold when I said this, all the other men in the room applauded. Everyone took my side in the debate and began shouting, '*Tom and Jerry* forever,' and 'fix my television now! I want to watch football.'

I was enjoying the time I spent with Jabbar, however, whatever he had in mind by taking me around to meet his Saudi friends to the exclusion of Black Saudis, it was not working for me. My time in the Kingdom was winding down and the window of opportunity to find the Black Saudi Community in Riyadh would soon close. One evening after leaving the home of yet another one of his friends, I got in the car and started the motor but after a second or two turned the engine off.

"What is wrong Mr. Adam," Jabbar asked?

Raising my hands inquiringly I asked, "Do you have any Black friends?"

"Yes, you are my friend isn't it?"

"Saudi - Black… Saudi… friends… Jabbar… and you know what I meant. Don't you have any Black Saudi friends?"

"Yes."

"Are you ever going to introduce me to any of them?"

His answer "Insha'Allah" of course, was not convincing. Insha'Allah could be the most powerful response an Arab could give or it could just as easily be a brush off. Since he seemed reluctant to talk about his Black Saudi friends I dropped the subject.

Two months of running around with Jabbar and I still had no idea where he lived, or anything about his family, or if he even had a home. To an extent Jabbar had become as big a mystery to me as the Black Saudi community. The only things I knew about Jabbar for sure was that he had tons of friends and that, as far as I could tell, he was an overnight guest in one of their homes every weekend.

We were into our third month of friendship before Jabbar finally introduced me to one of his Black Saudi friends. His name was Abdul and he had the best grasp of English of any Saudi I had met thus far. Talking to him was as easy as having a conversation with someone on the streets of D.C. It came as no surprise when he told me he had been to the States numerous times. The place where Jabbar took me to meet Adbul was a tea shop in a part of town I had never been before. Several of the men in the shop were using Hubbly Bubblies, so I decided to take advantage of this opportunity to communicate freely in English with a local and inquired about these mechanisms and how they worked. Abdul explained them to me in detail.

During our conversation I discovered Abdul was a newlywed and that is how we got to talking about romance and marriage. Abdul confirmed most of the observations I had made in the suqs about subtle interactions between males and females. I also brought up the option Muslim men have to marry up to four wives and asked, "How many wives do you plan to have." Abdul smiled and said, "That is something only the rich do. For me it is hard enough to live with one woman, why would I make my life miserable by marrying two and God forbid three or four?" We laughed like we were old friends.

Unfortunately, I think we were getting along too well for Jabbar's liking. He had said very little during most of the conversation, but it was at this point when we were laughing the loudest that Jabbar suddenly decided we had to leave. After a relatively short visit with Abdul, Jabbar whisked me away. He never took me to see Abdul again.

Jabbar's behavior was not surprising. I had known since my teenage years how possessive males can be when it comes to their friendships. But it was not until I met Abdul that I realized Jabbar was deliberately keeping me from his Black Saudi friends. Maybe he was afraid he would lose my friendship or that I would prefer to spend more time with other Blacks than with him. Whatever was going on in his head, it was clear after our visit with Abdul that Jabbar might not be my conduit after all to the Black community.

One Friday Jabbar asked where I lived. This was something I never expected Jabbar to ask, but I decided to show him my villa. He liked the place. We watched videos and talked about Black American history. Later that evening when I drove him to his destination I advised him, "now that you know where I live, you are going to have to take me to visit your family." He grunted but said nothing in response.

As far as I could tell, Jabbar was a confirmed bachelor just wandering through life. Reluctantly, I came to the conclusion he was not the kind of Black Saudi that could help me achieve my objectives. Considering how long it had taken me to meet Jabbar, I doubted there was enough time left for me to meet any other Black Saudis in Riyadh. Even though I was becoming disillusioned about finding the community, Jabbar had a few surprises for me up his sleeve as I would soon find out.

On a Friday not too long after our visit with Abdul, Jabbar had me drive into an older section of Riyadh. At a certain corner he instructed me to turn onto an extremely narrow street. Houses on each side of the street were little more than shacks and all of the residents were Black. This was my first venture into a Black Saudi neighborhood. However, as I drove forward the street narrowed even more until there was barely room to drive between the buildings. I figured Jabbar had me go that way because it was a shortcut of some kind and he was leading me through this narrow passageway to a regular sized road.

But when Jabbar started looking around, I got suspicious. To confirm what I was thinking I asked, "Do you have a friend on this street Jabbar?"

"Yes, and he is Black so keep driving ah-la-tool (straight ahead)."

"What if another car comes from the other direction? How will we get out of here?"

"No car is going to come. Just drive."

I was seriously worried about getting wedged between the buildings. The last thing I needed was to take the car back to Danny at the Motor Pool with the sides all scratched up and try to explain what happened. It was crazy to even think about trying to back out of the street, so I had no choice but to keep moving forward as carefully as possible. Three quarters of the way into the block Jabbar told me to stop. He then climbed right over the seat into the back, rolled down the passenger window behind me and stepped through the window into the front room of the home of one of his friends. The young man that came from the back of the house greeted Jabbar by pointing at my car and laughing like he had never seen a car at his front door before, which I doubt he had. Jabbar and his friend enjoyed the joke together as they walked away. I sat fuming and worrying about how I could get out of that street without damaging my vehicle. Mostly I was annoyed with Jabbar for bringing me to the home of a Black Saudi that he had no intention of introducing me to, because he knew I was not going to climb through the window into his friend's home and leave my car unoccupied and blocking the lane.

Fifteen minutes later Jabbar climbed back into the car and over the front seat then told me to drive on. Negotiating my way carefully, I managed to get to the end of the block without scratching the sides of the car. At the end of the lane I pulled onto a normal sized street and breathed a sigh of relief. Jabbar laughed. I glared at him. After a few minutes I calmed down and as I sat there simmering I reminded myself that this is what I had wanted, to spend time with local Blacks. The moment I accepted Jabbar's friendship, I exposed myself to customs and ways that were different from my own. Along with this came the possibility that some of the things Jabbar did or the things he might expose me to could include situations I did not agree with or understand. That is why, rather than complain to him, I chastised myself for not being more cautious about following blindly after Jabbar.

Silently I promised myself that from thenceforth if I had any doubts or misgivings about a direction Jabbar was leading me, I would voice those concerns and stand my ground. On the other hand holding onto our friendship was important, not only because I liked Jabbar but he was still my best chance of connecting with the elusive Black Saudi community.

I dropped Jabbar off at a restaurant that night and headed home. It was the last time we would see each other for several weeks. Had I known this before he got out of the car, I would not have been so quick to get angry with him.

Jabbar's subsequent absence left a void in my Friday evenings. I used the time to catch up on my journal and letter writing. Occasionally I played basketball with Dempsey or went to a party. Meantime, Jaylynn and I were growing much closer and I suspected she had fallen in love too.

Chapter 25

The Saudi Arabian government announced an all paid six week Arab language course to be held at the Arab Language Institute of the University of Riyadh. This course was specifically designed for western businessmen and we were extended a written invitation to attend. Classes would begin in two months and interested westerners only had to submit an application to the Ministry where they worked. As soon as I heard the announcement, I went to Abdullah Al-Basheer, asked for an application, filled it out, and returned it to him that same day. Abdullah immediately signed off on it and sent my application, along with his letter of recommendation, to the top floor to be reviewed, and hopefully approved, by Minister Al-Naseem.

After work that same afternoon, I pulled up to my compound and discovered I had a visitor waiting at the front gate. After an absence of nearly a month, Jabbar was back. Before I could get out of the car he came over, jumped into the front seat and started telling me about his trip to Jeddah. He said he been away visiting with some of his brothers who are children from his father's other wives. 'Women love my father' he bragged and explained that the elder Al-Bughawi was well endowed physically, and using his hands explicitly illustrated his father's capacity.

The motor was off because I had expected to go into my house when I got to the villa, but as I suspected when I saw Jabbar he wanted to pick up where we left off - running from one friend's home to the next. After lighting a cigarette, he said cheerfully "Come on then let's go."

Reluctantly I started the car and pulled into traffic, but warned him, "I cannot stay out all hours of the night with you this evening Jabbar." For the first time since we met, I was putting my foot down with him and I was determined not to let anything Jabbar said undermine my resolve. Whatever he came up with, I would be ready for him. Continuing, I said "Unlike some people, I have a job to go to in the morning. That reminds me, I have always wondered where you work Jabbar."

"I do not work."

"How do you survive without money?"

"You said your friend has a lot of videotapes, isn't it?"

Changing the subject, this was a tactic I was familiar with. My father was the champion of switching topics when conversations made him uncomfortable.

"Answer my question first, then I will answer yours" I said firmly.

Jabbar fell silent. It had never been that quiet when Jabbar was in the car. For a few minutes I was content to sit quietly and listen to the sound of the wheels rolling on the road. Once I saw that Jabbar had no intention of answering my question, I said, "All right then. Where do you want me to take you tonight Jabbar? Tell me so I can drop you off and get back home. I have a long day ahead of me tomorrow."

"Do you remember my friend Sami? Please take me to him."

"Okay."

The good news was I had succeeded in making my point to Jabbar. Going forward I would never have to argue the issue again of us staying out all night. It was an important step for me and I was proud of myself for gaining a measure of control in the friendship.

Chapter 26

For the first time since I left my parent's home, I was attending church regularly. Doreen Strong took her time about it but she slowly warmed up to me. Each week the physical distance that she established between us in the beginning, narrowed a little more. Finally she stood close enough to be able to distinguish my voice from other members of the congregation when we sang hymns.

That afternoon during the after service meal, the one Jaylynn liked to call brunch, she commented, "Adam, I never knew you had such a lovely voice. Pastor Strong have you heard Adam sing?"

"No."

"Come on Adam sing a hymn for the Pastor."

I never liked being the focus of attention in that kind of setting. My strategy in those situations was to stall. Because we were eating it was a simple matter of shoveling a fork full of food into my mouth. Chewing ever so slowly, I trusted I would be able to ride out this request long enough for someone to bring up a different topic. Once I finished that mouthful I reached for another. However, when I lifted the fork to my mouth Doreen scowled, "Don't you dare put another bite of food in your mouth. You are not going to get out of singing for Pastor Strong today no matter what tricks you try."

Pretending she had not caught me in time, I went ahead and forked this new load into my mouth.

"Let Adam eat his food in peace Doreen," Pastor Strong gently counseled. In my head I once again said a blessing for the man.

"Phillip, Adam is trying to be clever," she said playfully. Turning to me she added, "I have no idea what makes you think you can get out of singing because you have food that I cooked in your mouth, but you are wrong Mr. Sneed." While saying this Doreen walked up behind me, reached over my shoulder and lifted my plate away, then continued, "I promise you, you are not going to leave this house until you have sung for us today. Go ahead and finish that last bite of food, then I want you to come on over to the piano. I will have hymn number 153 waiting whenever you are ready."

Seeing I was not going to have any peace and it was no longer possible to finish my meal anyway, I got up from the table and walked over to the piano. Doreen played. I sang. My tenor voice filled the air and the patio became as quiet as a sanctuary.

I was a child the last time I sang in church. In my teen years I drifted away from religious music. Since my parents were too strict to tolerate secular songs in the house, most days when I felt like singing I had to suppress the urge. Like most people, I sang when I was in the shower but in my parents' home I had to keep my voice low so nobody would hear me. However, there were days when I was alone in the house. On those occasions, when the impulse hit me I raised my voice to the rafters. Once I was singing while mopping one of the rooms on the second floor of our house. Earlier I had washed the windows in that room and inadvertently left one of them open. A stranger walking through the neighborhood and stopped and called up, "Excuse me... excuse me." When I went to see what they wanted, she asked, "Was that you singing?" I shrugged my shoulders. "You have a beautiful voice," she complimented. "Do you sing professionally?" I was too shy and embarrassed to engage in that kind of conversation, so I closed the window and pulled the curtains shut.

The only other occasions I sang were when I got together with my closest friend, a kid we called O. Like me, O was shy. O and I only sang in private, and we sang all the popular tunes of the day. But other than singing with my friend, I kept that particular talent on the hush-hush. There were times in school when I had to take chorus, but I was able to blend my voice in enough not to draw attention and be noticed. One year though my music teacher heard me and was so impressed that she sent me to represent the school on the All-City Chorus when it performed at Steven Foster's Memorial Hall. Nevertheless, in the end I never gave much thought to performing on a stage.

That day in front of Pastor Strong and his guests, the richness of my voice surprised even me. Encouraged by the supportive 'Amen's' and 'sing to the Lords' being said, I really got into the hymn. Pastor Strong's smile could not have gotten any wider unless his head suddenly grew. Jaylynn, although she had heard my voice before, beamed with pride.

After the applause died down Pastor Strong stood and announced, "I think we have found a new member of the choir, would you not agree First Lady."

"I wholeheartedly agree Pastor Strong." The look Doreen gave me said loud and clear 'now you have been fully accepted by the church.' Her approval automatically removed all impediments in the congregation to my already blossoming relationship with Jaylynn. After that we began to openly do what church folk call 'courting.' I do not know exactly when Jaylynn fell in love with me, but I think it is safe to say it was before I sang at brunch that day. At any rate, after that the whole congregation actively promoted our romance.

Jaylynn and I were free to be affectionate inside the Strong's compound, and we took full advantage of that freedom. Still, I kept Todd Dearbourne's words in the forefront of my mind about limiting acts of affection to within the walls of western facilities. His counsel replayed in my head each time I caressed Jaylynn's face or took her hand in mine. There was also the fact that Jaylynn had been brought to Saudi Arabia to replace a woman who had gotten thrown out of the country for kissing a man in public. Jaylynn reminded me about that constantly.

When it came to taking precautions, Jaylynn and I were on the same page. I would never put her in a position where one of those old long bearded Mutawah's might take a swing at her. If that ever happened, I knew I would get into serious trouble because I was not about to let anyone hurt my love. For these and other reasons we took it upon ourselves to limit our expressions of affection to the confines of the Strong's compound. It did not matter where else we went, the APO, Headquarters' Rec Center to watch a movie or play video games, or wherever – unless we were in the Strong's compound Jaylynn and I kept our hands to ourselves. That took a lot of self control, but we never wavered.

On occasion Jaylynn and I teamed up against Mark Parsons, and whatever lady he was seeing at the time, and played doubles. Jaylynn though was not much of a tennis enthusiast. But even then, no acts of affection passed between us. Our sole love nest was the Strong's compound. We held hands during service, when I was not sitting and performing with the choir, and sat together at brunch often feeding each other playfully. We strolled through the neighborhoods inside the compound and sometimes played on swing sets. On weekends when she spent the night at the Strong's, I would stop by in the evening and we would go out for a walk. Gazing into the starry sky together was one of our favorite things to do, especially after I told her about the starry canopy I had seen in the desert on the way back from Dammam. We talked about driving into the desert one day and seeing that site together. Maintaining self-control was definitely tough, but our love flowered. Doreen encouraged us a great deal and having her approval made a big difference.

Around this time we started seeing each other on Wednesday evenings as well. Mostly we went to the Rec Center to watch movies but we also swam and played tennis with other couples including Dempsey and Mark and whoever they might be dating. From time to time we went dancing at one of the regular party places.

As the weeks passed I was seeing Jaylynn more and more in her own light. To me she was lovelier than Lovelen and I no longer made comparisons between the sisters in my head. To be sure I enjoyed the memories I had of Lovelen, but the only woman that filled my eyes and heart was the lady I met that night at the Vinnell compound.

Things were also improving for me on the work front. I had a staff of three and a dozen file cabinets in the Admin Room. But there was even more going on in my professional life. The Ministry managed construction projects in a number of cities, including Qatif, Hail, Al-Jouf, Taif, Jeddah, Dammam, Abha, Tabuk, Najran and Gizan. Al Dennison and Abdullah Al-Basheer and their staffs traveled to those places from time to time to perform on-site inspections. Although it was not part of my job description to participate in these trips, Abdullah was kind enough to suggest to Al Dennison that I be taken along occasionally. Privately, he confided to me that he did this because he wanted me to see other parts of the country.

That is how I got to see western Arabia. Traveling in western Arabia allowed me to confirm first hand what Ahdel had told me that night at Larry Corbin's house. There indeed were more Blacks in the West. In fact they were highly visible everywhere. But I never had the chance to meet any of them in person or to sit down with one of them and introduce myself. Typically we arrived in a town, were picked up at the airport, taken directly to the construction site, performed the inspection and returned to the airport – all within the span of a few hours. We were in and out of towns too quickly for me to meet and interview any of the locals.

Still I appreciated every opportunity I was given to travel with the engineers and never more so than the week we visited the site at Abha south of Jeddah. Abha sits in a mountainous region amidst some of the most striking terrain in the world. Greenery and fertile farm land is abundant in Abha due to the large amount of rain that falls in that area. We only stayed half a day before flying back to Riyadh, but it is a place I would love to visit as a tourist and stay long enough to do some serious sight seeing.

Contrary to what I had expected, there are a lot of interesting things about the various cities of the Peninsula. Prior to living and working in Arabia, I was of the opinion most of the country was dry and arid and that all Arabs lived under the same conditions weather-wise. Those early years in Arabia were truly educational because I got to see with my own eyes the wide variety of the Kingdom. Some cities stood on the shores of the Red Sea (Jeddah); or on terraced mountainsides that rose up from the sea (Gizan – here we saw young boys racing in small colorful sailboats along the coast); and in the east there were lovely towns right on the Gulf (Qatif and Dammam); in the interior cities were built on mountain ranges (Taif and Najran); in verdant valleys (Hail); in dry deserts (Riyadh); and I was really surprised at how cold it got in some parts of the country (Tabuk for instance gets cold enough at times for snow to blanket the ground). With so much variety in topography and climate I was forced to abandon my preconceived notion that the country was one big desert.

The rainy season began and, as always, brought cooler temperatures. That rainy season however, something happened in Riyadh that was extremely rare. It rained. Showers fell every day for several weeks. They only lasted for brief periods but at times the showers were intense.

One rainy morning Al Dennison followed me into the Admin office just after I got to the Ministry and asked, "So when are you going to bring her over to the house and introduce her to me and Marlene?"

"Excuse me, what are you talking about?"

"I am talking about whoever this girl is that has your nose so wide open that here lately it seems the sun sits back and waits for you to get to work before it comes out in the morning. It is as plain as the nose on your face; you are in love my man."

I blushed.

"O my God, now I have seen everything. A Black man blushing. I don't mean any harm Adam, but I did not know that was physically possible," Al snorted.

"I will talk with Jaylynn and see if we can work out a time to visit you and Marlene. Thanks for the invitation."

"That's her name, Jaylynn?"

"Yes."

"That is a pretty name. I suppose Jaylynn is as pretty as her name."

"Actually, she is the most beautiful woman in the world."

When Al walked out of the Admin Room he had a goofy smile on his face. Moments later my phone rang. It was Jaylynn.

Jaylynn had remained rigidly opposed to giving me the number to her dorm, but I made sure she had my work and home numbers. Occasionally she called me at the office, but most of the times we talked late in the evenings after her dorm mates had gone to their rooms. A couple of nights we even talked into the wee hours of the morning. Looking back on it, I think that was a mistake. Even so, she did not call nearly as often as I would have liked.

That morning the conversation went in a totally unexpected direction. "Can you pick me up after work?"

"Sure baby, where would you like to go? I hear there is a new film at the Rec Center tonight. They say it is supposed to be really good, so if you like we can do that or if you prefer we can play doubles with Dempsey and Lori again." Lori was the newest single Black American female in Riyadh. Best of all she worked at the APO. Dempsey hooked her the first day she landed in the Kingdom. Neither Lori nor Jaylynn were good at tennis, but Dempsey and I took on the challenge of teaching them the game. The four of us had played three matches so far, so I assumed Jaylynn would go for my suggestion that we play that evening, that is if she did not want to see a movie.

"No, I am not in the mood for going out tonight. I prefer to stay in. In fact I think it is time you showed me your villa. I will even cook us a meal, and since I have the day off tomorrow I might as well spend the night, so we can have breakfast together in the morning."

I gulped so hard, I thought I would swallow my tongue. Sweat burst on my forehead. Was she suggesting what I thought she was suggesting? Wait a minute, was the house presentable? Forget the house, what about Doreen Strong? I had enough experience with church people to know what would result if it ever became public that Jaylynn spent the night at my place. Then there was the question of food. She said she wanted to cook. Was there anything at the house worth cooking? Mentally I was babbling, though physically I was all for getting together with her. The overriding emotion hitting me, however, was panic because we were westerners having a romance in a restricted society. Too many things could go wrong.

"You did say you have two bedrooms right," Jaylynn fished innocently as if she had no inkling what thoughts were going through my mind?

"Yes, that is right… I did say that," I answered as if I was not quite sure that I had. Then I coughed to clear my throat.

"Then it must be true if you said it Adam… so please make sure the guest room is clean enough for a lady to sleep there. Abud is dropping me off at the APO. I will be waiting for you at 6:00."

For the rest of that day I got very little done because my mind was not on work. Obviously this was merely a social visit in Jaylynn's mind, so any thoughts about hanky-panky had to be dismissed. But I was not so sure I could be that near to Jaylynn, alone in my villa in the middle of the night, in a lonely desert, and our visit would remain platonic. A lot of questions were running through my head. Rather than obsess over it, I decided to wait until later to start worrying about something that might never become an issue.

I rushed home after work and spruced up the guest room, and a few other parts of the house, then headed over to the APO. Jaylynn was standing alone outside the facility when I drove up. This meant one of two things, she had already sent Abud away or someone other than Abud had driven her to the APO and she had gone into the theater long enough to convince the driver she was there to watch a film.

Jaylynn got into the back seat and handed me a note. As we got underway she explained, "That is a list of things I need you to pick up at the Commissary and the PX. Just to be safe, I want you to drop me off at your villa first and then you can go shopping. That will give me time to go through your house and check for all the evidence other women left behind in your private little love nest."

I ignored her joke, putting on an air of confidence that I had nothing to hide. At each red light and stop sign, I took a glance at her shopping list. I could not believe some of the items she had written. "Wait a minute, do you really expect me to go into the PX and ask for all these things?"

"Think about it Adam. If I packed any of that stuff at the dormitory, what would the rest of the nurses think? Martha especially, she was best friends with the nurse that got deported. I have to be careful around her. Everyone thinks I am going to spend the weekend with the Strong's, and I want them to keep thinking that. If you have a supply of the things I need at your place, it will be easier for me to visit and spend the night whenever I get the chance."

When I sighed she asked, "Is there something wrong?"

"Baby, I never expected things to get this complicated."

"Enjoying the company of a female in this country is not easy, but I think you agree it is worth it even if it means making a few sacrifices."

"You are right about that, I do not mind sacrificing for a night like this. But I am glad you have all this figured out because it is much too complex for me."

"We have to cautious my darling."

"Caution is definitely our watchword," I agreed with enthusiasm. I also thought of an item she had not put on the list. Maybe I would not need it, but it could not hurt to be prepared.

When we pulled up to the villa, I was stunned to see Jabbar waiting at the gate. As usual he had shown up unannounced following a long absence. However, on this occasion his timing was terrible and completely unappreciated.

Jaylynn immediately got nervous. "Who is that man standing there waving at you Adam?"

"That is my Black Saudi friend, the one I told you about. Jabbar Al-Bughawi."

"The dancer?"

"Yes, that's him."

"Wave to your friend and take me back to the facility right now. You can get the things on that list some other time. We will get together on another day."

"Sweetheart, please calm down. Whatever we do, we cannot let this guy see us panic. He will think we are up to something, and Jabbar can be very suspicious. Besides he has already seen you. Let me introduce him to you at least and then I will take you back. Are you okay with that?"

"I guess."

Jaylynn was not keen to meet Jabbar. After I got out of the car and headed toward him, a new plan came to mind. Instead of introducing him to Jaylynn I would find out what he wanted first, and if he just wanted to visit his friends I might be able to talk him into waiting at the villa while I took Jaylynn back to the APO. Jabbar and I shook hands.

"Jabbar where have you been," I asked with as much interest as I could fake?

"I was in Jeddah visiting my brothers."

"You seem to go there often. How many brothers and sisters do you have?"

"Let me think. My father has four wives and children by all of them. Really I do not know how many children my father has. Twenty – thirty - who knows, it is like that here you see."

"Four wives, he is up to the maximum."

"Like I told you before, my father is special," he said with a licentious laugh.

"What about you, do you have a mother?"

"No, I do not have a mother… what do you think? Everybody has a mother, isn't it? That was a stupid question Mr. Adam."

The question had come out wrong because I was nervous. "Forgive me Jabbar, I meant to ask does your mother live here in Riyadh."

"Yes she does and that reminds me, I need you to take me to my mother's house one day soon. She has been calling all around Riyadh asking for me. I know she wants something so I must go and find out what it is so she can stop worrying my friends to death."

This was a first, Jabbar inviting me to meet his family. Maybe my luck was about to change.

"Who is that in your car Mr. Adam? Why is she wearing an Abbaya? I do not think she is Muslim, maybe she is American woman? Is she pretty? Are you two doing things, huh," he asked with a wink of his eye?

"She is American, and we are friends. Sometimes I drive her to a compound outside of Riyadh. I ran into her just now and have to take her to our post office near Airport Road. I had to stop by the house first to get something. Come inside with me, this won't take but a moment. When we come back you can meet her if you like."

"I definitely like," he said and headed straight for the car. I had never intended for him to go to the car without me and did not like what was happening. But there was nothing I could do. To panic would only make things worse. All I could do was count on Jaylynn to handle herself. I watched helplessly as he got into the front seat.

When I heard Jabbar introduce himself, I rolled my eyes. Knowing the two of them, I had a pretty good idea how that conversation was about to go.

Why did I tell Jabbar I had to get something out of the house? Now I had to think of something to grab that would make sense when I took it out to the car. An idea came to mind and I looked around for a book. As I scanned the living room I spotted a copy of a *Reader's Digest* magazine with a cover article about Sudan. I grabbed it, counted to ten and headed back to the car.

When I got in, I was delighted to find Jabbar having a hard time of it because my girl was peppering him with questions. "What do you mean you do not work? How do you take care of yourself? Do you have children Mr. Jabbar?"

"No, I do not have children."

"Good, because I would hate to think you are like those Brothers in the States who refuse to take care of their children."

"This is not America. It is very different in Saudi Arabia. We do not do things like that here. Some men here do not live with their wives and children, but we do take care of our families."

"Some men do not live with their families? Then where do they live?"

"Any place they want. How's that," he snapped! Jabbar was not used to conversing with females who were not related to him and he was quite annoyed that an outspoken foreign woman wanted to criticize him over his employment status.

I handed Jaylynn the Reader's Digest and started the motor. For the rest of the trip Jaylynn remained silent, but when I took a quick glance at her through the rearview I could tell, despite her Abbaya, she was smirking. I looked forward to her call later that night because I wanted to know everything she and Jabbar had talked about while I was in the house.

After dropping Jaylynn back at the APO, Jabbar directed me to where he planned for us to go that afternoon.

It had rained heavily earlier in the day and all over town locals were celebrating the large puddles of water that had collected. The city did not have a sewer system yet, because it rained so infrequently and from what I had been told there still were no plans drawn up for one. As a result, the few times it did rain runoff water accumulated in huge puddles. It was funny to see motorists deliberately speed through puddles near curbs just to splatter any pedestrian who happened to be nearby. Nobody minded and many of the adult Saudis were dancing in the puddles anyway like children do back home when a fire hydrant is opened on a hot summer day. Scores of young drivers threw caution to the wind and plowed through the puddles at high speeds. Batteries often shorted out when water sprayed on them from the undercarriage. Instead of getting upset when that happened, the Saudis simply pushed the stalled car to the side of the road and promptly went and got another vehicle to continue their fun. There were scores of abandoned cars littering streets all over the city.

That afternoon Jabbar took me to a part of town a few blocks east of Television Street, and instructed me to park near a cluster of homes at the base of a low hill. "Come with me Mr. Adam."

We climbed the hill, cut through a narrow alley and walked into a crowd of males, all of them cheering wildly. Their attention was focused toward the bottom of the hill where a second crowd of males had gathered not far from where I had parked. We could not see everything that was going on so Jabbar grabbed my arm and shouted, "Follow me this way, it will be better. You will see everything."

Jabbar led me to a house nearby where he knocked at the gate. After we were welcomed inside, Jabbar and I followed our excited young male host as he raced across the courtyard and up an outdoor staircase to a second floor balcony. From there we had a view of the full length of the hill. At the base a crowd of males was standing around an exceptionally large puddle of rainwater. At the top of the hill a long row of cars was surrounded by a heaving mass of young men and boys all jostling to cram into one of the vehicles. At the front of the line a Cadillac rocked violently as guys competed to get inside. Once no more bodies could fit, the driver took off down the slope and pushed the gas pedal to get up to top speed. At the base of the hill, when he reached the large puddle, the driver slammed on brakes and turned the wheel. This caused the vehicle to hydroplane and spin nearly one hundred eighty degrees. Spectators at both ends of the hill shouted and cheered.

The next car pulled forward and wrestling began anew for a chance to take the trip downhill. Soon I realized the objective of this activity was to push the car into the biggest spin and the more violent a car spun when it hit the puddle, the louder the accolades earned by the driver. One driver successfully pushed his car to make a 360° turn and the crowds at both ends of the hill, as well as spectators looking on from houses along the block, all lost their minds. A 360 was rare. During the time we were there, only that one driver managed to pull it off. Jabbar assured me competition to ride with him the next time would be intense. Because of the violence of the spins, centrifugal force always threw the passengers to one side of the car squeezing them into a tight bunch. None of the riders seemed to mind. The thrill of the action was what they loved.

"Do they have anything like this in America," Jabbar asked with the confidence of a man who already knew the answer to his question?

"No, in America we would be concerned that a car might spin out of control or a battery could stall and the vehicle ends up plowing into a crowd, like that one at the bottom of the hill."

"You Americans cling to life like it is the only thing you have. Your life does not belong to you. It belongs to Allah. If you die, so what, you return to God. That is the way of the world."

It was a waste of time getting into a philosophical argument with Jabbar, so I did not respond. Arabs simply reasoned differently from

Westerners. I was amused though at the kinds of automobiles participating in the fun on the hill. None were what we would call lemons. In fact, there were so many Mercedes Benzes and Cadillac's that it was hard to take in the reality that the Saudis could afford to subject such expensive machinery to that kind of devil-may-care activity. Modern machines had given the Saudis fancier toys to play with in their quest for distraction.

The ages of some of the drivers, though, that was a little disturbing. Some appeared to be no older than eight or nine. Shorter boys creatively tied attachments to their feet to extend their reach and thus be able to operate the accelerator and engage the brakes. Males of all ages were participating, most as passengers and competition was fiercest to ride with the youngest drivers. Often younger boys were forcibly pulled out of a car kicking and screaming by older males who got in as passengers instead. After all the months I had lived in Riyadh and the many young men I had met and spoken with, I understood this behavior. Younger drivers presented a higher level of risk, and thrill seeking was a big part of the lives of these sexually repressed young men. What else was there for them to do in the desert? Before I met Jaylynn there were times when even I, with all the options at my disposal, sometimes struggled to make it through the day without succumbing to the doldrums.

Jaylynn chuckled when I described the scene on the hill to her over the phone that night. "At least your friend exposed you to another facet of Saudi culture that you would not have known otherwise."

"I would rather have been with you."

"Think about what you would have missed had you not gone with him."

"I am thinking about what we are missing because you are not here."

"What, dinner and a guest sleeping in the other room? I hardly think that is worth more than what you got tonight."

Afraid to say more, for fear the wrong thing would come out, I changed the subject. "If Jabbar ever introduces me to other Black Saudis that will be a miracle," I sighed. My comment reminded me of what he had said earlier about his mother. "By the way, tonight he told me he wants me to take him to see his mother. Things could be looking up."

"Good. Then all you have to do is be patient. Once you meet his mother that will be your official introduction to a Black Saudi family, and who knows where that could lead. Does he have brothers and sisters?"

"I know he has brothers in Jeddah, but he never mentioned siblings here in Riyadh. Say, what were you and Jabbar talking about when I went into the house?"

"Actually he did not have a lot to say. Remember I told you Saudi men and doctors talk to me all the time at the hospital, so I pretty much knew what to expect from Mr. Jabbar. All I had to do was ask the right questions. I started out slow, asking about his country. He said he did not know enough English to give me good answers to that question. Then I thought about something you and I have talked about many times. I asked if he was old enough to remember slavery. Adam, your boy's face lit up like a candle. I thought he was going to spill his guts for a moment there. But after a second or two he shot back a curt 'yes.' You know me. I can take a hint. I did not press him. Then I asked what type of work he did. When he told me he was unemployed I kind of flipped out. You heard the rest."

"He admitted he is old enough to remember slavery. Now that is interesting. I will have to explore that further with him when, or if, the right moment ever comes."

"Our plans were scuttled tonight Adam, but we should be better prepared next time as long as you remembered to stop by the Commissary and PX to pick up those items I asked you to get. Did you?"

"Sure babe, I got everything."

"Really, what was the total bill? I want to pay you back."

"I do not remember. I will check the receipt later, but baby you do not have to pay me back. Forget about the money. How about we say good night? I have got to get some sleep. We have tennis practice in the morning."

"Just make sure you have all those things on the list for the next time we get together. Speaking of sleep, I noticed your villa sits next to a Mosque. Do the morning and night prayer calls ever bother you?"

"There is a Mosque next to my villa?"

"I guess that answers my question. Prayer calls do not disturb you then."

"Not since my first day here. I tuned those out early."

"Hopefully I will be able to sleep through them too when I spend the night."

"Trust me you will. I have just the thing to knock you right out."

"Adam I hope you are not talking about anything nasty. You do not know me well enough to say those kinds of things to me."

"Jay-Jay what is so nasty about warm milk and a shot of rum?"

"You have alcohol?"

"Oops."

"Oops nothing, spill the beans."

"Some of us get alcoholic beverages through the Mission, but the distribution is carefully controlled. First of all out of respect for Saudi law, and secondly to make sure none of it gets supplied to an alcoholic. Everyone that signs up for it is closely monitored."

"Well that makes things a little more interesting."

"I certainly am glad to hear you say that."

"I will say good night to you Adam Sneed, and I look forward to coming over after work soon."

"It is a date Jaylynn Sinclair. Oh by the way you said you wanted to cook. What would you like me to pick up from the Commissary?"

"I thought you said you bought everything on the list?"

"I meant did you want anything else, you know like something that you did not put on the list."

"Sure that's what you meant. Okay, do they have pork?"

"Yes."

"Wonderful. I am simply dying for bacon and eggs."

"Then bacon and eggs it is. I will have everything ready for next Wednesday."

"Adam I did not say I was coming over next Wednesday. I work in a hospital remember. I have a crazy schedule and rarely get time off on Thursdays. Maybe I will be able to take a day off a few weeks from now. Sweetheart, I will let you know early enough so you can pick up the bacon."

"Okay baby."

'Pick up the bacon,' that expression became our special code. Each time Jaylynn called, I listened to her every word in hopes that she would slip those four wonderful words into the conversation. It was tough waiting to hear her say them, but I remained hopeful.

❧❧❧❧❧❧❧❦❦❦❦❦❦

Dating in Riyadh was a very different experience. It was odd always having Jaylynn ride in the back seat or waiting for her to wrap up in black cloth from head to waist before we went out in public. Still, to be brutally honest, I developed a great affection for her Abbaya. In its own way, it turned into a special treat.

On Friday's when I picked Jaylynn up at the APO, I spent the drive to church anticipating our arrival at the compound gate. That was where what I came to call 'Jaylynn's routine', always got underway. She would get out of the car; flash her ID to the guard; climb into the front seat next to me; then remove her Abbaya. Every week that was my special moment because I would get my first view of what she was wearing that morning and how she had styled her hair. There was something about the Sinclair girls when they got all gussied up that made a man happy to be alive. Whatever Jaylynn wore I would keep that look in my head until the next Friday because I knew Jaylynn would come out with a totally different look the following week. She seemed to have an endless variety of outfits and hairstyles and all of them were tantalizing to my eyes. Knowing that the efforts she made with her appearance were solely for my pleasure, prompted me to be creative in expressing appreciation. Saying 'Jaylynn, honey, you look nice today' was not good enough. I worked at being innovative with my compliments. In fact I kept a written log to make sure I did not repeat the same compliment twice. I did this because I wanted her to know that her stylishness was precious to me and that I regarded her efforts highly. For example, Jaylynn knew about Lee Williams' repeated invitations to hunt for desert diamonds so one of my compliment s to her was, 'The reason I never go with Lee is because I have already found the most valuable diamond this desert has to offer and that is you Jaylynn.' Maybe those words were not very slick and perhaps they were a bit corny, but trust me, they worked.

When it came to her hair styles, for a long time I wondered if she did her own hair or perhaps a nurse coworker helped her out. Eventually I asked and she told me First Lady Doreen Strong was her stylist. Whenever she needed to get her hair done she would ride out to the Strong's compound. And she always got her hair done on Wednesdays. If she spent the night, Pastor Strong would drive her back to the dorm the next morning in time for her to get to work. The Motor Pool knew Pastor Strong well and trusted him. He was the only other person who took Jaylynn to her dorm other than her regular Motor Pool drivers. She also told me that on the night we first met, the reason she left when she did was because she had to meet Abud so he could drive her out to the Strong's for her regular hair appointment with First

Lady Doreen. Before she and I started dating, Jaylynn spent whole weekends with the Strong's when her work schedule permitted. Now that we were together, the plan was for her to start spending her free weekends with me.

At any rate, Friday mornings never really began for me until Jaylynn unveiled herself at the gate to the Strong's compound. That became one of my favorite moments.

Church service was awesome the weekend of our failed hookup at my villa, although I thought I noticed the ever protective Doreen Strong giving us a few weird looks. I wondered if her intuition was telling her Jaylynn and I had been up to something. Our body language may very well have given her a clue, but thankfully we made it through service and brunch without being raked over the coals.

Week after week I longed for Jaylynn to call and say the magic words 'pick up the bacon'. Waiting to hear those words made the weeks drag by. On the day she finally gave me the signal, I was totally primed for our date. It was a Wednesday afternoon and this time my plan was ready. I would go to the Commissary first, pick up the pork and anything else we might need, drop it at the house, which, by the way, would give me time to take care of any surprise visits by Jabbar, and then I would drive to the APO and collect Jaylynn.

I was so excited for our date that I left the Admin Office fifteen minutes early. Down the stairs of the Ministry I raced and out the front door. But when I looked over to where I had parked, I stopped in my tracks. Standing next to my car grinning brightly, was the predictably ill timed Jabbar back after yet another long disappearance. After the obligatory greeting ritual, I asked, "How did you find out where I work?"

"I was talking about you with some friends. One of them works here and that man knows you. He said good things about you Adam. I told him I already know you are a good man. When I came back from Jeddah, I think maybe I surprise you so I come here today. By the way, some of my friends want to see you dance. One day you and me dance for them, isn't it?"

Friendship is highly valued among Arabs and it means much more than merely hanging out together. To be a friend calls for loyalty and at times sacrifices and friends are not chosen lightly. In our culture the closest thing I can think of, that resembles friendship as Arabs know it is what we call patriotism. It is common for networks of friends to be fiercely loyal to one another in the so-called 'Third World.' This makes a lot of sense when you consider the fact that most of those lands are ruled by absolute monarchs and president's-for-life. Loyalty to a friend is more natural than blind obedience to an unchallengeable ruler. That is also why attacking someone in those parts of the world is the same as declaring war on whole networks of people.

Conversely, if you do something nice for one member of a group you might be asked to do the same for all or parts of the group – like dance for them. Yet even if you are not requested to do something for everyone, the group will honor you simply because you were kind to their friend. That is why when Jabbar said we must dance for his friends; I understood he was not asking if I would be willing to dance. Rather, he was informing me that we were going to be dancing for them. Refusing was pointless and would be considered rude and unfriendly.

As was his habit Jabbar got into the car without asking if I had plans. I was about to tell him I could not hang out with him that night when he said, "I want you to take me to see my mother."

Extremely curious about this request, I asked "When?"

"Now, okay, yala let's go."

Could he be serious? Instantly I was excited and wanted to get going before he changed his mind. But a voice in my head said, 'you know you can't meet Jaylynn and go to the Al-Bughawi residence at the same time.' My mind raced to come up with a solution. There was no way I could let Jabbar ride with me to the APO, so that option was out. One look at him in my car and Jaylynn would back out of our date again. Maybe I could talk Jabbar into waiting for me at the Ministry, run over to get Jaylynn, drop her off at my place, then come back and take Jabbar to see his family.

To be honest I was annoyed with Jabbar for walking in and out of my life at his leisure, as if he expected my world to stop just because he decided to make an appearance. There was absolutely no awareness on his part that I might have other plans, or simply might not be interested in what he had in mind to do. On top of that, Jabbar had my phone number. He could always call ahead rather than just show up unannounced.

Still I could not deny my interest in what he had in mind to do on that particular day. I had been waiting for a chance like this since before I arrived in the Kingdom. It had taken more than a year and a half to get this close to connecting with the Black Saudi Community in Riyadh and the odds were stacked against me if I missed this opportunity. Sure, I could hope to meet another Black Saudi, but how long would that take? Or maybe before my tour ended I would get to Jeddah, where Black Saudis were in greater numbers. Nevertheless, on that day I had a wonderful evening planned and nothing and no one was more important to me than Jaylynn.

"Jabbar, I really want to meet your family but I have something to do right now. If you do not mind, I will drop you somewhere and come back to get you in about an hour?"

"Okay, take me to my mother's house then go. You do not have to stay."

"Jabbar I have wanted to meet your family since I first met you, so I do not want to take you over there and leave right away. The problem is, I was not expecting you this afternoon and I have something else planned. All I need is twenty minutes to take care of it. If you wait here, I will come back and take you to see your mother. Can we do it that way?

"You can take me to my mother's house, isn't it, and then go do what you must do. I will take you to see my mother some other time."

"Sure Jabbar. Let me guess when - a year from now? I will be back in America by then. After all these months of knowing you, it is only now that you have decided to take me to see your mother. Only God knows how much time will pass before you go back to see her again?"

Laughing he answered, "Now you get the point. Only God knows, Insha'Allah!"

I did not like this plan of his for me to take him to see his family then rush back to the APO to get Jaylynn. I continued to weigh my options. But the more I thought about it the stronger the feeling I had that I was about to get into trouble. Last minute changes to any plan involving Jaylynn could be tricky, as I had already experienced. I was highly suspicious that if I took Jabbar to his mother's house I would not get back in time to meet Jaylynn. However, unless I got to Jeddah any time soon, this could be my last chance to meet a family from the Black Saudi community in Riyadh. My hands were tied. I could make no other choice. Jaylynn will understand I told myself. "Tell you what Jabbar, I will take you to your mother's house and stay a few minutes, but I will have to leave you there. I am sure you will be able to find some other way to get to wherever you plan to go when you leave your family tonight."

"No problem," he said grinning with satisfaction.

Perhaps he thought he had successfully manipulated me into doing what he wanted, but I figured once I found out where his family lived I could return on my own if Jabbar never got around to taking me back there again.

Chapter 28

As we drove to the Al-Bughawi residence, the miles piled up and the reality set in that I would never get back in time to meet Jaylynn. I followed Jabbar's directions to the east side of town and an hour or so later we rode into an area with large palatial homes and properties that covered many acres. Back home we called places like that estates. The only difference was the architecture. Massive walls protected these properties and entrance gates varied from elaborate and creative to styles that reflected an earlier period in Arabian history. I expected to drive through this area until we reached a humbler community, but at the gate to one exceptionally large complex Jabbar instructed me "turn in here".

"Is this where your family lives," I asked in disbelief?

Jabbar answered "yes" but sounded annoyed.

The complex was magnificent. 'They must be rich,' I thought to myself but dared say aloud.

Whatever Jabbar's reasons for avoiding his family, I began to suspect they were closely linked in some way to the mystery behind my inability to locate the Black Saudi Community in Riyadh. This made me very excited because I believed a puzzle that had stumped me for a long time was about to unravel. I also knew at that point, that I would never have dropped Jabbar at a residence like this and drive away after a few short minutes.

The guards reacted warily at the sight of an unfamiliar vehicle pulling into the entrance. One of them cautiously approached on the driver's side, alert and fingering the trigger of his automatic weapon. Needless to say, I was nervous. Slowly I lowered my window and Jabbar leaned toward me so the guard could see his face. Relieved, the guard relaxed and smiled as he and Jabbar exchanged greetings. After signaling his companion to raise the bar, he waved us through the gate.

As we entered the complex, my eyes widened in astonishment. The entire compound was professionally landscaped and an army of gardeners were busily attending to palm trees, shrubbery and numerous flower beds. In addition, there were a half dozen or so water fountains all designed in Middle Eastern motifs that added to the artistry and aesthetic beauty of the grounds. One fountain consisted of as a group of seven stone camels standing in a circle facing outward in the middle of a large basin with water pouring out of their mouths into the basin. Another fountain was a palm tree with sheets of water running down the trunk. My favorite was a basin with seven dolphins lined along the outer rim of a basin all facing inward. Streams of water shot out of their mouths and crashed together in the air above the bowl. Gravity caused the majority of the water to fall into the basin below but the heavy spray from the impact of the seven streams colliding spewed a refreshing mist out into all directions of the compound.

The residence was beautiful and quite impressive. Truly a lush oasis in the middle of the desert. Just after we passed through the gate the road forked. On our left three large mansion-sized buildings stood on the north side of the dolphin fountain. The right fork splintered into numerous side streets all lined with humble abodes that I presumed were the residences of the servants of the household.

Instead of taking the right fork, Jabbar pointed me toward the three large structures to our left. As we neared the rear of the middle structure I saw a tennis court. Directly across from the court was a little house exactly like the abodes in the section on the right fork back near the entrance to the complex. Jabbar directed me to park by the little house.

The nets were down on the tennis courts but a pretty little girl was using them for a roller skating surface. Jabbar waved to her when he got out of the car. The little girl nearly lost her balance returning his gesture.

Seconds after Jabbar knocked at the little house, a girl of about 13 opened the door. One look at Jabbar and her eyes widened with shock. I could tell they were related the instant I saw her face. This girl was not wearing a veil, which I assumed was because of her age and the fact she was relaxing in her home. Either way she did not seem at all flustered by my presence.

Realizing her older brother was standing in front of her, she let out a shriek of delight then stretched to the tip of her toes to reach up and embrace the much taller Jabbar. Upon releasing her hold on him, the girl turned and raced inside heralding the news that Jabbar had come home. As I followed Jabbar into his family's residence he whispered, "That one is Nura, my baby sister. She gets too excited about anything." Jabbar was trying to appear irritated, but I had never seen him smile the way he did that day.

A comely young woman of approximately 17 approached next. Like her younger sister, she too was not wearing a veil so I had a full view of the distinctive Al-Bughawi features in her genetic makeup. As with her younger sister, the young lady did not get ruffled at the sight of a strange male standing in the foyer with her older brother. However, in contrast to her sibling any elation at seeing Jabbar flashed all too briefly and her smile quickly turned into a scowl. No translation was necessary for me to understand the reasons behind the withering scolding she began to heap upon Jabbar. She wagged her finger at him so fast and hard I thought it would fall off. Jabbar, despite the embarrassment of being dressed down in front of his guest by a younger sibling, was happy to see her. Sweeping her up into his arms and spinning in a circle Jabbar proclaimed giddily, "This is ya uchti, my sister, Jammilla. As you can see, she likes me too much."

Her name fit her, for the girl was beautiful. Not as lovely as Jaylynn, but very good looking. Breaking free of his grasp, Jammilla automatically switched languages and objected in English, "No, no, no, do not believe him I do not like him at all. He makes my mother cry every night. Um, she worry too much. Jabbar is not good man."

"Yes, yes, yes, save it for some other time... Jammilla this is my friend from America, Mr. Adam. Now go make tea for my guest."

Jammilla cast a glare of pure disdain at Jabbar. I could not help but smile because I knew that look. I had seen it before, many times and it was at that moment even before I was formally introduced to Jabbbar's family that I began to get a warm familiar feeling that said to me 'Adam, these are your people'. Jammilla's face softened as she turned to me with an approving smile that she made sure Jabbar knew was solely for my benefit.

"Your guest," she queried Jabbar? "When did this become your house? Make tea for your own guest lazy man." To me Jammilla grinned and said, "Welcome Mr. Adam. It is very nice to meet you. Come, sit and have some tea. Nura hurry bring..."

Jammilla's instructions were unnecessary for Nura was at that moment returning from the interior of the house with a silver tray loaded with small handled drinking glasses and a silver teapot.

I was ushered into a spacious area that appeared to serve as the living room and reception area for the family and its guests. An older woman wearing a colorful bandana around her neck, exactly like the ones I had seen on the women sitting on the curb outside the ancient bazaar, was sitting on the far side of the room amidst a heap of cloth and sewing implements. A third young girl sat in the middle of the floor. This third girl was older than Nura but younger than Jammilla. It looked like the girls had been shelling peas when Jabbar and I knocked on the front door.

Jammilla presented this third girl to me as, "my sister Samirah."

Samirah held the back of her hand up to me, as if expecting me to kiss it in the French manner and in a comical imitation of Tallulah Bankhead declared, "No, don't call me Samirah. Call me Fifi dah-ling."

Nura and Jammilla laughed hysterically and Jabbar said, "Mr. Adam, I should have warned you about that one. Fifi Dah-ling is crazy."

Samirah, or perhaps I should say Fifi Dah-ling, never spoke again the rest of that visit and by the end of the evening I came to realize she was actually quite shy. The few times I caught her eye she blushed and quickly turned away. In time I learned that Samirah loved western movies, particularly old Black and White films from the Golden Era of Hollywood. I was not too surprised by this because I had heard the Saudis loved American films. With video players in wide use in Arabia, videotapes were in high demand. Films from India and Europe were also in circulation, but American films were highly prized.

"Come meet my mother Mr. Adam."

Jabbar kneeled and kissed the old lady with the colorful bandana tenderly on her forehead. She smiled briefly as he explained, "Ya Umi, hatha sadiq min Amreeka, ismu Sayeed Adam (Mother, this is my friend from America, his name is Mr. Adam). Mr. Adam, this is my mother Yewande Al-Bughawi."

Mrs. Al-Bughawi looked up at me with a face filled with love and brimming with sweetness. She did not have a wrinkle in her skin save for dimples when she smiled. Her eyes though were weathered from years of life. A shrill high pitched sound came out of her mouth as she uttered in English "morning."

"That is the only English word she knows," Jabbar whispered.

Mrs. Al-Bughawi reached for my hands and pulled me to a kneeling position on the floor beside her. Staring affectionately into my eyes, she rocked slowly back and forth. Unlike her face, her hands were knobby and scarred from a lifetime of hard work. For me, looking into her eyes was like peering into history. It was as if our common ancestries were reconnecting after being apart for many centuries. This endearing woman reached inside me and touched my soul with the force of her spirit.

Why had Jabbar waited so long to introduce me to these wonderful people? More importantly, why did he avoid his family? The Al-Bughawi's seemed perfectly lovely.

Jammilla served tea, first to me, next her mother, then to her sister Samirah and finally Jabbar.

On taking my second sip, I looked up and saw Nura leading another family member, a male, into the room. This man was closer to my age than Jabbar, and he approached with outstretched arm. I stood and we shook hands.

"Hello, I am Waleed, Jabbar's brother. Welcome to our home Mr. Adam. Are you hungry? My sisters can fix food, yani anything you like."

"No thank you Waleed. I am not hungry."

Waleed sat on the floor next to me and his mother rose and moved to a far corner of the room where Nura, Samirah and Jammilla were relocating to resume shelling peas. This resulted in the traditional demarcation between males and females. Jabbar sat next to Waleed but continued to eye his mother anxiously, wondering I was sure what had prompted her to put out an APB on him. So far she was acting as if she could care less that he was in the house.

"Ya sheikh," Waleed grumbled, "Nura has already told me koola-shay, yani everything there is to know about you, so there is no need for you to tell me ay-shay, yani anything. I know you very well so you might as well ruuh, go away now," he chuckled. "La yimkin, yani it is not possible for me to learn anything new about you thanks to Nura. Females, my God, they can talk. It is like this, sowa-sowa, in Amreeka with the females, correct?"

I liked Waleed. His random mixing of English and Arabic was entertaining and at the same time educational. There was no doubt in my mind I could learn much by spending time with this family. Right away I started thinking of ways Waleed might be helpful in my quest to learn how life had changed for Blacks in post-slavery Arabia.

In response to his inquiry I said, "I guess I can safely answer that question here. Yes, some women in America are known for doing a lot of talking."

From across the room came a sultry retort from Jammilla, "I heard that Mr. Adam."

Waleed and I laughed. Jammilla's personality reminded me a lot of Jaylynn. The two of them would definitely hit it off if they ever got an opportunity to meet, and yes I was sure they could talk for hours.

"How did you get mixed up with this bad character," Waleed asked pointing to a worried Jabbar who was still taking glances toward the other side of the room.

As I related the circumstances of our first meeting, Jabbar interrupted from time to time to add embellishments that I could tell did not impress Waleed. Waleed then inquired about my job and how I had come to Saudi Arabia. To these questions I provided general information without going into substantive detail.

"Mr. Adam, I have many questions about Amreeka but my English is mo-qwayis, yani, not good," Waleed stated.

"I am also interested in learning about your country Waleed."

"Good, then you come to visit and we talk… if we talk many times, yani, my English will be better and maybe you learn little Arabic too, Insha'Allah."

"Insha'Allah, that sounds wonderful. I would like that very much."

"Meantime ... I really like that word meantime," he laughed. "It is very nice English word. I like how it sounds when you say it. Listen... 'mean... time' Waleed whispered, enunciating the syllables softly as if they were sacred. Then he roared with laughter. "It is like the time is mad at you for something and gets very mean. Yani it is not happy time but mean... time. Ya sheikh, there are many English words like that and I really like them. I say them all the time but sometime I am not sure what they mean. Anyway, I want to say, meantime, yani, when my" turning to Jabbar for help Waleed muttered, "esh is mutha akhuwiya mulad bil Inglizi?"

"Baby brother," Jabbar translated.

"Yes, when my baby brother is home, his name is Tayyib, he speaks English very well, Tayyib is maybe 17 or 18, he can be yani our," turning again to his brother, "Jabbar, esh is mutha mutarjim bil Inglizi?"

"Bil Inglizi, translator," Jammilla yelled from across the room.

"Thanks ya uchti but your name is not Jabbar," he chastised playfully. "Okay, Mr. Adam, when Tayyib is here he can be translator for, yani, you and me – that will be a good thing."

"That sounds like an excellent plan Waleed."

Over the next few hours Waleed struggled bravely to converse with me in English. Jabbar translated what words he could and Jammilla assisted from time to time as well. All of us were groping in the dark, but we did not do half bad. I really appreciated their attempts with English but was terribly embarrassed by my meager Arabic. I had high hopes that my Arabic would improve if I got approval to take the language course at the University of Riyadh.

The evening was delightful, particularly because I got to meet Waleed. As usual our conversation came to an abrupt end by the one thing you could always depend on to disrupt any activity in the Kingdom – prayer call. It was impressive how the family sprung into action to prepare to go to pray. I decided it was as good a time as any to take my leave but as I was about to make my excuses Jabbar stood and announced "ya Umi bi ruuh (mother, we are leaving)."

Waleed pulled Jabbar aside and quickly whispered something in his ear. Meanwhile Jammilla shook my hand and said "Good night Mr. Adam." Nura did the same but spoke in her native language, which I repeated phonetically, "Tisbah al nuur." Mrs. Al-Bughawi giggled and uttered her sole English word "morning."

Waleed held on to our handshake until I promised to come again. He assured me "you can come anytime. Do not wait for Jabbar. Meantime, I will talk to the guards. They will let you inside the gate any time you want to come. Bayeet baytak – yani, my house is your house. Ya sheikh, you are long way from your country without your mother and father and brothers and sisters, so now you have us, we are your family in this country." Waleed's genuine empathy toward a fellow Black who was a foreigner far away from his family, nearly brought tears to us both. Finally, he squeezed me in a bear hug.

While I was saying goodbye to Waleed, Jabbar fidgeted nervously. His mother still had not told him why she had been asking around for him. I got the impression she had every intention of going to prayer without giving him a second thought. Jabbar did not give up but began pleading with her, insisting she tell the reason she had sent for him. I thought she was going to ignore him altogether and leave the room, however, she paused, walked up to Jabbar, smiled, reached up to clasp his face in her hands, pulled his head down to her level and kissed him on the forehead. Jabbar looked puzzled. His mother laughed and was still laughing when she walked out of the room.

What I witnessed between them seemed clear enough. Yewande Al-Bughawi was a mother that wanted to know if she still had enough influence in her wandering son's life to get him to come home if she summoned him. I think she was more than satisfied the moment he walked through the front door, just knowing he was alive and well. Bringing an American friend home was a bonus and may have assured her that Jabbar was staying out of trouble and not hanging around the wrong kind of people. I assumed that was the reason she searched my eyes when she pulled me to the floor next to her. Whatever she saw in me, it was enough for her to accept me as the kind of associate she preferred Jabbar to have. Bottom line, the APB was a litmus test, and it had proven successful. Yet, even though what happened was pretty cut and dry to me, Jabbar continued to look puzzled and frustrated.

When we drove out of the gate the guards waved goodbye. Jabbar only grunted.

There was something else that I noticed about Jabbar during our visit with his family. Not once did Jabbar light up a cigarette. Waleed would tell me later that his family had tried for years to get Jabbar to quit smoking. He was the only member of the family that had the habit. The reason Jabbar did not smoke in his mother's house was because the family banned him from doing so. Later, when I felt the time was right, I prohibited him from smoking in my car.

Shortly after driving through the gate, I remembered Jaylynn and slapped my forehead with the palm of my hand.

"What, you forgot something isn't it," Jabbar asked?

"I was supposed to meet somebody this evening. I will call them when I get home."

"It is that girl I met at your house, isn't it?"

"Yes."

"What is her name again?"

"Jaylynn."

"Kiss her one time and she will forgive you," he snickered then added, "Kiss her two times and she will love you all the night."

Jabbar had assumed correctly that Jaylynn and I were more than casual acquaintances so before he had the chance to get too inquisitive, I changed the subject. "Jabbar I want to ask you something, but I hope you will not get offended by my question."

"What is this word offended?"

"It means to get upset, be angry… something like that."

"No, I will not be angry, you can ask me anything."

"Why do you stay away from your family?"

"Look where they live," he shouted pointing back in the direction of the compound!

"Yes, in a nice home inside a palatial complex. I have to tell you, I was impressed. What is wrong with where they live?"

"Mr. Adam, you do not understand. You do not know how long my family live in that house and work for that family. Listen. When I was little boy, Black people we slaves in this country. Then Prince Faisal say Black people no more slaves, I was seven maybe eight years old. Waleed he ten, I think. I say nothing to my mother or Waleed, but I walk out that gate, the same gate we go through tonight. I want to see if anybody try stop me. Guards look but say nothing. I go stay three days. When I go home, my mother, oooh she very, very angry. My brother he hit me many times but I only laugh. He hit – I laugh. He hit – I laugh. We do like that long time. Waleed get tired, he say, 'why you laugh when I hit you?' I say, 'Prince Faisal say you free! What you do? Nothing. Not me. I go and come anytime because I free. Now I come home and what you do. You hit me. So I laugh because this first time free man beaten by slave in this house.'"

It was a jolt to realize that when I was ten years old, an eight year old on the other side of the world was testing the validity of an edict on freedom made by a powerful monarch. Historically, with respect to the African Diaspora, the actions of young eight year old Jabbar Al-Bughawi were both unheralded and heroic. I was moved by his story. That young lad had, at age eight, provided one the clearest attestations I had ever heard in support of the innate desire in all humans to live free. The eight year olds comment to his ten year old brother, however, that a free man had been beaten by a slave tickled me so I started laughing.

"Waleed he laugh too when I say this,' Jabbar informed me. "We both laugh long time. Then he take my hand and say 'come.' He take me to my mother and he say 'ya Umi, me and Jabbar we go out but we return soon.' So we walk, holding hands, out to gate. Waleed say hello to guards, then we walk out that place together. We walk maybe one kilometer then Waleed take me back. Waleed say to me, 'I do this thing because I want to show you how free man works. I am free. Like you, I come and go when I want. But I do not hurt my family or make my mother cry all the night. That is what you did Jabbar. You left this house three days and nobody know where you go. Everybody worry, think maybe you dead. What you did was wrong. And you are wrong when you say free man beaten by slave in this house today. A bad boy was beaten by his brother because the boy did not respect his family. Jabbar listen to me. I want you to know I am very proud for what you did and reason you do it, but not how you do it. If you go away again and not tell your family, I promise, you will have to pay too much for your freedom. You will think you slave again and this free man will beat you.' So I say to Waleed, 'I went away three days because I do not like this place. This family slaves here too long. I want to go out. You watch. When I get big, I go out and I stay out.' But I learn two things that day Mr. Adam. I was wrong to hurt my mother and Waleed he proud of me."

I intended to muse privately when I said, "You were trying to show your family that this place reminds you of slavery, so you do not want to have anything more to do with it," however, without thinking the words actually came out of my mouth.

"That's it," Jabbar agreed.

"And that is what you have been telling your family ever since." I could not help but smile at Jabbar. After being around him all those months, I could easily see him at age eight boldly walking out of the residence of the people that once owned his family. His reaction to the edict fit his personality and his story made such a deep impression on me that I felt a rush of pride toward this fellow Black of the African Diaspora. Whether he realized it or not, at eight years of age Jabbar became one of our heroes. He may not have been a hero on the level of a Crispus Attucks, Rosa Parks, Martin Luther King, Jr. and a host of others, but he had their spirit and at a very young age had exhibited an inspiring level of courage.

Everything I thought about Jabbar changed after that. It was a delight to discover my friend was much deeper than his life style indicated. Out of respect and homage I instinctively reached out to shake his hand. Our eyes met and a look passed between us that said more than either of us could have articulated with a thousand words. It was a Black man to Black man moment that crossed all the cultural, geographic and historical barriers the world outside of Africa has erected to separate Black people from our common heritage.

"Jabbar you are amazing," I said. "But where did you go in Riyadh all by yourself at age eight, and what were you doing for three days while your family was at home worried sick about you?"

"I walk long time and get very tired and very hungry. I am so hungry I could eat... what is this thing bil Inglizi... I do not know... we call it konzia... it is harram for Muslim... mamnua yani."

"Are you talking about pork?"

"Yes, that's it. I am so hungry if somebody give me pork, I eat it ala-tool, straight away, no problem. But I keep walking. Then I smell food, so I follow my nose to this place where I see many people. They dance and sing and have much food. It is wedding. I see the food but I am Black so if I go inside oooh wheee big trouble. But this boy, my age, he see me. He come and ask, 'what is your name.' I say to him Jabbar. He say, 'my name Sami.'"

"Wait. Is this the Sami whose house I take you to sometime?"

"Yes that is the one. Sami he say come play with us. So I go. Many boys there and they play football. I play too. Then they want to drink something and say, Jabbar you come. We go to the place of the food but they give me water. I take the water but my eyes only look to the food." Pointing to his abdomen, Jabbar further explained, "When I drink the water something inside me do something very loud."

I translated, "Your stomach growled."

"Yes, my stomach growled like... esh es mutha bil inglizi... lion, that's it. It growled like lion. So Sami ask if I want food. I say yes. He say it-fadle, welcome, eat. I very happy. But when his father see me he come and say, 'Sami who is this Abidan?' Sami say, 'he is my friend Jabbar.' Then father say, your friend Jabbar must go home because this your brother's wedding. Tell him come back bah-d bah-d bukra (the day after the day after tomorrow), yani after two days. But I see where people dancing so I run to that place and I dance too. Sami's Father he very angry. I think, maybe he do not like Black people. But when he see me dance, he like it very much. After that he say okay you can stay. Wedding party three days, I stay three days. Then I go to home."

"So that is how you started dancing at weddings."

"That was first time, yes."

I had asked Jabbar why he stayed away from his family and, unknown to him, his response had provided a very big first piece of the puzzling mystery behind the Black Saudi community of Riyadh. But I wanted to know more.

"Jabbar if your family can leave at any time, why have they stayed in that place all these years?"

"Everybody in Saudi Arabia is Muslim, but not all people good. Some Black families work for bad people. We lucky, the Rashid family always good to us. They love my mother. Many times my mother say she will move, but the Rashid talk to her and she change her mind and stay."

"Do you think they will ever leave that place?"

"Waleed tell me tonight they will leave soon."

"But the Rashid will try to talk her out of it again, right?"

"This time they will move. Tayyib he finish high school soon."

"Is that what they been waiting for all these years, for Tayyib to graduate?"

"That is not it. You see, in Saudi Arabia when a boy finish high school the government give him 30,000 Riyals. When he finish college he get 100,000 Riyals and some land so he can build house or business, whatever he want. Waleed finish high school and college so he put 130,000 Riyals in bank and he has land. Now Tayyib finish high school so he put his 30,000 Riyals with Waleed's 130,000 Riyals in bank. Waleed is building new house on his land. The house will be finished soon and my family will move out of that place. Whole family will live in this new house, even my sister in Egypt will come back to live in that place."

"You have another sister?"

"Yes, her name is Hawwa. She older than Waleed."

"What about you, will you live in the new house?"

"Insha'Allah."

What Jabbar told me about Saudi boys getting money after completing specific levels of education, had my head spinning. This was the way to integrate a disenfranchised community into mainstream society. With money and land, Black families could not only shed the stains of slavery, they could eliminate its odors as well and take back control of their lives.

I thought about my six siblings. Had we grown up in Saudi Arabia, as much as 970,000 Riyals, the equivalent of $320,000.00, would have been generated between us. There were a million things my family could have done with that kind of money. What a revelation, and to think I would never have known about these things had I canceled my contract. It had been important after all that I came to Arabia and sought out Black Saudis. Enlightenment was intoxicating and I was hungry to learn more.

"What about you Jabbar? Did you put 30,000 Riyals in the bank?"

"I did not go to school."

Even if it put Jabbar on the spot I had to ask. "Why didn't you go to school?"

"I do not want to talk about that," he answered curtly.

"Fair enough - is Tayyib planning to go to college?"

"Yes he will go to college."

The natural follow-up question was to ask if Saudi girls received educational incentives too, but I decided not to ask Jabbar if his sisters earned incentives money. I had already put him on the spot about his own education. Asking him to admit his sisters brought money into the family coffers, when he himself had not might be too humiliating for him. I would ask Abdullah Al-Basheer about it the next chance we got to talk. If my suspicions were right about the girls, then the potential financial gain in the Al-Bughawi family after 19 years of freedom was astounding after adding the earnings of all the siblings together. Historically, these kind of educational and financial opportunities were unprecedented among any group of former slaves.

Learning about the system the Saudis had in place was a watershed moment in my tour. Their programs ran rings around anything I had heard of anywhere. Prior to that night the only thing I had been aware of about Saudi government programs was that they were funneling billions into developing a modern infrastructure. Now I knew the government was also investing real money and economic power directly into the hands of its citizens. Incentives to get an education and acquire skills was good for the population and it accommodated the national goal of building an indigenous workforce. It was a win-win situation for the government and its citizens. With a national workforce in place they could phase out the two million strong communities of foreign workers in the country and recoup billions into the national treasury. The government could take money currently being spent on housing, food, management, salaries and security to cover foreign workers and redirect those funds elsewhere and thusly foster further economic growth.

I thought back to Faisal's 1962 edict freeing Blacks. That decree could not have been timelier. Citizenship gave Black families like the Al-Bughawis, full rights to participate with fellow Saudis in the huge task of moving as a nation into the modern world.

Another aspect of Black freedom that was significant and affected my search for the community in Riyadh, was the amenability of former slave owners to continue sheltering their former slaves until Black families were able to stand on their own. The acquisition of education, skills, money and property were tickets to a life of economic independence.

Considering the large number of former Black slaves in Arabia, there was no telling how many housing starts were underway at that very moment in the Kingdom. I could only admire Saudi Arabia now that I knew Black Saudis had risen to a level where they were also making contributions to the country's growth. And considering the fact that education is free in Saudi Arabia, citizens would have to spend the rest of their lives paying back loans.

Jabbar's revelations that evening were the starting points to clearing up the mystery of why I had so much difficulty locating the Black Saudi Community in Riyadh. Simply put, at the time of my tour the community did not exist - at least not in the traditional sense. Until they could stand on their own feet, many Blacks apparently had continued to live and work for their former owners. Therefore, since Riyadh was the seat of government in Arabia and the traditional stronghold of the House of Saud, a large number of former Black slaves still lived in the palaces and royal residences of Saudi princes and princesses. Obviously, the chances of me running into Blacks living in palaces were slim. Fahad's invitation to visit his home was quite fortuitous in that it led to my meeting Jabbar, a Black Saudi whose family did not work for members of Saudi royalty. Working for the Rashid's, however, did not mean the Al-Bughawis were employed by a family of commoners. The Rashid's were formerly rivals of the Saudis in Eastern Arabia and still possessed considerable wealth.

The idea that Blacks in Arabia will eventually evolve into a separate entity or true Black Saudi Community appears doubtful because Saudi Arabia is one of the strictest Muslim countries in the world. If you ask any Saudi, Black or White, they will tell you their country is monolithic when it comes to race. 'We are all the same in Islam,' they insist. From the perspective of a western Black, I felt their viewpoint on race was more idealistic than actual. As far as I was concerned, a distinction will always exist between Blacks and Whites so long as the term Abidan is used by Arabs. Or it is possible that the only people who are sensitive to that term are Blacks from the West, like me.

When all is said and done, I had nothing but praise for the Saudis because they treated their former Black slaves equitably when they offered them the opportunity to participate in and benefit from the country's modernization drive. Certainly, what Blacks in Arabia received was better than promises of 40 acres and a mule, affirmative action, welfare and reparations combined.

The information I received that night was overwhelming. It was a lot to absorb and I knew I needed to learn more about the country. Even as I pondered over the things Jabbar shared with me, I realized not everyone in the country was benefiting from the programs. There were exceptions. For example, questions were raised in my mind about that poverty stricken neighborhood Jabbar had me squeeze my car through the day he climbed out of the window into the front room of his friend's home. Why weren't they benefiting from the government programs? While driving around town I had seen White Saudis living in squatter's tents right in the city. Once I parked and walked through one of these small tent cities and confirmed those people were living in squalid conditions. In addition, I had questions about people who were too old to go to school when slavery ended or who were childless and never had offspring to send to school. What were their chances of attaining economic independence through the education incentives program? Were there other programs available in lieu of education incentives? Obviously I did not have enough information to even begin assessing Saudi society or the status of Blacks in post-slavery Arabia. Nevertheless it made sense, at least from what I had learned to that point, that a percentage of Blacks would likely remain dependent on their former owners for the balance of their lives.

There was an interesting offshoot from Jabbar introducing me to his family. The man did a 180 with respect to his attitude about taking me to meet other Blacks. We continued to visit his friends in the city only now he included stops at homes of his Black Saudi friends. Many lived in situations like his family, as residents in the homes of former owners and like the Al-Bughawis were pooling their funds and planning to build their own homes.

A number of the young Black men I met were members of the military, which meant their families had never been slaves in Arabia. It was explained to me that only men of the Saud tribe and members of the tribes that allied with Ibn Saud when he took over the country were permitted to join the military. These Blacks descended from free men who belonged to tribes that had been loyal to the Saudis prior to 1932.

෧෧෧෧෧෧෧෧෧෧෧෧෧෧

Chapter 29

I dropped Jabbar off at a ma'taam (restaurant) on Airport Road and hurried home to wait for Jaylynn's call. It came shortly after I got into bed.

"Adam, you are finally home. Where have you been, I have been calling all evening. Are you okay?"

"Yes I am fine."

"Thank God you are safe."

"Of course I am safe. Jaylynn - is something wrong?"

"Listen carefully Adam because I do not have a lot of time and I cannot stay on the phone long. I am at the APO. Dempsey is here with me. I am using his phone. Adam, they are watching me - the hospital. An agent has been assigned to follow me. Someone spread a rumor that I am seeing a man and that we are not married. Remember Martha? I told you about her. She is the best friend of the nurse that got kicked out of the country. I suspect Martha is behind this. She does not know anything about my personal life, not really, but she will always resent me because I replaced her friend. I was probably on her hit list before I got to Riyadh. If she is the person behind this, it is being done out of spite. Abud, the driver I told you about, the one I trust, alerted me to what is going on when he drove me here tonight. He urged me to be careful. I assured him I was not meeting anyone and was only going to the APO to watch a movie. I told him he could either wait or come back in two hours. When I went inside the theater I sent for Dempsey and asked him to meet you at the gate and let you know what is going on. I made him promise that whatever happened, he should make sure you did not come into the theater while I was there. He said he would try to talk you into riding out to your Rec Center, or do something else to get you away from the APO facility. Then when I came out of the theater after the film, Dempsey was still waiting for you to show up. We have been calling your house ever since."

"Jaylynn, I never made it to the APO tonight."

"Oh my God Adam, were you stopped?"

"No, don't be alarmed. Nothing happened to me. Jabbar is back in town. I was on my way to my car after work and there he was at the Ministry waiting by my car in the parking lot when I got off work."

"I did not know he knew where you worked."

"Neither did I, so you can imagine how surprised I was to see him there. Jaylynn he asked me to take him to see his family tonight."

225

"So you went with him then. Good."

"Hold up. Why aren't you angry? Baby, I stood you up."

"Adam Jabbar's timing was perfect, for a change. No I am not angry. Your friend may have saved us from a world of trouble. There is no way I can be mad at him for that."

"Here I have been worried all evening that you were going to call and read me the riot act tonight. Come on, tell the truth Miss Sinclair. You would not be reacting this way if you had not found out you were being followed, am I right?"

"Possibly, but chances are had we gone through with our plans we both would be in jail right now. No Adam, I am happy you got to visit Jabbar's family. I know how important it was for you to meet them. Like you have said many times, we will never get the chance to come to Saudi Arabia again. I am not upset about our date. Even if I was not being followed, I would have known automatically that something had come up when you failed to show. Trust me honey, I am not about to forget where we are. And don't you forget for one minute, that I support your efforts all the way. I want you to learn as much as you can while you are here. You should know by now I will always stand behind you, and support you in whatever you do. Plus, what you are doing benefits me too. I am learning a lot of wonderful things about Saudi Arabia thanks to you, and not just me, Lovelen and Barry also. I could never go into the places you get to see, or do nearly half the things you do. So I depend on you for enlightenment about what I am beginning to see really is an incredible country, despite its determination to keep single people apart."

"Jaylynn you are such a wonderful woman. Believe me darling, I will make up for tonight a hundredfold when we get together."

"That is another thing. I do not think it is a good idea that we see each other – not for awhile at least. Not until all this suspicion goes away. I plan to stay away from Pastor Strong's compound too as a further precaution. The last thing I want is for them to get dragged into this. I am so afraid Saudi agents will follow me out to their compound, maybe take down license plates of members of the church and trace them back to their companies. As it is, I am not too sure they are not planning to go out there anyway."

"Nobody would be in trouble for attending Christian services on an expatriate compound, would they?"

"No, but a witch hunt is underway to try to catch the man I am supposed to be seeing so there is no telling what trouble they might cause for members of the church. I simply do not want to take that risk. Adam, I need you to go along with me on this and stay away from that compound for the time being. Will you do that for me?"

"Anything you say baby, of course I will. Prudence is our watchword, remember. Okay, so what do we do now?"

"For the time being we will communicate through Dempsey. He has agreed to funnel notes from me straight to you and you can leave notes for me with him at the APO."

"This puts a permanent barrier between us."

"I know honey, it sucks. But you know what they say – absence makes the heart grow fonder."

"Sure but do you know what frustration does to the body? I am going to go crazy not being able to hold you in my arms or kiss you or hear you say pick up the bacon."

"Be patient my love. Think of how special everything will be when we finally come together. Meantime we just have to persevere."

Hearing Jaylynn use the word meantime brought my conversation with Waleed back to mind and I laughed. She asked, "What is so funny Adam?"

I started relating the events of that evening and she enjoyed them immensely, especially my descriptions of the Al-Bughawi family members. Jaylynn was quite amused by Samirah, aka Fifi dah-ling, and liked the idea of one day getting to meet Jammilla.

"If you can arrange that, I would love to talk with Jammilla. She needs to know that what you said about American women talking a lot is not true."

"Hey, I was just going along with Waleed, you know, trying to make a good first impression. I am sure you will get to meet Jaylynn and the two of you will set the record straight. Of course, in view of the present situation it could be awhile before the two of you can do anything like that. By the way, I feel the same way about the Al-Bughawi's as you do about the Strong's. I would not want Jabbar's family to get caught up in our problems either. From what I have learned from Jabbar and Waleed thus far, Black Saudis are still finding their freedom legs in this country."

"Adam, promise me you will be careful."

"I will do my best dear, and you do the same."

"This is the last time we will be able to talk on the phone for a long time so make sure you keep me updated about your visits with the Al-Bughawi's, and everything else in your life when you write to me."

"Of course I will. I love you."

"I love you too. I have to get out to the gate because Abud has been waiting for a long time. Do you want to speak with Dempsey?"

"Yes."

She said a quick "goodnight" and handed him the phone.

I asked Dempsey to make sure Jaylynn got off safely and call me back afterward to solidify the set up for our message exchanges.

Chapter 30

At the Ministry, I spoke with Abdullah Al-Basheer and asked him about the education incentives. Abdullah confirmed the system was in place and that it had been established to promote education and stimulate the development of a skilled domestic workforce that would in time eliminate the need for foreign laborers. Al-Basheer also clarified that these distributions were not simply handouts but interest free loans to be repaid at a later date and, yes, girls also received awards. On the other hand, he admitted that so far no government agency or procedure had been established to collect on the loans.

"Could the government change its mind and call in these loans at some point in the future," I asked?

"Possibly, but chances are that will not happen for a couple of generations if at all."

Other Saudis I spoke with about these programs informed me that they considered these government programs as a means to share the oil wealth. As one young man explained it, 'the oil does not belong to the Saudi family. It belongs to everybody in Arabia.'

Putting wealth into the hands of the common citizen was an excellent way for the Saudi government to invest in its own future. Not only was this good strategy in support of the nation's economy, it also encouraged loyalty and cooperation with the royal family by the present population and future generations.

Minister Al-Naseem approved my application for the six week Arab language course at the University of Riyadh. Classes were to begin in a month and would take place two evenings out of the week at the University's Arab Language Institute.

On the morning that Minister Al-Naseem's approval came through, Khaleel came to my office and informed me that I was wanted downstairs. Khaleel did not know who had sent for me, but his instructions were to take me to a specific room on the first floor. Before going downstairs I stopped by Al Dennison's office to inform him that I had been summoned by the Saudis.

"Who could be calling for you on the first floor," Al wondered aloud?

"I have no idea, but I wanted to alert you before I went down."

"I suppose you will have to go and find out. Keep me posted."

Khaleel led me to a room that I had observed in passing many times. The reason it had caught my attention was because a lot of activity went on in and around it. A stream of young Saudi males were constantly going in and out of that room throughout the day. From what I had overheard, these guys formed the messenger corps for the Ministry. If something had to be transported around town or delivered to another Ministry, these young men made the trip. Unsurprisingly, they owned the smallest and speediest cars in the parking lot.

One young man welcomed me in halting English saying, "Ahmed, he come… moment, please sit, take your rest."

The half dozen or so other males in the room were occupied reading the *Saudi Gazette* or *Al-Jazeerah* newspapers.

The young man who first greeted me spoke up again. "My name uh, Tawhid (t-ow-heed), nice to meet you Mr. Adam."

"It is nice meeting you too Mr. Tawhid."

"Um, this Falah (fah-lah)," he said pointing to one of his coworkers, "and this Abdul-Haqq (ab-dool hawk), this Mudar (moo-dar), and this Abdul-Ahad (ab-dool ah-haad)." I shook hands with each man as they were introduced.

"Moment, Ahmed he come," Tawhid repeated.

As I waited, I felt a bit nervous about what might be in store. I did not know any of these young men, although I had seen a number of them from a distance.

After a lull of five minutes a side door burst open and in charged an effervescent young man who walked right up to me with outstretched hand

and in a bubbly manner introduced himself. "Ahmed Al-Saud (awk-med aul-sow-uud) is the name. You must be Mr. Adam."

I was astounded to hear an Arab speak English with a cockney accent. As I shook hands with him I responded, "Yes, my name is Adam Sneed, Jr. Nice meeting you Mr. Ahmed."

"From the look on your face I'd say you are wondering about my accent. I studied in England and spent a lot of time in Piccadilly Square, but that's another story," he chuckled with a wink of his eye. "To get to the point, you probably want to know why we asked you to come here today."

Ahmed had a disarming smile and happy eyes. I was quite amused with his manner and animation.

"We just had a meeting upstairs. Minister Al-Naseem told us you applied for the Arabic course for western businessmen at the University of Riyadh. Minister Al-Naseem also said that in all the Ministries in the city of Riyadh, you are the only American that applied. This has made us very proud. We also want you to know that we have been watching you Mr. Adam, and have come to respect you a great deal because you have shown a lot of interest in us. Most Americans that come to Saudi Arabia only come to make money. You are the first American to come to this Ministry who asked about us and our customs. This makes us very happy. Since you are so interested in us, we want to honor you in some way. My friends and I have been talking, trying to think of something we can do to show how we feel about you. Tell me, have you ever heard of Cupsah?"

"No, I have never heard of it."

"It is a formal meal for when we celebrate something. We would like to invite you to a special dinner in your honor. Would you accept our invitation and be our guest of honor?"

"Thank you very much for your kind invitation. Yes, I would love to come."

"Good. Everybody here will be at the dinner. You have already met Tawhid Al-Nedjaris; the dinner will be at his house. He lives not far from here. Pick a day when you want to come and we will meet you here at the Ministry and take you to his house."

When I returned to the third floor I told Al Dennison about the dinner invitation.

"Congratulations," Al responded.

I did not mention that the invitation was the result of my being the only American in the city to apply for the Arabic language course at the University.

After work that evening, I went to visit the Al-Bughawis. Waleed had lived up to his word because the guards remembered me and as soon as I drove up to the gate I was motioned right through. As I pulled up to the house, Waleed was coming out.

"Mr. Adam, it is good to see you again. Now I have business at the airport. Go inside and sit, drink tea, eat if you like and when I come back we will talk."

"How long will you be gone?"

"Not long. Maybe you like to come with me? We can talk while I drive."

For the second time since coming to Riyadh, I was a passenger in a car driven by a Saudi. I just hoped Waleed was as obedient to traffic laws as Abdullah Al-Basheer had been.

As soon as Waleed stepped on the gas, I knew I was in trouble. Waleed was a typical Saudi driver. To say I was nervous does not come close to describing the terror I felt as he zipped through the streets running red lights and stop signs, jumping from one lane to the next and repeatedly coming within millimeters of hitting bumpers or scraping side mirrors. We reached the airport much faster than we would have if I had driven. I was white-knuckled from gripping the seat and my nerves were shot. Waleed parked in the lot and said he would be right back. His business took less than ten minutes.

On our way back to his house, Waleed asked where I lived. When I suggested we could stop by my villa if he would like to see it, he accepted. The first thing he noticed when we walked in the door was a videotape lying on the coffee table. He picked it up right away to inspect. It was a new movie that was making the rounds in the expatriate community. I had picked it up at Larry Corbin's house the previous day. Larry said everyone was giving it high praises. The film was called *Carbon Copy*. Waleed saw the face of a Black actor on the cover and got very excited.

"Ya sheikh, I love films with Black people in them. Can I watch this film with you now?"

"Sure," I said and put the film in the video player.

"Who is this actor? I have not seen his face before?"

"Neither have I. Larry Corbin, the guy I got the film from, said he is a new so this is his first movie. Let's see, his name is," after reading over the cover I announced, "Denzel Washington."

Waleed and I watched Mr. Washington's debut film together. We both loved it and Waleed said, "Ya sheikh, very good this man. Helowa jiddan (very sweet) yani I like him too much. I want my family to see this film."

I agreed and told him, "This guy is incredibly talented Waleed. I can tell he is going to have a great career."

Waleed drove me back to his house so I could get my car, but I stayed to watch *Carbon Copy* again. I was not about to let that videotape out of my sight. I also hoped to find his younger brother Tayyib at home. Jammilla said he was out hunting Jerboa in the desert with the Rashid brothers. My second sitting through *Carbon Copy* was more enjoyable than the first because I got to watch it with Waleed and his family. Jammila, Fifi and Nura loved Denzell Washington and raved "very handsome this Black man." Waleed, agreeing with my earlier comment, said "I believe this man is going to be very great actor."

Between that visit and the start of Arabic classes at the University, I visited Waleed several times. On each occasion we muddled through conversations as best we could. The going was slow, but I was learning quite a bit about the eldest Al-Bughawi brother. It was obvious early on that I had more in common with him than I did with Jabbar. Waleed was as passionate as I was when it came to the challenges Blacks face as free people, particularly in lands where their ancestors originally arrived in chains. We definitely saw eye to eye on that score. Even more impressive to me was the extent of his knowledge of Black American history. But there was one thing I noticed about Walled that had me puzzled. Whenever I swung the conversation toward talking about Black history in Arabia, his responses only went to a point then stopped. He never gave out a lot of details. It was as if he knew more Black American history than that of his own people. Lovelen, if she were permitted to come to Arabia, would probably have been able to get him to open up a little more. But when he and I talked, I always had the feeling he was holding some things back.

Dinner with my Saudi co-workers was set for a Wednesday after work. We rendezvoused in the Ministry parking lot as planned.

Tawhid's home was a five minute drive from the Ministry. Everyone I met the day I was summoned to the first floor was there - Falah, Mudar,

Abdul-Haqq, Tawhid, Abdul-Ahad and Ahmed Al-Saud. I also got to meet Tawhid's younger brothers Nasser, Khalid, Mansur and the youngest, eight year old Ajib.

Like typical Saudi homes, Tawhid's house was surrounded by a wall. Inside the gate we crossed a courtyard to the front door where we took off our shoes and sandals. From past experience I was familiar with socializing Arab style, but this was different. Cupsah was special and more formal than a regular meal. So I waited and watched for cues as to what I should do next. Professional attendants, hired for the occasion, arranged a lovely setting and began the ceremony by bringing each guest a bowl with a steaming hot towel in it for us to clean our hands.

For the next twenty minutes we engaged in light chatter. Three attendants entered the room carrying a large tray on their shoulders on top of which was a mound of rice sitting on a bed of carrots, peas, corn, lettuce, tomatoes and cucumbers. Sprawled across the top of the rice mound was a half of a lamb. The meat was roasted in herbs and spices. The aroma was exotic. Everyone, including me, was anxious to get started. Young Ajib demonstrated for me how to kneel and the posture I should assume to partake of the food. I did not understand his words, but his gestures were easy to follow. Once I was in place, the rest of the guests took their positions. Steaming towels were handed out a second time for us to once again clean our hands. Next bowls of soup were brought out and placed in front of each guest along with a glass of water and fruit. Tawhid jumped up like he had forgotten something and surprised me when he came back with forks and knives and placed them on a napkin next to me. The way he handled them, I could tell he did not have a clue how they were used.

Ahmed officially began the meal by offering to show me, as the honored guest, how to eat Saudi style. "Of course you can use the fork and knife if you prefer, but so that you know how we do it in Saudi Arabia I will demonstrate how to eat with your hand." He tore off a piece of meat then grabbed up a handful of rice all of which he squeezed into a tight ball in the palm of his hand. Using his thumb like a lever he then deftly flipped the ball of rice and meat into his mouth. I copied his lead as best I could, but was clumsy at it and dropped most of the rice on the floor. Everyone else reached into the serving tray and the meal was underway.

Should I eat the Western way or continue trying the local method? Looking at Ahmed, I shrugged my shoulders and said "When in Rome" and tore another piece of lamb off with my hand. I spent most of the meal fumbling with the technique and dropped more food than I realized. The trick was to squeeze the food into a tight enough ball so that it would not fall apart before you popped it into your mouth. Eventually I came up with a workable strategy that allowed me to eat a reasonable amount of food. I wish I had known what I was doing because everything was so tasty. The meat was seasoned very nicely and the rice was unlike any I had ever eaten.

During the meal I was introduced to another interesting Bedouin custom. Intermittently someone tore off a piece of lamb and tossed it in front of me. This puzzled me until Ahmed explained, "That is our way of honoring a special guest. By taking the offering, whenever someone tosses you a piece of meat, it is like accepting a personal invitation from that individual to share the meal together." Over the course of the evening everyone ripped off a bit of meat and tossed it over to me. Even young Ajib tossed me a piece of lamb and gave me the nicest smile when he did so that was full of warmth and hospitableness. I truly felt honored to be among them.

Ahmed took a moment to explain an aspect of Saudi eating etiquette that I had already figured out on my own. "I don't know if you noticed, but we are all eating with the right hand. So make sure you do not reach in to take food with your left. If you eat with your left hand, nobody will invite you to eat with them again."

Al Dennison's explanation of the Arab's preferred method of cleaning themselves after defecating had paved the way for me to figure out this cultural no-no on my own, so Ahmed's explanation did not catch me off guard. I did ask, "What happens if a person is naturally left handed. Does that present a problem when he or she is invited to dinner?"

"No. Once you reach a certain age everyone that knows you and your family would be aware that you are left handed. But I will tell you something you might find interesting. Thieves get their hands cut off here after they are caught stealing a third time. After the third time we figure they are incorrigible. The problem is that, the right hand is always amputated. This means for the rest of that person's life he has to use the left hand for everything – if you know what I mean."

"Yes, there is no need to go into details on that Ahmed. I have already been thoroughly educated on that matter."

The other guys grabbed their noses, wagged their left hands in the air and made related gestures when Ahmed translated our discussion.

"That is the main reason why thieves are never invited to dinner. Another thing about being a thief, people will not marry your sisters if you have any because they believe that kind of thing is hereditary."

"Your culture is quite interesting. A person could do things here that would bring shame on his whole family and it would literally take generations for his relatives to live it down. Crime really does not pay here."

"That is true, and if you notice we have very little crime. Most of the time when we hear about a crime on the news, it does not surprise us that it was done by a foreigner because many of them do not know our laws. But for the most part this country is very safe. Even now you will see women walking around early in the morning wearing gold and other jewelry and nobody bothers them because our penalties for crime are harsh and swift."

Ahmed was right. I had recently heard of a Philippine man getting beheaded for a crime. He broke into a jewelry store, robbed the place and killed the proprietor. Within weeks of the robbery, he was caught and executed. There was no long jail time while waiting to be brought to trial and no long appeals processes that could take decades. It was swift justice, as the crossed swords and palm tree emblem of the country represents.

"In some ways our societies are alike, but we are very different when it comes to crime" I said. "For instance, my brother or sister could steal something and get caught and I might be embarrassed to see their faces on the evening news. But for the most part, I can go on with my life without having to suffer because of their actions. So in America we have a measure of insulation from bad decisions on the part of a relative."

"Do you know what we young Saudis like most about American culture? The way Americans fall in love and get married. We do not have that here. Our parents arrange our marriages for us. They pick the bride, pay the dowry, or we pay it ourselves, and then we get married. Most young guys like me and Tawhid, would prefer to get our wives American style. You know, meet a girl, fall in love, court her and then get married. But here it is almost impossible to even see a girl, let alone meet her and get to know her well enough to propose marriage. But things are changing, slowly. For instance, until recent generations it was not customary for married people to even see each other naked. In fact I doubt my grandfather ever saw my grandmother naked."

"How did they manage that? I mean the fact you are here proves they…" I glanced at young Ajib kneeling next to me and finished "had children." Delicately, I added, "They had to be able to see what they were doing."

"In past generations, husbands and wives usually did not live in the same house, or tent, as the case may have been. It was like that here in the Middle East for centuries. When my grandfather wanted to see my grandmother he went to her house and she waited for him in the bedroom. They never turned on the light, so everything happened in the dark. In fact they never got completely undressed. She would lie on the bed; he would go in and do what he had to do then leave. My father and his siblings grew up in my grandmother's house but only got to see my grandfather occasionally whenever he came by. Some people in Arabia still live that way as a matter of fact."

"Are you married Ahmed?"

"Yes, I am. I got married two months ago. But my marriage is nothing like my grandfather's. My wife and I stay in the same house and we definitely see each other naked," he added with a laugh. "Actually, when it comes to sex we are curious about everything. The things we see people do in sex films, we try it all."

When Ahmed translated our conversation for the rest of the guests, there were hoots and wolfish howls, nods of agreement, thumbs up gestures and a couple of mildly lewd hand and pelvic motions to confirm agreement with everything Ahmed had said.

Following the meal, we stood up and the attendants came and took away the large platter with the remnants of the food. While Ahmed explained that the leftovers would be given to the poor, young Ajib suddenly shouted to Tawhid, "shy-eef" and pointed to the area on the floor where I had knelt to eat.

Everyone started laughing. Looking down I saw that the blanket we had knelt on was completely unsoiled with the sole exception of the spot where I had eaten. Kernels had been dropping from my hand the whole time and now a perfect half arc of rice marked the aftermath of my first attempt at eating Saudi style. Talk about being embarrassed. I felt like a child that had eaten without a bib. I made less of a mess when I used chopsticks for the first time.

"Next time I will do better," I promised.

As I was leaving, Tawhid grabbed my hand and invited me in his best English. "Bayeet, baytak. My house, you house. Now come anytime, no invite, just come, anytime. Um, now we brothers."

These ordinary Saudi citizens had shown me hospitality and warmth that I would never forget. But I knew what they had done was not considered extraordinary. Sure they honored me for showing an interest in their culture, but it was simply part of their tradition of extending kindness to strangers. What I enjoyed most about that evening was their openness with regard to their culture. They shared much with me and I left Tawhid's home feeling less uninformed about the country and the visit reinforced in my mind that I had been blessed to have been offered an opportunity to come to the desert kingdom.

Not surprisingly, my life at the Ministry changed dramatically after that. Dozens of my Saudi co-workers now considered me a friend and a brother. I could no longer show up for work, walk into the building and go straight up to the third floor. Every day I first had to stop and greet my friends on the first floor and before long, Saudis I had not met that worked on the second floor began to greet me too. All of them smiled and spoke to me as if they had also shared Cupsah with us that evening.

One morning while visiting my friends on the first floor, Barakah Derar, Abdullah Al-Basheer's Deputy, came into the room. His arrival prompted a celebratory reaction as everyone in the room jumped up and patted him on the back.

A beaming Ahmed informed me, "Barakah here is the hero for the whole city of Riyadh today."

"Really, what did he do?"

"He helped Hilal win the game last night against Naddy Nasser, our hated rivals."

"You play football Barakah?"

"Yes, I do," he admitted humbly.

"What position do you play?"

"Backup goalie; the regular goalie was sick so I had to play yesterday…"

"Yes, and he won the game for us Mr. Adam. We are very happy today and proud."

"Awesome. I am proud of you too Barakah."

"Would you like to come to see me play sometime?"

"Yes, but in all the time we have known each other, you never mentioned that you played professional football. Not even when I visited you in your home and we watched matches together on TV. Barakah, why didn't you tell me you were a goalie for Hilal?"

"I don't know," he answered sheepishly.

"If you had, I would have told you what I know about football in your country. In fact I have known about the Hilal-Nasser rivalry for a long time. Nasser's colors are red and black; Hilal blue and white. Most Nasrawi (noss-r-ow-wee - Nasser supporters) live in Jeddah but there are a few neighborhoods in Riyadh that favor Nasser. But if a car with Nasser markings and colors is ever parked in a Hilal neighborhood it will get vandalized." The translation of this latter comment incited rowdy cheers from the guys, many of whom had blue and white Hilal team memorabilia and decorations inside and on the outside of their vehicles. Continuing I said, "Riyadh on the whole staunchly supports Hilal. Am I correct in all of that Barakah?"

"Yes, and I am impressed."

Ahmed, intrigued that I had knowledge of the local sports teams, inquired, "Who told you those things about our clubs?"

"An American coworker, on the curriculum side of the project, has a Saudi friend who plays for Nasser. I met him one evening when I was visiting my coworker. The player's name is Ahdel. He told me about the Hilal-Nasser rivalry."

"Ahdel Al-Zacharie," Ahmed asked?

"I do not know his last name."

"Maybe it was Ahdel Al-Ghosaibi," Barakah suggested. "There are several players on Nasser named Ahdel.

Ahmed continued to translate our exchange to the other coworkers and at one point several of the guys interrupted asking all at once, "Sayeed Adam, Nasrawi o la?"

They wanted to know if I supported Club Nasser, probably thinking I automatically did so because most Nasser players were Black.

I answered honestly, "la (no)."

"Inta Hilali?"

Again I said no.

"Then that settles it, you have to be Hilali Mr. Adam to support your coworker Barakah. Is that okay with you," Ahmed asked?

"Sure," I said smiling at Barakah. When Barakah and I shook hands Ahmed announced, "Sayeed Adam Hilali." The room erupted in a song I would soon be singing alongside thousands of Hilal fans at Riyadh stadium. "Oh oh abyad azrag ajnabi, oh oh abyad azrag ajnabi," clap, clap, clap, clap "Hilal," clap, clap, clap, clap "Hilal." Roughly translated they were singing, oh, oh white and blue we love you, oh, oh, white and blue we love you, then they would clap four times and shout Hilal. The clapping and shouts cadence went on until it gradually wound down.

Ahmed next translated a tirade from Tawhid who chided, "American football is not the real football, kurat al gadem. They should call it hand ball, kurat al yad, because you use your hand not your feet." I could only laugh at this critique of our brand of football. Ahmed promised that one day we would all get together and go to Riyadh Stadium to watch Hilal play.

Two weeks remained until Arab classes were to begin at the University. With Jaylynn keeping a low profile at the hospital, my Friday mornings were free. For a period I went through church withdrawal and actually looked around for another Christian group to join until I could get back with Pastor Strong. I located Christian services in several expatriate compounds around Riyadh, some for Catholics, Baptists, Jehovah's Witnesses, an Ethiopian group whose services were in Amharic, and a group from the Philippines that held services in Tagalog. After all my due diligence, I wound up not attending any of them. Without Jaylynn, church was just not the same. However, something serendipitous came out of my excursion into the Riyadh Christian community. One of the Jehovah's Witnesses I met was a fellow Black American who had a green thumb like no one I had ever known or even heard of. This man was so successful at farming that he was able to grow a magnificent vegetable garden right out of the desert sand around his villa. His collard greens were the rage of his compound and everyone raved about the time Saudi Ministry of Agriculture officials came to see his garden and discuss his farming strategies. I told this man about Doreen Strong and how she missed fresh greens. He extended an open invitation for me to come and get collards at any time. I planned to take him up on his offer when I started going back to church at the Strong compound. The collards would be my gift to First Lady Doreen.

To fill my Friday morning gap, I spent more time on the tennis courts. Most days Dempsey and I hit volleys at the APO and afterward I would go to his apartment and read any notes from Jaylynn she may have passed to him. One thing I never did was take her notes out of the facility. It was a precaution I took on the odd chance I might get stopped and searched. Jaylynn and I agreed on the strategy, even though we acknowledged it was probably overkill with respect to being cautious. We felt an overabundance of caution was appropriate for the duration of our time in the Kingdom.

One Friday I went to meet Dempsey but he was not on the court. A coworker of his, who noticed me standing around, came over and asked, "You are looking for Dempsey Stevens, aren't you?"

"Yes."

"He is over on the basketball court on the other side of the compound."

When he saw me coming toward the court, Dempsey shouted "Time out."

"Sorry man, I called your villa but you had already left. As you can see we are running full court today. A lot of guys are coming out to play these days. Everybody is hyped because the International Military Basketball

Championship is being hosted by Saudi Arabia this year. The tournament starts in a couple of months. Have you seen the new sports arena they are building over by Crown Prince Fahad's new palace?"

"I thought that was being built for tennis. I mean I heard Saudi Arabia is hosting a tennis tournament and have invited Gene Mayer, Andres Gomez and other big name players to compete."

"That's true but actually there are a number of sports venues being planned for the new arena, including the Military Basketball Championship."

A major basketball tournament in Saudi Arabia – that was interesting. I hung around the court to see if I could get into a game. While waiting I talked with several of the guys and they filled me in on some of the details about the upcoming tournament. A team from the U.S. was competing that would consist of All Stars taken from all branches of the military. I was not surprised to hear the American team was the odds on favorite to win the tournament.

☙☙☙☙☙☙☙☙☙☙☙☙☙☙☙

Chapter 31

Saudi Arabia earned extra kudos from me on the day videogame parlors opened in Riyadh. With Jaylynn's tour winding down, I planned to take full advantage of the parlors in my spare time in the coming months. They would come in handy in keeping me occupied during her absence.

At the first parlor I visited, I stood back and watched to gauge how the Saudis were reacting to the machines. It was evident most of the younger boys already knew how to play the games. Some of them were as skilled as some of the best young players in the Western world.

The second parlor I walked into was crowded with an older set of Saudis. Most were in their early twenties. One group of three friends drew a lot of attention. Two were Black and the third looked like he had aspirations of becoming a Mutawah some day. In face he already had a good start on a Mutawah-style beard. One of the Black Saudis was thin and dark like Jabbar, only not as tall. He seemed to have his hands full playing Pac Man. I could not see what he was doing from where I was standing, but every time the ghosts caught Pac Man and that weird melting sound occurred, the young man made some kind of jerking motion that sent his friends and onlookers into hysterical laughter. I had to find a better angle so I could see what he was doing. From my new vantage point I could see that every time this young Muslim got caught by the ghosts, the jerking motions were caused by his

240

version of performing the Stations of the Cross. What amused me even more was how quickly his hand moved and the odd way he made the sign. First of all, his hand was no more than a blur but I laughed even harder when I realized he was making the sign of the cross perfectly backward. It was like a blitz by a dyslexic Catholic. Perhaps he had seen sports broadcasts from the West and how athletes commonly make this sign before a major event or after scoring a goal. Watching him was enough to make anybody laugh. I laughed too and this caught the attention of the three friends. After introducing ourselves they told me they had guessed I was American. The other Black Saudi of the trio had an older brother who spent a lot of time in the United States and preferred to dress Western style.

Hassan was the name of the aspiring Mutawah. Yushua was the one that played the role of a dyslexic Catholic, and Kardal had the brother who often traveled to America. Hassan, Yushua and Kardal became running partners of mine over the next few months. They were a load of fun. We went to video parlors all over town and I also accompanied them to the first bowling alley built in Riyadh. That was a wild evening. Watching the Saudis try to bowl wearing their Thobes was hilarious. The guys missed far more pins than they knocked down but seemed to enjoy the game. One of the funniest incidents was when a kid of around 12 left the 7-10 split. He was so angry that he turned around, faced his friends and gave an impassioned five minute lecture on the impossibility of making that spare and said "this game is ridiculous". A companion of his stepped up and offered to roll a second ball down the alley simultaneously, and suggested that each of them should aim for one of the remaining pins. The kid adamantly refused that idea and pushed the reset button.

I got the chance to speak with Kardal's brother briefly on a couple of occasions. His name was Nadeem. As I had been told, each time I saw Nadeem he was dressed like a Westerner. Nadeem told me he had visited Washington, D.C. several times and that he liked Black American culture. Among all the Black Saudis I met, Nadeem was probably the most Westernized. The guy was smooth and rather seasoned from all his travels.

Some days Hassan, Yushua, Kardal and I sat around talking instead of going to a video parlor or some place else. As is common with men everywhere, our conversations often gravitated to sex. I was surprised at how forthright they were when talking about sexually transmitted diseases among Saudis returning from abroad. They told me that locally, King Abdul Aziz Hospital had the nickname the Herpes Clinic. Jaylynn never mentioned anything about STDs at the hospital, but she only dealt with female patients and had no access to units of the hospital where Saudi males were treated. Predictably, the religious Hassan was staunchly opposed to premarital sex. He stunned me thoroughly one day when he jokingly said "I know you Mr.

Adam, you are probably the kind of guy that used to hang out on Share-ah Arba-atasher." My jaw dropped like it weighed a ton when he said this. Share-ah Arba-atasher was Arabic for 14th Street. In those days 14th Street was the heart of the red light district in the nation's capital. Hassan soon learned that he should not have told this little joke, because it came back to bite him. I questioned him, "What do you know about Share-ah Arba-atasher Hassan"? He tried to deny any personal knowledge of the area, but it was too late. Yushua and Kardal had learned a lot about 14th Street from Nadeem, but I added a few details and soon the tables turned on Hassan as his friends began to tease him mercilessly. That day Hassan got a new nickname - Hassan Herpes Hussein. Since his friends' roll their R's, when they said this name it had a dramatic flair.

A few months after they opened, the Saudi government shut down the videogame parlors and I went into mourning. After a short lifespan in Arabia, it was decided the parlors were a bad influence. They were wrecking havoc on the society. Young boys developed the habit of hanging out at the parlors and that is where their families would find them after the boys failed to show up for dinner as was the custom. In a land like Saudi Arabia, the reaction from the authorities was predictable. To be honest, I had seen trouble coming because of what I observed as the video parlor craze spread. Not only did the government close the parlors, they also placed them on the banned list.

෯෯෯෯෯෯෯෯෯෯෯෯෯෯෯

Chapter 32

Two days before the Arabic course at the University of Riyadh was to begin, I visited the Al-Bughawis. I hoped to spend some time with Waleed and perhaps finally get to meet Tayyib. Mrs. Al-Bughawi answered the door, welcomed me inside and went to get tea. I quickly realized everyone else was out and the mother was alone in the house. As kind and sweet as Waleed and Jabbar's mother was I did not want to sit around sipping tea and listening to her constantly saying 'morning'. It was cute, the way she said it, but a steady diet of them would surely drive me nuts.

As gracious as I could, I turned down the traditional offer of tea when she brought out the tray and headed for the door. Yewande, however, was insistent, so I sat down hoping to get away after a brief stay. I swallowed a couple of gulps as we sat in silence, which I appreciated. After a few minutes I stood up and slowly turned toward the door. Yewande jumped up and started yammering frantically and gestured for me to sit back down chanting 'akel,' 'akel.' It was their word for eat. She was proposing to bring me food.

242

Shaking my head, I said la shukran (no thanks) and again made a move toward the door. In desperation she tried to grab me but I eluded her grasp while politely excusing myself again. Yewande then lunged at me. Quickly I shifted my body and her fingernails scratched harmlessly across my belt. She charged forward but a couple of quick steps backward, a quick wheel on my heels and I was out the door all in one motion. Yewande raced after me. So I started sprinting leisurely, thinking the old lady would not want to waste her limited energy chasing after a strapping healthy young hulk of an adult male like myself. But Yewande hiked up her dress and that barefoot older woman, 58 years old according to Waleed, showed me what a woman her age, size, health and strength could do. I would guess Yewande weighed around 225 pounds and she was no taller than 5', if that much. Yet, in a matter of seconds she pushed me to my top speed. I was running as fast as I could and yet I repeatedly felt the old lady's fingernails scratch at my belt nearly seizing me. Several times I was forced to turn on the afterburners at the last possible instant just to keep from being nabbed. As we raced through the complex, Yewande laughed and giggled like a school girl on the playground with her friends. She was having fun. I was getting stretched.

As I ran from Waleed's mother, the thought crossed my mind that it was a good thing Barry or any of the guys I played ball with back home, could not see me at that moment. There was no telling how long and hard they would have laughed. Thinking about them made me cringe and I knew I would never mention this incident in any of my letters. Never would I have imagined that I would meet Black Saudis, end up being chased through a compound by one of its senior citizens and barely be able to outrun her.

I hate to admit this, but it took every ounce of energy I had to keep ahead of that old lady. I think if I had tried to turn my head to see if I was putting any real distance between us, I would have been caught. The sound of her footsteps on my heels and that cackling laugh of hers were enough to let me know she was matching me stride for stride. I simply had to keep moving.

I ran so hard I entered that zone runners get into when they are totally committed in a race. That is why it took a few moments for me to realize the chase was over when she finally broke off the pursuit. Eventually the sounds of my footsteps were the only echoes I was hearing. Yewande was at her front door by the time I slowed down and looked back. She waved goodbye and closed the door.

Winded, but grateful she had given up the chase, I headed back to my car. It was a huge relief that Yewande had given up, because I was not sure I could have run that hard much longer. As I neared my car I kept a wary eye on the Al-Bughawi's front door, just in case Yewande jumped out and tried to renew the chase.

Wiping sweat from my brow I unlocked the door, but just as I started to get into the car I heard the sound of music. The sound was a little distant and vague but the song sounded familiar. Hesitating, I cocked my head in the direction it was coming from and realized the sound was getting louder. Somebody was heading in my direction. Moments later I recognized the song and whoever was coming they knew all of the words. Man, were they singing them loud. My curiosity was piqued. I closed the door and waited because I had to see who this was singing along with the legendary James Brown and boldly telling the world they were proud of being Black.

A teenaged Black male stepped around a nearby corner and headed toward the Al-Bughawi residence. He had a medium sized boom box perched on his right shoulder and the way the kid was dressed he could have stepped right out of South Chicago or off the streets of Harlem. At first I assumed he might be another Black American friend of the family, but a closer inspection of his face told me exactly who he was. When he caught sight of me, his face exploded in a smile. Walking right up to me he said, "You must be Mrrrrrr. Adam."

I loved his accent and the way R's rolled off his tongue. In response I said "and you must be Tayyib Al-Bughawi."

Holding out the palm of his hand for us to slap fives he confirmed, "At yourrrr serrrrrvice soul brrrrrotherrrrr."

"So what part of Chicago are you from man," I teased. He laughed with delight.

Tayyib, realizing I was on my way out of the compound protested, "Where are you going Mr. Adam? Come, let us sit and talk. My mother will get us tea." Dutifully I followed Tayyib into his house. As soon as we walked in the door a grinning Yewande jumped up from the floor, clapped her hands and cackled with delight as she ran to prepare tea.

Tayyib had no idea what was going on with his mother. Shrugging his shoulders he turned to me and quipped, "Women, you can't live with them - you can't live without them." It was amusing to hear this western platitude come out of the mouth of a young Black Saudi. It was at that point I understood why his mother had struggled so hard to keep me at the compound that afternoon. The family had often talked about how disappointed I would get when I stopped by the house and discovered Tayyib was not there. Tayyib had also mentioned how eager he was to meet me one day. Yewande knew we were all frustrated. On that particular day, she realized Tayyib was in the compound when I stopped by and made up her mind that he and I were going to meet. Had she been able to communicate this to me, of course, I would have been more than happy to cooperative with her invitations to sit and drink tea and would not have put her through that ordeal of chasing me through the compound. Or was it the other way around, and she had put me through an ordeal? Either way I had to give Waleed's mother a lot of credit. She really showed me something that day and for as long as I live, I will never again make any assumptions about the stamina or capacity of an older person.

As I had been told, Jabbar's youngest brother had an extensive grasp of English. We talked effortlessly for several hours. Tayyib confirmed he was in his final year of high school and shared with me his favorite activities which included swimming and accompanying the Rashid boys of the main household on overnight trips into the desert to hunt jerboa. On most of my previous visits they had been out in the desert. Tayyib also enjoyed local broadcasts of American TV programs like *Bonanza, Little House on the Prairie* and the cartoon *Tom and Jerry*. He did not have to tell me that he loved Western music, especially Black American artists, but I was impressed at how many artists he knew. In addition to James Brown he was also a big fan of Michael Jackson and the Pointer Sisters.

When I mentioned that I played tennis in my spare time, he surprised me with his knowledge of the game and the level of his interest. Tayyib was a big fan of the Wimbledon tournament and an avid follower of the careers of Borg, Ashe, Connors and his all time favorite player Ile Nastase. He laughed when I told him my Aunt's pet name for Ile was Nasty.

Toward the end of my visit Tayyib asked, "Are you Christian, Mr. Adam?"

"Yes I am."

"Why? You should be Muslim. Look at what White people did to Blacks in America. How can you accept their God? Islam is a religion for all people. It does not matter what you are, White, Black, everybody is the same in Islam."

"As I understand it, Arab Muslims were enslaving Blacks centuries before Europeans started coming into Africa," I said in response.

"Who told you this thing? It is a lie. Islam is a religion of brotherhood. There are no slaves or hatred because of the color of your skin among Muslim people. Let me tell you about Islam, Mr. Adam..."

"Maybe next time Tayyib, talking about religion takes a lot of energy and thanks to your mother I don't have much left right now."

"My mother, what did she do?"

"Nothing really, I was just kidding."

As much as I enjoyed visiting with Tayyib, I left the Al-Bughawi residence with the distinct impression the youngest son was naïve about history. Even so, that was not my reason for refusing to discuss religion with him. I held back because of his age. From my experience, I knew families typically do not want outsiders talking to their children about religion, especially if the outsider has views that are different from the teachings they have instilled in their child. Nevertheless, there were facts of life Tayyib obviously had not been made aware of, or it was a matter that he simply had not yet faced certain situations. He had some growing up to do.

As I was leaving, Tayyib requested "Next time you come, please bring American films so we can watch them together, especially films with Black actors in them."

"Your brothers and sisters have already asked me to do that, and as I promised them, I will try. Problem is there aren't that many films with Black actors in circulation here in Riyadh, at least not as far as I know. But I will ask around."

"Uh, we have already seen *Shaft* and *Superfly* too many times. Films about the family would be better, if you please."

The guards noticed I was laughing when I drove through the gate and they began to laugh, which tickled me even more.

When I left the Al-Bughawi residence that day I was feeling good about finding in one family, three brothers who could give me separate and distinct views of the community. Jabbar was my conduit to young adult males in the city. Waleed and I could exchange cultural and historical information from our respective communities, and Tayyib, with his excellent command of English, would bridge the language barrier between me and his brothers plus provide a window into the lives of Saudi youth.

One thing I could say with one hundred percent accuracy, Black Saudis were more up-to-date on Black American culture than we were on theirs. I was also seeing with each visit to the Al-Bughawis, and other Blacks that I was meeting, more and more similarities between Black Saudis and Black Americans.

There were still many questions I wanted to find answers to, but time was running out on my contract.

Later that night, I wrote down the details of my first meeting with the elusive Tayyib Al-Bughawi and passed the note to Dempsey to deliver to Jaylynn. Her response read, "It took a long time for you to finally meet Tayyib. Now that you have, wouldn't you say it was worth the wait?"

❧❧❧❧❧❧❧❧❧❧❧❧❧

Chapter 33

Arabic class at the University provided the kind of structure and discipline I needed for a serious study of the language. Our professor was from Nigeria and spoke seven languages including Spanish, English, Arabic, Italian, Hebrew, Yoruba, and a second tribal dialect. Students haled from various parts of Asia, the Philippines, Europe, Africa, and one that I would get to know very well was of Lebanese extraction. His name was Joseph Feda. Joseph was born in the United States, but his parents were Lebanese citizens. He had come to Saudi Arabia to work in one of his father's jewelry stores. The senior Feda had shops in several Middle Eastern countries and also in Los Angeles, California. Now that his father was approaching retirement, the family expected Joseph to take over the business. After years of putting if off, Joseph was finally trying to learn the language of his heritage. That is why he joined our class.

Two of my classmates were brothers from the breakaway province of Eritrea in Ethiopia. The first weekend after the course started, the brothers invited me to a wedding. The ceremony was beautiful and one of the brothers came dressed in traditional native apparel. I learned a dance during the reception where everyone moved around in a circle and at a given point stopped, pumped their shoulders up and down while gradually squatting lower and lower. After they squatted as low as they were going to go, they slowly rose back up, bumped shoulders with the nearest dancer then resumed dancing around the circle. The dance was not as easy as it looked, but it was a lot of fun.

At the Ministry, Al Dennison and Abdullah Al-Basheer wrapped up the paperwork for a year extension of my tour and presented it to me. No sooner had I signed it, they hinted they would not mind if I signed on for a second two-year stint at the completion of the extension.

I did not want to think about returning to Arabia for a fourth and fifth year, at least not until Jaylynn and I clarified our plans for the future. Recently in my notes to her, I had been reminding her that the Ministry had asked me to stay a third year. Her return notes confirmed that her plans had not changed. She would be returning to the States at the end of her tour. That is why I was not all that enthusiastic about coming back for a fourth and fifth year. The thought of being half a world away from Jaylynn that long did not sit well with me, especially since I had not yet brought up marriage and was not one hundred percent sure she wanted to be my wife. Carl Scott was right an emotional attachment had undermined my commitment to the project.

Before all that trouble started for Jaylynn at the hospital, things had gotten pretty serious between us and that is why not being able to see and talk to her freely was so tough on me. I knew we felt the same way about each other, and though we had not discussed marriage formally there was no question in my heart that Jaylynn was the woman I wanted to be with the rest of my life. To me the bond between us already felt permanent.

As the Military Basketball Championship tournament approached, the games became the talk of the expatriate community. Not much was being said about the tournament among the locals, but that was no surprise. Tournament authorities expected little interest from Saudis, even though a national team was competing. Basketball had not caught on in the Kingdom and a large turnout of fans was not expected.

Late one evening in June, I had just gotten into bed when the phone rang. "Hello," I answered.

"Adam."

"Jaylynn, it is so good to hear your sweet voice again. This is a wonderful surprise. I take it things have cooled down at the hospital, is that why you are calling?"

There was a long pause on the other end. "Jaylynn, sweetheart, is everything okay?"

"Adam… King Khalid died today."

"Oh no."

King Khalid had been widely loved by his subjects. He would surely be missed. Thankfully, the Saudis were well organized when it came to the royal succession. Crown Prince Fahad had been chosen years earlier as successor, so there was no reason to fear a power struggle among the surviving Princes. Their political organization was comforting because I could only imagine the chaos that would result if the government fell and we had to be evacuated, plus worrying about Jaylynn's safety would make such an event even more stressful.

Jabbar stopped by my villa the next day and informed me that his family's move to their new house was on hold. "There is no way my mother is going to make this move during the mourning period for the King," he explained.

The country slowed down for a few weeks as it mourned the death of one monarch and installed the next. By the time things returned to normal, all attention in the expatriate camp had turned to the military basketball championships. Tickets to the games were free. I did not plan to see all of the matches, but I arranged to be there opening day.

Chapter 34

Ticket agents and arena personnel had not expected much interest locally still they were noticeably disappointed over the low turnout. When I arrived, there were no other fans at the gates but I was still excited to be going into the new arena. An attendant escorted me to the section where I was to sit. There were plenty of empty seats, so I had my pick of whichever one I wanted.

It was a typical sports arena with large seating sections along the sidelines and additional seating behind the baskets at each end of the court. Non-Saudis, like me, were seated in one of the sections along the sidelines. Saudis were directed to seats across from us on the opposite sideline. Team benches were at floor level in front of the Saudi section. All total there may have been half a dozen spectators in the section with me. We looked like tiny dots lost among approximately five to ten thousand vacant seats. Saudi nationals on the other side, I estimated numbered somewhere between fifty and one hundred. The national team was not scheduled to play on opening day. I assumed that might have contributed to the small turnout.

Two Arab countries opened the tournament. During the game, it was so quiet in the arena that it sounded more like a scrimmage being held at a local gym. Each bounce of the ball echoed thunderously through the chasm of the virtually empty arena. None of the handful of spectators in the stands got into that first match, however, the atmosphere in the arena completely changed for the next game. This match was the one I had come to see.

A team from another Arab land came out on the floor and was greeted with a sprinkling of applause on the Saudi side of the arena. I stood up proudly in anticipation of welcoming the team from the United States. When they were introduced, the arena came to life in a big way for the first time that day. A thunderous chorus of boos rained down on the court. Clearly the Saudis had come to support their Muslim brothers. This did not surprise me insomuch as the Arab rule of 'me against my brother, but me and my cousin against you' was likely in effect. Despite their rancor toward the U.S. team, I made up my mind that I was going to let the players know they were not completely without support in the Kingdom. Though alone on my little island, I proudly cheered and applauded the U.S. team and being outnumbered did not make one bit of difference. Ask anyone that knows me and they can tell you how vocal I can be at a sporting event, and particularly at a basketball game. Believe me when I tell you, nobody in that arena had any problem hearing my voice. I can state categorically that on that day in Riyadh, the Saudis found out how loud I can get.

From the opening tipoff, the Saudis were fully energized in their support of their fellow Muslims and the arena began to sound like a sporting event actually was in progress. Unfortunately for the Saudis, it was only the team from the United States that gave me, their lone fan, anything to cheer about. That the other team did not belong on the same court with the Americans was painfully obvious. The U.S. athletes made a statement that game. People had been saying all along that they would be the team to beat. The players were letting everyone know that those statements were not mere hype.

As the game progressed and the U.S. players did what they do best, neither they nor I were aware that something was going on in the arena that day that in the long run would have the biggest impact on the entire tournament. In fact, every American in the arena that day, and particularly me, had already begun to play key roles in a drama that would continue to unfold throughout the Kingdom over the course of the coming two weeks.

When an American player dunked the ball, blocked a shot or made a steal - I let out a resounding cheer. On the other side, the Saudis waited patiently for an opportunity to cheer for their Muslim brothers. Unfortunately U.S. defense was too strong. Nothing the Arab team did, gave the Saudis a reason to celebrate. That side of the arena fell completely silent. Meanwhile I was really enjoying myself as I put on quite a show across from them. Had I known how tired the Saudis were getting of hearing my voice, I would have screamed even louder. But I was about to find out how they felt. After one of the players on the U.S. team executed an exceptionally spectacular dunk, I screamed and jumped up and down like it was the greatest play in history. Once I was satisfied that I had rewarded the play and the player sufficiently I sat down. At that point, a voice from the Saudi side of the arena rang out loud and clear 'why don't you shut up!'

Talk about waking the dead. The Saudis sprang from their seats cheering, whistling, dancing and applauding – not for the battered team down on the court – but for the guy who heckled me. You would have thought a rock star had come into the stands. They gave each other high-fives, pointed at me and laughed derisively.

This outburst was not surprising in view of what I had experienced from the Saudis thus far in Arabia, and I was relieved that they had finally woke up on that side of the arena. In the spirit of competition, I accepted this challenge. As I waited for the Saudis to enjoy their moment and settle down, under my breath I whispered the immortal battle cry of Bugs Bunny... 'Of course, you know this means war!' Once the arena grew quiet again, I counted to ten then shouted back, 'you shut up!'

That really cut it. A barrage of raspberries flew at me from the Saudis and the onslaught went on for at least two minutes. Then in the midst of this salvo from the Saudis, something extraordinary happened. Down on the arena floor players on the U.S. bench stood up and applauded for me. For the first time in my life a team I was rooting for, returned the gesture by cheering in my support. 'Tell him brother.' 'That's right, that dude should be the one shutting up, not you.' 'At least you have something to cheer about.'

No American in the arena realized it at the time, but we had just triggered the unlikeliest rivalry of the tournament. A battle was about to begin that would rage for the balance of the competition. Lines had been drawn on the basketball court between the teams and fans of the United States of America and the Kingdom of Saudi Arabia. Although the U.S. and Saudi teams had never played against each other, by the time the sun set that day overwhelming support for a showdown between them would erupt all over the Kingdom.

Before my confrontation with the heckler, the American players had been cruising on auto pilot. The dynamics in the stands now had them fully energized and they began to play like men possessed. I was right in sync with them, giving every great play and defensive gem my full and frenzied support. They were feeling me and I was feeling them.

No one in the arena had to be told the U.S. players had turned up the heat in response to the jeering from the stands. Everybody knew it. Yet, the Saudis did not back down. Personally, I was proud that these talented Black American warrior athletes had circled me in a protective emotional ring of defiance in that hate-filled arena far from our homeland. But to be quite candid, I also admired the Saudi that heckled me. If I were in his shoes I would definitely have done the same thing. Actually, in the long run he did more for the tournament than anyone because he lit the spark that got the crowd going, pumped up the players on the court and, as a bonus, inspired every other team in the competition. Had I met him in person, I would have happily shaken his hand. By telling me to shut up, he became responsible for all of the fireworks that followed. That is why the next two weeks ended up being more memorable than anyone in Saudi Arabia, including me, ever expected.

At the end of that day's matches, I waited outside the arena hoping to meet the U.S. players. When they came up the ramp from the team locker rooms, the first thing they did when they spotted me was laugh. One of the forwards said, "Man, we never expected to get any support out here, you were right on time. You really got us fired up. What is your name?"

"Adam Sneed."

"The guys call me Silver, this is Big Man, and that is Kirk coming up the ramp. I know you liked the way we stepped things up after that guy told you to shut up."

"That was awesome. I was real proud of you guys."

It was great meeting those guys and for the two weeks the team was in the Kingdom, I rolled out the red carpet for them. However, as I mentioned earlier, something profound was taking place that day that neither the U.S. players nor I were aware of. In fact, I would not find out about it until several months after the tournament was over.

The local Saudi television station had assigned reporters to cover the games that opening day. Since I had not purchased a television antenna, I never watched the local news. That is why I missed the report about the tournament that aired on television that night. Months later I would learn that highlights from the opening games were broadcast nationwide. Camera shots revealed how small a crowd had turned out for opening day, but the primary focus of the report was on what reporters described as the story inside the game – namely, the acrimony between Saudi spectators and one lone supporter of the American team. The report informed the nation that if the U.S. team kept winning, as expected, then that lone American fan would have plenty to cheer about. But, if the Saudi team was as good as everyone in the Kingdom hoped, it just might win out in its bracket and challenge the Americans for the title.

The report was accurate enough about the U.S. team and naturally optimistic with respect to the home team's chances. But what threw Saudi and arena authorities for a loop was the reaction to the report in the Riyadh community. Young Saudi males took to heart the statement that their team might challenge the Americans in the finals.

Saudi Arabia's team was scheduled to play its opening contest on the second day of the tournament. I can only imagine their surprise to come on court and be greeted by thousands of their countrymen who had flocked to the arena to give them support. From that day through to the end of the tournament, attendance climbed steadily each day. Saudis not only came out on days the national team played, they showed up in force as well on days the U.S. team competed. In the latter case, they came for the express purpose of rooting against the Americans and for whatever opponent the U.S. faced off against.

Sometimes when I look back on those two weeks, I regret my decision not to get an antenna. Nevertheless, television had once again made its power felt in Saudi Arabia. I was there when it happened, right in the midst of it all. I was a major player in the drama that ensued, but for the most part completely missed out on the impact the games had locally. Talk of the tournament became the hottest topic in the country. King Faisal's bones surely had to be dancing in their grave. I am sure the Saudi government could not have been more pleased about the way things turned out and the level of interest the games generated.

Compared to opening day, the third day of the tournament was quite a contrast for me personally. It began with arena attendants extending a delicate apology to me when I arrived. Pulling me aside they explained, "The otherrrr day we made a mistake. You have to sit with the otherrrr Amerrrricans." Indirectly it was an admission that they had jumped to conclusions about my nationality. Nevertheless, when the attendant said I had to sit with other Americans, I took it as a figure of speech and not a statement of fact that other expatriates were actually inside the arena. To my surprise and joy, when I got to the section reserved for Americans about a dozen fans were sitting there. We did not know each other, but I am sure the Saudis thought we did once the U.S. team hit the court. Although we had been strangers before that day, our Country's long basketball tradition allowed us to organize familiar cheers and present a wall of support for the team.

At the end of the first week of play, three of the U.S. players joined me for lunch on Thursday afternoon. I took them to a Lebanese restaurant in my old neighborhood near the airport. Big Man, the 6'9" center, Silver, a 6'7" forward and 6'0" guard Kirk were my guests. They enjoyed the meal, but we had barely finished eating and I was paying the waiter when Al-Asr prayer call rang out. The owner, as customary, locked the front door and began closing the window shutters. Kirk and Big Man grew agitated and questioned what was going on. I explained the ritual of prayer call and assured them we only had to sit tight for about twenty minutes. The players, however, did not like the idea of being locked inside and particularly did not appreciate being told they could not leave. Big Man and Kirk made such a fuss that the owner let the four of us slip quietly out the back door.

Perhaps our behavior was disrespectful, but in defense of the players they had far less exposure to the country and its traditions than those of us who were long termers in Arabia.

Midway through the second week of the tournament, the Saudi and American teams were still unbeaten in their respective brackets. It was beginning to look like a championship confrontation between them might actually take place. For the Saudis to reach the finals, however, they had to get past another highly vaunted team in the tournament. The Sudanese had drawn a lot of attention as well because they boasted the tallest player in the tournament. He stood a towering nine feet tall. His knees were the size of a grown man's head and he had feet that looked like canoes. Saudi fans swarmed him before and after games to get him to pose for pictures with their children.

Around town the Saudis put on a brave face, but I knew they were worried. Debates raged about the team's chances against the Sudanese. In the tea shops it was generally conceded the match would likely be very close. Others quietly expressed fear that the Saudis would lose in the final seconds.

I attended the Saudi Arabia vs. Sudan match mainly because I wanted to see how the Saudis played and to get a heads up on the level of competition they might present against the Americans. I was in the midst of thousands of Saudi fans who had no idea that I was the guy they had seen cheering on the television report.

The match was a rout, which for me was a huge disappointment. I had hoped the game would be exciting, competitive and a cliff hanger that might not produce a winner until the final buzzer. Sudan's nine-foot center could not pick up his huge knees or move those boat-sized feet fast enough to help his teammates against the best competition they had faced to that point in the tournament. The Saudis were simply too fast. Most of the game the Goliath sized center was left marooned at the offensive end of the court. Rarely did he bother to run to the other end and help out on defense. The few times he started out for the defensive end, the Saudis had scored and were already on their way back to defend against his team's offense. For most of that game the giant's teammates were forced to defend against the Saudi offense a man short. It was worse than a 5-on-4 power play in hockey. The swiftness of the Saudi guards took its toll at both ends of the court. Naturally, Saudi fans were delighted. All around me they screamed feverously as their players ran rings around the Sudanese Center. Not only did the thousands of Saudis in the stands have a lot of fun, that game sent the whole country soaring with confidence that their team had an excellent chance to win against the real behemoth of the games - the Americans.

Once the semifinal matches ended and a championship tilt between the United States and Saudi Arabia became a reality, tickets to the game became more valuable than desert diamonds. If you did not have a ticket to the final, you had to watch it on television because hanging around outside the arena hoping to convince someone to sell their ticket would be a waste of time. The Saudi vs. U.S. final promised to be magical.

A few days before the championship game, the Arabic language course at the University ended. To celebrate, I hosted a graduation party for my classmates and instructor. You can imagine their surprise when they arrived at my villa and discovered several members of the U.S. basketball team there whom I had invited as special guests. They were the toast of the party and my classmates could not thank me enough for the opportunity to meet them.

On the day of the championship game, the arena was packed to the rafters. Never would I have imagined that a day would come in Riyadh when I would see thousands of Bedouins packing a stadium to watch a basketball game. When I got there Saudi fans already had the place rocking. I knew it would take more than a handful of expatriates to represent in that hostile environment. When I got to the U.S. section, I was ecstatic to see that several hundred fans had turned out from the expatriate community. There were plenty of us to hold our own against the overwhelming numbers in the arena. We were awesome. Our long basketball heritage came through loud and clear and the game was a classic, in fact much better than most expected. From the opening tip to the final basket, the arena was jumping and fans were treated to a sporting event that pretty much lived up to its publicity. Amazing efforts and jaw dropping plays by both teams drew enough noise from the crowd to register off the sound meters. We waved our little American flags and chanted popular cheers in an atmosphere that reminded me of an Olympics event. The Saudis played far better against the Americans than I am sure anyone thought they would, but were not good enough to win. Still the Saudi team earned a lot of respect that day. As had been predicted from the beginning, the U.S. team won the title. The expatriate community held a victory party for the team at the APO Facility that evening.

For the two weeks the U.S. team was in Riyadh, the starting five spent much of their free time with me. I tried to convince Jaylynn to come out of her dorm and at least meet them, but she was even more nervous about being seen in the company of these highly visible athletes. As Jabbar had done with me in the early days of our friendship, I took the players all over town to see the sights and I introduced them to some of my Saudi friends. They sat and drank tea in the homes of Abdullah Al-Basheer and Waleed Al-Bughawi. And for a final touch, I took the guys to my tailor and had them fitted for Thobes to take home as souvenirs. My tailor was astounded at their height and said he had never made Thobes that size before.

⊱⊱⊱⊱⊱⊱⊱⊰⊰⊰⊰⊰⊰⊰

Chapter 35

The six week Arabic course at the University was over. I learned just enough Arabic to realize how much more I needed to study. My hope was that the Saudi government planned to offer follow up classes. If they did I would definitely sign up.

I was sad to see the U.S. Military basketball team leave the country, but I had high hopes the Saudis might invite more U.S. teams to the Kingdom.

Even now I believe exhibition games between NFL teams would go over big in cities like Jeddah and Riyadh.

But for me, life suddenly became humdrum. Jaylynn was still laying low and I was developing a severe case of boredom.

A week after the U.S. team's departure, I grabbed a couple of films and drove over to visit Waleed and his family.

"Mr. Adam, where are your American friends," Tayyib questioned as he met me at the front door?

"They have returned to the United States."

"Ah, your team won the championship mabruk (congratulations)!"

"Did you get a chance to go to any of the games Tayyib?"

"No, we have been much too busy." Putting a finger to his lips, Tayyib leaned close and whispered, "we are moving away from this place in two weeks."

I already knew about the move but it was apparent Jabbar never told his brothers that he had mentioned it to me. Feigning surprise I said, "Really! Where are you moving?"

"Waleed has built a house for our family. It will be ready soon. Can you take us there now to see it?"

"Sure."

"Remember it is a secret," he said softly and slipped back inside the house. It had to be a very big secret for the Al-Bughawi brothers to ask me to take them there rather than to be seen driving out of the compound together in Waleed's car. I felt honored that they had invited me to see the new house, and the memory of my first experience riding with Waleed made me appreciate even more that I had been asked to drive them there.

Moments later Tayyib and Waleed came out and quietly got into my car. Tayyib sat in the back and Waleed got up front and muttered "Ruuh (let's go), ya sheikh, drive!"

Outside the gate I followed Waleed's directions to the soon to be new residence of the Al-Bughawi family. It was the first home Waleed and his family would own in the history of their tenure on the Arabian Peninsula. They had every reason to be excited. I too was excited, but excitement turned to elation when I discovered their new home was less than two miles from my villa. The Al-Bughawis were going to be my neighbors.

Though humbler than the lavish surroundings of the place they were moving out of, nothing but pride registered on the faces of Waleed and

Tayyib as they stepped through the gate into the courtyard of their future home. Being there to see their faces that day was one of the highlights of my tour. Workmen were completing the final stages of construction, so Waleed did not want to stay long. He did not want anything to slow their progress.

When we got back to the compound, one of the Rashid brothers was on the tennis court roller skating with his young sister. Tayyib informed us he was going to join his friend but suggested, "Why don't you come and watch Mr. Adam?"

I gestured Saudi style for Tayyib to hold on a moment. When I opened the trunk and pulled out my own roller skates, Tayyib shouted "Yes!" As I put on my skates, I suggested "why don't you bring your boom box and a couple of cassettes over to the tennis court. I want to show you how we skate in America." I grabbed a few of my favorite cassettes out of the car as well.

Within minutes the four of us were skating to James Brown. After demonstrating some of my favorite moves, which Tayyib and the Rashid boy copied perfectly, I put on the Emotions song *Best of My love* and taught the boys how to skate triples. They caught on quickly and soon we were doing some of the stunts triples teams do in the States. While we were skating, I happened to look up at the balcony of the main house and saw a number of people watching us including Mrs. Rashid. At the end of the song they gave us a round of applause.

I was impressed with the athleticism of Tayyib and the Rashid boy. They had me doing things I had not done in years. I felt like an old man when we finished, and I knew I was going to be in a lot of pain the next morning.

The little Rashid girl asked to skate triples with us, but I was afraid she might get hurt. Instead, I said "let me show you how pretty little girls like you skate in America." I put on Heatwave's *'Always and Forever'*, and skated around with her like she was a beautiful princess. The routine we skated brought an appreciative ovation from the family. Right afterward Mrs. Rashid called her daughter into the house. I suspected the sight of the young girl skating with a foreigner, who was also a man, might have been too much of a departure from their customs. It turned out I was wrong. Tayyib told me later that Mrs. Rashid enjoyed watching me and her daughter skate together.

After skating, Tayyib and I went into the house and sat down with Waleed and the rest of his family to watch the films I had brought. No mention was made of the new house, but the undercurrent of excitement in the room was palpable. I was very happy for the Al-Bughawis.

A few weeks later the family moved out of the Rashid compound in the middle of the night when everyone in the main house was asleep. Mrs.

Rashid was sad when she learned they had relocated, but sent a nice house warming present. Later she would visit them in their new home.

☙☙☙☙☙☙☙☙❧❧❧❧❧❧❧

Chapter 36

Swimming every day had done wonders for my body. I do not exaggerate when I say I was in the best shape of my life. Certain ones of my fellow expatriates had also taken note of my improved physique.

At Headquarters one morning there was a card in my mailbox from the ELCR, the 'Expatriate Ladies Club of Riyadh'. It was an invitation to a luncheon the following Thursday at which I was to be the guest of honor. According to the card, it was an informal gathering and specifically stated 'no special attire required' and 'if you so choose, you can wear jeans'. The invitation was completely unexpected but the fact it was from a women's club aroused my suspicions.

I did know a member of that club - Marlene Dennison – so when I got to the Ministry I asked Al if he knew anything about the luncheon.

"I haven't heard a thing about it, but I will call Marlene and ask when I get the chance."

The mystery intensified later that day when Al reported "Marlene does not know anything about it either. There is a possibility she really does know and is not going to tell me. It could be one of those hush-hush club matters. But I have to say, I cannot imagine what they might want with you. I guess the only way you are going to find out what this is about is to go and see for yourself. I have to confess though, I am a little jealous I did not get invited. Man, you are going to be in hog heaven with all those good looking gals. Plus you get a free meal in the bargain."

Skeptical, I grumbled "I just don't know about this Al?"

"It's just a bunch of women Adam, how bad could it be," he counseled.

'Just a bunch of women, how bad could it be?' Boy would those words come back to bite me in the butt.

The luncheon was held in a villa at the Dennison's compound just across the drive from their home. A nicely dressed middle aged woman opened the door when I knocked. I did not know her, but she gasped when she saw me in the doorway. I was wearing jeans and a white short sleeved fishnet body shirt that accentuated my abs, bulging chest muscles and upper arms.

258

After she regained her composure her face warmed into a sweet smile and she welcomed me politely, calling me by my name I might add. The place was packed with females. I never would have guessed there were that many Western women in all of Riyadh. A few of the faces were familiar. Most were strangers, but from the way they smiled and greeted me when I walked in you would have thought they knew me better than I knew myself.

Unlike me, they were all dressed like it was a formal affair and the spread laid out for lunch was like something fit for a king. During the meal I was fawned over and the ladies went out of their way to make sure I had my fill. It was the closest thing to what I had imagined a harem would be like in Arabia. From the moment I walked in the door until my last bite of food, anything I asked for was provided right away. To be honest, it felt nice to be pampered by so many lovely hands.

Under different circumstances, being the center of that kind of attention would have made me very happy, and while I can admit I was enjoying myself I was becoming increasingly wary of whatever the motives might be that were behind this little soirée. Every wink and flirtatious smile, of which there were many, sent red flags popping up in my head. It was obvious they wanted something. Whatever it was, they were setting me up for it royally. Though I had no idea what it could be, my instincts told me it had to be something highly unusual and likely outside my comfort zone.

At a certain point, two members of the club gave a signal and the room fell quiet. A quorum of the ELCR was now in session. It was at that very moment that, for me, the luncheon took on a sinister feel. I had the eeriest feeling. A vision of the courtroom scene in the film 'the Devil and Daniel Webster' flashed in my mind. Nobody had to tell me whose soul was about to be put on the auction block that day. The ladies were ready to make their presentation. I looked around the room at all the pretty faces.

The two lead representatives came over, sat down, one on each side of me, and introduced themselves as Marie and Pauline. There I was flanked by two beautiful, curvaceous women with the friendliest faces while fear rippled the length and breadth of my spine. Tried and true survival instincts screamed, 'Adam, get out of there!' But I could not get my feet to move, not yet, not until I found out what this was about. I simply had to let the scene play out. I did not want to spend the rest of my life wondering what these ladies had been up to, or regretting that I had missed out on something special.

Both spokespersons grew agitated and nervous all at once, which did not bode well in my mind. Finally Marie, in a professional yet soft voice dripping with femininity, said "Adam we are very pleased that you accepted our invitation to lunch, which, as you know, was held in your honor. Now that you have eaten and relaxed a bit, I am sure you would like to know why we invited you here today."

Maintaining a steady gaze, to mask my growing apprehension, I nodded in the affirmative.

"First of all, let me assure you it is nothing bad or harmful. You see… oh, please forgive me Adam… Pauline, I think I over rehearsed… sorry Adam… just how shall I put this…?

"Why don't you start by asking him the question we talked about Marie," Pauline suggested helpfully.

"Good idea. Adam…" then after a slight pause, she blurted out in a single breath, "Have you ever heard of the Chippendale Club?"

O my God! Stuck between shock and bewilderment, my jaw fell immobile. What these ladies were about to ask was something that never in my wildest dreams would I have expected anybody to suggest, especially in of all places, the center of the Islamic world – the Kingdom of Saudi Arabia.

Mustering her nerve, Marie forged ahead. "We are starting our own Chippendale Club here in Riyadh and would be honored to have you as our very first dancer. So what do you think? Does that sound like something you would like to do? There will be plenty of perks."

Perks! I'll bet! Speechless, I panned the room eyeing all the nicely dressed ladies, all of whom wore wedding bands. Some were married to colleagues and associates of mine. Several of them I saw week in and week out. I knew right then my relationships with them had changed forever, because I would never be able to look any of these women in their eyes again. Scarier yet, I recognized one of the ladies from Pastor Strong's church.

Images filled my head of these ladies of polite society jostling to stuff dollar bills in my jock strap while I gyrated to sexy music. Thinking about the possible repercussions made me shudder. If my colleagues discovered their wives were starting such an enterprise and, more importantly, that I was the one doing the dirty dancing for them, what would they do to me? I was certain it would only be a matter of time before this little escapade became public. And when everyone at church found out I had become an exotic dancer, First Lady Doreen would crucify me and worst of all I would lose Jaylynn.

When I managed to regain my voice, slowly and in an even tone I said "I've… got… to… go." A chorus of protests and pleadings followed, but I retreated straight to the front door. The wife of one of the tennis players I had competed against during the tournament intercepted me just as I was turning the knob. Attempting to reassure me that dancing for them would be okay she said, "Adam, we are not asking you to do anything bad or something immoral. We simply want you to dance, that's all."

To satisfy a personal curiosity I asked, "why me? There must be plenty of guys here that would jump at the chance to accommodate you ladies. What made me your first choice?"

Wagging her head sassily, she slapped me on my backside and in a bawdy tone crowed, "Because we want to see you shake that tight ass sugar!" Screams, whistles and shrill hoots erupted when she smacked me on the butt. The looks on the faces of all these sophisticated ladies was all I needed to propel my precious body the rest of the way out the door.

Whether the ELCR, aka the connoisseurs of lust, ever got Chippendale Riyadh started or not, I never found out. If they did, they kept it a tight secret.

As I drove home, I thought to myself that it was a good thing Saudi men were not available for these women to interview. I could easily see Jabbar, Tawhid or almost any of the other young men I had met in Riyadh, eagerly agreeing to dance for them.

Though I have never regretted my decision to turn down that invitation, I actually think dancing for them would have been a lot of fun. But eventually I would have had to tell Jaylynn about their offer. I wanted to make sure I could talk about it with a clear conscience.

☙☙☙☙☙☙☙❧❧❧❧❧❧❧

<h1 style="text-align:right">Chapter 37</h1>

Two months before the end of her contract, Jaylynn called with good news. Suspicions about her had dissipated and she had not been followed in over a month. We were happy with these developments but agreed it would be wise to take our time about getting back to our former routine. We would limit our phone conversations to brief discussions, no more than twice a week and she would never again call me from her dorm. That meant she would only call me from the APO. Each of us would return to the Strong's compound but we would not start out attending services on the same weekends. After alternating Fridays for a while, we would reevaluate the situation and try to determine if it was safe to resume attending services together.

Even with these strategies in place Jaylynn went further with her vigilance. That first week she only called me at home once. Over the first two weeks after giving me the okay, I got a total of three phone calls from her and two of them came into my office at the Ministry. Yes I was happy to hear her

261

voice, but the intervals between our conversations were tougher on me than when we were communicating through notes.

On my first trip back to church, I scored big points with Doreen Strong when I handed her a large bag of fresh collard greens. To sweeten the deal I stopped by the Commissary and picked up a pound of bacon. The following week I brought another batch of greens and promised to bring more. I planned to do this as long as I had my secret connection.

At the third service I attended, Jaylynn was in the compound. Whether she was ahead of schedule or not, I did not know. We had not had that conversation to decide if we should begin attending services together again. I was too happy to see her to worry about a schedule.

Jaylynn looked better than ever, and it was more than the fact I had not seen her for so long. Jaylynn really looked good. She was wearing a new outfit that was tight and right. Later she told me Lovelen mailed to her for the special occasion of our reunion. I grabbed her right in front of the First Lady and we gazed into each other's eyes. It was tough, but I kept it cool until we were able to steal away for a private moment. When we finally got to kiss privately, it was as exciting as our first time and in my heart the commitment to be with her the rest of my life was sealed. Jaylynn owned me body and soul.

As the final weeks of Jaylynn's tour passed, it grew harder for me to come to grips with the reality that she would soon be leaving Arabia forever. I made plans for us to do a number of things together before she departed. One of those things was to take her to see a play. There was a group of performers in the expatriate community that put on plays from time to time and recently had begun a run of the play *The Fantasticks*.

Jaylynn looked spectacular, as usual, the night of the show. It was a nice change of pace for us both plus it felt good to be at an event with a crowd of Westerners all dressed up for an enjoyable evening. Pauline, the lady from the ELCR, was there with her husband. Our eyes met but she quickly turned away. I guess Pauline was thinking the same thing I was, that we shared a dirty little secret. Jaylynn was at my side when I walked past them and I kept my head held high. I was confident one look at my girl would be enough for Pauline to realize I had something much better going for me than anything the ELCR could offer. Jaylynn was the only woman I would be dancing for in a jock strap.

Though I had known about *The Fantasticks* for years, I had never seen the play. I did have a general idea what the plot was about and knew the show opened with a solo by the main character. When the lights dimmed, the actor playing he role of El Gallo walked out on stage. Recorded music started playing and he began to sing. As I listened to the first few refrains of his rendition of the song 'Try to Remember', my eyes widened in disbelief. Peering through the darkness, I strained to see the face of the man singing on the stage. It was difficult to believe what my ears were trying to tell me. Was it him? It sounded like him, but the face was not familiar. I was struggling to read the program in the darkness until a stray ray of light from the flashlight of an usher fell on the page. It flashed briefly but long enough for me to verify what I had suspected. Next to the role of El Gallo was the name Olophius Freeman. O, my best friend from childhood, was in Saudi Arabia.

Reading his full name on the program felt funny. From the first days of our friendship, nobody called him Olophius. That was too much of a mouthful for a classroom of six year olds. Everybody called him O. We spent our entire school career together and I hadn't seen O since we graduated from Allegheny High School.

As O belted out the song, the audience became transfixed. His voice was as beautiful as I remembered and more powerful. Jaylynn squeezed my hand and nestled closer. Under my breath I said, 'Way to go O, thanks.'

Not many in our circle knew about O's voice when we were growing up. The only reason I knew was because he and I were close friends. From time to time O and I got together and sang, but always in private. We sang the popular tunes of the time, including songs by The Righteous Brothers, The Temptations, We Five, Smokey Robinson and the Miracles, The Four Seasons, and The Four Tops.

O did a wonderful job in the role of El Gallo that night and I was excited about the prospect of seeing him backstage after the show. Unfortunately, there were so many well wishers it was impossible for me to get back to see him. I did not have a lot of time anyway because I had to get Jaylynn to the APO to catch her ride to the dorm. Jaylynn had introduced me to Abud a few days earlier. I could see why she liked and trusted him. Abud was decent. She had arranged for him to pick her up after the show that night, so I wanted to make sure we got to the meeting point on time.

At the next performance of *The Fantasticks*, I was in the audience again. This time I got backstage after the show. O's back was turned to me when I spotted him.

Ordinarily I would never erupt in song in front of strangers, although doing so among a group of thespians did not seem very much like a walk on the wild side. I could not think of a better way to reunite with O than to sing one of our old favorites. When I sang the opening words of We Five's 'You Were on My Mind', O jerked around and that wonderful smile I remembered from childhood spread across his face. Right away he joined me. It was as if the years since the last time we sang together simply evaporated. A couple of his fellow performers picked up the song and we fell into each other's arms. O and I shouted, hugged and shook each other almost senseless.

I stepped back to take a good look at my old friend. O had grown up to be quite handsome. His looks had been a big problem for him throughout his adolescence so I was truly happy for him, and relieved.

"What are you doing in Riyadh, Ad-man?"

O was the only person that called me Ad-man. Jaylynn came close the day she suggested calling me Ad. "I suppose the same thing you are – working," I answered.

"Of all the plays, in all the deserts, in all the world, you had to walk into mine," O said in an attempt to mimic Bogart. My Bogart was always better than his.

"Do the world a favor and don't let this acting thing go to your head. It is good to see you man. How long has it been?"

"Since high school… about eight years, although not too long ago I saw a guy on the news who I thought could have been you. He was certainly acting like you. This fellow was at the new arena watching the International Military Basketball Championship tournament and rooting for the U.S. team. A couple of our sports reporters were there to cover the story. That was you?"

"I am afraid so, but I had no idea there was a report on the news about the tournament."

"Oh yes, it was a big story all over the country."

"That's wild man. I wish I had known. So you are working in television?"

"That's right. Ad-man you and I have some serious catching up to do, but we will never get it done in this chaos. Can we get together this weekend, maybe for dinner and we will talk then?"

"I wouldn't miss it for the world. Are you familiar with The Empty Quarter Inn?"

"Perfect choice - how about Thursday at 5:00, will that work for you?"

"See you Thursday."

As I drove home, memories flooded my head as I thought back to the first time I laid eyes on Olophius Freeman. It was at church the Sunday of Labor Day weekend of my first grade school year. The Freeman family had just moved into the Manchester community on the Northside of Pittsburgh.

They were the newest members of our congregation. I was glad to see that a new boy my age had come to church that day, but my mind was elsewhere. All I could think about was opening day at Conroy Elementary that coming Tuesday.

On Tuesday morning I saw Olophius Freeman again when he walked into my new classroom. I decided right then that he and I were going to be best friends. In my six year old mind it made perfect sense. Our families went to the same church and now we were going to be in the same homeroom. Later when the teacher read off our names, everybody laughed when she called out Olophius Freeman. After school I told him "your name is too hard to say. I am going to call you O instead."

"Okay," he agreed. From that day everybody called him O.

We were close from the start and for years everything was great. Then puberty set in and my classmates and I started changing from little boys and girls into teenagers. Every fall on the first day of school, boys and girls liked to show off the physical changes that had taken place with their bodies over summer vacation. Guys grew taller and girls became curvier. Nothing, however, ever seemed to change with O. Everybody knew O was different. He simply would not grow but remained small in stature and boyish in appearance.

Before age eleven a guy might get away with looking soft but not after that, especially not in our old neighborhood. To make matters worse he was pretty in the face. O had long eyelashes, soft pink lips, and smooth skin that never had a blemish or suffered from bouts of acne. These physical features made it impossible for guys to accept O as an equal.

Despite being rejected by almost everyone, O tried his best to fit in. He ran harder and played rougher than he should have and hid the pain when he got hurt. I hate saying this, but O lacked too many things in the masculinity department. Yet, he acted like a boy, talked like a boy, even liked girls just like a boy is supposed to. But his soft features and pretty looks were the bane of his existence.

Needless to say, O had a tough adolescence. He was never popular. The older he got, the more of an outcast O became. Nobody talked to him or said anything about him, unless it was to say something disparaging. In Junior High kids had a popular saying when they saw him coming down the hall. They would shout, 'Oh no—here comes O!' Honestly, if the school had put O in a classroom by himself he would not have been more socially or physically isolated than he already was. Truth is I was O's only friend.

Everywhere O went, guys harassed and berated him. Once time it even happened at church. I will never forget that Sunday. Shortly after service Deacon Moffett said, loud enough for everybody standing around to hear, 'O you look more like a girl than a boy.' O was sixteen years old when Deacon Moffett said that. As far as I was concerned, there was no excuse for the Deacon to make that statement in front of half the church. Deacon Moffett was an adult and a leader with responsibilities, including the responsibility of setting an example of tolerance and tact for the rest of the congregation.

O, humiliated and hurt, ran out of the church and got into his father's car. I followed after him and we sat together until his family was ready to go home. O was fit to be tied. We both were. At first I thought he might even cry, but I was proud he never did. I think if he could have gotten away with it, O would have picked up a brick and bashed the Deacon in the head. Had I been older and strong enough I might have punched Deacon Moffett myself. But the sad truth is Deacon Moffett was right. O was much too soft looking for a Black male.

I tried to stand up for O, but the few times I did he pleaded with me not to get involved. In school he rarely let me get near him. "Keep your distance Ad-man," he would say. "I do not want anybody mistreating you on account of me." O was that kind of guy. He looked out for me better sometimes than I did for him.

When we hung out together it was usually at church, because that was the one place we could talk freely without drawing too much criticism or attention – most of the time.

Obviously everybody thought O was queer. But I am positive nobody had a shred of proof about which direction he leaned sexually. I was his best friend and had no idea about that part of his life. Quite naturally, since I spent time with O, suspicions arose about my sexual preferences too. It was that 'birds of a feather flock together' mindset. What saved my reputation was that I always had girl friends. This kept the talk about me on the rumor mill pretty tame for the most part.

Once or twice someone came right out and asked, "Is O gay?" I was brutally honest when I answered I did not know. But there were times when I tried to assure people that O liked girls. It was an impossible sell. Nobody ever saw him with a girl or knew him to have a girl friend. Ironically, this was not for lack of effort on his part. I may have been the only person among our peers who knew O was desperately in love with Penelope Wilson, the smartest girl in school. O had a crush on Penelope that lasted from first grade all the way through high school graduation. Like me, he was shy, but probably worse than I was and he never really told Penelope how he felt. Once he wrote a note to her once, but that did not turn out well. She turned it in to the teacher and O received a mild reprimand. In all the years he obsessed over Penelope, she never gave him the time of day. O's mistake had been to think smart girls liked smart guys. Since Penelope was so smart, his strategy to get her attention had been to keep his grades up in hopes of impressing her. Good grades backfired on him because they turned out to be as bad for his reputation as his looks. Being smart and pretty was two strikes against him. O simply could not win. That is why I think O liked the song 'You Were on My Mind' as much as he did. Whoever wrote the song likely did not have the issues O faced in mind, but the words resonated with him for some reason. I think they expressed what he felt, but could never articulate as poetically as the group We Five.

There were days when I got more than the usual amount of flack because of my friendship with O, and when that happened I deliberately avoided him. O always seemed to be able to tell when I was feeling self conscious about our friendship. But he never complained or called me Judas. That is why, to this day, I think of O as the most courageous, dependable and trustworthy friend I ever had. I always had a lot of respect for the guy and loved him like a brother.

❦❦❦❦❦❦❦❦❦❦❦❦❦❦

Chapter 38

At The Empty Quarter Inn I got an even better look at O. The metamorphosis he had undergone over the past eight years was remarkable. All the softness he had in his youth was gone. O was not pretty anymore. Now he was outright handsome. Talk about turn about. Growing up, males looked at O with disgust. Now it was likely they looked at him with envy. O was still short though, that had not changed and his hair was different. He used a hair-relaxer now and he wore a stylish beard. If O was to put on a Thobe and Gutra he would make a dashing figure of an Arab sheikh.

The first surprise of our conversation was finding out O also lived in the nation's capital. He moved away from home two weeks after high school graduation and settled in D.C. six years before I arrived in Chocolate City.

"You were going to tell me how you got to Riyadh," I reminded him.

"I was working for a law firm at 14th and I Streets downtown. A number of the firm's clients were connected to the television industry. I don't know if I ever told you this, but I have always been fascinated with television. Do you remember Frederick Lawrence?"

"Yes, he went into journalism and became a reporter for KDKA."

"I ran into him downtown one year when I was in the Burgh visiting my folks. We had lunch together and afterward he invited me to his house. His place was fabulous. I told Fred about my interest in television. He gave me a few suggestions on how I might get started in the business. When I got back to D.C., I followed through on his advice and took some courses. One of the firm's clients wrote a letter of recommendation for me and that led to an internship. After that Channel 3 hired me as a Teleprompter technician and in time I branched into camera work and editing.

"Promoters came to the station from time to time to film plugs for some product or program. One day a guy gave a presentation about job opportunities overseas. Saudi Arabia's modernization program caught my attention. I approached him after the taping and told him how much I enjoyed his presentation. He took my card and promised to call if he came across anything that fit my skills set. Six months later he phoned and told me the Saudis were starting an on-the-job training program in their television industry and were recruiting professionals to assist. So I applied. I was hired and two months later I was here in Riyadh.

"Now you Ad-man, what has happened in your life since high school and how did you wind up in Saudi Arabia?"

I delved into my history starting with college graduation, my work with East Coasts Contractors, how I met Barry, and my recruitment by IPC. I did not mention Lovelen or Jaylynn because something told me to hold back that information. Later that evening I would realize it was a wise decision. Next I shared with him some of my experiences since coming to Riyadh. When I told him about being invited to Fahad's house to meet his little brother and mentioned they lived near Television Street, O interrupted to say "That's where I work, you know."

"O, it's crazy the way you and I have been moving in parallel universes since we finished high school. We both moved to D.C., we both came to Saudi Arabia, and we both have been traveling around the same vicinity here in Riyadh. That is uncanny my friend."

"It is something to think about Ad-man. Okay, back to your story, why did your friend's younger brother want to meet you?"

"Bashir, his little brother, is a Michael Jackson fan. Get this, he assumed because I am Black all he had to do was ask and I would get up and dance like Michael Jackson."

"That is funny. Poor kid had no idea what he was saying when he asked you to dance."

"Forget you man. Whether you believe it or not, I do all right on the dance floor. Anyway I got more out of the visit than I expected. After watching me dance, Fahad rigged a competition between me and a popular local wedding dancer. This guy turned out to be a tall lanky dark skinned brother named Jabbar. We hit it off great and he became my first Black Saudi friend. Jabbar has been taking me all over Riyadh ever since, and I have met a ton of people. His family is really nice too."

"You have a Black Saudi friend here in Riyadh? That's quite an accomplishment. I have never met a Black Saudi in this city."

"I can believe that. It took me over a year to meet Jabbar, but he was not the first Black Saudi I met. The first Black Saudi I met was a guy from Jeddah. When the Steelers played the Rams in the Super Bowl one of the Black Americans in our project invited me over to listen to the game on Armed Forces Radio. The Black Saudi from Jeddah was there. I asked him where all the Black Saudis were in Riyadh, because I was beginning to think they did not exist. He assured me they were around but said there were more Blacks in the west and especially in the cities of Mecca and Jeddah. A year later I met Jabbar. But not long after I met Jabbar, my boss at the Ministry started taking me along with him on inspection trips with the engineers. Once I started visiting our sites in the western part of the country, I was able to confirm for myself that there are plenty of Blacks out west. I still have not seen Jeddah, and that city remains at the top of my list of places to see before I leave Arabia."

"I know a lot of Black Saudis in Jeddah," O announced.

"Really, how did you meet them?"

Before O could answer our waiter interrupted to ask how much longer we would be. O and I had talked so long that we lost track of time and did not realize how late it had gotten.

"I live nearby. Why don't you come over to my place so we can do some more catching up?"

"Let's go."

🙞🙞🙞🙞🙞🙞🙞🙜🙜🙜🙜🙜🙜🙜

Chapter 39

O loved the villa. "This is sweet Ad-man. How did you manage to get a hook-up like this?"

"Believe me, I pinch myself every morning to make sure I am not dreaming."

"What is your neighbor like in the other villa?"

"That house is vacant; has been since I moved in."

"You have your own pool too? Man what a setup. I could have a ball in a place like this."

"This is my private oasis," I said as I unlocked the front door. "Come on in. Can I get you something to drink?"

"Vodka on the rocks would be fine, thanks."

"Coming right up," I said with a laugh.

"That's right Ad-man, play the game right down to the end," O said, obviously convinced I was joking about the drink.

I brought out a bottle of Smirnoff and asked, "Is this to your liking?"

"Dude, you weren't joking! How do you get booze here?"

"That is one of the perks that come with this job. Do you want it with ice?"

"Sure throw a few rocks in there, thanks."

I placed the drink on a coaster in front of O. He took a sip and said, "Man that is nice… I can see now I am going to be visiting you often."

"You are always welcome here O."

"Thanks buddy, now back to our conversation. Where were we when we left the restaurant?"

"You were going to tell me how you met your Black Saudi friends in Jeddah."

"I had been in the Kingdom about six months when the station sends me to Jeddah on a two week assignment. The only people I knew in the city were my coworkers, and they were all new to me too. Every day when I got off work, I drove straight back to the compound. It was boring. There was nothing for me to do with my spare time, and nowhere to go because I was afraid of venturing out on my own for fear of getting lost. Jeddah is nothing like Riyadh. It is very cosmopolitan and the place is huge. But the steady routine of waking up, going to work, and returning to the compound every day was wearing me down. In Riyadh I had outlets, performing in the theater group, going to our Recreation Center to watch movies, or attending one of the many parties that get thrown here every week. After a week in Jeddah I was developing a serious case of cabin fever. Help came that first Wednesday when one of my British coworkers surprised me by inviting me to go with him to a party. I accepted right away. We get there and all I see is White faces, as usual, but I figured being there was better than sitting around the compound with nothing to do. A little while later a brother walked through the door. He was the first Black American I had seen since coming to Arabia. I think he was just as starved to see my face, because we were instantly drawn to each other like magnets. His name is Edward Lawson. Ed works at our Embassy in Jeddah. After a few minutes we left the party. That night, like your friend Jabbar did with you, Ed took me around to meet some of the local people. During my second week in Jeddah, Ed and I went out every night and he introduced me to brothers from everywhere. I am talking Black Saudis, Blacks from at least a dozen African countries, and Black American Muslims who are in the Kingdom taking Islamic studies. The night before I flew back to Riyadh, Ed and a big group of his friends all got together on one of the plazas downtown. In Jeddah hundreds of guys go downtown and hang out on the plazas just sitting around talking. We blew on Hubbly-Bubblies and talked about our homelands and what life is like for us here in Arabia. It was beautiful Ad-man, and empowering in a way that is hard to put into words. It felt like a Confederation of Black Nations or something the way we were all from different lands but communicating with a common understanding. Most of us were descendants of people who had been taken out of Africa in chains, but all of the Africans were from countries that had once been colonized by Europeans. So we all had things in common. Now whenever I get the chance, I fly to Jeddah and hook up with Ed and the guys. It is a lot of fun."

"That sounds awesome. I want to sit in with you guys too. Can I go to Jeddah with you?"

"Tell you what I will do, I will call Ed, tell him about you, and let him know ahead of time when we are coming so he can arrange to get all the guys together."

"O, something happened to me not too long ago that I want to run past you. Listening to you just now made me think of it and I think you may be the perfect person to share this with. Before I tell you about it, I want to ask you something - have you ever been to Mecca?"

"Are you crazy? No way. I did not come here to get my head chopped off. I am surprised you even bothered to ask that question. You know non-Muslims are not allowed in Mecca."

"You're right, I do know that. In fact I wrote Mecca off as a place to visit before I came to Arabia. But the reason I asked if you have ever been to Mecca is because a few months back a Saudi invited me to go to Mecca."

"You are kidding. Who invited you?"

"This guy my friend Jabbar knows. Jabbar and I were on Sitteen (60th) Street one day when I was waiting at a red light and this Black Saudi pulled up next to us and honked his horn. I looked over but did not recognize him. But I suspected Jabbar knew him because down on the seat he was motioning with his hand for me to drive on. That told me he did not want to talk to the guy. So I pulled away when the light turned green but this guy followed us to the next light and honked his horn again. Jabbar asked me to pull over but says, 'I will talk to him very fast then we go. I do not like this man.'"

"Before Jabbar can open the door to get out of my car, this guy has already parked his car and come over. He jumped into the back seat and started talking to Jabbar and the way they were talking I got the impression they had not seen each other in years. They laughed and talked for a minute or so, exclusively in Arabic. O, it is kind of hard to explain how I knew this, but Jabbar did not want me to know what they were talking about. I could tell he was trying to use words that he thought I did not know. They talked for several minutes before the guy got around to asking about me. Jabbar had never introduced us and I think that made the guy very curious to find out who I was. Jabbar had to tell him something so he said my name quickly and tried to get their conversation going again. It was obvious to me Jabbar wanted to get away from the guy and did not want him to say anything to me. But once the guy knew I was American, he switched to speaking English. Right away he started asking questions about America, how much does a ticket cost to go to the U.S.; how long could he stay if he went for a visit? Then he wanted to know how long I have been in Saudi Arabia. Now, I did not know anything about this guy, but I was beginning to dislike him myself. Something about his manner just did not seem right, you know. It felt like I was talking with a con man and who was ready to try to run a hustle of some kind on me at any moment. Then this guy asks, 'would you like to go to a party?' Up to that point Jabbar had stayed out of my conversation with him, but I sensed when the guy mentioned a party that Jabbar got antsy. Frankly I was not even curious to know where or when the party was being held, so I told the guy no thanks. But he persisted 'man you will like this party it has girls, sex, hashish, beerrrra, anything you like. You can come with me and my friends.'

"At this point Jabbar asked, "Where is this party?"

The guy says 'in Mecca.' Now in my mind I am thinking he is either lying or the guy is some kind of a nut case. So I am getting ready to tell him, 'I am not Muslim' but before I can say anything, Jabbar shouts 'Mr. Adam is Christian. Christian people are not permitted in the Mecca, isn't it?' That, I figure, is the end of the conversation. But this guy says, 'no problem for you Mr. Adam. Just put on a Thobe and gutra and nobody will say anything to you. If they do, just say Allahu Akbar a shadu illah wa Muhammad rasull allah three times and you will be fine.'"

"Again I turned down his offer and Jabbar tells him we have to go. As soon as he got out of the car Jabbar says to me 'ruuh, yala nimshi.' He really wanted to put distance between us and that guy. As we were driving away Jabbar explains, 'there are good people and bad people in every country. That man is a bad person. He should never have invited you to go to Mecca.' I assured Jabbar that I would not have gone to Mecca under any circumstance even if he or Waleed invited me, because I would view that as gross disrespect for his country's traditions. I told him, 'I do not want anybody to come to my country and disrespect our customs so I would never do anything like that while living in Saudi Arabia.' Jabbar smiled and said, 'very good Mr. Adam. I like that.' But I have always wondered about that invitation. It seemed like an odd thing to say so casually to a foreigner and a non-Muslim at that. Furthermore, I could not imagine the kind of behavior he mentioned actually going on in Mecca. In the end I figured the party was probably in a suburb and not in the city itself. Even then, I would not have gone because the things he invited me to participate in are not my idea of fun. I have never done drugs and I would never dream of committing crimes in a foreign country, especially not here in Saudi Arabia."

"Ad-man, you might find this hard to believe but parties like that have happened in Mecca," O stated. "I heard about them from my friends in Jeddah."

"Are you serious?"

"Yes, but they cannot happen there any more," he said with a hint of nostalgia.

O's statement had me puzzled and intrigued. I now knew that the invitation to party in Mecca had been genuine. But I wondered what O meant when he said those kinds of parties cannot happen at Mecca any more.

"Sounds confusing I know. I can explain. First let me ask you something. Have your Black Saudi friends told you anything about their history in this country?"

"Not much."

"During one of our sessions in Jeddah, the Black Saudis got to talking about things that none of us in the group; that is us Blacks from outside Saudi Arabia, had ever heard before or read in any history book. Are you familiar with the Island of Zanzibar and its connection with Black slavery?"

"O, do not get me started on that subject. My African Studies professor would rant class after class about the Arab slave trade and the Island of Zanzibar."

"Did he ever talk about what happened to the people they took away?"

"That was a mystery that had him and a lot of other people baffled. He said Arabs had a 700 year head start over Europeans in taking our people from Africa but nobody can figure out where they took all those Africans and why there aren't at least one or two Black communities, at a minimum the size of the Black American community, here in the Middle East or other areas just outside of Africa.”

“That is interesting Ad-man, because what the Black Saudis told us that night might provide some of the missing pieces to that puzzle. Did you know that Muslims making the pilgrimage to Mecca have to pay a tax?”

“No, I never heard of that.”

“It is called the Hajj tax. Black Saudis told us that a long time ago Muslims paid that tax by bringing slaves to Mecca. They did not know when the practice started or how long it lasted, but they did say it stopped long before the Saudis came to power in Arabia. How it worked was like this, Muslims would sail from Persia, India, Asia, Europe, North Africa and other lands to the Island of Zanzibar, purchase a slave, sail up the Red Sea to Mecca, drop the slave off in payment of the Hajj tax, circle the Kabba seven times, then return to their homelands. In some ways it sounds a lot like the Triangle Trade in the West.

“Once the slaves reached Mecca they were told they no longer had citizenship in any country and were now the property of Islam. Our Black Saudi friends explained that these people were considered, not slaves, but gifts that belonged to the religion. Over the centuries the population at Mecca grew as more Africans were brought in. Some thought there were African families living in that city that may have had residency at Mecca 1,000 years or longer.”

“When Ibn Saudi took over the country, I am not sure he knew about the population of Africans at Mecca. And even though nobody knows when the practice of bringing slaves to Mecca to pay the tax ended, I think it is a fair assumption that Ibn Saud would have shut it down if it had been ongoing when he came to power. In fact, the Saudis brought a completely different type of Islam with them from the East.”

“That makes sense,” I said. “I can see Ibn Saud ending a practice like that, especially given the fact the Saudis are the ones who ended slavery in the whole country 30 years after taking over.”

“True, but the facts are those Africans were in Mecca when Ibn Saud came west, so he inherited that situation. Keep in mind though they were not considered slaves, but gifts. In fact, from what I understand, these Africans, for the most part, never totally abandoned the superstitions and traditions of their ancestors. If they converted to Islam, it may not have been a conversion that took root in their hearts. So the guy who invited you to a wild party in Mecca was inviting you to go into the Mecca ghetto.”

“I see, but you said those kinds of parties cannot happen anymore at Mecca. Why not? Wait, before you answer that, let me ask another question first. I am not sure you have the answer to this, but do you know what happened to the Africans when Faisal issued his edict ending Black slavery?"

"Sure, I can answer that. Nothing, they were viewed as gifts remember, not slaves. The edict did not cover them. Remember, when they arrived at Mecca they were stripped of national identities and told they no longer belonged to any country. They were not even considered citizens of Arabia."

"Interesting, okay back to my first question, how were those wild parties stopped at Mecca?"

"The root of the answer to that question connects to that fellow who took over the Grand Mosque in the fall of 1979. You said you were here when that happened, right?"

"I had only been in the Kingdom nine days when the attack took place. I remember the event vividly. We had a translator at the Ministry at the time named Mohamed Al-Hamidi. He and I became friends for awhile. Mohamed was the first person to tell me the events at Mecca could lead to a war. He had a lot of contacts in Riyadh and thanks to Mohammed I learned some of the details of what was going on at Mecca."

O then asked, "Did anyone tell you about the prophecy in the Quran about the Mahdi and that the guy leading the takeover claimed he was the fulfillment of that prophecy?"

"Mohamed took me to visit a Muslim student that had been evacuated from Mecca. Believe it or not that student was a White American Muslim studying here in the Kingdom. He told us in detail about that and how the battle the Mahdi is supposed to initiate at Mecca would begin against hypocritical Muslims."

"Good, then you already have the background to the story. According to my Black Saudi friends the government was never convinced they caught everyone that followed this man. They believe he had additional supporters hiding out in the Mecca ghetto. Of course if you think about it logically, the government has a good argument. Hundreds of guys followed that man into the Kabba and took enough provisions and ammunition to hold off the Saudi military a long time, even longer than they ultimately did. These guys fully expected to defeat the Saudis and fulfill that part of the prophecy before branching out from Mecca to conquer the rest of the world. An effort of that magnitude would take coordination and logistics on a scale much broader than the confines of the Grand Mosque. These guys had to set up somewhere before launching their attack on the Mosque so they exploited the ghetto to use as their seat of operation. The idea that every one of his supporters followed him to the front line of battle there inside the Mosque seemed far fetched. Some believe that as many as were inside with him, if not more, were outside waiting for a signal to reinforce the group, either if things went bad during the fight against Saudi forces or to spearhead the breakout from Mecca to the rest of the peninsula. If what the government believes is true, their biggest problem would be tracking all of them down and rooting them out of Mecca. To do that in a ghetto of that size would have been virtually impossible and bloodier than I think the Saudis wanted to see happen. The rebels could have hidden out in the ghetto for a long time but a lot of innocent people would have been killed if government forces moved in to force them out."

"Hold on O. I can understand the government wanting to round up all the people who supported this guy, but didn't the movement fizzle once this guy was killed? He is dead, right? What could any remaining followers do that would threaten anybody?"

"Yes he is dead. But if you remember about 2,000 years ago another man here in the Middle East was executed after claiming to be a foretold prophet. A few days after he died, a small band of his followers claimed he had risen from the dead. That started a movement that has since swept the globe. Sound familiar?"

"Of course, Christianity, so are you saying these guys at Mecca were claiming the dead professed Mahdi has been resurrected?"

"No, I have not heard that. But one thing I do know, the Saudis would never sit around and wait for something like that to happen. Since they could never root a secret society of unknown size out of the ghetto, they decided to tear the whole place down. Actually, I think they have wanted to clean up the city from the beginning but out of compassion for the Africans they let them stay rather than disrupt their lives. What happened with this professed Mahdi forced their hand. They started clearing out the ghetto a few months ago and are sending all those families of Africans that were brought here as gifts in past centuries, back to Africa as we speak."

"What?"

"You heard me correctly. They are deporting all of those Blacks in Mecca back to Africa."

"Where in Africa are they sending them?"

"That was another dilemma the Saudis had to resolve. Neither the Africans themselves nor the Saudis know from what part of Africa their ancestors were taken. Plus, none of the Blacks have passports so they cannot claim citizenship anywhere on the continent. I was told the Saudis negotiated with a number of East African nations to take these people in, so they are being repatriated into several countries."

"Wow that is a stunning story. I never dreamed something like that could happen to any Black community anywhere, especially not in this century. How did the Africans react to the order to leave the country?"

"They refused to leave, so the government set a deadline. The Africans were warned if they did not leave voluntarily by that date the military would force them out. The deadline came and passed and the Africans were still in the city. So the military surrounded the ghetto and after a short battle forced the Africans out of the city."

"How large of a population are we talking about?"

"The Saudis never give out those kinds of statistics, but after all these centuries I would not be surprised if the population numbered in the millions. Ed thought it was important that I see what was happening with my own eyes, so he invited me to Jeddah last month. We went to some of the Embassies where the refugees are being processed out of the country. It was a sight to see. Thousands of women and girls of all ages crying and begging for help. We had to climb over them and their possessions to get through the crowds. Apparently, they had to leave in a hurry so they grabbed what they could when the soldiers rounded them up. I really got nervous when I did not see any males in the crowds, of any age. But Ed reminded me the Saudis always separate the sexes. He said the men were likely sent ahead to get things ready for their families."

Needless to say the information O shared with me was shocking. My heart went out to the Africans at Mecca because twice now in their history their families had been forcibly uprooted and sent off to unknown destinations. First they were put in chains in their homelands in Africa and brought to Arabia. Now they were being deported out of Arabia at gun point and sent back to a continent on which their ancestors at some point in the distant past had claims of citizenship. Which was worse, I wondered, to be sent back to an ancient homeland that you knew absolutely nothing about or to languish in a city for 1,000 years or longer with no chance of ever becoming a citizen of any country?

Of course there was more to the events at Mecca than O and I could possibly know. I was impressed that Black Saudi citizens, though not a part of the group at Mecca, were interested enough in what happened to the Africans to share that information with fellow Blacks from other parts of the world. This spoke volumes about the kind of people they were and I hoped to meet some of them one day.

Lovelen had asked what I would do if I awoke one morning and heard a royal decree reinstituting slavery in the Kingdom. In all the scenarios we debated, not once did we consider the possibility of Blacks being sent back to Africa. Now that this had happened to the Africans at Mecca, I could not help wonder if it was possible for something like that to happen to other Black communities, ours in America for example. Was it possible that a matter of national security could arise in the United States that would force the nation to choose between its survival and the continued tenure of Black Americans in the country? If a decision was made to send Black Americans to Africa, how would we react? Would we do as the Africans at Mecca did and refuse to go? If we resisted repatriation, could the U.S. military, with its ranks filled with Black Americans, be expected to carry out an order that would force millions of Black families out of the country?

The plight of the Africans at Mecca underscored a problem that is prevalent among Blacks all around the world. We have no idea where most of our people ended up when they were taken from Africa. Even at this late date in history, obscure communities of Blacks still exist. But what if that group of Africans at Mecca had been more visible to the world? Perhaps other nations or groups may have been in position to offer alternative solutions for the Saudis and the Africans to consider that might have avoided loss of life among those who resisted the deportation.

For far too long other people have controlled the telling of our story and history. Learning about the events at Mecca, reaffirmed for me how important it is that we take control of our own legacy, past, present and future. Our ancestors were enslaved by the millions in past centuries and much of the evidence about the details of those times was destroyed. But today Blacks around the world reside as free citizens in the lands where their ancestors first arrived in chains. This gives us, their descendant's unique opportunities to reconstruct the history piece by piece if necessary. The dispersion of Africans in past centuries has resulted in a global community of a sort in this modern world. With global communications, it would be easy to reconstruct lost history by coordinating the stories of these dispersed groups around the world. In that way we could compile a more complete and reliable accounting of what occurred in the past. Communications and other technologies could serve to our advantage in an effort of that magnitude. The opportunities are there for us. The question is what will we do with them?

"Ad-man, I am surprised your Black Saudi friends never told you about these things."

"Actually Jabbar's older brother Waleed has been very judicious when it comes to saying anything about the history of Blacks in this country. Jabbar though told me an amazing story about how he reacted to the edict ending Black slavery here. He was eight years old when Faisal issued the edict. Young as he was, Jabbar walked right out of the compound where his family had been slaves for years. He was testing the edict to see if it was true. But he left the compound without telling his family. Then he made matters worse by staying away three days. Waleed beat him pretty good when he got back but Jabbar just laughed through the whole beating. When Waleed asked why he was laughing, Jabbar told him 'this is the first time a free man has been beaten by a slave in this house.'"

O laughed as hard as I did when I first heard the story. "Man that is awesome. Eight years old, huh… sounds more like a full grown freedom fighter. Oh yes, I have got to meet this brother. He sounds magnificent."

"Jabbar is pretty wild, but you will love the whole Al-Bughawi family. They are good people. Just wait until you meet Fi-Fi Dahling."

"Whoa, who is that?"

"I am not going to spoil it for you. Wait until you meet her."

"Sounds like you are having a great time with Black Saudis here in Riyadh Ad-man."

"They are an amazing people and a lot like us. They love our music and everything Black Americans do. Waleed and I watch a lot of Black film together and at times he tries to tell me things about their history, but like I said he holds back for some reason. But you should hear what he has to say about the films we watch. He is so well informed about what is going on in the Black community in America that his reactions to situations in those movies are exactly the same as ours. He even understands what is meant by Blackploitation. I am telling you, just from being around Black Saudis I can say with certainty they really know us. It is sad that so little is known about them outside of Arabia."

"That is because they have no voice and there is no free press here," O commented. "Black Saudis are probably one of the most underreported communities in the world. Like you, when I first got here I had no idea slavery had recently ended or that a distinct group of Black citizens lived in this country. Once I found all of that out, I wrote to the station back home and suggested we do a story or a series on them. So far there has been no interest."

"If they ever decide to do something, give me a call. I would love to help."

"Sounds good Ad-man, hey, I feel like a swim. Do you mind if I use the pool?"

"Not at all, be my guest."

"Come swim with me, we can swim nude the way we did in High School."

It was true we were not allowed to wear swim trunks in high school, but now we were grown men. "O, you obviously missed the sign when you walked in the gate, the one that says 'No skinny dipping allowed by order of the management.' You are making me nervous man. If there is something you need to tell me; please do it now. There were a lot of rumors about you in school, but I always gave you the benefit of the doubt. Have you changed on me man?"

O was laughing so hard he could hardly get the words out when he said, "I was joking Ad-man. I have a pair of trunks in my car. I'll be right back."

"Okay, I will grab my trunks too. Maybe we can race laps like we did in school."

Running into someone I knew as a child could have turned into a big disappointment, but this had been special. After many years apart, my friendship with O was as strong as ever. It was as if we picked up right where we left off. As adults, however, our time together would be much better than what we had to deal with as children.

After swimming we sat on the side of the pool and talked. That is when O started recounting his sexual escapades. The man had been with females of all types, shapes and races. I considered the possibility he could have been exaggerating, or outright lying as men often do, but he was too detailed in describing his love making. A couple of times he went into such explicit detail about the ways he positioned the legs of a girl that I found myself getting aroused just listening. The way O talked about women convinced me my friend had turned into a wolf and mentally I gave myself a pat on the back for not mentioning Jaylynn. Maybe I would tell him about her in time, but not that night.

After the swim, O showered and got ready to leave. We exchanged phone numbers and set up a time to meet so he could take me to see where he lived. Right before he left, O surprised me by asking, "Ad-man do you play tennis?" I was happy to hear he played. We agreed to set up a match when he finished his engagement with the *Fantasticks* and reaffirmed our commitment to take a trip to Jeddah together.

After O left, I thought about the Expatriate Ladies Club and how O might react if they ever asked him to dance for them. Now that he had come out of his shell and had turned into a wolf, my guess was he probably would have jumped on top of a table and started performing for them right on the spot. Some really wicked stuff started running through my head and the more I thought about it, the more afraid I became just thinking about O dealing with the ELCR.

Two days later I pulled a business card out of my wallet and telephoned Darrell Jenkins. He was happy to hear from me and affirmed, "Yes, I know Ed Lawson very well. Make sure you give me a call when you and your friend come to town. Maybe we can all get together for lunch or something."

A trip to Jeddah promised to be a lot of fun. I looked forward to sitting in on a session of the Conference of Black Nations with O, Ed and their African, Black Saudi and Black American friends.

🙟🙟🙟🙟🙟🙟🙟🙝🙝🙝🙝🙝🙝🙝🙝

Chapter 40

Ramadan in Saudi Arabia is unlike anything anywhere on earth. Faithful Muslims do not eat, drink, smoke or engage in sex from sunrise to sunset for the entire month. After sundown they do all the things they normally do, but during the day Riyadh is a virtual ghost town. Come evening the town springs back to life in a big way.

At the Ministry there was concern that people might pass out in the heat due to weakness from hunger. That is why most of our Saudi coworkers did not come to work during Ramadan. Those that did only stayed briefly. Conserving energy, particularly during the heat of the day, was the rule of thumb during Ramadan. Westerners benefited from there being fewer cars on the roads because it was slightly safer to drive.

Commencing at sundown people got together and basically made up for the abstentions during the day. Living through that holiday in Riyadh was what I always imagined life in Transylvania was like with everybody sleeping during the day and only coming out at night.

Pious Muslims were more moderate in eating and drinking after sundown, in keeping with the spirit of the holy month. They were highly critical of those who reveled overnight and overindulged in food to the point they could do little else but sleep through the following day. Recommended activity for daylight hours was meditation and discussions on the Holy Book.

Out of respect for the religious observation, I did not visit any Saudi friends during Ramadan. Even so, I was certain the Al-Bughawis would not be reveling after sundown. The family was always fastidious about going to prayer, so I imagined their holiday was being spent in serious meditations. Tayyib was the family Mutawah, an honored designation reserved for the family member most dependable in getting everyone to answer prayer call. He would be particularly alert to make sure the family got to prayers during

281

this sacred period. Undoubtedly he and Waleed were taking the lead in reading passages from the Quran during the day.

Ramadan was followed by the festival of Eid, during which celebration some Arabs strung lights on their residences and places of business. Some parts of Riyadh looked a lot like communities in America during the Christmas holiday.

After Eid, I took O with me to introduce him to the Al-Bughawis. When we pulled up to the house, Waleed and his family were loading up the car. He was taking his mother to visit the Rashid's and invited us to go along. "We will not stay long," he promised, "and your friend can meet Tayyib. He is there now playing with the Rashid boys."

When we arrived at the compound, Tayyib and the Rashid brothers were on the tennis courts with a large group of their friends. They were trying to show twenty or so boys how to skate triples. A large audience had gathered to watch, including many of the servants that worked in the compound. As soon as Tayyib saw me he shouted "that's him, that's Mr. Adam." Tayyib and several of the boys rushed over to the car and pleaded with me to bring my skates and help them learn triples. "What's going on Ad-man," O asked? I gave him a quick recap of what happened with me, Tayyib and the Rashid brother and sister. Then I asked Tayyib if O could borrow a pair of skates from one of his buddies so we could show them a few things.

"What makes you think I can skate," O questioned with a sly grin?

"O, you have lived in D.C. longer than me. Get real man."

He laughed and laced up a pair of skates.

Tayyib put on James Brown and he and his friends started skating. O reminded me "if you still have that K.C. and the Sunshine Band cassette I loaned you in your car, bring it over. There is a song on that cassette that is perfect for skating."

I skated back to the car and got it. At the end of the James Brown song, O put on 'I'm Your Boogie Man'. That song really got the crowd going. The balcony of the main house was crammed with onlookers. I took a chance and waved to Mrs. Rashid. She smiled and waved back.

O and I put Tayyib in the middle and made a couple of circuits of the court demonstrating favorite moves of Triples teams. Once they caught on, a few of the other boys joined in and soon there were three sets of trios skating around the court.

At one point O broke away, skated up to one of the Saudi onlookers and snatched his gutra and ak-gal. When he put it on, Tayyib and I adjusted to have O skate between us. Watching that gutra billow in the wind as we rounded the court energized the crowd and the place went crazy. The rest of the Saudi boys rushed on court to join in and turned the court into a real skating rink. I think it was the first time in their lives they experienced the power of a group of skaters working together in synchronized fashion. For me being with them reminded me of an army of Bedouins charging across the desert sands only instead of camels and stallions we were rolling on skates.

The little Rashid girl brought a cassette out of the house and Tayyib put it in the machine. It was Arab music that was perfect for skating (Jalsat music was something I would hear more about a little later). The crowd loved it and for the first time since arriving in Arabia I heard females sound the high pitched ululations or Zaghareet trills that Arab women are famous for at celebrations. O and I had a blast with those boys. We skated only as long as our old bones allowed before leaving the court to the youngsters.

When we skated off the court, Waleed pointed a finger at me, laughed and said, "ya sheikh see what you started."

Waleed left his mother and sisters at the Rashid compound and we followed him back to his house. Once we sat down and started our visit, Waleed expressed shock over O's hair. "Ya sheikh, yani, what is this? How can you have hair like a White fellow? How is this possible? You know sometimes I dream I have hair like this. In the dream my hair moves in the wind just like a White man."

O assured him, "Your dream can come true. I can fix your hair this way if you like."

That is how a date was set for O to relax Waleed's hair. Frankly I was glad Waleed agreed to do it. The first time I saw him without his gutra I was convinced a comb had not touched his head since birth. Why bother combing your hair when you could keep your head covered with a tawkeeya and gutra all day?

On the day O gave Waleed the treatment, the first thing Waleed said when he finished was "ya sheikh I cannot feel my hair. Where is it? Am I... esh is mutha..."

"Bald" I hinted.

"Yes, am I bald now?" Pointing to O, he said, "If I am bald I will cut this man".

His wife Asimah came in the room. She was the first family member to react to his new hairstyle. Asimah laughed like it was the funniest thing she ever saw in fact she doubled over with laughter. This made Waleed nervous and afraid to look in a mirror. Then Jammilla, Samirah and Nura came in the room. They celebrated like their brother was a movie star, rubbing his head and making the biggest fuss over him. Fifi ran and got a mirror and put it in front of him. His reaction was the same as his wife's, he laughed. Then he said, "Wait, ya sheikh, come with me."

O, me, and the Al-Bughawi sisters followed Waleed outside. "Watch this," he said as he danced and twirled around shaking his head around so that his hair tossed effortlessly on the wind. We got a big kick out of Waleed's show but it only lasted five minutes. Afterward he said, "Okay, now get it out. I don't want this thing. If I go to work like this all of my friends will laugh and talk and talk and never shut up."

O tried to convince him to take a few days to get used to it, but Waleed was adamant. "I want it out," he screamed. O instructed him, "wash your hair repeatedly over the next several days, in time the relaxer will come out and your hair will return to its former state."

"Meanwhile, yani, I will put my gutra on my head and not take it off," Waleed promised.

When we left the Al-Bughawi's, O and I kicked around the idea of bringing Black American hair stylists to Arabia. A few days later when the topic came up again, we decided to table the idea until we talked to a few more of my Black Saudi friends and got their opinion. We did not know it at the time, but a powerful seed had been planted that day.

᪥᪥᪥᪥᪥᪥᪥᪥᪥᪥᪥᪥᪥᪥᪥

Chapter 41

Tawhid Al-Nejaris constantly reminded me about his standing invitation to revisit his home. At the Ministry he mentioned it at least twice a week. One especially dull weekend I took him up on his offer.

Getting to his street was easy. It was not that far from the Ministry and everything about the night when I was the guest of honor for Cupsah at his home was still fresh in my head. However, after I parked and got out of the car and looked around I noticed for the first time since coming to Riyadh a quirk about the city. There were no street signs on the back roads and none of the houses had numbers on them. How I missed these major differences in our cultures I did not know. Now I had to figure out which building, out of a row of houses that all looked the same, belonged to Tawhid and his family.

As I surveyed the block, a memory from Junior High came back to mind. I had a classmate who was a Jehovah's Witness. His name was Jack Robinson. All the guys called him Jackie. Jackie and I used to talk about his religion, nothing serious, but once I asked if he ever got nervous knocking on the doors of strangers. He told me the first door in the morning was always the hardest but after that it got easier. He said people usually became friendly once they realized he was not a bill collector or a detective searching for a suspect and only wanted to talk about the Bible.

Jackie may never have done religious work in a foreign country, but there I was facing a city block of identical gates in a land where people did not speak my language. I had two options – take up the challenge of knocking on every door until I found Tawhid or turn around and go home. As I approached the gate that my best guess told me belonged to Tawhid, I whispered under my breath, 'Jackie, if you can do this, I guess I can too.' When I knocked a young boy around the same age as Tawhid's youngest brother Ajib opened the gate. To prevent a prolonged conversation, I limited my statements to English as I explained my reason for knocking. I figured, whether he understood me or not I could leave quietly and quickly. He reacted in traditional Bedouin fashion, extending his family's hospitality. "Malish, itfaddle, ijlis, wa shrub shaiy (No problem; come in, have a seat and drink tea)." The way this young boy extended hospitality, however, was no mere repetition of age old custom. This youngster conducted himself with all the authority and responsibility of being the only male in the home at that moment. Even the youngest of Saudi boys are sometimes called upon to stand in for older siblings or fathers when no other males are present. On occasion they have been known to drive the family car to take their mother's to market. From what I had seen during the rainy season, I was aware that young Saudi males started honing their driving skills at an early age.

No sooner had the youngster invited me in for tea, he turned and shouted "ruuh, hut a shaiy (hurry, get tea)" to his mother. All along she had been hiding behind one of the columns on the porch of the main house just across the courtyard. When I spotted her she was holding her veil over her face, but at her young son's bidding the woman literally raced away at a dead sprint just to prepare tea for a stranger that had called at her home. Backing away, I excused myself as graciously as I could. The young boy, in turn, in a very polished manner blessed me and closed the door saying, "fi amanilah (go with God)."

Relieved that I had gotten out of that situation with relative ease, I went to the next house. This time a tall Saudi gentleman, probably no older than 27 years of age, came to the door. Again I avoided using Arabic as I explained my situation. The young man listened attentively then in clear English responded, "That's okay you can knock on any door until you find your friend. Nobody will bother you."

I commended him on his excellent command of English, to which he revealed, "I attend university in the States. I am home on vacation."

"Sorry I disturbed your evening."

"No problem. Why don't you come in, sit, and have some tea."

It was the identical invitation the youngster had offered at the previous house. Again I declined and told him, "Your neighbor made that same offer. I really appreciate your kindness but I think I should keep moving. My friend lives along here somewhere. I am sure I will find him soon."

"Okay. But like I said, feel free to knock on any door. Nobody will harm you. God be with you my friend."

My Jehovah's Witness friend had been right, after the first door it got easier. It also helped that the people of Riyadh were so friendly. I approached the third door brimming with confidence. No matter who answered or what language they spoke, I felt I would be able to handle the situation. I knocked and was pleased to see that this time it was young Ajib who opened the door. Surprised, he turned and shouted excitedly, "Tawhid, Sayeed Adam fil baab (Tawhid, Mr. Adam is at the door)!" Immediately sounds of people rising to their feet and slipping on sandals fell on my ears. Ajib turned back to me and as he opened the gate wider said, "itfaddle, ijlis, shrub shaiy." Tawhid rushed to the door, embraced me, took me by the hand and led me inside.

It was a wonderful evening during which I learned a little more about Tawhid's family. Mansur, the second youngest brother at age 15, was in secondary school. He played soccer and ran track. Khalid, an 18 year old, was the religious one of the family, the family Mutawah. Nasser, a few years younger than Tawhid, was the quietest of the brothers. He smiled a lot but said very little.

My visit lasted for a little under two hours and I had the rare honor of meeting Tawhid's father when he stopped in for a visit. This was an added treat for everyone. Though he did not stay long, I enjoyed watching him interact with his sons. Listening to them singing songs that had been passed down for generations was a wonderful experience.

On my way home I thought again about how much I would have missed had I not come to Saudi Arabia. I had met many wonderful families, but Tawhid Al-Nejaris, Waleed Al-Bughawi and Abdullah Al-Basheer would stand out for the way they welcomed me into their homes and treated me like an honorary member of their respective families. Perhaps every Saudi I met would not have treated me the way these three men had, but I had no doubts the majority of the people on the Peninsula would at least have been just as kind as Tawhid's neighbors. Bedouin culture shone through that night in all its strength. Kindness to strangers is innate to Saudis and has been ingrained in their psyche. It was impressive to see in action.

I did not visit Tawhid as often as I stopped by the Al-Bughawi's, but that was not the last evening I spent in his home. He always welcomed me when I stopped by and each time I learned a little more about the family, thus further enriching my Arabian experience.

Barakah Derar was scheduled to start at goalie for Hilal the following Thursday. Tawhid, Ahmed Al-Saud, Abdul Haqq and Mudar took me along with them to Riyadh stadium. The moment we walked in, I knew I was among 30,000 serious Hilal fans. It was like a Steelers or Redskins home game. Before the game the guys took me down on the field to visit Barakah, which was a special treat for us all. Barakah was as mellow as ever and I think his cool demeanor contributed to his successes on and off the field.

The game began and as the teams played, spectators chewed on sunflower and pumpkin seeds or pistachios. Guys were spitting hulls everywhere. A lot of them fell on me. At first I took offense, but as I looked around I saw it was not just happening to me. My friends were being pelted as well and none of them were getting upset. I attended several games and in time picked up the habit myself, chewing the hulls off seeds and spitting them out to land wherever they may.

Barakah played well that day and Al-Hilal won the match 1-Nil. We were all very proud and celebrated his victory together at the Ministry the following Saturday.

Chapter 42

Joseph Feda, my Lebanese friend from Arab class, helped me pick out an engagement ring. Once I made up my mind that I was going to ask Jaylynn to marry me, my heart pushed me to propose before she left Riyadh. I presented the ring to Jaylynn three weeks before she was scheduled to leave the Kingdom. Jaylynn loved it and admitted she had dreamed about us getting married. But she said "I do not think it would be wise to make a commitment like that at this time. We have only known each other less than a year and will be living on opposite sides of the planet for the next 12 months. As relationships go, ours has a pretty thin background." I understood how she felt. It was the Middle East. Anything could happen and she was right, we only had a short history together. I asked her to take her time and think about it a little more before stamping her decision as final. She agreed to discuss it again before she left.

A few days after that conversation, I arrived at the Ministry one morning and as I finished my rounds saying good morning to everyone, I was heading for the stairs when an unfamiliar Saudi walked up, flashed a friendly smile, then handed me a piece of paper. It was a map. Instinctively, I turned it over. On the back was a printed announcement in English that the Ministry was hosting a picnic the following month at a place called Mej-ma-ah. The American staff was invited to attend. According to the directions, the picnic area was near the Kuwaiti border. When I read that, I figured most of the American staff would not be going. Driving around the city was scary enough. Many of my fellow expatriates might conclude traveling long distances on Saudi highways just to eat a meal was not worth the risk.

When I got to my desk I called O and asked if he would like to ride up to Mej-ma-ah with me.

"A picnic sounds like fun but I am surprised the Saudis thought of it and even made the suggestion."

"Actually this might be reciprocation for a picnic the Mission hosted at the Recreation Center my first summer here. We invited our Saudi coworkers and their families to come. I do not think they were impressed. I got to the Center late, but when I walked in the first thing I noticed was that all of the Saudis were clustered around the shallow end of the pool. At the other end, near the entrance to the shower rooms, the Americans were putting on a square dance exhibition for a couple of the upper echelon Saudi managers from the Ministry.

"The Saudis at the shallow end looked bored out of their minds and the ones at the other end watching the square dancing, seemed a little uncomfortable. I looked around and wondered if anyone noticed that none of the Saudis had brought their wives. There were no little girls there either, only a few young Saudi boys running around at the shallow end where their fathers were keeping wary eyes on them. Saudis Tayyib's age swim at school. Older Saudis, like the men I work with at the Ministry, had a different upbringing. Swimming was never part of their lives. Many of them are deathly afraid of drowning. I could sense their fear as I looked in the faces of the men sitting around the pool.

"One of the Saudis, a manager I had seen around the Ministry from time to time, really put me on the spot. When he saw me he jumped up and shouted, 'Good, Adam is here, now we can get this party started.' Just that quick someone dropped a Michael Jackson cassette into a player and the Saudis at the shallow end of the pool got up and started dancing. The transformation was so sudden it was like someone had flipped a switch. One minute they were moping around and the next they were dragging me into a Soul Train line. There was no way I could stay because I knew what would happen if the party at the shallow end of the pool upstaged the square dancing at the other end. Somebody was going to get upset and if they saw me in the middle of it I knew where the finger of blame would be pointed. I think I might have been in the Rec Center all of four minutes before I got out of there."

"Wait a minute Ad-man, are you telling me American couples were dancing together in front of the Saudis?"

"That is exactly what they were doing. I think the idea was to introduce the Saudis to a bit of American culture and I know what you are thinking, the Saudis may have been offended. The fact that none of them brought their wives should have given us a clue that they were not going to abandon their traditions just because they were inside one of our facilities. Still, I applaud the effort that was made to reach out to our Saudi coworkers. Perhaps more thought should have gone into the planning, but we tried, and I think that counts for something. Like I said, the invitation to the Ministry picnic next month may be pay back on their part."

"It sounds like the Saudis did not enjoy the evening at your Rec Center."

"Of that I am not sure. Remember, I did not stay long. Maybe things got better after I left. There was not a lot of talk about the picnic afterward. At any rate, something tells me the picnic at Mej-ma-ah will be a lot of fun."

ੰੰੰੰੰੰੰੰੰੰੰੰੰੰੰੰ

Chapter 43

Two weeks before the picnic, I stopped by the Al-Bughawi's to visit Waleed and his brothers. One of Waleed's White Saudi friends was talking with him about a private matter when I walked into the reception area. Waleed explained to me that his friend was in love. "But he has a big problem, ya sheikh. A Saudi Prince wants to marry the same girl he loves. The Prince is very rich so he can give bigger dowry to family of the girl. My friend does not think he can marry this girl and he loves her too much. He wants me to help. Insha'Allah I will see what I can do. I know a man who is very good with this kind of problem. We go to him now. You can come if you like and you will see, okay?"

I was fascinated. This was a side of Waleed I had not known. Not once had I imagined Waleed to be a man of such deep counsel that people in the community sought him out for advice, especially advice on affairs of the heart. I was proud, and yes I wanted to go along. But I insisted we ride in my car.

Along the way we passed the building where I had seen dozens of women entering and exiting and presumed was a prison. Waleed confirmed it indeed was a prison – a prison for women. "Many women get arrested for shop lifting," he informed me. "If a woman is caught stealing a third time she will get her hand cut. But not all these women you see are thieves. Most of them have come to bring them prisoner's food because if they do not do it the prisoners will not eat anything. Maybe that woman over there is daughter or sister of prisoner or maybe she is her friend."

"You said if they do not bring food, the prisoners will not eat. What do they do if they have no family members or friends to help them?"

"People come to sell food in the prison, but if them prisoners have no money, yani, they must trade something to get the food."

"What can they trade if they do not have money?"

"Ya sheikh, I do not know about these things but I think when people get very hungry they will do, yani, anything to get the food."

"Is it like that at all prisons?"

"Yes, it is like that."

Waleed's information reaffirmed Todd Dearbourne's warning about the undesirability of going to prison in Arabia in his welcome speech.

The house where Waleed took us was three doors from where Mohamed Al-Hamidi, our first translator at the Ministry, lived. I was tempted to knock on his door to see if he had moved away, and if not say hello. But I did not know how long Waleed's business would take so I dismissed that thought. At the house Waleed took us to, an older Black Saudi between 40 or 45 invited us inside. We followed him down a narrow hall to a sitting area at the back of the house. Waleed's friend and I were served tea while he and our host went into another room to talk privately. The young lovesick Saudi seemed quite nervous as we waited. Ten minutes later Waleed returned and pulled his friend aside. They spoke briefly and the young man got up and walked out of the house.

"What is going on," I asked?

Waleed explained, "My friend he must decide what to do. He go out to think."

Up to that point I was having a hard time trying to imagine what this older Black man could do for the heartsick young Saudi. Everything about him seemed fishy to me. Like Waleed's friend, I was nervous, only for different reasons. After a few moments of silence I asked, "Waleed, what can this man do to help your friend in this situation?"

"He talks to the ginna."

"Ginna, what's that?"

"There are good ginna and bad ginna."

"Are you talking about genies like in Aladdin's lamp?"

"Yes that is the word, genies. You call them demons. There are good ginna and bad ginna. He talks to the good gina. Come let us go see what my friend will do."

Waleed led me back toward the front of the building. Half way down the narrow hallway he stopped at a door that we had passed when we first entered, opened it and said "This is where he talks to the ginna." We were in the middle of a framed house with walls and a roof but that door opened to what looked like a cave that had been carved out of solid rock with a hand pick. It was the spookiest thing I had ever seen. Quickly I slid past Waleed and, as a friend of mine from South Carolina used to say, I hog-shagged out of there. Waleed raced after me laughing so hard he was barely able to stay on his feet.

Back at the car, I was gasping for breath when I asked "Waleed are you serious? What does this creepy guy plan on doing for your friend? Man, I shudder to think what goes on in that room. He talks with demons! Good Lord, this is some crazy stuff."

"He say if my friend pay 100 Riyals the Prince will never get, esh is mutha bil Inglizi when your zuber goes like this?" Waleed made a gesture that implied he was talking about an erection, which is the word I gave him. "Yes, the Prince will never get erection again and my friend can marry this girl he love too much."

"Waleed I have to tell you something, and I mean no harm in saying this but you must be out of your cotton picking mind to bring your friend to a man like that. I cannot believe you did this." Thankfully Waleed's friend turned down the offer. He told Waleed "if I can get the ginna to do something that bad to the Prince for 100 Riyals, imagine what the Prince can get them to do to me with all the money he has."

Wise young man.

A couple of days later two of the Al-Bughawi siblings returned home after long absences. Jabbar came in from off the streets and the oldest sibling, Hawwa, returned from Egypt where she had lived many years.

It was good to see the family come together to enjoy the success, pride and joy of owning its very first home on the Arabian Peninsula. This was a landmark moment in their history.

Jabbar had told me some time back that Hawwa would come home when the family moved into the new house. He never knew the exact date of her return but by coincidence I stopped by the morning following her late night arrival in Riyadh.

Jammilla excitedly introduced us saying, "This is our brothers' friend, Mr. Adam. He is a Black American."

Hawwa grunted, "So what! I have seen Black Americans before. And we are Black Saudis – what of it?" She walked away as if she had little interest in anything I might have to say.

When Jabbar and I had a chance to talk, I asked "Are you home to stay?"

"That was my plan until this morning."

"Jabbar don't tell me you have changed your mind about staying already."

"I almost have."

"Why, what happened?"

Pinning his eyes on his sister, Jabbar followed Hawwa as she moved from room to room. He was like radar tracking its target. Leaning toward me he confided "starting tomorrow I am going shopping to find a husband for Hawwa." We would have laughed openly, but Hawwa happened to look our direction at that precise moment. I nearly swallowed my tongue to hold back from snickering.

Five minutes later Waleed came in and whispered, "If we ever get this sister married and out of the house, it will, yani, be a miracle." Fortunately for Waleed his day-to-day life would only be mildly disrupted by his older sister's return. As the oldest male, and a married man, Waleed carried a lot of clout in the family. Plus Hawwa did not want to tangle with Waleed's wife. Asimah was a formidable young lady. She and I rarely interacted, but I liked her personality. She complimented Waleed perfectly and was very attentive to their daughters Keera and Suriya.

I did not stay long that visit. When Tayyib escorted me across the courtyard to the front gate, I was surprised to see sadness in his face. As I got into my car, I motioned for him to come over to the window.

"What is the matter Tayyib? This is a special day for your family. Why do you look so sad?"

"It is just that Hawwa came home last night and already this morning we want her to go back to Egypt." With a sly grin he leaned closer and whispered, "She is too bossy."

"I get the impression the only person who enjoys having Hawwa around is your mother."

"Yes, my mother, sweet woman… but confused somewhat… you see…" Tayyib was laughing as he spoke and had a hard time getting his words out. I allowed myself to laugh a little while keeping an eye on the front gate, in case Hawwa came outside.

"Tayyib, I am going to get out of here before you get us both into trouble young man."

For the first time since meeting the family, I was happier to be leaving at the end of a visit than when I arrived. One thing I knew for sure, Waleed and Jabbar would need a lot of luck getting that sister married.

੫੫੫੫੫੫੫੫

Chapter 45

At the last Friday service in the Kingdom that Jaylynn and I attended together, I introduced her to O. He behaved himself, probably because I gave him stern warning ahead of time that I would clock him if he tried to hit on my girl.

After the service I brought up marriage again and presented the ring to Jaylynn for the second time. Honesty I expected her to balk, as she had done previously, but she accepted enthusiastically. I was bubbling over with love as she ran to tell the Strong's and show off her ring to members of the congregation.

"My only regret," said Pastor Strong "is that the wedding will not take place here. But I am happy for the both of you, and you have my blessing."

First Lady Doreen was very pleased about our engagement and in a departure from her usual inquisitiveness, said very little that afternoon. Jaylynn's going away party turned into an engagement celebration. I did not enjoy it much myself because I was thinking about the year ahead without the love of my life. I dreaded that she was leaving. But I was determined to stand strong even when I saw her off at the airport that coming Thursday.

For the rest of that week we talked on the phone every night and she called my office every day. "I have never been happier," she kept repeating. I said the same. Wednesday afternoon she called me at the Ministry for the last time to confirm our meeting at the airport the next day. It was on that occasion I inquired why she changed her mind about getting married. She told me Lovelen reminded her that 'you two will be apart for a year. Long distance communication will either strengthen the relationship or weaken it. Being engaged could also be the glue you guys will need to hold you together. Look at it this way, if you grow apart you can always end the engagement.' Jaylynn said she thought her sister's advice was sound. I agreed.

I was invited to a party at Waleed's house that night, so I exchanged telephone kisses with Jaylynn and we said goodnight. We would see each other for the last time in Arabia, at the airport the next day. Before I left for the Al-Bughawi residence, I took another look at the present on the coffee table that I would be giving Jaylynn the next day. It was my final bon voyage gift. Joseph Feda had ordered it special for me all the way from Beirut, a gold necklace with two gold camel-shaped ornaments that had our names inscribed on them.

Rahman Al-Gamed and Waleed Al-Bughawi had gone to college together. Rahman was the best man at Waleed's wedding. Waleed was now returning the honor, for Rahman had gotten engaged. That night Waleed was throwing a Saudi style bachelor party.

The festivities were in full swing when I arrived. Laughter, toasts, well wishes and reminiscing lasted all evening and into the early hours of the morning. When the party wound down, Waleed's sisters prepared rooms for the guests to stay overnight. I was about to leave when Waleed commented, "You have never spent the night in my home. You are my brother too, please stay." In the spirit of brotherhood, I accepted his invitation.

In the morning when I got up, Nura advised me that all of the other guests had already left and her brothers had gone somewhere with the groom-to-be.

The only people in the house were Waleed's sisters, his mother, his wife and daughters, and me.

Nura and Samirah brought breakfast and hot tea. I thanked them but first checked my watch to make sure I had enough time for a meal. When I finished breakfast I got up to leave.

"Where are you going Mr. Adam," Jammilla asked?

"I have to get to the airport. A friend of mine is going back to America today."

Jammilla looked like she wanted to say something, but stopped. She had a look of confusion on her face but quickly left the room. I went to the front door. It would not open. Someone had locked it, from the outside.

Nobody was around so I called for Jammilla. Nura came instead.

"What is the matter Mr. Adam?"

"The door is locked. Open it please. I have to go."

For all the reaction I got from Nura, I might as well have turned to the door and said open sesame. My words simply had not registered with Nura. "Please bring the key so I can get out," I prodded to get her moving.

Hawwa came into the room. "What is the problem? What do you need Mr. Adam? Have you eaten?"

"Yes Hawwa, I had a nice breakfast thank you. There is no problem. I just have to leave. I am meeting someone at the airport in about an hour."

"Waleed will be back soon."

Hawwa said this as if that was the answer. Problem was it had nothing to do with unlocking the door. "Excuse me Hawwa, I need to go now. Would you please unlock the door?"

"I cannot unlock the door Mr. Adam."

"Why not?"

"Waleed has the key."

"But he is not here."

"That is why I tell you he will be back soon. He went with his friend to the suq."

"Maybe I am not making myself clear. I have to be at the airport in about an hour. It is going to take at least thirty minutes to drive there from here, plus I have to stop by my house on the way to get something, so I need to leave now."

"I understand Mr. Adam, but we do not have the key. Waleed has the key."

"Wait a minute. Are you telling me nobody can get out of this house until Waleed gets back?"

"Yes, that is it."

My heart sank. I knew at that moment, come what may, I was not going to get to the airport to see Jaylynn off. Something more pressing, however, began to worry me. "Hawwa tell me something - what would this family do if a fire broke out while Waleed is away? How would you guys get out of here? Every window in this house is cut at the top of the walls and none are large enough for anyone to squeeze through even if you had a ladder. Not even Waleed's little girls could squeeze through those narrow slits. What would you do if there was a fire?"

"Fire, what fire? Where is the fire?"

"I did not say there is a fire Hawwa. I asked, 'what would you do if a fire started.'" The picture of the fuselage of the burned out plane sitting on the remote runway flashed in my head sending a shudder through my body.

"You are mezhknown (crazy), there is no fire Mr. Adam."

Hawwa was absolutely right. I was crazy. Crazy for having forgotten where I was. Why did I keep forgetting the most fundamental lesson about her country? It was a developing land. Lee Williams had tried to tell me, 'new buildings - old minds.'

The situation I faced that morning reminded me of the car accident Lee Williams once told me about when an entire family was wiped out in a terrible collision with a fuel tanker. The driver of the Cadillac had put drapes over the windows to keep outsiders from ogling his wife and daughters. Waleed was a product of the same culture. Like every indigenous male, his main goal was to protect the females of his family. But locking them inside an impenetrable building was not the right way.

Arguing with Hawwa was definitely something I wanted to avoid. First of all, it would be a waste of time and mental energy. More importantly, I was locked in a house with her and that was not a good thing. The only choice left for me was to wait and pray that no emergencies occurred. While waiting I concentrated on what I would say to Waleed, if I lived to see him again. Somehow I had to get him to recognize the danger inherent in that situation. Over the months I had known him, Waleed had impressed me as a reasonable man. I trusted that he and I would be able to talk about the problem rationally.

ৰ্ফ ৰ্ফ ৰ্ফ ৰ্ফ ৰ্ফ ৰ্ফ ৰ্ফ ৰ্ফ ৰ্ফ ৰ্ফ ৰ্ফ ৰ্ফ ৰ্ফ ৰ্ফ

ৰ্ষ্ণৰ্ষ্ণৰ্ষ্ণৰ্ষ্ণৰ্ষ্ণৰ্ষ্ণৰ্ষ্ণ

ৰ্জ্ঞৰ্জ্ঞৰ্জ্ঞৰ্জ্ঞৰ্জ্ঞৰ্জ্ঞৰ্জ্ঞৰ্জ্ঞৰ্জ্ঞৰ্জ্ঞৰ্জ্ঞৰ্জ্ঞ

As far as Jaylynn was concerned, she would be in the air more than 15 hours counting her cross Atlantic trip and connecting flight to D.C. Since she would not get to Barry's house until early the next morning, I would have to wait until them to talk to her. That gave me plenty of time to worry about what I would tell her. As far as the necklace was concerned, I would hold on to it until I could give it to her in person when I returned to the States.

Two hours later Waleed inserted his key in the lock. When he opened the door he greeted me with a big smile that I did not return. This was not out of anger. It was just that my mind was on Jaylynn's flight. She had been airborne by then a little over an hour. I could only imagine what went through her mind when she realized I was not going to show up at the airport to see her off. In eleven hours she would land at JFK. After a three hour wait, she would take a connecting flight to D.C. Having lived in Riyadh, I trusted she would understand when I told her what happened. But telling my fiancé 'I was locked in my friend's house with his family' was going to be the oddest excuse I ever had to give for standing someone up.

Waleed sensed something was bothering me so he asked, "Ya sheikh, what has happened? Did Hawwa say something to you?"

"Waleed, I need to talk to you and it is very important."

"Okay," he said and sat down next to me. "What is wrong my friend?"

"Waleed, I was unable to leave this house today until you came back just now because I and your whole family were all locked inside this building. Now, if..."

That was as much as I needed to say. Waleed, an employee at the airport, had a direct tie in to the events surrounding the country's first air disaster. Slapping his forehead with the palm of his hand he said, "ya sheikh you are right. I should have left the key with my wife. I am going to get keys made today and, yani, thank you so much for telling me this thing. Anything could happen, a fire or something like that, and poof, I would lose my whole family. I am so very sorry that I put you, yani, in this position today. Please forgive me, my friend."

I do not mean to sound condescending, but I was proud of Waleed for how quickly he perceived the potential danger he had exposed his family and me to that morning. The fact that he had not anticipated this beforehand was not important. The country was changing. It was going to take time for thinking and habits to adjust to new structures and systems. I felt good knowing our conversation may have saved the family from having to learn this important lesson in a horrible way. Missing Jaylynn's flight was worth at least that much.

In the wee hours of the next morning, I got through to Jaylynn and we talked. Contrary to my worries, she was very understanding and ended up consoling me instead. She assured me, "I understand perfectly what you went through yesterday. Remember I lived over there too. Now you have an idea what I went through dealing with women who do not trust modern medicine and prefer to apply traditional remedies. And I am sure you have not forgotten what happened to you at the DMV. All of this is part of their growing process and you can be proud that you made an important contribution. What you said to Waleed may have altered the family's future and averted an inevitable tragedy."

That conversation made our emotional bond even stronger and gave me a nice push to get on with the third year of my tour with her not being around. But I could already predict my telephone bills were going to be sky high over the next twelve months. Calling my fiancé long distance was going to be a big expense, but I did not care. Knowing Jaylynn would have my back no matter what happened over the coming year, made me a little less worried about feeling lonely. I had a good feeling about our future together and could readily see mutual benefits from both of us having lived in the Middle East.

Chapter 46

The Ministry picnic was another portrait of Bedouin hospitality. However, getting there was a different sort of picture.

The drive to Mej-ma-ah was long but the Saudis assured us it would be worth the ride. They touted the region as one of the best places to see in the Kingdom, particularly following the rainy season when an abundant growth of vegetation blanketed Mej-ma-ah. Nomadic Bedouins drove their herds through the area every year so Headquarters advised those of us going to the picnic to be alert for encounters with nomads. They also warned that we should not expect these Bedouins to be like Saudis that live in the cities. Perhaps the threat of running across nomads was an additional reason some Americans stayed away from the picnic. But for me, the prospect of seeing real Bedouins up close living Arabia's old ways before that way of life faded into history forever made me that more eager to go.

The picnic was a two day affair. Our schedule was to drive up on Wednesday after work, sleep in tents overnight and enjoy a feast on Thursday before returning to Riyadh.

O and I were very enthusiastic when we started out that Wednesday. We tried our best to follow the map but after two hours we were lost. Whereas the information about the picnic had been clear enough, the map itself was difficult to follow and had Arabic markings that I could not decipher. Rather than turn back to Riyadh, we kept going convinced that enough Americans would be traveling to the picnic that we would eventually run into someone we knew. Unfortunately, we never saw another American on the highway. In fact nearly an hour passed before we saw our first vehicle and it was a pickup truck pulled off onto the shoulder of the road. I stopped to ask them for directions. Of the four young Saudis in the truck, none spoke more than a few words of English. One young man, however, exclaimed, 'you Jabbar friend. I see you - Jabbar, me Jabbar friend.' His face was not familiar but I figured we must have met during the early days of my friendship with Jabbar when he was taking me around the city introducing me to his Saudi friends. It was nice to be remembered, but trying to explain to them that we were lost was getting us nowhere until I mentioned the name Mej-ma-ah. As soon as they heard that name they began to laugh and chatter excitedly. It turned out we were all heading to Mej-ma-ah. They invited us to follow them.

Once again I found myself driving like a maniac trying to keep up with a Saudi on the highway. After sunset it got a little easier because I did not have to match their speed. The weather was clear so all I had to do was keep the truck's tail lights in sight. Forty-five minutes after the sun went down the truck's left signal light flashed and our guides veered sharply off the highway about a quarter of a mile ahead. Until we reached the spot where they had turned off the road, O and I did not realize they had driven onto irregular terrain. My car jostled violently as I drove over mounds of hard sand, brush and large stones, which gave my shocks a workout. The truck handled the off road conditions superbly and bounded across that terrain for ten rugged minutes at pretty much the same speed as when they were on the highway. With the pickup kicking up so much dust it was déjà vu for me, bringing back memories of the sandstorm coming from Dammam. Abdullah Al-Basheer's words came to mind 'Just keep on the tail of that truck.' The land finally leveled and the drive got a lot smoother. Five minutes later the pickup came to a stop. After getting out of our vehicles, one of the Saudis untied a live lamb that had been resting in the bed of the truck. He took it to a nearby bush and slaughtered it in preparation for the next day's meal.

O and I stood trembling in the cold desert night air as the young Saudis pulled materials off the truck and began setting up a medium-sized white tent. We watched in admiration as they put it together in less than ten minutes. Even more extraordinary was what we found when they invited us inside. It was phenomenal. Not only was it warm and roomy but the interior was arranged as cozily as any living room I had ever seen. There were portable lamps; a nice carpet covering the desert floor, dozens of pillows for us to lean on, and on the fire in the center of the tent, a kettle of tea was brewing along with a pot of rice. Flaps on either side of the tent served for windows. Had we been blindfolded and taken to that tent, there is no way O and I would have known we were in the middle of a desert.

After feeding us, the entertainment began and it went on until early in the morning. They sang and danced while one of the boys strummed a pot-bellied banjo called the Ute (oot) and another young man beat on a goat-skin drum. They sat together in a row swaying back and forth in unison as they played and sang their songs. The highlight of that night was when they put down the instruments and did this rhythmic clapping routine with their hands. It was fascinating. Each man had a different cadence to perform and when they put the cadences together the parts were coordinated right down to the final clap. Those four young men performed an amazing composition with the precision of a symphony orchestra using human hands instead of musical instruments. O and I failed terribly when we tried to clap along with them. It was not as easy as it looked. Later I learned this form of entertainment has been handed down among the Bedouins for generations. They call it Jalsat. Today I buy Jalsat music over the Internet and from time to time sit back listening to it and reminiscing about that night in Mej-ma-ah.

Our hosts asked O and me to sing. It took some time for us to agree on a song but once we got that straightened out we filled the air with the sound of the Temptations 'Just My Imagination.' They enjoyed our performance and applauded vigorously. Then they grabbed their instruments and sang the same song. Turns out it was one of their favorites as well.

Around four in the morning, the party ran out of steam and we settled down to get some rest. I slept like a baby.

Next morning I was the first to get up. I stepped outside to breathe the cool fresh air and shake off the cobwebs. As I looked around I saw we were in a lush field of knee high grass. Even more astonishing, Bedouins had moved into the area overnight. We were surrounded by seven large brown nomad tents, each at least five times larger than the one we were in. Herds of camels, lambs and goats were grazing nearby under the watchful eyes of young Bedouin lads. It amazed me that all their activity had taken place without disturbing our little tent with its slumbering occupants. Their stealth was impressive, but the fact that they had not molested us in any way or treated us like we were trespassers underscored the respect they showed us that night. It also made sense that the four Saudis we came with had pitched a white tent. As city dwellers, they would have anticipated nocturnal encounters with Bedouins in that region and came prepared.

Just as I was thinking about finding a spot to relieve myself, a couple of veiled women carrying water jars on their heads walked up from behind me and strolled past our tent. They headed toward a group women cooking outside one of the large tents. All of the adult males were clustered together at a separate tent away from the women, but I could not tell what they were doing. I called O so he could take a look while I went to finish my previous thought of taking a leak. O was enjoying the sights when I got back. Around that time I spotted something a little peculiar. There was another large tent, very similar to the Bedouin's tents, sitting far off by itself about a football field away. A number of people were moving in and about this solitary tent, but not all of them looked Arab. One of them had blonde hair, which was unusual for Arabia. After a few seconds I recognized him. I called to O, "see that guy with the blonde hair over there. That is Howard Seymour, the Director of our project. Call it fate or whatever, but these guys have led us to within sight of where we are supposed to be here in Mej-ma-ah."

O and I said goodbye to our new friends, thanked them for their hospitality and joined the Ministry picnic.

There were no wives at the picnic, so we Americans had learned a lesson. When O and I shared our experience from the little tent the previous evening, Howard assured us the same scenario had played out over the same period in their tent with our Saudi coworkers and their sons.

The meal that afternoon was a feast. There was so much food it was almost sinful. After eating I pulled my football out of the trunk and we showed my coworkers how to play the game American style. O ran patterns and I threw passes. The Saudis watched for a few minutes then joined us. Soon they were throwing tight spirals just like quarterbacks in the States. Younger boys took off their sandals, hitched up their Thobes and raced like rabbits barefoot across the sand to catch passes. Only rarely did one of them drop the ball. It was like they had been playing football all their lives. Some of them were very talented and I am sure would have caught the attention of college recruiters.

The picnic was a wonderful and unforgettable experience. Everyone had a good time.

Chapter 47

Early in November of 1981, my two-year contract officially ended. I submitted an end-of-tour report to Al Dennison and began my year extension.

Unless I signed up for a second tour, I would be leaving the Kingdom forever in less than a year, and the countdown had already begun. Thinking about it made me a little sad because I had grown to love Saudi Arabia. I knew that no matter where I went the rest of my life, Abdullah Al-Basheer, Majd, Barakah, the Al-Bughawi brothers, Tawhid Nejaris, Ahmed Al-Saud, Hassan, and a host of others would remain close to my heart as central figures in my wonderful memories of the desert kingdom.

After all was said and done, a tour in Saudi Arabia was quite an accomplishment for a kid out of western Pennsylvania. But I am American so the day would inevitably come for me to pack up and return to my country. A wonderful future awaited me back home, one that I would spend with family, friends, and three of the dearest people in my life. Lovelen and Jaylynn were making plans for a double wedding ceremony and trying to decide on maids of honor. Jaylynn wanted to invite the Strong's and have First Lady Doreen serve in some capacity in the wedding party. A double wedding meant Barry and I would either be each other's best man or pick separate ones. We opted for the latter. He had plenty of friends to choose from and I knew who I wanted to stand with me on that special day.

A full schedule awaited me over the next few months. The Ministry was sending me to Abu Dhabi to attend a computer show and canvas for an Arabic/English system. Once a system was purchased, cabling diagrams for the Ministry building would need to be drawn up, approved, and the physical instillation implemented. All of this promised to keep me very busy. Meantime, the Admin Room, which had come a long way since the days when my desk and chair sat dwarfed in emptiness, now boasted twenty file cabinets and five desks. I had a staff of three consisting of a secretary, a translator and a file clerk. A second secretary and an additional file clerk were being recruited to occupy the other desks. We would be fully staffed in the very near future.

Shortly before my trip to Abu Dhabi, O called. "Ad-man, I know you are about to fly to Abu Dhabi, but can we set a definite date to go to Jeddah. How does your schedule look?"

"When I get back from Abu Dhabi I will be swamped with a ton of work. It will probably be at least two months before I can even think about planning a trip."

"Two months works for me too, because it looks like my schedule will be opening up around that same time. What do you think about setting up a trip between two and a half to three months from now?"

"That sounds about right."

"Good. Ed asked me to tell you the group is planning to hold a debate about Blacks outside Africa returning to live in the motherland. This debate will be based on what happened to the Africans at Mecca. They want you and me to talk from the Black American perspective on what our community would do if a matter of national sovereignty arose and Black Americans were forced out of the country and sent to Africa."

"I can think of one person who would be perfect for that debate, but she would not be permitted to participate because she is a female."

"You're talking about Jaylynn's sister, right?"

"Exactly, in fact I would not be surprised if Lovelen debated something like that already when she was in college. Maybe I can get her to help me organize my arguments. That would be okay, wouldn't it? To get her help, I mean."

"Sure, why not. They don't care how we prepare our arguments. I'm sure they will be happy if we just show up. By the way Ad-man, since I started going to church with you every week I have been getting a lot of invitations to parties and dinners from members of the congregation. Those people do not know me very well, but I think because they see me with you all the time they feel I am safe. Anyway, I got an invitation that I want to ask you about. It is from a lady who gave it to me on behalf of her club. Have you ever heard of a group called the Expatriate Ladies Club of Riyadh?"

It took all the strength I had not to laugh, but I was determined to remain neutral as long as possible about this particular affair.

"That group has come to my attention before. As a matter of fact, my boss' wife belongs to that club. Why, what's going on?"

"Nothing, I just wanted to know if you knew anything about them that's all. They have invited me to be the guest of honor at a luncheon. I just thought you might know something that might help me decide whether or not to accept."

"It's just a bunch of women O, how bad could it be?" I wanted to laugh so bad that holding it in made me ache.

After hanging up with O, I started worrying that O would respond to the ladies as I believed he would and then hold back the details when I asked him about his experience with them. Then again, knowing O, he would probably be so excited that he couldn't wait to tell me everything.

Later that day Al asked me to come to his office. Abdullah Al-Basheer was with him when I entered the room. They spoke with me for twenty minutes about the status of the project and emphasized how much they appreciated my contribution to the effort. I was not surprised when they offered me a second two year tour that would begin after the end of my year extension. If I accepted, I would be taking a trip back to the States for rest and recuperation and return to Saudi Arabia afterward. I did not commit to anything right then, but promised I would think about it and get back to them.

That night when I called Jaylynn to tell her about the offer, she surprised me with the suggestion 'why don't we get married when you return to the States and then go back to Arabia together?'

[END OF PART I]